Best
Henry

CONALL

THE PLACE OF BLOOD

RINN-IRU

TITLES BY DAVID H. MILLAR

Conall: The Place of Blood - Rinn-Iru
Conall II: The Raven's Flight - Eitilt an Fhiaigh Dhuibh

Conall

The Place of Blood

Rinn-Iru

David H. Millar

Conall: The Place of Blood - Rinn-Iru
Copyright © 2014 by David H. Millar
Revised March 2015

All rights reserved. No part of this book may be reproduced or transmitted in any form or by any means, electronic or mechanical, including photocopy, recording or any information and storage retrieval system now known or to be invented, without permission in writing from the publisher, except by a reviewer who wishes to quote brief passages in connection with a review written for inclusion in a magazine, newspaper, blog or broadcast.

A Wee Publishing Company
Houston, TX, USA
http://www.aweepublishingco.com

Paperback ISBN 978-0-9916640-0-9
eBook ISBN 978-0-9916640-1-6
ISBN-10: 0991664000
ISBN-13: 9780991664009
Library of Congress Control Number 2014905121
A Wee Publishing Company, LLC, Houston, TX

Conall: The Place of Blood - Rinn-Iru is a work of historical fiction. Apart from obviously historical figures and places, all names, characters and incidents are either the product of the author's imagination or are used fictitiously, and any resemblance to actual persons, living or dead, establishments, events or locales is entirely coincidental.

To Stephen

ACKNOWLEDGMENTS

Thanks to the many friends and colleagues who were a constant source of support and encouragement and who suffered through the many drafts. Special thanks to Lauren who cajoled me to begin writing and was "rewarded" by being elevated to the position of chief editor.

A big thanks to Eddie Kelleher, Visiting Scholar of Irish Language and Literature at the William J. Flynn Center for Irish Studies in Houston, Texas for providing many of the Gaelic pronunciations. Apologies where my interpretation of his sound files are not quite accurate!

Contents

Titles by David H. Millar	ii
Acknowledgments	vi
Contents	vii
Pronunciations	xiv
Chapter 1	1
Part 1: Fate	5
Chapter 2	7
Part 2: The Southern War	25
Chapter 3	27
Chapter 4	45
Chapter 5	57
Chapter 6	66
Chapter 7	72
Chapter 8	87
Chapter 9	109
Chapter 10	129
Chapter 11	139
Chapter 12	154
Chapter 13	166
Chapter 14	179
Chapter 15	184
Chapter 16	206
Chapter 17	213
Part 3: The Trail North	227
Chapter 18	229
Chapter 19	233
Chapter 20	246
Chapter 21	265
Chapter 22	277

Chapter 23	295
Chapter 24	301
Chapter 25	313
Chapter 26	328
Chapter 27	338
Chapter 28	359
Epilogue	366
Notes	369
Suggested Reading	374
The Characters	375
About The Author	379

Pronunciations

My personal belief is that Gaelic as a language was never meant to be spoken, but always sung. To hear it spoken it strikes me as quite a harsh language; to hear it sung it is simply beautiful. Just listen to Clannad, De Dannan, Mary Black or Enya.

Furthermore, to view written Gaelic and then hear the pronunciation is the ultimate in confusion. Below is a listing from a variety of sources with suggested pronunciations for the main names, place names and phrases used throughout the story. I am very open to better suggestions for what should be the best pronunciation of Ancient Irish Gaelic.

That said, I am reminded of the occasion when I visited a famous distillery in Ireland. After the distillery tour the marketing director was asked by a whiskey aficionado as to what was the proper way to drink the brew. His answer, "I don't care how you drink it or what you mix it with. Just drink it!" So in that same vein, feel free to pronounce the Gaelic in a way that gives you the most enjoyment.

Abha na Sionainne	OW-wa nuh SHUN-in-nah
Ailill Mac Máta	AHL-il mak MAWta
An trua (the unfortunate)	an TROO-uh
Ard-Righ (High King)	AWRD-ree
Ard-Righan (High Queen)	AWRD-ree-an
Aedh Ruad	EE-th ROO-uh
Aengus Ruad	ENG-yus ROO-uh
Aes sídhe	ASH shee
Áine	AW-nya
Aodh Mac Eochaidh Fionn	AWD mak OHY-fin
Baeth	BEE
Beacán	B'YAG-awn
Bedach	BED-da
Bean-sidhe (foreteller of death)	BAN-shee
Bealtaine (festival)	BYAHL-tih-nuh
Bitseach	BIT-shuk
Bodhrán (Irish drum)	BAR-awn

Bohd Carraig	BOW'D KAR-ig
Bog ar aghaidh	BUG R AH-eed
Borbcas	BUR ub-kiss
Bras	BRASS
Breácan	BREK-awn
Bréanainn	BRAY-an-in
Bricriu	BRICK-roo
Brighid	BREED
Brion ó Cathasaigh	BREE-un o-KAS-akh
Brocc	BRUK
Bróga	BRO-gah
Brónach	BRO-nakh
Caher Conri	KAH-r KUN-v'yuh
Caomhnóirí	KWAYV-nor-ee
Carn Tigherna	KARN T'YER-na
Carraig na Caillí	KAH-rihg nuh KAL-y
Cathán	KA-hawn
Cathán o Bric	KA-hawn oh BRIK
Cathal	KA-hul
Ceannairí céad	KAN-ari KAYD
Ceannairí na míle	KAN-ari nuh MEE-le
Cearbhall ó Domhnaill	KYAR-ull oh DON-al
Céili	KAY-lee
Chomhairle	an HOR-ya
Chrúachain	KROO-uh-shan
Cian Craobhach	KEE-in CRAY-v-akh
Cimbáeth	KIM-boy
Cinn péinteáilte	KEEN PENT-or-tah
Clárach	KLAWR-akh
Conall Mac Gabhann	KON-ul ma GAWN
Connachta	KAWN-ah-ta
Craic	KRACK
Craiftine	KRAFT-in
Cret	KRET
Cróeb Ruad	KROO-v ROO-uh
ó Cuileannáin	o QUILL-an-awn
Curach	KUR-ah
Curraghatoor	KURRAKH-toor
Cúscraid Mac Conchobar	KOO-skri MAK KRUH-who'r
Deaglán ó Neill	DEG-lawn o NEE-ul

Deda Mac Sin	DAY-da MAK SHEEN
Dithorba	DEE-tor-va
Do mo dheirfiúracha	DUH muh GRA-fur-akha
Dún do bheal	DOON duh VAY'l
Do theach do rialacha	Duh HAAK duh REE-aha
Danu	DAH-noo
Emain Macha	AV-in MA-sha
Eirnín	ER-neen
Eochaidh Ruad	OHY ROO-uh
Eoghan ó Liath	OH-in o LEE-ah
Ériu	AY-roo
Fachtna	FAH-na
Faolán Ó Floinn	FWAY-lawn o FLIN
Fearghal ó Maoilriain	FER-ul o MWAY-ree-an
Fiach	FEE-akh
Fidchell	FEY-hil
Fionnbharr	FYUN-var
Geis	GEH-sh
Gheasa	YA-suh
Ghlean Athain	GLAN AHA-in
Gleann na Muice Duibhe	GLOWN nuh M'WIKA DIV-ah
Gleann Baile Éamonn	GLOWN BALL-ya AY mon
Gleannta	GLOWN-tah
Go raibh maith agat	GUH RAW MA AG-ut
Halla Mór	HALLA MOHR
Íar Mac Dedad	EER MAK DAY-da
Imbolg	IMBOL-ugh
Ionsaí	UN-see
Knockadigeen	K'NUK-a-DIGEEN
Labhraidh	LA-ra
Laighi	LA-hi
Lugnasad	LOON-a-sad
Macha Mong-Ruad	Maha MUNN ROO-uh
Medb	MAY-ve
Medb na pluide cairdiúil	MAY-ve nuh PWEE KAR-doo-ee
Midi	MI-th-i
Mongfhionn	MUNN-yung
Mooghaun	MOO-awn
Mórrígan	Moe-rig-gAHn
Nathair	NAH-hihr

Niall ó Bric	NEE-ul o BRIK
Nuadha	NOO-a
Odhrán Mac Seáin	UR-awn mak SHAW-in
Olcán Ó Floinn	UL-cawn o FLIN
Oisín	USH-een
Óenach	OH-n-ah
Onchú Ó an Cháintigh	UN-choo Awn HAWN-tyg
Phortaigh na Cullen	FUR-tyg nuh QUILL-an
Póg ma thoin	POHG muh HOE-in
Portach an Choirr	PURR-tahk an HOW'R
Ráth	RAW
Ráthgall	RAW-gal
Ráth na Conall	RAW nuh KUL-al
Ráth na Lairig Éadain	RAW nuh LAR-ig AY-dan
Rí ruirech	REE ROOR-akh
Rí túatha	REE TOO-ah-ha
Rinn-iru	RIN CREW
Ronan	RO-nawn
Ruiri	ROO-ree
Samhain	SOW-wen
Seanachaí	SHAWN-a-Kee
Seanán	SHAN-awn
Sidhe	SHEE
Siollan ó Dubhghaill	SHULL-awn o DOO-l
Sláine Ulfhada	SLAWN-yah UL-ada
Slántu	SLAWN-tu
Sleibhin	SHLAI-veen
Sráidbhaile de Bhiotáille	SHROID-boll-yah du BOT-oyyah
Striapach	STREE-ah-pah
Tadhg ó Cuileannáin	TYG o QUILL-an-awn
Taobh Builleach	TAV BWEEL-ah
Tara	TAR-a
Toirneach	TOR-nah
Torcán ó Dubhghaill	TURK-awn o DOO-l
Treasach	TRAS-akh
Uallach	OOL-akh
Uallachán	OOL-akh-awn
Uiscí na fathach	ISH-key nuh FAH-ahka
Ulaid	ULL-a
Urard	UR-urd

CHAPTER 1

390 B.C.

The black battle horse snickered and pawed at the dirt. Instinctively, the warrior leaned forward to stroke and pat its black velvet neck. "Patience, Toirneach, soon... very soon." From his vantage point on the high ground where the tents of the kings and nobles were pitched, Conall Mac Gabhann contemplated the barbarian army assembled on the banks of the Allia.

Over twenty thousand warriors had gathered; many having crossed the Alps and then Northern Latium from their homeland in Gaul. Now they were camped within sight of the gates of Rome. They were tall, powerful and proud warriors distinguished by tribal paint, hair style and color, and weaponry. Apart from their nobles, most wore little by way of clothes. Many chose not to wear armor. They congregated in families and clans, but fought fiercely as individuals for glory, survival, plunder and women.

Conall looked to the center and smiled as he studied his own army. The "Warriors of the Wall" as they had become known. Battle-hardened over the past thirty years. With the exception of a cohort of cinn péinteáilte – the painted ones, most wore leather body armor inlaid with iron scales. A few had chain mail. Their helmets, although functional, had grown more ornate and fantastically decorated over time. He had permitted this; it had proved one way for him to identify particular warriors in battle.

Familiar, oblong, curved shields emblazoned with a black

raven on a field of red, rested at their sides. Sheathed in beautifully designed and crafted leather scabbards, were double-edged short swords sharpened to a vicious cutting edge. When in formation, each man or woman, carried four javelins – three for throwing, one for stabbing. Most carried a preferred weapon – their favorite axe or longsword, for when they were allowed to fight with no constraints. Many had several daggers and knives of various shapes and sizes for throwing, stabbing – or just carving food.

Distinctive in their armor and weaponry, Conall's warriors, many from the land of Ériu, contrasted starkly with their Gaul comrades. His army, while seemingly at ease, stood alert in comparison to their allies, and retained their well-ordered formation. Behind the front two rows, each containing a thousand men, another three thousand formed up as two columns, each with two rows of seven hundred and fifty warriors.

Marked by the red and black foxtail crests of their helmets, a thousand cavalry guarded the flanks of his men. They carried smaller oval shields, javelins for throwing and longer swords or long-handled axes for slashing. All were safely secured on either side of their mounts - for now. Conall had conceded long ago to Mórrígan's wisdom on archers, especially since his travels through Albu, Iberia and Gaul. He now had two hundred with him, carrying composite bows of wood and bone slung across their backs and quivers full of the signature black-shafted arrows with their red and white fletching.

His men shared their good-natured craic, laughing at the constant flow of insults and at the bare arses and genitals flaunted by the main army of Gauls. Conall still considered them Gauls, not true Celts. For their part, the Gauls looked disdainfully on their heavily armored allies, but both sides remembered the bitter battles fought between these former adversaries, now united against a common enemy - Rome. The insults masked a high level of respect for each other.

Brennus, the leader of the Gauls, or to be more accurate the Senones, was a tall warrior with piercing green eyes. His shoulder length red hair was crowned by a winged helmet. Tugging on a great red beard, he looked grim. His honor had been deeply offended by the behavior of Rome and, in particular, by the Fabii brothers sent as envoys to him at Clusium. These Romans were foul-tempered and arrogant men. Not only did they negotiate in bad faith, but one, Quintus Fabius Ambustus, had speared and slain a chieftain of Brennus' when confronted.

The tall Gaul nodded to Conall and then pointed at the Roman army. "Maybe we can do without your men today. There aren't that many Romans to fight." Conall nodded, somewhat in agreement. The Roman legions were understrength, numbering only around thirty thousand men. The Gauls and Celts had roughly the same numbers, but were vastly superior warriors. Conall wanted his men in the front, though. He needed to be first into Rome. After thirty years, he had business to bring to a close. And one final vow, one geis to complete.

Conall grinned wolfishly, "Of course you could, but how many do you want to lose against the Roman phalanx, Brennus? If my men are killed, then there will be more plunder for you. And if I'm killed, then you can rest easier at night." Brennus had witnessed many times what Conall's army could do against his own elite warriors even when well outnumbered. He had lost too many warriors to Conall and his commanders, the feared ceannairí na míle. Thus, while Brennus respected him, he did not trust him, and had no love for either Conall or his men. He would be more than happy to see them culled and even happier to attend Conall's funeral pyre.

He smiled, "Would I really be rid of you even in death? Let's see if the Romans can teach you some humility, Conall Mac Gabhann. Get your men ready to march."

Conall watched the campfires being doused as dawn approached, their light slowly replaced by the crimson sunrise. He reflected on the journey that had brought him to this point.

PART 1: FATE

CHAPTER 2

415 B.C.

There were twenty in the hunting party. Apart from Fearghal ó Maoilriain, who at thirty summers was the eldest and assigned by their community to make sure no-one got lost, injured or drowned in the excitement of the hunt, the rest were aged from ten to eighteen summers.

The band looked to Conall as their leader. He was quiet, determined and embarrassed by the loyalty his friends tended to give him. At almost eighteen, he was the oldest, by a few cycles of the moon, over his friend, Brion ó Cathasaigh. He wasn't the tallest, the best muscled or perhaps even the most cunning of the group. Yet Conall had an aura of quiet confidence.

In contrast to his red-haired, pale skinned friends, his face was framed with dark, brown hair flecked with highlights of auburn – a gift from his mother. His swarthy skin was inherited from his father and meant he could take advantage of the summer sun without burning. His eyes were his most striking feature, varying from deep blue to steel grey. All who knew him were aware that when his eyes were grey, his jaw set and his words few, there was no moving Conall from his chosen course of action.

Mórrígan, who was Brion's sister, was the only girl. At fifteen summers, Mórrígan could hunt better than most and, taking her cue from the goddess she was named after, preferred male company to her sisters or other women in the community. She was also the only rider and, by far, the best archer. Appointed as unofficial scout, she cantered ahead of the group, keeping a watch for unfriendly strangers or animals. No one took her role quite that seriously. They had made this journey many times. Besides, Fearghal had brought his brace of wolfhounds to alert them to any wild boar, wolf or bear they might disturb.

Fearghal hurried them north-east along the meandering path from the coast. It was late in the afternoon, and he wanted everyone back before sunset. Fearghal ó Maoilriain was somewhat of a mystery. No one really knew how he came to be with the little community. Standing a full head taller than all of them, he was built like a seasoned oak – hard, sure-footed when needed, and with arms that would reach out and box ears without warning. His limbs were those of a warrior - covered in scars.

Rumor had it that Fearghal came from the North – from beyond Gleann na Muice Duibhe – the Black Pig's Dyke. The Dyke was the great earthworks that marked the boundaries of the Ulaid territory. He had a mysterious red branch entwined around a long-sword tattooed onto his right upper arm. No one asked about this; everyone respected his privacy. Fearghal was the only one with a "real" weapon. It was a long-sword sheathed in a beautifully crafted leather scabbard, and was always strapped to his back. The tang of the sword itself was enveloped with stag's antler smoothed with age and use; it was finished off with a blood-red ruby. The blade always oiled and honed sharp.

It would not have been a long walk back as the crow flies, but for the hunting party, there were sand dunes and the wildwood with its dense undergrowth to navigate before they reached home. About fifty people, from newborns to grandparents, lived in the three large shelters that formed the heart of their home. Each house was a simple round structure, built from rocks found in the nearby fields, and a mix of turf, sod and thatch for the roof. Yet the houses were more than able to withstand the cold, harsh winters or the odd bear scavenging for easy food. Everything was infused with the rich, aromatic fragrance of burning peat.

Sitting atop a natural hill, the settlement had a perfect view of the surrounding area. The site was ringed with a dirt bank crowned with a wooden palisade. The stockade was built not for military fortification, but to dissuade wolves and other wild animals from entering. A ditch ran along the outside of the bank and served as the sewer. Most times the cold air kept the smell down and at least the waste nourished the blackthorn trees planted to discourage unwelcome visitors. Mountains to the west guarded the rear and sides of the settlement and to the east was a large, almost level, area that had been cleared of trees. A few fields of crops had been planted; small groups of sheep and cattle grazed on the grasses and bushes.

While there were always skirmishes in the region, for the most part the settlements and farms were ignored by the itinerant bands of warriors. When they were not required by their kings and nobles, the warbands fought each other, went on cattle raids or got drunk. To a warrior, there was little point in fighting peasants. There was no honor in it and it was no way to gain a reputation. Very few poems were sung about warriors beating up on the local workers. If they called, it was likely they needed weapons sharpened or mended or they just wanted some food and beer.

The community, to which the hunting party returned, was different. It was protected under an agreement with the local rí túatha. These chieftains liked to be called "kings", but were really just the more successful rogues, warriors or politicians. The rí túatha, in turn, pledged their allegiance – for what it was worth, to the region's ruiri or king. In this region that was Eochaidh Ruad who resided in Carn Tigherna, the hillfort a day's ride to the west.

Eochaidh held real power in the south of the island. His own oath was given to the rí ruirech of the Connachta, Ailill Mac Máta and his Queen, Medb, who lived at Chrúachain.

Of course, all the kings were subject to the High King or Ard-Righ. Cimbáeth, the leader of the Ulaid, had reigned for almost twenty years as Ard-Righ and resided behind the defenses of the Black Pig's Dyke.

The value of the community was in their skills. There were many mines for copper in Ériu, but none for tin. To make bronze, and hence bronze weapons and armor, tin had to be imported from the larger island to the east. Supplies of tin were not guaranteed, trade was often disrupted and the cost was high. The discovery of large iron deposits in the mountains behind the settlement had changed all this. In the hands of a skilled blacksmith, iron could be worked from being a hard, but brittle metal to one that was tougher, more durable and able to hold a sharp edge. Bréanainn Mac Gabhann, Conall's father, was famed across Ériu for his skills as a blacksmith and a weapon-maker.

Leather armor, much sought after by the local royalty, was crafted, by Brion's father in a second roundhouse. In the third, a woodworker built the box-wagons that were drawn by mules or oxen and often laden with goods for sale. Bréanainn and the woodworker also made the spoked, iron-rimmed wheels for the battle and ceremonial war chariots favored by the local kings and warlords. The village was considered neutral territory in the region, because it was so valuable to everyone.

The hunters broke from the forest, crossing the grassland that led home. It had taken many years to clear the thick undergrowth, thorn bushes and trees from the land to make it suitable for cattle and crops. Being close to the coast, the climate was well-suited for farming, although even here the chill never quite left the air. It was almost harvest time and the grass was long, ready for cutting to feed the livestock during the winter. A thousand paces distant, the settlement was clearly visible. Hunting horns blasted out a warning of their arrival. Oddly, today, there was no response and no familiar blue smoke rising from the peat fires.

Hauling the fruits of the hunt behind, they moved closer.

Then the hounds started growling, a low, full-throated rumble. Mórrígan's horse stopped, snorted, tossed its head up and down and refused to go further. It was then they noticed the grass, flattened as if by a large band of people – and there were deep wheel ruts in the dirt. Fearghal dropped to his knee, his longsword sliding out of its scabbard in one fluid movement.

"Down, all of you, and be quiet. Something's wrong. Conall, go right, keep down and just watch for anything." Conall nodded, and gripping his hunting spear moved a short distance away. "Brion, the same, but left. Mórrígan, quiet that horse and hobble it. The rest of you go back to the forest edge and stay under cover." They had never seen Fearghal this serious and were too stunned to make any objection or ask questions.

Calling his hounds to him, Fearghal knelt and they watched as he whispered to them. The hounds belonged to Fearghal and were the only property, apart from his sword, that he had brought with him from the North. He sent them off towards the settlement and watched as they bounded swiftly forward until they got to within a few hundred paces of the community. Then they slowed to a cautious walk. Fearghal observed, considering. He whistled instructions and the dogs separated and circled the ditch before entering through the gateway and moving into the yard. Everyone waited. There was a pause and then came the hounds' howling —full of mourning, anger and sorrow. It was the sound of death.

Fearghal looked at the young hunters, "Conall and Brion, forward with me. Mórrígan keep the rest here." Brion ó Cathasaigh was slimly built and taller than Conall with auburn-red hair braided into several lengths that touched his shoulders. He looked at Conall, uncertain of what was happening, but sensing that nothing good lay before him.

There is calmness in death. This, Conall's first time, was not to be his last. As he walked through the open entrance into the main room of his home, he was at first filled with a sense of serenity and stillness. The evening sun shone through the open door lighting up the dust particles that danced in the beams of light. Sword in hand, Fearghal followed close behind.

The tranquility of the moment was brief, shattered by the potpourri of death. The smell of burnt flesh drew Conall's eyes to the forge and the body of his father shackled to the iron corner posts. Tendrils of smoke still rose from what remained of his clothes, his back burnt and in some places charred to the bone. The metallic smell of blood now enveloped Conall as he followed what remained of his father's eyes to the oak table.

His mother, Brónach, was drawn across it, her hands still held in place by two iron nails hammered through flesh, her head turned towards her husband. A dark stream of blood from her slashed throat had spread across the table, flowed over the table's edge and soaked into the dirt floor. Her skirt had been ripped apart; the bruising and blood telling its own story.

Conall turned away, embarrassed that he was looking upon his mother's partially naked body, and was greeted by the sight of his twin sisters. They lay in the corner with their throats cut and their bodies tossed aside. At least they were very young and had been spared anything else.

Brion stumbled through the entrance, his eyes streaming with tears after having been to his own home. He started to speak, but his eyes took in the appalling tableau in front of him. "The Goddess preserve us," he whispered hoarsely. The shock had him stumbling back out the door where he threw up, his retching broken only by sobs.

Fearghal watched silently, taking in the awfulness of the scene before him and beginning to mourn the loss of his friends and those he considered his family. In his warrior's soul the stirrings of vengeance made their presence felt, but he watched, waiting to see how Conall reacted. A sigh of relief escaped him as he saw the young man fall to his knees, sobbing, a flood of salty tears joining the blood on the dirt floor.

He was saddened, if not surprised when Conall arose, his grey-blue eyes taking on a dark and haunted look. "I swear by the Hag, that we will hunt them all down, kill them all - and their families, Fearghal. I don't care how long, but they all die. No mercy." Fearghal lamented the change in his young ward, but could not argue with him.

"Keep my little brother away from this. He shouldn't see our parents and sisters like this."

Putting his hand on Conall's arm, Fearghal spoke quietly, but with authority, "First, we give them a good parting to Tír inna n-Óc. Then we prepare for what's to come."

At that moment, Fearghal knew that all of their lives were at risk. Whoever had carried out the butchery had planned on killing everyone. Without a doubt, they would be back to complete their mission.

It was a somber supper. All were shocked at the sudden loss of their parents and families. Mórrígan had been tasked with keeping the younger ones away until the bodies were washed and dressed for burial. They knew from the tear-stained cheeks and grimly set jaws of their older friends that something terrible had taken place. The flickering flames from the fire emphasized each one's tormented thoughts. There was no priest to say words over the bodies, so Fearghal had stumbled over a few sentences. None dared to enter their homes, haunted as they were by the spirits of the dead.

Fearghal looked around the group. "So what do we know?"

It was a question meant to divert conversation and thoughts. Not expecting an answer, he continued, "Whoever did this was known. There's no sign of force. The stockade is untouched. There's no sign of a battle. Whoever it was, they were welcomed into the settlement as friends, and then they slaughtered everyone."

"They're coming back, aren't they?" Brion looked nervously at the faces of his friends as he voiced their thoughts. "They can't leave us alive. But why... why did they do it?"

Conall looked to Fearghal, "Likely it has something to do with the weapons and armor stockpiled in the cave at the foot of the mountain. The swords and shields my father forged, and the armor Brion's father made."

"Yes. It can't be the whole story, but my guess is that Eochaidh Ruad coveted the weapons and armor, and didn't want anyone else to know why or what use they were to be put to. And he didn't want to pay for them. Few can fathom how that man thinks, but he almost certainly gave the order for the settlement to be destroyed."

Fearghal thought for a moment and snorted derisively. "But they hadn't bargained on your fathers storing them in a different place, not under the settlement along with the usual stores. Your fathers were wise."

"Our fathers are dead," snapped Mórrígan.

"How long do we have?" asked Cathán ó Bric, who at ten summers was one of the youngest. He looked at Fearghal and the older boys, hoping for a reassuring answer, but suspecting it was not to come.

"It's a day's ride back to Carn Tigherna along the lower route, but most will be walking. So, say one and a half days to get back. They'll make their report to Eochaidh, get fed and get new orders. That probably gives us three days, maybe four if we are lucky, to prepare. If they take the high road then maybe we'll have an extra day."

"Prepare?" Once more, Mórrígan turned on Fearghal, spitting out each word with venom. "Prepare for what Fearghal? What can we do? Half of us are just children."

Fearghal's patience with Mórrígan had worn thin and he glared at her, "Many of those that are coming will be no older than you." Looking around the frightened band, he held their attention, "You were privileged. Were it not for your fathers many of you would already be dead or in the warbands of the local chieftains." His tone was harsh as he finished, "You will fight or you will die."

Conall stood, his body bathed in the red-yellow colors of the roaring fire. His friends were changing. Bitterness burned in their bellies and dark shadows were enclosing their souls. With a note of resignation and defiance, he spoke, "Fearghal is right, we fight or we run and are hunted down. Either way, their swords and spears are coming for us. I say we stand and fight."

He paused to let his words sink in, then continued. "The settlement is on high ground and has a strong, if not very tall, fence. We have the weapons and armor made by our fathers. We've all played at being warriors and practiced with the weapons and the new armor that our fathers made. We never thought we'd need them for real, but Fearghal is a warrior. He'll tell us what needs to be done."

At that moment, Conall Mac Gabhann became the leader, and no one dissented.

At first light, they tramped to the cave behind the settlement to retrieve the weapons and armor. With no oxen or cattle to pull the wagons, it was hard work and would take several days, but no one complained. All were glad to have something to take their minds from lost family and friends. Mórrígan was sent with the hounds to reconnoiter the land, just in case Fearghal had got it wrong and the raiders came back sooner.

Fearghal directed the younger ones to sow the ground to the left and right of the gateway with caltrops. Simple and very effective, caltrops were two iron nails bent and welded together – with one sharp end always pointing upwards. This was to force the attackers into a narrow corridor in front of the gate, where he reckoned the javelins could do maximum damage. They could not hope to stop the attack, but they might slow it down. That was the basic strategy - slow them down... survive... maybe kill a few.

The ditch around the settlement was populated with the sharpened stakes that had been stockpiled as replacements for the palisade and livestock fencing. Hay was forked into the ditch and covered with lamp oil and grease. Inside, logs and boulders were rolled against the fence to provide a platform for the defenders. By the fourth sunrise, the settlement was fortified as well as it could be with what was to hand.

"Seems like good work." Conall commented, inspecting the results of their labors.

Fearghal grunted, "With twenty men I could hold this ground for as long as I wanted. It's a perfect position for defense. But look around you. I see the sons of peaceable craftsmen – not warriors. We have eight who haven't seen fifteen summers. Half of the others can't even see over the fence without standing on something. We can slow the attackers down, but they will get through and then it's warriors against boys. Unless the goddess smiles on us, it will not be a good day."

"They'll fight, and fight well no matter their age. They know what was done to parents and friends. They'll give no quarter, because they expect none to be given."

"I hope so Conall. Now, let's go see how we can use the fancy armor and weapons that your fathers made." Fearghal shouted out to the others, "Right, you lot! Get over here and get equipped."

Normal sized armor looked ridiculous on the youngest. So they donned the leather play armor and helmets that their parents had made for them because they fitted well, and the iron plates, sown between layers of bonded leather, made good protection. The young ones were given hunting bows and quivers of arrows. Swords or spears were too heavy for them, so they were armed with daggers.

The craftsmen had been experimenting with several types of armor, their work inspired by stories of warriors in far off lands told by infrequent travelers and crew members from Phoenician or Greek trading ships or the odd shipwrecked sailor. Brion, Mórrígan and Conall put on iron ring mail suits. Only three suits had been made, as they took much longer to forge than the other armor. The mail was a tunic of iron rings alternating in rows of closed flat circles and riveted rings. The tunic covered the upper half of the body down to just below the crotch. It was worn over a soft leather shirt and pants to help prevent the skin chafing. The mail was reassuringly heavy and very flexible. Whereas Brion and Conall's suits were a reasonable fit, Mórrígan's needed cinched with a tight belt to make it practical.

Fearghal favored the other armor, which was simpler to make and lighter, but he swore it would stop blows better than the mail. It was made of leather, reinforced with small iron pieces, like fish scales, sown between and over the leather layers. Preferring his long-sword, he left the swords that Bréanainn had forged for the others.

These new swords were constructed from iron with a narrow tang that passed through a wooden handle. This had a long leather thong tightly wound around, ending with a pommel holding the handle to the blade. The blade itself was leaf shaped and waisted, with a midrib for added strength. Most swords were at least an arm and half long, but these were smaller – more like an arm's length. The swords were kept sharp from waist to tip. They were vicious blades made for close fighting - for slashing and thrusting. Fortunately, the design also meant that they were much lighter, which now proved a major advantage.

The shields were made to complement the swords. They were about two-thirds the height of a warrior – from chin to knee. Oval shaped and slightly curved, they were comprised of three layers of birch strips, and covered front and back with wool felt, which was doubled over the rim and stitched on. The grip was reinforced with hand-forged iron. Two cross-strips of iron with a decorative, yet very functional boss at the center finished off the front face. The group had practiced being warriors sometimes with these shields and swords and knew that they were meant to work together. The shields formed a solid protective wall and the short swords were used for killing and maiming.

Next were the helmets. These were simple iron bowls with leather flaps to protect ears and were fitted with chin straps to make sure they stayed in place. In truth, they were designed to prevent injuries when hunting or riding. Now it was hoped they could deflect a sword blow. As a finishing touch, layers of wool felt and leather were wrapped around calves to help prevent being disabled by a low sword slash.

Complaints and cries of how cumbersome and heavy the armor felt filled the air. Unmoved, Fearghal ignored them or growled, "Get used to it. It may save your life." Before they settled down for the night, stacks of javelins were arranged behind the fence. These were for the older ones who had the strength and the height to throw them over the palisade.

The sixth sunrise came too swiftly. Everyone woke hoping that there would be no trouble, but the hounds' barking soon put paid to that desire. Led by a chariot, a force of about fifty men was advancing across the open grassland. A few were on horseback, but most were on foot. Their laughter could be heard a long way in the still, cold morning air and even at a distance, their walk and positioning showed they were not expecting much resistance. They were carrying mostly swords and spears. Some had small shields, but few had any level of body armor. A good number wore only pants, showing off battle hardened and scarred upper bodies. Still others displayed their tribal loyalties with faces painted in blue or red designs. Many were young, and more than a few were no more than thirteen summers.

Their leader, Olcán ó Floinn rode in a chariot drawn by four mangy-looking horses. The chariot was much more of a status symbol than a practical offensive battle-cart. There was no possibility that the heavy box, with its solid, iron-rimmed wheels would make it up the slope of the hill without either rolling over or tipping out its driver and warrior occupants. Fearghal was confident that the few riders present would dismount before battle, since very few warriors chose to fight from horseback.

Halting about a hundred paces from the community gate, Olcán jumped off his chariot and paced forward carrying his sword and shield. He was tall and impressively built. Amulets had been stitched onto his hardened leather tunic it to ward off evil spirits as well as the gold and silver chains that proclaimed numerous successes in battle. His arms were covered in bands of bronze, gold and silver, but otherwise he bore no armor. Red, waist length hair was braided so that it wouldn't be a hindrance. More than a few foolish warriors had perished when their hair was grabbed in a fight or trapped by low-hanging branches when travelling through the dense forests. Olcán had forgone the use of pants and as he strode to within thirty paces of the gate the massive, scarred muscles on his thighs and calves were plain to see.

He shouted in the direction of the gateway, "I am Olcán ó Floinn. I wish to speak with your leader. Let's talk and settle this quickly and peacefully."

The gate swung open and Fearghal walked down the path, his hounds close to heel. As he got closer, Olcán sneered. "Not you, Northerner, you have no rank here. You know the way of things. Send me whoever is the leader of the settlement now. If he is willing, I'll fight him man to man. If he wins, you all go free. If not, well, he'll not be worrying about what happens to the rest of you."

Livid, but bound by protocol, Fearghal walked back and said, "The Goddess go with you, Conall."

Conall took a deep breath and strode out of the entrance towards the warrior. A javelin rested in his right hand as if he intended to use it to stab. His sword hung in a leather scabbard from his belt; his shield was carried on his left arm. To anyone watching, it appeared that Conall had no idea what he was going to do. It looked a novice stance.

Olcán anchored his feet, tensed his muscles and observed Conall approach. He grinned widely as a young boy of eighteen summers and slightly above average height came towards him wearing a red-brown tunic and carrying a spear and an oddly-shaped shield. The boy was muscular, but soft, not hardened through battle, and his skin was unblemished by sword or spear. His hair was dark brown and short, barely touching his shoulders. The warrior laughed, taunting Conall, "That spear will not save you from the reach of my sword, boy. Let's you and I talk and maybe we can find a good way out of this."

At fifteen paces Olcán considered the unusual shape of Conall's spear. Unlike the normal flattened head, this had an arm's length of iron shaped into a sharp spike. It dawned on him, that it was designed for throwing. His assessment quickly changed, seeing not a boy, but a warrior, bearing down on him, perfectly balanced, his grey-blue eyes sharp and focused. He watched, as if in a dream, as Conall's grip on the javelin effortlessly changed from carrying to throwing, his arm rising up in one fluid movement as he released the weapon. Instinctively, Olcán began to turn and crouch, swinging his shield across his body, but he knew, as he watched the javelin's spinning flight, that he had left it too late. It was he who had made a very basic mistake and underestimated his enemy.

Cursing his stupidity, he growled, "Shite," as the tip of the javelin carved a piece from the edge of his shield before piercing his leather armor. Ribs cracked at the impact and he felt sharp pain as the weapon punched through his chest, emerging from his back in a spurt of blood, torn flesh and cloth. Impaled and in shock, Olcán slumped to his knees and waited. His dimming eyes strained to focus on the young man who now stood before him, sword in hand.

"This is for my mother, father and sisters, you bastard." Conall's sword sliced the air, the sun glinting off the unused, polished surface. The edge met Olcán's neck and Conall's arm jarred as the sword tried to carve a way through, but was resisted by bone, sinew and muscle. Hot blood spurted from torn arteries, splattering over him. He tried to pull the sword out, but found he needed to put his foot on the warrior's chest to twist and pry away the blade.

The difficulty of removing a blade from a man's torso was the first of many harsh lessons that Conall was to learn. The second was how difficult it was to cleanly remove a head from a body. Conall hacked at the neck until the head was freed. Then, holding it by Olcán's long, red braids, he turned, spat on the lifeless corpse, and threw the head towards the band of attackers. Cheering immediately broke out behind the stockade as he walked back through the gates. Stunned silence and uncertainty was the response from the attackers.

Cassius Fabius Scaeva, mounted on what he considered to be a poor specimen of a horse, regarded the scene with some trepidation. This was supposed to be a simple mission. Slaughter the community, take the weapons and armor, pay off the barbarians and travel back to Rome with an army of mercenaries.

His mission orders had actually been to negotiate and pay the blacksmith for the armor and weapons; however, he needed money and swiftly concluded that he could get it by killing what he deemed to be inferior, and largely unarmed, barbarians. In Eochaidh Ruad, he had found a willing accomplice.

Cassius was neither well-liked nor loved in Rome. His exploits and debauched tastes had rapidly outgrown his inheritance and his ability to obtain credit. Being a member of the noble and influential Fabius family, he still had a last recourse in the person of Marcus Fabius Ambustus, Pontifex Maximus of Rome. However, Marcus had ambitions for himself and his three sons, and did not particularly want Cassius anywhere near Rome. So Cassius had been given a choice. A slave galley to Egypt or the mission to this land the barbarians called Ériu to secure a supply of weapons, armor and men. There was also the implied third option of finding himself in a warm bath with his wrists opened.

As he looked at the tall, lean warrior beside him, Cassius was well aware that Faolán Ó Floinn's brother that had just been beheaded. Of the two brothers, Olcán had been the warrior, but the red-haired Faolán had a natural ability to lead the pack and was commander of Eochaidh's forces. As he looked on the tightly drawn muscles of Faolán's face, Cassius was unable to resist putting his Roman foot in his mouth as he remarked condescendingly, "So this was your brother's great plan." Barely had he finished when a fist wrapped in iron-studded, leather strips broke his nose and several teeth. He found himself sprawled on the ground, struggling to stem the flow of blood from his face with his purple robe.

"One more word, Roman, and I'll spread your guts out on the ground and leave you for the wolves. I didn't like the agreement my king made. Personally, I thought we should just slit your throat and take the gold. We had no quarrel with these people – until now."

Faolán turned to his second-in-command. "Take charge of those bastards. Hit the settlement hard now. No prisoners. Kill them all. Burn the settlement to the ground. I'll hold the rest in reserve. If I need to use them and you are still alive, I'll put your head on a spear." Treasach gave Faolán a sour look, but nodded, grabbed his spear and trotted across open ground until he reached the warriors milling around in front of the settlement. He was of stocky build and average height, his body hard and muscular. Treasach was memorable for his hair – dark brown at the roots going to blonde at the tips. Unfortunately, the constant use of lime wash to bleach his hair also made it stand up stiff as a board – although it did make him look a good hand taller.

There was no love lost between Treasach and his men. He chose to lead by brute force and severe punishments for failure rather than respect and esprit-de-corps. But he had a reputation for standing his ground and all knew he would not be easy on anyone who tried to retreat. Treasach barked at his men, "Faolán wants the settlement taken. Now! What are you bastards waiting for? Are you hoping the children will surrender? Move forward. I'll gut anyone looking back." Cursing him, the warriors spread out in a skirmish line and moved towards the settlement. The noise of axes, spears and swords slapping against shields was heard in the settlement as the attackers picked up their pace.

The cheering died down as a blood soaked Conall re-entered the settlement. "Well, so much for negotiating our release," Fearghal remarked sarcastically. "I guess diplomacy will not be a great strength of yours!"

In shock and unable to speak, Conall trembled at the realization of what had taken place. Unable to set his sword down, his knuckles were white from the vice-like grip. "Here, drink this. It will help." Fearghal handed over a jug and Conall took a mouthful. Moments later he was coughing and spluttering as the liquid burnt a track down his throat.

"What was in that?" Conall croaked.

Fearghal laughed and slapped Conall's back, "Oh just a wee Northern recipe passed down by my father. I keep it for special occasions. We'll drink more tonight – if we're still alive."

"They're getting closer, Fearghal." Brion called from the stockade.

"Bar the gate and move the wagons against them. You four get into the wagons with Conall and me. Brion, take three with you and spread out on the right side of the stockade. Brocc, take three and hold the left. Mórrígan spread your archers either side of the gateway, but keep behind the others. Just keep shooting until you exhaust your supply of arrows. Then hide. As for you three…" Fearghal peered sternly at the youngest who stood terrified and close to tears. Then he grinned. "Keep a watch on the back gateway. Shout if you see anyone get close to it."

Fearghal shook his head as he surveyed his defenses before climbing onto the wagon. Taking a deep breath, he roared "Mac Gabhann abú," slamming his sword hilt rhythmically against the wooden side of the wagon. "Mac Gabhann abú, Mac Gabhann abú." It took Conall a few moments to realize that Fearghal had taken his father's name and made it into a battle cry. Tears welled into his eyes as he hoarsely took up the shout, slapping his javelin against his shield.

Soon all the group from youngest to the eldest was yelling, "Mac Gabhann abú. Mac Gabhann abú."

Conall looked around his friends, "Remember our mothers, fathers, sisters and brothers. Show no mercy. None will be given. The goddess of the woods and the waters be with us." He turned and faced the oncoming warriors.

PART 2: THE SOUTHERN WAR

415–411 B.C.

CHAPTER 3

415 B.C.

On a raised bank, just a short distance from the edge of the forest, Faolán's mount grazed on sweet autumn grass.

"Shite!"

From his vantage point, Faolán could quite clearly observe the skirmish. He could also hear the battle cry resounding from the settlement as his men approached. Cassius had remounted and was again beside Faolán. He measured his words more carefully this time, although they were slurred due to his swollen and painful jaw.

"Surely you don't see a problem in taking the settlement. After all, they are just a handful of children and a lone warrior, not fighters."

"Arsehole! No wonder they sent you on this mission. Your masters must have wanted you out of the way and I can see why." Faolán looked contemptuously on Cassius, "Take a hard look at their position. The settlement doesn't have a high stockade, but it's built on a dirt bank on a natural hill and is surrounded by a ditch, which no doubt, holds some surprises. My men will be fighting uphill - and a pretty steep hill at that, all the way to the gate. Those so-called children have access to the best weapons and armor available. Much better than my men, as you well know. Your master's gold paid for them."

"And... They have a warrior chieftain in Fearghal ó Maoilriain from the Ulaid. A people renowned in this island for their fighting skills. I've interrogated some of his comrades. So far none have given up anything about him except that he is the best warrior in Ériu and commands their unswerving loyalty." Cassius made no comment as Faolán paused.

"Now, they also have a hero. That "boy" took down one of the best chieftains in this kingdom, as natural as it comes. If we don't kill Conall Mac Gabhann today, then we'll have much more trouble coming. It won't take long before superstitious peasants start believing he is some ancient god or hero reborn. You better have more gold in your bags, Roman. This will have a high price."

Cassius smiled through bloodied teeth, wishing he could slide the dagger he was fingering between Faolán's ribs. Faolán looked at him, seeing a coward with no honor, "I know what you're thinking, Roman. Just try it."

The raiders' pace quickened. Some cursed as the sharp points of caltrops pierced leather boots and flesh forcing them back onto the heavily rutted pathway to the settlement. As they came closer to the gate, Mórrígan and her young archers went to work. Scattered showers of arrows fell on them. Not enough to do any major damage, but enough to slow their advance and make them more cautious. In return, the raiders swore and shouted in anger and frustration. A few with spears halted and hurled them, but they fell short or glanced harmlessly off the fence. At twenty paces, Fearghal lifted his first javelin, balanced it in his hand, and launched it at the pack leader. The missile took the raider in the chest, driving him back into the warriors that followed.

"They're in range. Throw your javelins."

Along the stockade, javelins were lifted and heaved at the pack of men charging up the hill or trying to cross the ditch. Young muscles strained and burned, unused to such activity, but with jaws set and teeth gritted, the defenders kept up a steady volley. Men screamed as iron spikes punched holes in their flesh. Some died, but more fell, disabled by the shafts and were trampled by their comrades.

The pack steadily edged closer to the gate as the stock of javelins diminished. A few picked up the thrown javelins and tossed them back, but the angle was not great and most fell short or became lodged in the wooden gate and palisade.

"Keep a javelin for close range," Fearghal shouted as the pack came within five paces of the settlement fence. While their numbers had been reduced by death and injury, there remained over thirty snarling men moving forward, determined to complete the job.

"Fire the ditch Mórrígan. Now!" At Fearghal's order, Mórrígan dipped arrows tipped with oil-soaked cloth in the brazier behind her. She flinched in pain as the flames licked at her fingers before each arrow was released. The straw and wood in the ditch smoldered, then burst into flames, filling the area in front of the stockade with thick smoke. Surprised at their resourcefulness, Treasach cursed the settlement defenders as he drove his men forward.

"Who will sing stories of you if you're beaten by children?"

As they reached the gate, some of the men split off left and right jumping into the ditch. Amid the smoke filled air the first few died, impaled on unseen wooden stakes. Those following used their comrades broken bodies to bridge the ditch. Throwing axes were launched. Screams from within the compound told Fearghal that some had found their mark.

Brion looked down at his young friend. Niall ó Bric had an axe head buried in his chest. In the last convulsions before his spirit departed, he grabbed Brion's arm and cursed the attackers. Brion swore, gritted his teeth and drove forward with his javelin. His first lunge glanced off the shield of Niall's killer. Quickly recovering, Brion thrust hard once more, catching the warrior as he lifted his arm to strike. The javelin punched into the man under his armpit. Bellowing in agony and spitting blood flecked with foam, as his lungs and heart were pierced, he fell back. His body hung, suspended above the ground, impaled on a wooden stake. Brion swore as his javelin, embedded firmly in the man, was torn from his grip. Pulling his sword from its sheath, he readied for the next attacker.

On the left side of the gate, Brocc ó Cathasaigh, a thin, wiry lad who, along with his twin Mórrígan, had been looking forward to his sixteenth summer, was fighting an increasingly desperate battle as more attackers reached the palisade and were able to bring their axes into play. He wailed as an axe head pulled his shield down just enough for the adjacent attacker to slice a deep cut down his arm. As he stumbled back in pain, Siollan ó Dubhghaill took his place. His reward was to receive a blow from an axe that spilt the front of his helmet and opened up his skull.

As Siollan fell, Brocc snarled and swung his blade wildly at his slayer. The attacker was unbalanced and stretched over the stockade; more startling, he looked no older than Brocc. A first slash left the attacker's hand joined by a flap of skin to his wrist. Looking into the young attacker's shocked face, Brocc drove his sword point into his mouth and up into his brain. Blood and gore soaked him and the surrounding fence. His lips, now drawn back into a ferocious grimace, accentuated his normal sharp features as he swung at yet another attacker.

Though occupied by stabbing and raining blows on a stream of assailants, out of the corner of his eye, Conall could see the mass of men crowding against the stockade and gateway. Increasingly frequent shrieks of pain told him he had lost more of his friends who, if not dead, were wounded badly enough to be of little use.

"We can't hold them Fearghal. They'll just pick us off one-by-one. We need another plan."

Fearghal shouted over his shoulder, "This fence was made for keeping animals out, not an army." He grunted, shoving back a wounded attacker and ripping his sword through the man's belly as he fell. "It's not strong or high enough to be a real defensive position. And if I know anything about battles, there's bound to be a reserve pack waiting in the forest."

"Well if we can't hold them off we need to meet them. They won't be expecting that!" Conall glanced at Fearghal hoping for an answer, but Fearghal was busy stabbing at a huge, half-naked warrior. The man was covered in coarse red body hair, sported a massive red beard and was missing half of his rotted yellow teeth. He was roaring and hacking double-handed at the gate with an enormous battle axe. The man took hit after hit without it slowing him down.

Fearghal couldn't get a clean stab at him, over both the wagon and the gate, and was loath to give up his javelin. "This bastard will have the gate in pieces soon, Conall – if not with his axe then with his stink – he mustn't have bathed since he was born. You're the smart one. We need a plan. Think of something and make it quick."

Conall looked feverishly over his surroundings looking for inspiration. He glanced at his parents' home, immediately filling with anger at losing them, then he thought of the games his father used to have them play with the new armor and weapons.

"Fearghal, the wall. The wall."

"You're not making much sense. I know the stockade is coming down and when it does we're in deep shite."

Conall groaned and shook his head, "Sometimes you're an eejit, Fearghal. Think about that game my father taught us to play - the shield wall. We form the wall then take the battle to them. You know how difficult you found it to break the wall when it was formed and kept together. The space between the gates could be spanned by six of us in a front row. We can use Mórrígan and the wolfhounds as a diversion to distract them on their flanks while we regroup."

Totally unconvinced that it would work, but equally convinced they were all going to die, Fearghal grunted, "Why not?"

Mórrígan and the hounds were dispatched out the rear gates and raced around to the ongoing skirmish. When she was within range, Mórrígan screamed a torrent of insults at the attackers and sent flights of arrows from her diminishing stock. Teeth bared, the hounds snarled and snapped continuously as they closed with the fighters. In reply, the attackers hurled insults at Mórrígan and rocks at the circling hounds.

The commotion, however, was a sufficient distraction. As the wagons were rolled aside, defenders were called off the stockade and formed up in two rows of six. The biggest and oldest stood in the front; the back row's job was to steady and strengthen them.

Fearghal grumbled that he had a stick in his hand rather than his longsword, but stood steady with Conall to his left. Brion took up position on Conall's left; Brocc was placed on Fearghal's right and the ó Cuileannáin brothers, Labhraidh and Fionnbharr, stood at the ends of the row.

Conall yelled at the remaining younger ones to pull aside the bar on the gate. As the gates swung open, Conall looked to his friends who were now covered in cuts and blood. "Lock shields," he shouted. "Javelins ready. Move forward." The small wall of shields moved into the gap to face assailants whose expressions reflected surprise and confusion.

"By the Hag, what is going on?" Faolán muttered to himself, as he watched the gates of the settlement swing open.

"Maybe they intend to surrender to your superior tactics?" Cassius ventured, his voice dripping with sarcasm.

Faolán ignored Cassius this time, deciding to cut his throat later. He turned to Sleibhin – a huge mountain of a man, and brother of the equally huge and hairy attacker who was still threatening the gate. "Move the rest out. I don't like the way this is going. There are too many surprises for my liking." The remaining warriors moved out from the trees to the edge of the fields and waited for instructions.

Further along the forest edge, the wind whipped up the edges of a black cloak draped over the shoulders of a solitary rider. The cloak's deep crimson lining, flipped over by the breezes, contrasted against the velvet black coat of the magnificent horse on which the rider sat. He had chosen his position with all the care of his heritage – and trade. The afternoon sun blinded Faolán and Cassius from uncovering his position while he observed all that took place with a high degree of interest.

Nikandros was a stranger to Ériu. A Spartan, he had travelled to the Roman Republic after the Peloponnesian War in search of new challenges. He was thirty summers old, tall and muscular with long, black, naturally curled hair and a short beard. His skin was tanned golden brown from spending most of the time outside in much warmer climates.

Even in the cold of Ériu he only wore a lightweight, dark red tunic just long enough to cover his genitals. His armor – bronze cuirass, greaves and helmet - was carried in a pack lashed to his horse. He had left his favorite weapon – his beloved doru, in Rome, and now only carried his sword. The xiphos was a double-edged sword used for cutting and thrusting, and hung from a baldric under his left arm. His wide circular shield, made of wood and leather, and faced with bronze, was slung over the side of the horse.

He was a mercenary by circumstance and had met his current employers - Marcus Fabius Ambustus, and his eldest son Quintus, in a skirmish with bandits outside of Rome. They were impressed with each other and Marcus offered him work. Soon, Nikandros became known as Marcus' shadow, gaining a reputation for resolving disputes. Indeed, his method of conflict management was to ensure the other party was never seen again.

Unsurprisingly, Marcus did not trust the idiot Cassius to do a good job, act wisely or to protect his interests. And given the sensitivity of the mission, and Marcus' position as Pontifex, he decided he needed insurance. That insurance was to send Nikandros, with gold and instructions, to make sure there were no loose ends. So far, Nikandros was not impressed at the turn of events and knew Marcus would not be pleased. At this moment, it seemed to Nikandros that he was looking at a tangle of loose ends.

He reached behind him and drew a bow from its cover, two arrows followed. The bow - a gift from a Mongol Khan many years ago in celebration of a job well done, was the latest addition to his weaponry. It was made from birch, sinew, and the horns of a sheep. Though lighter and shorter than most, the bow had a range far in excess of anything owned by the local warriors. Nikandros watched and waited.

Surprise soon turned to anger and Faolán's attackers hurled themselves at the shield wall. Their combined weight drove the wall back a pace, yet it held across the gateway as the back row steadied the front. Those in the front hoisted their javelins and started to stab the attackers. Screams of rage rose as iron spikes punctured and ripped flesh. Blood spurted onto arms, faces and shields from gouged faces and necks. One warrior screamed as an iron spike found the soft flesh of his eye, bursting it and mangling his brains as the spike was pushed through his skull. Another howled as a spike tore his neck. Blood spurted several paces from a slashed artery and his body soon fell to the side as its life drained away.

A roar came. The pack parted and moved aside as the unwashed, red giant forced his way forward again. "Shite Conall," Brion shouted, "what will take that bastard down?"

Fearghal shouted, "Front row throw your javelins before he gets too close." A flight of six javelins whipped through the air. Three struck the giant, but he kept moving forward, albeit slower with the javelins embedded in his limbs and shoulder. He stopped, grunted, snapped the javelin shafts and then lifted and swung his battle-axe.

The axe caught the edge of Fearghal's shield, almost tearing it from his grip and pulling it downwards. But it left a gap that allowed Brocc to chop down hard with his sword. The blade sliced through the muscle and tendons of the giant's exposed arm. He bellowed and tried to bring the axe up again for another strike. This time, Conall thrust forward with his sword as the giant exposed his fat belly. The blade punched through the giant's stomach, emptying his guts on the ground as Conall twisted upwards and wrenched the sword out. At the same time, Fearghal slashed across the giant's chest opening a wide, bloody gash that exposed white ribs. The giant dropped to his knees as the stench of his shite filled the air; then fell forward to die.

The remaining attackers, stunned at the turn of events, made to run away. A spear thrust from Treasach tore out the throat of the nearest one.

"I told you I'd kill anyone who ran. Now get back and earn your gold. Kill those bastards."

Cursing Treasach and the defenders equally, the warriors once again turned to the shield wall. The wall braced itself for the next onslaught holding fresh javelins passed forward by the back row. This time the attackers had to scramble over the bodies of their fallen comrades and fight on ground that was slippery with blood, shite and entrails. As they hit the wall, unbalanced, they were stabbed again and again by the iron spikes. The wall held.

Frustrated and enraged, Faolán's men kept coming, but made little impact. This was not the way they knew to fight and they were uncertain how to combat it. There was no room for them to get behind their enemy. Several more fell to javelin thrusts sinking into soft flesh and muscle, or cracking ribs and other bones. They soon gave up and retreated. Treasach, thinking of the threat to his own life if he failed in his mission brandished his spear and shouted at them to get back and fight.

This time, the snarling pack of bloodied warriors united to face him with raised swords, spears and axes. Treasach stepped back a few paces to get on solid ground and snarled, "Try it you sons of whores. How many of you want to die?"

The pack halted and stood to the side of the pathway. One of them shouted, "Then you fight them. Show us how it's done, big man."

Faced with no choices, Treasach swore at the men and strode toward the shield wall. When he got to within five paces he halted. He had seen what the young warrior had done to his chieftain earlier so he was not altogether keen on facing him. On the other hand, he had also heard stories about Fearghal ó Maoilriain, but hoped they were exaggerated tales told by drunks and slaves.

Treasach called out, "Fight me Fearghal ó Maoilriain, if you're not a coward. Fight me, and if you kill me, you can all go free. You have my word."

Fearghal turned to Conall, "You know he's lying, don't you?"

Conall nodded, "But if you kill him it may give us a break. The rest of his men won't fight on."

Fearghal agreed, "Well I'm not fighting with this little sword." He turned to Brocc and handed him his short-sword and shield. As he strode forward to meet Treasach he reached behind and his longsword slid smoothly from his back-scabbard. Treasach dropped his spear and took up an axe, balancing it in his right hand; his round wooden shield swung across his chest for protection. He was the same height as Fearghal, but much heavier. They circled each other,

Treasach wary of the sword's longer reach.

At the edge of the woods, Faolán and Cassius could only watch as the two men faced each other. Cassius looked at Faolán and smiled, "Would you care to wager on the outcome? Five gold pieces says that your man dies."

"Dún do bheal – shut your mouth," Faolán snarled at the Roman, but in truth he was thinking the same. This was not turning out to be a good day. By his estimate, more than half of the men who had been sent to take the settlement were either dead or wounded.

Furthermore, as he looked to the sky beyond the settlement he saw that dark threatening clouds were coming in from the west, replacing the earlier sunshine. The rumble of distant thunder confirmed in his mind that the omens were not particularly good. He was also starting to consider how this would look to Eochaidh Ruad. The king would not be happy. With some resignation, Faolán signaled his remaining men to move forward.

As Fearghal lifted his longsword up into a striking position, Treasach sprang forward. He was surprisingly fast for a man carrying his weight, and struck first with his shield, forcing the iron boss into Fearghal's chest. Fearghal grunted in pain. Treasach swung his axe around in a low arc, thinking to slash across Fearghal's legs, but was hit hard on the head as Fearghal brought the longsword's pommel down on Treasach's skull.

Stunned and feeling blood trickle down his face, Treasach regretted not wearing a helmet. However, his skull was thick and his mind cleared quickly as he instinctively changed the direction of his axe and scythed upwards to slash Fearghal's side. He smiled as he felt the axe strike, thinking that he had wounded the northerner. Instead, as he stepped back and glanced down, he saw that his axe was as clean as when he had started.

Fearghal grinned ghoulishly, "New armor. You should try it."

He moved forward, sword gripped in both hands and pointed at Treasach's chest. Treasach blocked the thrust with his shield, but Fearghal was already turning around, moving to his right and around Treasach's back. The blade swung low across the back of Treasach's legs and its sharp edge sliced effortlessly through leather pants. Treasach howled as he felt the sword tear through muscle and warm blood flowing down his calves.

He stumbled and turned to face his opponent, but Fearghal was moving faster and had changed direction. The longsword's razor sharp tip cut along an exposed neck, and then opened up a bloody gash on his opponent's forehead. Blinded by blood and pain, Treasach cursed, shouted and attempted to strike out at Fearghal who kept on moving and changing direction. Like a wasp, the sword point stung wherever it saw weaknesses.

With further stabbing wounds to his legs and arms, Treasach knew he was not doing well. He was losing blood, breathing heavily and tiring fast. Finding it difficult to hold up his shield, he tried to change his grip for a better balance. It dropped just enough for Fearghal. The longsword's point slashed across Treasach's upper chest, and he felt his flesh open up. Blood drenched his torso, and the shield slipped a fraction more. It was more than enough.

Fearghal took a step forward and his sword swept in a long arc through the air parallel to the ground. The weight and momentum of the blade carried it through Treasach's neck severing his head from his body. Blood fountained upwards as his heart beat for the last few times. Seizing a discarded spear, Fearghal spiked the head and raised it into the air with a roar of "Mac Gabhann abú."

At that, the remaining attackers turned and fled back towards the forest.

Faolán cursed as he watched his men scatter and run from the settlement. He considered having them executed immediately, but thought he might need some of them another time and probably sooner than he would like. Instead, he consoled himself by taking note of who he would hang later as an example.

Cassius watched in amusement, and with some degree of pleasure, at Faolán's growing angst. Rubbing salt into the wound, he sneered, "So, what will be our story when we report to Eochaidh Ruad? I presume we're returning to Carn Tigherna now, rather than taking a second beating from the children in the settlement."

Aiming to plant his fist once more into Cassius' face, Faolán slowly turned to face the Roman. He should have gathered his men up and done exactly as Cassius suggested. Take them back to the fort and get new orders from Eochaidh, but he was angry, proud and stung by Cassius' words. He bridled at the inference that he was a poor leader and a coward. Jumping down from his horse, Faolán strode forward.

"Move the men out," he barked at Sleibhin. "Put the bastards that ran in the front row. If they object, kill them."

A large drop of rain on his face and thunder in the distance reminded Faolán that the weather was changing fast, and not in his favor. Dark clouds now covered the sky and in a short while the land would be sodden. A strange white mist was making its way down the mountain at an unnatural speed. Soon it would engulf the settlement. The flashes of lightning that appeared to dance on the mountain peaks behind the settlement just about sealed the list of ominous signs. However, he was committed and Faolán was, by any standards, a brave warrior and a loyal subject. He stomped onward.

Fearghal's celebrations were short-lived as he watched the reinforcements crossing the open ground towards the settlement. He anxiously looked at Conall who appeared to be of the same mind at their expected fate. Totally focused on what lay before them, neither had noticed that the weather had changed until a flushed Mórrígan rode up and shouted, "Storm coming." In the midst of battle no one realized that the weather had shifted from sunny to overcast. Mórrígan stood up, her feet lodged in her mount's leather belly straps, and pointed at the mist rolling down the mountains.

"Never seen that come so quick before. Strange things are happening today."

"Hopefully the rain will make it more difficult for them than us. Form the wall. Mórrígan, pick up any arrows you can and stand behind us with your bow. Fearghal, call your hounds to heel. I think we're going to need them." Conall looked at his friends, exhausted, covered in blood, and suffering from bruises and sword and axe cuts. They were no longer children; their spirits were troubled knowing they had killed today.

"Friends, we've had a hard few days and none that we deserved or expected, but we've fought these bastards before and we can do it again. Remember your parents and families." Conall took his place in the shield wall and watched as the next wave of warriors moved closer. Behind him, the fog continued to roll in. It finally stopped when it had covered the stockade and gate, and lay almost on top of them.

An unearthly scream froze everyone, attackers and defenders alike, to the spot. As one, Conall, Fearghal, and Faolán muttered, "Shite!" Cassius looked confused; Nikandros struggled to steady his horse. The scream came again. This time louder, piercing eardrums and setting hearts to thump much, much faster, until the men thought their chests would burst open.

Cassius and Nikandros could see better from a distance, but were not sure they could believe their eyes. The mist had stopped and possibly even retreated slightly to reveal a stooped, grey-cloaked figure, staff in hand, who appeared to hover over the gatepost. One after another, the attackers breathed the same word, afraid to say it aloud, "Bean-sidhe," dropped to their knees, eyes fixed on the ground, not wanting to look at the apparition. The harbinger of death was among them and they were scared shiteless. To a man, they crawled away on their bellies until only Faolán and Sleibhin were left standing before the shield wall.

Then, in contrast to the scream, the apparition spoke in melodic, siren tones that floated on the wind. "Walk away with whatever honor you have left, Faolán. It is not your time to die – unless you want me to make it so. And make no mistake: if you choose now, the worms will feast on your flesh. Take this message to Eochaidh Ruad. Tell him the aes sídhe are not pleased. He has violated the gheasa that made him prosperous. The blood of this community is on his hands. It must and will be paid for – blood for blood. Now go."

With little choice, Faolán bowed his head and retreated to the woods where his men waited. He mounted his horse and started on the path back to Carn Tigherna. Cassius, not knowing what to make of these strange events for once chose prudence and kept quiet for the rest of the journey.

At the distant tree-line, Nikandros decided that he needed to know more of what was happening before planning on his next moves. He took up the reins of his horse intending to take a path round the rear of the settlement. The horse went as far as the edge of the trees then stubbornly refused to advance. As he tried to move the beast, he thought he heard a word carried on the wind, "No." Shaking his head in disbelief, but needing time to think, the Spartan turned the horse around and slowly trotted deeper into the forest.

Not one person dared turn around for fear of what they might see. The wolfhounds, curiously subdued, sat beside Fearghal. They looked up at him, almost willing their master to say something. He didn't. Then a mocking female voice said, "Well, Fearghal ó Maoilriain or whatever you're calling yourself, it has taken me a long time to find you. Now, since I've saved your lives, the least you could do is introduce me."

Fearghal looked at Conall and Brion, shook his head in resignation and muttered, "From the cauldron into the fire."

He turned and bowed to the figure that still seemed to float over the gatepost. "Let me introduce you to the Sidhe, Mongfhionn, who at various times has been, and may still be, queen, bean-sidhe, seanachaí, Druidess and giver of geis. She can be both a true friend and an implacable enemy. Do not under any circumstance trust her!"

Mongfhionn cackled provocatively, "Didn't you leave one thing out? Embrace me, lover!"

Even in the midst of the death and carnage around them, first Mórrígan and then the rest started to giggle then laugh out loud as the tension was relieved. Fearghal just glowered, then grunted and studied the ground intently.

Conall turned to the cloaked and crooked figure and bowed, "My lady, we thank you for your help. Without your intervention we would surely have died today."

Acknowledging Conall, Mongfhionn said, "Good timing and illusions work well on the feeble-minded. Today was not your time to die. The goddess has work for you to accomplish, but your thanks are appreciated." Looking at Fearghal she said, "And it's more than some have given."

To Conall she continued, "I am sorry that I was unable to be here sooner to help your families. I have some words to say over them so that they will rest in peace, but before that, there are the practicalities. You have bodies to strip and behead."

Shocked, Conall, mouth open, was about to protest, but Mongfhionn continued, "Come, come Conall Mac Gabhann. You may not have fought in anger before today, but surely you know what happens after battle. The dead are to be beheaded so that their spirits will not haunt the living and their heads need to be staked to strike fear into your enemies. If any are alive, although I very much doubt it, they must be killed or sacrificed, as you have no keep for prisoners. Also, how do you propose to feed your "army"? You'll need silver, gold, weapons. Indeed, anything that can be traded. So, you will search and strip the bodies for trophies of value."

As suddenly as she had appeared on the gatepost, Mongfhionn now stood beside Conall and Fearghal, her face still shaded by the hood of her cloak. Brion whispered to his sister, "Crone or goddess, Mórrígan?"

Their rescuer had given the impression of being old, stooped and needing the staff to lean on, but as she straightened up, she stood almost the same height as Fearghal. In her right hand, the solid oak staff, just short of her own height, looked more like a weapon than a crutch.

Fearghal shrugged in resignation. "She's right, Conall. You're no longer simple villagers. As for me, it seems I can't escape that which I left behind." He turned, headed to the nearest body and started to strip anything valuable from it. When he had finished, he used the longsword to behead the warrior.

"There's a big difference between fighting and looting bodies," Conall retorted as he set his shield down and with a look of total distaste, chose a corpse and followed Fearghal's lead. Soon Brion, Brocc and the rest did likewise. Away from the heat of battle, the sound of retching, and the stink of vomit, soon filled the air as the unhappy band set about their work.

When they had finished, a row of stakes displaying the fallen's heads lined the pathway to the settlement. A pile of valuables and weapons collected lay on several shields. Unfortunately, for them, two attackers had survived. Their wounds had made them unable to crawl away. Mongfhionn ordered that they be dragged to the center of the settlement.

"Now let's all get inside. We have business to take care of to keep the goddess happy, there are wounds to dress, and friends to send to their gods before the sun sets." Mongfhionn turned and led the way back into the settlement, and the gates were closed.

The dead - Niall, his brother Ronan, and Siollán, were all fourteen or fifteen summers old. Their friends stood silent as the Sidhe prayed over them

> *Trí shúil bhé, a bhfuil grá aici dom,*
> *Trí shúil an bhanfháidh, a thugann treoir eagnaí dom,*
> *Le cairdeas agus gean,*
> *Le do nádúr diaga, mo bhandia,*
> *Líon ár riachtanais.*

Go dtuga tú cosaint dár laochra ar lár;
Agus i gcosaint, neart fiartha dá n-aistear.

As the flames licked around the funeral pyre, Mongfhionn turned to Conall and Fearghal, "Bring the prisoners." She stood before the three dwellings in which so much evil had been committed. The prisoners trembled and looked wretched, under no illusion as to their imminent fate. Mongfhionn looked at them unsympathetically, "At least you will be able to do one good deed before your journey to the Other-world."

Conall, shocked at the brutality of what happened next, saw the flash of a dagger and heard a gurgling sound as a blade was drawn swiftly across the prisoners' throats. Gouts of blood poured onto the dirt as the men died. Her hands soaked in their blood, Mongfhionn stood at the entrances of each home and smeared blood on the lintel and sides. At each she simply said, "Be at rest, go in peace." The red sun was slowly setting in the western sky as the Sidhe finished.

Fearghal turned to Conall, "She always had great timing. Mongfhionn will tend to the wounded as, among her many talents, she is a healer. Now let's eat. I'm starving. Then we all need a good night's rest. It has been a long day."

As it happened, the fair-haired, Fionnbharr ó Cuileannáin - a shy, slight boy of sixteen summers appeared to have a natural talent for healing. Mongfhionn guided him in the application of herbs, poultices and the use of a needle and thread to sew up the wounds of his friends. Of some concern to Conall, she also taught him a few chants in a language unintelligible to his ears. He wondered whether the Sidhe was a creature from Tír inna n-Óc or a much darker place.

Conall contemplated the scene before him as his friends, with pride, pointed out their fresh scars and bruises. The roaring fire in the center of the encampment gave comfort to all, as they ate and talked about the day that had past. Fearghal rarely took his eyes off Mongfhionn and it was obvious that they both shared a long history. From the occasional haunted look on Fearghal's face, not all of it was remembered with happiness. Yet Conall had a sense that they were opposite sides of the same coin.

Eventually weariness crept in, and the newly blooded warriors slowly drifted away from the fire. Mórrígan, Brion, Brocc, and their two younger brothers nodded to Conall and went to their home. Conall and his brother Eirnín looked at their dwelling, and for the first time since the awful discovery Conall thought of his parents without revenge in his mind.

"You cannot enter your home Conall."

Startled from his thoughts he looked at Mongfhionn with anger again burning in his eyes.

"Why? You've spoken to them and blessed their journey. Our home is at peace."

She looked at him and spoke softly, "Yes, they are gone, but they have left messages for us to find and decipher. They alone know who originated this treachery. Tomorrow, in daylight we will seek out what they have to say."

Conall looked in torment at his home and then at Mongfhionn and Fearghal. Shoulders slumped, he grabbed some skins and put his arm around Eirnín as they made their way to one of the wagons. Mercifully, they were quickly asleep. Fearghal whistled softly and his hounds took up guard positions close by.

Glancing back as she quietly made her way across the settlement, Mórrígan saw Mongfhionn reach out a hand and with her finger trace along the long scar on Fearghal's left cheek. In the light of the fire Fearghal smiled and took Mongfhionn in his arms. Mórrígan smiled as she went inside. This certainly was a side to Fearghal that no one had imagined.

CHAPTER 4

The next morning Mórrígan mounted up, took Fearghal's hounds and rode out to patrol. Mongfhionn, Conall and Fearghal returned to Conall's home. The others made a start on repairing and strengthening the defenses.

At the doorway, Mongfhionn held her hand up to forestall Conall from going inside. Eyes closed, and in a tone that made the hair rise on the back of their necks, she chanted. After a moment, the Sidhe slipped through the doorway. Stunned by the atmosphere of violence that pervaded the air, she wept as she felt how Conall's father, mother and sisters had suffered and were slaughtered. As she moved deeper inside, still chanting and praying, she felt her healing energies and life force drain away, until the beautiful woman was replaced by a crooked and stooped crone. She gasped as she absorbed the choking residue of death until she knew that the home was finally peaceful.

Exhausted and weak, she stumbled and grasped the table edge. Hearing Conall and Fearghal about to rush inside, she shrieked, "No! You will not cross that threshold unless you wish to die." Breathing hard, she gripped the solid oak table - the altar on which Conall's mother had been sacrificed. Her countenance lifted as the aged wood drew strength from the earth and became hers. She felt her skin and body restored and as she regained her vigor, she noticed a scrap of cloth lying on the floor. Mongfhionn thanked Conall's mother, spun around and strode toward the doorway.

Conall and Fearghal were brushed aside like chaff in the wind as Mongfhionn stormed out of the house. Her eyes blazed in fury and her appearance was terrible to look upon. Fearghal rolled his eyes, "We're in trouble now." Conall could only think that this was the first time he had actually seen Mongfhionn's head not covered by the hood of her cloak. He stared at her waist length, almost white hair shot through with streaks of red-gold. Her face was pale, highlighted by fiery red cheeks and full, blood-red lips; her eyes near black as the night sky.

"You won't see many with that coloring in this land, lad. Now stop staring, it's rude!" Fearghal chided.

"Fearghal, where are the trophies that were stripped from the bodies yesterday? I want to see them. Now!" They led her to where the trophies had been stored. Using her staff, she rummaged through the items until finally she uncovered a small purple velvet pouch. She tugged on the drawstring and pulled out a gold coin. Then she spat on the ground, turned to Fearghal and said but one word: "Romans."

Nikandros' plan had just gone up in flames and he must now decide on a new strategy. This disturbed him greatly, as he considered himself quite good at this particular game. From his vantage point, he curiously observed Mórrígan as she guided her horse along a well-trod pathway in the forest. He could see from her posture she was a confident and watchful rider, but was amused at the basic hunting bow that she carried over her shoulder. Not wishing to reveal his presence, he stayed downwind of the hounds that accompanied her.

A thunderous roar suddenly shattered the tranquility of the forest as a huge brown bear broke from the dense undergrowth and bounded on all fours in Mórrígan's direction.

Before Mórrígan or the horse could react, the bear was upon them. Roaring and growling, it rose up on its powerful back legs and with one blow knocked Mórrígan onto the forest floor. The horse tore off at a gallop, crashing through brush and branches, but the hounds, barking and snapping, placed themselves between Mórrígan and the bear. She lay on the ground unmoving, blood seeping from a deep cut on her head. The beast swayed and huffed at the dogs. Huge paws, with wicked curved claws, slashed the air as it tried to claim its quarry.

"Well it seems the gods have decided my next move," Nikandros thought, as he reached for his bow. He took three arrows out of the quiver and they flew in quick succession to lodge deep in the bear's neck. Maddened, the beast roared and clawed at the painful barbs. The hounds, sensing the animal was on the defense, circled then moved in closer, tearing and snapping at its lower body. They drove it back towards the bushes and further away from Mórrígan who still lay prone and senseless.

Nikandros approached from the side to face the bear. His own horse had seen battle many times and stood firm. He shot another three arrows. Two struck the bear's chest. The third found the bear's left eye, but the Spartan knew the arrows would only anger and slow the beast down. At best, they might persuade it to run away, but they would not kill it. Cursing that he did not have his doru, which would have given him more range, he quickly unclasped his cloak, and dismounted. Grabbing his shield and sword, he charged the bear.

Fortunately, the hounds sensed no threat from Nikandros toward their mistress and ignored him as they continued to harass the bear. Nikandros slashed and stabbed, trying to avoid its razor sharp claws, but luck still was with the beast. Blows from its powerful paws thudded against the Spartan's shield, and as he moved in closer, the bear pierced his defenses, raking his arms and naked chest.

He grunted in pain, feeling warm blood flowing, but the hunter in Nikandros sensed that the bear was at last weakening. Memories of his trials against nature to prove his manhood in the mountains of his native Sparta flooded his head as he pressed his attack. As the bear shambled backwards, Nikandros seized his opportunity, leapt forward and plunged his sword into its chest. The bear bellowed and then collapsed, its heart pierced. In an instant the hounds were on it, tearing at its throat until it was a lifeless carcass.

Bending over Mórrígan, Nikandros sprinkled water from a leather pouch onto her face. Her eyes opened briefly. Seeing a golden-skinned warrior who wore very little clothing bent over her only served to convince her that she had passed over into Tír inna n-Óc. Her hand made to touch the Spartan, but fell back as she relapsed into unconsciousness. Nikandros gathered her up in his arms, grunting in surprise at her weight. He laid her down again, looked under her tunic and smiled. "Chain-mail, very clever – and fortunate."

Forewarned, he took a better grip, hoisted her up onto his horse and lashed her to it with leather thongs. "We'd better get you to your friends." Before walking his horse, he put on his full armor, grimacing as the cuirass pressed against his clawed chest. "Might have to fight my way out of this," he thought, as he led the stallion towards the settlement. The hounds followed at a watchful distance.

They were gathered around the huge iron cauldron in which simmered a thick mutton stew for the evening meal. Conall was getting concerned at the absence of Mórrígan and was about to suggest that they should go search for her when Mongfhionn looked to the sky, paused, and then turned to him, "Beware of salvation in burnished gold and red. Its path has not been chosen and so can yet be a trap or a blessing."

Fearghal rolled his eyes, "See what I mean? She can never talk straight." But Conall's gaze was leveled on a black horse being walked towards the settlement. Its reins were held by a man who appeared to be clothed in gold, wearing a red cloak.

"Weapons and shields. Form the wall, we have a visitor. Let's be cautious until we know his purpose." Conall led his friends outside the settlement, halting about ten paces from the fence. Mongfhionn stood to the side, smiling in anticipation.

Nikandros walked to within twenty paces of the warriors and then halted. He tethered his mount, unclasped his cloak, and laid it over the horse's neck. Then he took off his helmet, shaking his hair loose. He moved deliberately and showed no fear or hesitation as he approached the young warriors.

He called out in a strange accent, pointing to his horse, "I believe that this young woman is a friend of yours. You should get her some attention quickly if you value her life. She had a hard fall and took a knock to her head." Conall and Fearghal strode towards the Spartan.

"You'd better explain yourself," Fearghal growled, his hand reaching over his shoulder for the long sword, "Or we'll have another head on a stake."

"Put the sword away, Fearghal. If the Spartan had meant trouble, you would have known about it long before this and he wouldn't have brought Mórrígan back." Mongfhionn nodded to the Spartan, took the reins of his horse and led it back into the settlement, "Fionnbharr and I will take care of Mórrígan." Left standing a wary distance apart, Nikandros and the group of warriors regarded each other.

"What in the name of the Hag is a Spartan?" Conall asked Fearghal.

"How should I know? Maybe we don't get out enough! He speaks strangely, and he sure knows how to dress up well, although that tunic doesn't leave much to the imagination." Fearghal looked the Spartan up and down, only now noticing the long red claw marks on his arms. "Well, are you going to stand there all day or will you tell us what happened?"

Conall walked up to Nikandros and held out his hand, "Thanks for bringing Mórrígan back. We have food and beer in the settlement and it looks like you could be doing with some of Fionnbharr's healing herbs. You're welcome to stay until you heal."

"My name is Nikandros and, as the lady said, I am from Sparta. I will come in and eat, but if you eat bear there's a big one just beyond the forest that would make a good meal and a warm covering. I'll explain what happened on the way." He looked at Fearghal, "Your hounds are very well trained. Without them your friend would be dead." Fearghal ceased glowering and started to smile. He had been in more battles than he cared to remember and could recognize a fellow warrior.

"Let's go get the bear. By the way we can give you some more clothes if you're a bit short of them." Fearghal slapped Nikandros on the back as he walked past, laughing at his own joke. Nikandros just smiled and winced as he felt the wounds on his chest open up again.

The bearskin, stretched across two poles, still looked a ferocious sight in the light of the camp fire. There was an air of excitement at the arrival of the Spartan, and he was bombarded with many questions of his land, of its customs, battles and the people he had met and fought. Mórrígan had joined them. A length of grey cloth bound the poultice, prepared by Mongfhionn, to her head. She glanced shyly at her rescuer, embarrassed each time he looked up and caught her eye. Conall, watching this tableau, felt strangely unhappy and refilled his wooden mug with beer.

Taller than most, Mórrígan had flaming red hair and green eyes that contrasted against her pale, almost white, skin. She had a very pleasing body, as Conall recalled from the time he had stumbled upon her bathing in a nearby river. He had been unable to take his eyes off her firm, but ample breasts as she rose out of the water - her nipples erect from the chill of the morning air. The thick bush of red hair between her legs made him stir uncomfortably.

She had laughed when she saw him, but didn't break her stride as she made her way to the bushes where her clothes had been draped. As she dressed, she sang happily then turned around, winked, and walked away. It was the first time that Conall had considered Mórrígan as anything other than one of his closest friends. The feeling disturbed him then just as much as it did now.

Fearghal had drunk a lot of his "special" brew, but not so much that he did not see what was going on. He looked at Mongfhionn and catching her eye, nodded towards Conall and then to Mórrígan and Nikandros. "I think Conall has a rival."

Mongfhionn laughed, "I think Conall has just been reminded that someone he has taken for granted as a friend can be a lot more. He has no worries and if Mórrígan plays this right, she too will get what she has always wished for. As for Nikandros, he has much deeper thoughts and conflicts to resolve. Just as you have, Fearghal."

Mongfhionn took up her staff and rose. In the light of the fire, her demeanor had changed from Druidess and seanachaí to a more commanding and somewhat imperious bearing. "We have things to discuss that can wait no longer. It would appear that the killers of your families were paid by Roman gold and that at least one Roman was here." Taking the scrap of purple cloth from a pocket, she continued, "Conall, your mother held onto this as she died, so that you would have a clue to her killers. The gold coins from the dead confirm its source. The choice is yours and yours alone, as to what you will do about this. My warning is that you should think hard about the path of revenge, for it is a long and lonely journey."

She paused and took a deep breath, "Know this also; if you choose this path, neither you, nor your sons, can ever return to Ériu and they will never inherit from their father – this is your geis. You will find what you seek, but consider this. It may not be worth as much as you will sacrifice.

It is also true that by slaying Eochaidh Ruad's men you may have already set your destiny. The king will neither forget nor forgive this insult. To fight Eochaidh, you will need many more men than this loyal, but small and inexperienced band of friends and would-be warriors. Even with the counsel and support of a renowned warrior such as Fearghal ó Maoilriain, you will not prevail against the army of Eochaidh - unless you have an army also. Know this too; even should you triumph over Eochaidh, your quest will not be ended, for he takes instruction from a higher king."

Conall gazed long and hard into the fire, watching the flames flicker and the sparks leap up and disappear into the darkness. He remembered happier days, but his dreams were now haunted with visions of his slaughtered family. He had killed men for the first time in his life and truth be told, he was good at it. While he was not as experienced as Fearghal, he was a natural fighter. A sword felt good in his hand, although it disturbed him how much he had enjoyed the fighting - and the killing.

"I took an oath to hunt down my family's murderers, and the murderers of my friends' families. I'll keep that promise. None of us wanted this, but none will walk away from our duty. We'll fight and we'll win or die. And I will accept what geis is laid upon me to succeed."

As he looked around the fire, he saw his younger brother Eirnín nod grimly, unsheathe his sword and hold it up. One by one, the rest followed and Conall knew their swords were his to lead. Looking in turn at his friend, Fearghal and then Mongfhionn and Nikandros, Conall spoke, "We will need help in battle, and wise counsel from ones who are more experienced, but I also see shadows behind the smiles of my old and new friends. Perhaps we can support each other along the path to our separate fates."

Fearghal broke the subdued silence that had descended. "Well it seems we have a quest to accomplish. I think I might know where we can get some more men. Eochaidh has slaves working his lands. They are special – Northerners like me and fighting men. Eochaidh has them chained together to prevent them from escaping and to humiliate them. They are watched over by a small guard of Eochaidh's men, although I'm sure that we can handle those.

We need to free them before the winter snows come, and they are locked in Carn Tigherna's cages. My advice is that, in a few days, we travel west along the valley, the grazing land for Eochaidh's cattle that leads to his fort. We will have to be fast, as we cannot risk an attack from the men at the fort. Only the eldest should travel with us. The rest will stay with Mongfhionn and Mórrígan. They can keep working on shoring up the defenses here."

Concerned, Conall looked at Fearghal, "What if others decide to attack while we're gone? We can't leave just the women and children to defend the place."

Fearghal roared with laughter, "Be wary of insulting the powers of the Sidhe. Isn't that right, old woman?"

"And you beware of taking liberties Fearghal ó Maoilriain – old woman, indeed."

Though Mongfhionn bristled at Fearghal, she smiled at Conall, "I think I can come up with a few diversions to frighten away any unfriendly visitors. And it will give Mórrígan and me time to have a long conversation about how she should use her undoubted talents. She has a lot to live up to with that name – in battle… and in bed." At that, Mórrígan coughed nervously and was thankful that the rosy glow of the fire disguised her burning cheeks.

Conall turned to Nikandros, "This is not your fight friend. We're all grateful for you saving Mórrígan and are in your debt. We will not think ill of you, if you choose to remain at the settlement."

Not fully sure why he felt such an affinity for Conall and his friends, Nikandros smiled and unsheathed his sword, "I need the exercise. And since when does a Spartan refuse a fight?"

Roughly a half-day's walk wide and a brisk march of two days in length, the valley was a lush, flat land bordered with steep-sided mountains and several narrow passes. Herds of cattle grazed contentedly and flocks of skittish sheep scrambled from one tuft of grass to another on the rock covered slopes to the south. The shimmering silhouette of Carn Tigherna was just visible in the distance. A river snaked lazily along the valley floor.

After gifting a gold torc to the water gods, Conall's band crept along the banks of the river until they were within a javelin's throw of the slaves. The sun was high as the group approached; making it unlikely the slaves or their keepers would spot them.

The slaves toiled under the constant lash of birch switches and whips knotted and studded with metal pieces. Shackles bound their hands and feet, rubbing flesh raw. They looked clumsy, having just enough freedom to complete their labor if they coordinated their movements with each other. A few snarled and hurled curses at their keepers and were rewarded with deep red welts on exposed skins - for all were naked.

Children from nearby farms and villages sat on the nearby grassy slopes. They laughed and threw stones and cow-shite at the helpless men. Young girls and women giggled, and pointed at the men's cocks. Others, more forward, teased the captives showing their tits and bare arses. All were disappointed by the almost total lack of interest shown by the slaves, and bored with the lecherous comments from the guards.

In all, there were thirty prisoners and ten guards. Conall thought that it seemed a lot of guards for the number of prisoners, especially since they were so thoroughly bound. He nodded at Nikandros. The

Spartan already had slipped his bow from its sheath and had arrows stuck in the dirt, waiting. He had insisted that he could use his bow from much farther away, but Conall needed to be within javelin range to hit the guards hard and quick. Nikandros rose up. As quick as taking a breath, three arrows left his bow and found their targets. Guards fell, clutching bloody chests, as iron arrowheads first pierced, and then punched a path through flesh and bone to exit from their backs.

Startled, and blinded by the sun, the remaining guards swung round to locate the attackers. They were met by a flurry of javelins and another flight of Nikandros' arrows. Iron javelin heads plunged into the guards' flesh amid screams of pain, killing some instantly and crippling others. Gouts of blood splashed the green pastures with red. Shrieks of horror at the carnage arose from the nearby children and women. Some fled, but others were terrified, rooted to the spot.

Quickly assessing their chance for escape and realizing that if they did not lend a hand in the battle, then they might find themselves on the wrong end of a stray javelin, the slaves seized their opportunity amidst the chaos. Guards were dragged to the ground and kicked senseless with hard-calloused feet or strangled with the chains. Wounded guards were dispatched without mercy as the prisoners turned the guards' own daggers on them, slitting their throats or plunging the blades deep between ribs. The slaughter, for no one could call it a fight, was over as quickly as it had started.

As he walked towards the slaves, Conall took note that they had efficiently relieved the guards of weapons and wrenched javelins from lifeless bodies. Though shackled, they had taken up a defensive stance. "That's far enough," the spokesman of the group called out in a broad northern brogue. "We've been fooled before and aren't looking to repeat that mistake. You're obviously no friend of Eochaidh, but who are you? And more to the point – what do you want with us?"

Fearghal pushed his way forward. "That's not a very polite way to greet your commander. Is it, men?" To a man, the freed slaves dropped to one knee and swung their arm across their chests in salute. "Oh get up!" Fearghal growled to the speaker. "We're well beyond that nonsense, Cúscraid Mac Conchobar." He embraced Cúscraid and then stepped back a pace. "Explanations can come later. Right now, we need to get far away from here before those screaming women and children bring Eochaidh's soldiers down on us."

Cúscraid nodded and with a glint in his eye and a quick fist smashed Fearghal in the jaw. "If we're all equals now, then that's for leaving us in the shite for so long."

Staggering from the impact, Fearghal rubbed his chin and laughed, "I suppose I deserved that – just don't try it again."

"Enough!" said Conall. "Let's move. We can get acquainted on the way back to the settlement."

Still shackled, after discovering that none of their guards had a key, the men made to move forward with Fearghal and their rescuers. Suddenly, they shouted, "Grab the women!" and charged towards the remaining women on the hillside who had been too petrified to flee. Moments later, over half of the former slaves had thrown kicking and screaming young women over their shoulders.

"In the name of the gods, what are you doing?" Conall shouted at the men.

Cúscraid laughed and winked, "Let's call it compensation for a long time as a slave."

Conall shook his head, "That's all we need – now Eochaidh has another reason to attack us." Irritably, he looked at Fearghal, "They better fight as well as you claim, because it looks like we're going to need them very soon."

The former slaves, stark naked, yet triumphantly hefting their prizes, took up an awkward shamble. As they passed by Conall, one pointed at Nikandros, "Where'd he come from with skin that color? He'd better get some decent clothes for the winter."

An incredulous Brion raised his eyebrows, "He's one to talk!"

Days later, it was a strange and loud group that shambled,

stumbled and clanked through the gateway of the settlement. The former slaves were tired, but shouting and joking. The stolen girls had stopped screeching, but were now whimpering and crying, as they could guess their fate. At the sound of the wailing, not knowing what to expect, Mongfhionn and Mórrígan came rushing out to the gate. Mórrígan turned a deep pink when she realized the men marching past her were naked, but Mongfhionn took it with equanimity, "Get these men some pants. We've had enough of a display for one day. Put those girls down. I suppose they will come in useful for cooking and washing – and likely other pursuits as well."

She smiled at Fearghal, "I see the slaves all bear a marking that I've seen before. It looks like the one on your arm. You know the geis and the terms for your return – I cannot change that. You know what was agreed. When are you going to tell Conall? He is, after all, your new 'king'."

Being reminded of things that he had not truly considered for a long time made Fearghal uncomfortable, yet he looked Mongfhionn in the eye as he spoke. "Conall has too much on his mind, and too much to accomplish right now. My – no, both your and my "challenges" would be a distraction for him, and are secondary to his needs. I am a king and so is he, one destined to be a great warrior and high king, although sadly not in these lands. He has no experience, but is a natural warrior. You and I will need to guide him to reach his destiny – regardless of past geis. Agreed?"

After a moment, Mongfhionn said, "Agreed."

Fearghal called out to Cúscraid, "Which one of your men is the smith? We need to get the forge going and those shackles off your men." He noted Conall's pained look as he contemplated someone else using his father's forge and tools. "It has to be done Conall."

Conall nodded, and then looked to his friends, "We need to plan our next moves."

CHAPTER 5

The next months were spent preparing the defenses of the settlement, now reborn as Ráth na Conall, before winter set in. A large structure of stone and wood where everyone could eat, drink, talk and if they wished, sleep – the Halla Mór or Great Hall, was quickly erected. As the old community had only made use of a small area of the hilltop, there was an abundance of space. Additional buildings to house the new arrivals were quickly erected within the palisade.

In the evenings, Mongfhionn stood on one of the long wooden tables in the hall and revealed another side of her character, regaling her audience with stories of Ériu's ancient battles, gods and heroes. She also had collected an apprentice in Tadhg ó Cuileannáin, who was particularly skilled with words and poems.

Tadhg had begun composing a great story to immortalize Conall. More often than not, he was accompanied by his brother Craiftine's harp as well as the drumming of bodhráns. As the beer flowed, the throbbing beat of the bodhráns and the sound of harp music got much louder.

The Sidhe did not always have the audience completely to herself. She was well-matched by Nikandros, who enthusiastically told tales of his home, and of great land battles with hundreds of thousands of warriors, and battles on the seas with thousands of galleys. Nikandros' preferred story though, concerned a small band of Spartans who had held back the great Persian army at the strangely named Thermopylae. It soon became a favorite of the fort's residents.

Even the weakest of the rescued warriors was fit for work after a few weeks of good food and exercise. Cúscraid took on responsibility for strengthening the fort and under his direction the palisade's fortifications underwent dramatic changes. Conall was delighted that his friends were being included in everything and soon stopped thinking of the two groups as separate units. He was also amazed that the previously homesick, kidnapped girls now willingly helped with the chores.

In a few months, and in time for the first real snowfall of winter, the settlement had become a real fort. A deeper ditch, two men wide and one deep had been dug out and populated with sharpened stakes and thorn bushes. The newly constructed rampart of stone was several feet thick. The fence had been replaced with a double row of wooden stakes, behind which was a platform running the circumference of the defenses. The gateways had been strengthened with wood and iron; lookout posts giving good sightlines were erected. Stacks of weapons were placed strategically around the fort. During the months of back-breaking work, Conall and his friends discovered and strained muscles that they never knew existed. They and the former slaves soon proudly flaunted their work-sculpted torsos.

Out of respect for Fearghal, Conall had not inquired about his relationship with the new men, although he was very curious about their deference to him. He figured that Fearghal would tell him when the time was right. Conall was somewhat frustrated that, apart from a few minor skirmishes with local bandits, there had been a lull in fighting. They had not even attempted to harass Eochaidh Ruad – apart from the occasional cattle raid. In later years, he was to reflect that he should have simply thanked the Goddess for giving him and his men a time to rest and prepare.

It troubled Nikandros that his loyalties had undergone a major change, but in his new friends he appeared to have found what his spirit had missed from his homeland – a new sense of purpose. Now his challenge was training Conall's "army".

The Spartan had found it relatively straightforward to meld Conall's shield-wall tactics with his experience of Greek and Roman battle formations. Under Fearghal's watchful eye, Nikandros trained the men to where they were well-used to their new armor, weapons and battle tactics. Since there would be many times when they had to fight out of formation, he also encouraged the men to hone their individual fighting skills. The blacksmith was kept busy making "weapons to order" – mostly axes - of all shapes and sizes.

Nikandros had decided that Mórrígan should use a 'proper' bow and encouraged her to lead a group who would focus on archery skills. Conall, Fearghal and Cúscraid were skeptical, as no true warrior in Ériu fought from a distance. However, as they watched the small band craft their bows and then practice with them, they re-evaluated their misgivings. Nikandros' oft told stories of mounted archers causing the destruction of mighty armies added to the allure. Mórrígan also kept up her horse riding, taking Fearghal's hounds with her most days to patrol the area around the fort.

Meanwhile, local farmers had slowly returned to the area and visited the "ráth" more frequently. They had known Conall's father and had been horrified at what had happened to the settlement and its inhabitants. Not being fighters or even armed, they could do little to help. With Conall's permission, they started to prepare the land around the fort for planting the next season's crops. They also provided cattle, bread, milk and cheese. In turn, the new blacksmith at the fort helped the farmers with repairs to their tools.

The influence of the fort and its men soon spread, dissuading the presence of outlaws and bandits. The farmers were grateful for this as were their daughters, who suddenly found themselves in the midst of hard-bodied warriors with needs to fill. It was not long until Conall supplied the farmers with additional cattle, since his men had taken up the age-old pursuit of cattle raiding outside of what they considered to be their own territory. The farmers then sold or traded the cattle – probably back to the same people from whom they had been stolen and supplied Conall with more goods and services.

Often, when not training or making plans, Conall was to be found gazing towards the valley that led to Carn Tigherna. He had come to accept that his army was no match for the thousands of warriors that Eochaidh Ruad could call upon, particularly not in a battle on open ground. Now he was concerned that Eochaidh would attack before he had a chance to build up strength. He looked south to the narrow strip of land between the coast and the mountains and pondered how to forestall that from taking place.

Although the distance between Ráth na Conall and Eochaidh's fort was not great — a warrior could march it in two days - there were several places in the valley that were narrow and bordered by steep rock faces. Perhaps, Conall mused, they could accomplish something at those points. Lookouts, rotated frequently due to the cold weather, were positioned about a half-day's ride to the north and south to keep a watch on any movements from Carn Tigherna.

In Carn Tigherna, Eochaidh Ruad had been in a constant rage since the defeat of his men by those he considered a pack of children. When Faolán had passed on the Sidhe's message, the king had at first been very afraid. He had withdrawn into isolation for a full cycle of the moon, for he was well aware that he had broken his vows. However, upon his re-emergence, his usual unpleasant demeanor and fierce temper were restored. His penchant to lash to lash out at everyone was unchanged, resulting in the immediate hanging and beheading of ten of Faolán's warriors and their families. Their heads now decorated the palisade that surrounded Carn Tigherna. Five more were executed when Eochaidh learned of the escape of the northern slaves and kidnapping of the young women. And now, the constant cattle raids on his herds by those same slaves were driving him to distraction.

He felt his authority, which until recently had been unquestioned, slipping. Worse, he detected a distinct change in attitude from the local chieftains, and was well aware of how long kings lasted when not feared by their men or the nobles. Eochaidh had personally cut the throat of the king who had previously ruled from Carn Tigherna. His anger not yet sated, Eochaidh sent Faolán out to enforce his will by destroying a small settlement, massacring its chieftain and warriors together with their families, but in his heart, he knew that this was not enough.

At times, Eochaidh looked upon Faolán with suspicion. Had his position been unassailable, he would likely have had Faolán's head on a stake along with those of his no-good men. However, his commander was the only person preventing a mass exodus of his army. Hence, Eochaidh stayed his hand.

As for the sniveling, condescending Roman, Cassius Fabius Scaeva, he tended to agree with Faolán that they should have cut his throat, taken his gold, and never gone near the blacksmith's settlement. The Roman never ceased to remind Eochaidh of his "duty", the bargain they had agreed and the considerable forces he could call upon, if needed. Eochaidh's usual sarcastic response was if Cassius' master had so many soldiers, then why did he need Eochaidh's men as mercenaries? In the end, Eochaidh gritted his teeth and hoped a fortuitous accident would rid him of Cassius.

From the huge, roughly-carved wooden seat which served as his throne, Eochaidh glared down at Faolán, "We have to do something. That young bastard cannot be allowed to slight me and flaunt his freedom to do what he wants. The locals have started to call him "king". What insolence! He raids my cattle and steals our women and slaves, yet we do nothing. I have several thousand men here and at least double that from the nobles, but what use are they?"

Faolán considered for a few moments, "We can't do anything now that the winter is drawing close. The pathways will be frozen or calf-deep in mud from hail and rain." He continued, choosing his words carefully, for he knew that he had lost Eochaidh's complete trust, "My spies tell me that the settlement is no more, but has been replaced by a ráth that would rival many in these parts.

Also, do not forget, my King, that the escaped slaves were no ordinary men. You know where they came from. Each is a Cróeb Ruad warrior. Their training for war commenced as soon as they could hold a wooden sword. Each is worth ten of our own. The valleys between Carn Tigherna and the settlement are narrow in several places; even a small band of determined warriors could hold a large army off at any of those locations. If we attack now, we may incur great and unnecessary losses."

Then Faolán added, "Such a venture may also leave you open to attack from some of your more powerful, but less than loyal nobles."

Exasperated, Eochaidh slumped back on his throne. He looked around the Great Hall with its walls hung with tapestries and trophies from past battles - all reminding him of what once was. Resigned, he asked, "Then what would you counsel, Faolán?"

Faolán gave the question some thought. He smiled wryly as he realized how cautious he had become of late. The rashness of youth and the blustering confidence of many battle successes was now tempered with a desire to survive. "We should wait until winter is over. Conall and his warriors will come to us. He has no gold and so can't buy men. His 'army' will remain small. He thirsts for revenge and sooner or later will lead his men to attack Carn Tigherna. Let him break his back on our ramparts. Then we can destroy him – and the rest of his warband."

Reluctantly, Eochaidh agreed, then called for a young slave to bring him food and drink.

"It's going to be a long winter."

The wine, warm bath, and the pleasure of being attended to by a bevy of naked female slaves soothed Marcus Fabius Ambustus. He was a Patrician, one of the Republic's aristocrats, and he simply could not imagine being an ordinary Roman, let alone a barbarian. What he could imagine was having much more power. His dreams were filled with schemes to expand his authority and influence as Pontifex. In the future, he saw his son, Quintus, as Dictator. Yes, he thought, the Republic would benefit from his nurturing and firm hand.

Marcus steadfastly believed his family should rule Rome and he was willing to do anything to make that happen. He had to be careful, however. Pontifex or not, one foolish misstep and his likely reward would be a warm bath colored red with his own blood.

Thus, Marcus cursed his moment of madness in trusting the ignorant and degenerate Cassius with what was a delicate mission: to secure arms and to hire mercenaries from a nation reputed as having the fiercest of fighters. The fool could not be trusted to do anything right. "The gods preserve us from family," he exhaled.

And now there was another disquieting possibility: what of the Spartan? Should he continue to trust him? He was ostensibly a friend, yet he was also a mercenary. Maybe another would make him a better offer. Maybe Nikandros would betray him. Was this another loose end?

Paranoia enveloped him as the Pontifex exited his bath and was dried by the lithe slave he intended to use later. He called for Primus Pilus, Spurius Sulpicia Longus, the first centurion from his personal guard. In the end, business was business. Nikandros was neither family nor Roman. Spurius was given his orders and commanded to make preparations for a sea journey. The following day, Spurius selected two hundred of Marcus' personal guard and dispatched messengers to the southern Italian coast to seek Phoenician or Greek galleys which would transport them to the Tin Islands in the spring.

It was a cold, mid-winter night as Conall lay alone on his bed of straw and rushes. His brother Eirnín no longer lived with him, preferring the company of friends over his increasingly intense sibling. Outside, the wind howled. Snow had replaced the rain and lay in deep drifts around the fort. Comforted by the skins and fleeces that weighed his body down and kept him warm, he reflected on past days. His two wolfhound pups had crept under the edge of the skins and were happily sound asleep, their warm fur resting against his legs. Conall considered what needed to be done after winter had passed and sometimes sighed despondently at the enormity of what lay in front of him.

Mongfhionn and Nikandros had told him about the Roman people. How and where they lived, the battles they had fought and won, and how they were governed. They also told him about the lands and barbarian nations that lay between him and Rome. Mongfhionn burned with a fierce hatred of the Romans - almost greater than his own, but declined to explain why. Nikandros as well was somewhat reluctant to go into detail, but had the look of a person wrestling with a great problem.

Conall thought long and hard on how he would punish his parents' killer, not just the men who slaughtered the settlement, but the one who gave the order. The one who paid with Roman gold and whose purple cloak threads Conall carried with him at all times. He had never been much beyond a few days ride from his home, but now he knew that he had to travel to distant lands. A shiver rippled along his spine and he pulled the coverings closer. He knew he needed men — many men — and loyal ones at that — but where could they be found? And where would he get the gold to pay them?

It struck him that only a short time ago all he had to think about were his chores and learning to be a good blacksmith, but now he had responsibility for a growing community of warriors, women and children. The duty weighed heavily on his young shoulders and he was thankful for advisors such as Fearghal, Mongfhionn, Nikandros and now, Cúscraid.

His forehead furrowed as he thought about Mórrígan. It annoyed him that she had been spending time with the Spartan. He knew that she was being taught skills with the bow as well as horsemanship, yet that was little comfort. Conall was jealous and could not see a way to resolve it. Oh, he had had plenty of advice from Fearghal and the other men. Even Mórrígan's brothers rolled their eyes and shook their heads when he spoke to or was near their sister.

He grunted in frustration at the thoughts that invaded his mind and taunted him. Feeling a blast of cold air, he grumbled that the skins on the door must have come loose. Then he felt his covers shift as someone slipped underneath. He groaned, "Not again." He had lost count of the number of times one of the camp girls had tried to get his interest.

Turning to face whoever it was, he spoke firmly, "I appreciate the offer, but no thanks. Go back to your friends."

"Well, Conall Mac Gabhann, is that any way to treat the woman who will be your queen?"

Conall sat up, startled beyond all comprehension. In the dim light he now recognized the outline of Mórrígan. She laughed at his discomfort, "Mongfhionn told me that I would eventually have to take control of things myself and by the Hag, she was right. Conall, you're becoming a great warrior, but you know little about women. You could have had me the day you saw me at the river, but no ... you had to just go all red and apologize."

Conall felt her straddle him and realized she was naked; the warm area between her legs rubbed along his now rapidly stiffening manhood. Instinctively, he reached up and cupped her breasts. Mórrígan murmured, "Now we're getting somewhere." She raised and then lowered herself down on him, feeling his hardness open her up and slide deep inside. Rhythmically, she rode up and down, groaning and going faster until she felt an intense burst of pleasure engulf her. They both gasped as she rode him harder until she had milked him and then collapsed on his chest, breathing hard.

"Next time, Conall, my love, you make the first move. You wouldn't want everyone to think I'm a striapach."

Conall sighed contentedly and hugged her until she could hardly get a breath. He smiled as he thought to himself that at least one problem had been resolved. Then he rolled over on top of her, spread her legs, and once again entered her. He was thankful that he had most of the night still remaining. And as he took her again, Mórrígan thanked the goddess that the risk she had taken had been more than worth it.

In the morning when Conall and Mórrígan arose and went outside, they were greeted by loud cheers and good humored shouts of, "And about time too!"

Embarrassed, Conall first looked at his feet, then breathed deeply, grabbed Mórrígan and kissed her. With a firm grasp of her hand, he asked, "What's for breakfast? I could eat a whole pig and we've both got big appetites this morning."

The cheers from the fort could be heard far away as they walked to the Great Hall.

CHAPTER 6

414 B.C.

Spring snows still lay on the ground and there were deep frosts at night, but the new season brought a freshness to Ráth na Conall and neighboring lands. It also brought rumors of war in Laighi – in the mid-east of the island. Curiously, Mongfhionn had an intense interest in these events and had long discussions with the infrequent messengers who stopped at the fort. There were stories that barbarian invaders had come from lands across the sea or that the Ulaid had crossed the Black Pig's Dyke on raiding parties. Some even said that an army had descended from the clouds. Tales of men and ancient deities freely mingled until no one was quite sure what was real and what was imagined. To the mid-west, it was believed that the Connachta were readying their defenses.

The distinctive smell of peat burning on many cooking fires filled the air, matched in intensity by the aroma of spitted swine and cattle roasting over the open fire pits. Freshly baked bread and goat cheese from the nearby homesteads were plentiful; hot soups or stews made with scraps of meat and whatever vegetables could be found, were always simmering in the massive iron cauldrons.

Knowing, but approving, winks and smiles were cast in Mórrígan's direction as it was not difficult to make out the increasing roundness of her belly. She was not alone in her condition. It had been a cold winter and Conall's men were certainly not known for their celibacy. Many of the young women were quite happy to exchange chastity for a warm bed.

In the Great Hall, Conall, Fearghal, Brion, Nikandros, Cúscraid, Mórrígan and Mongfhionn met frequently over beer and food to discuss plans and strategies. The desire to strike against Eochaidh Ruad had not diminished during the winter months. Conall had, however, been persuaded that it would be foolish to move against Eochaidh and his inclination to strike immediately had tempered. He knew they would be well outnumbered, since Eochaidh, with his nobles and chieftains, could likely assemble an army of five thousand or more warriors.

At times, Conall despaired at the enormity of the task ahead, but set his jaw in determination to find a way. After the tactical and planning discussions, he often felt as if his head would burst open at having to do so much thinking. In the privacy of their shelter, he confessed to Mórrígan that he was often torn between settling down and consolidating his territory, or continuing the fight for vengeance. He knew that the longer they all stayed at the fort, the harder it would be to motivate everyone on for future battles. But the hatred Mórrígan felt for the killers of her parents was a deep and bitter well. She had no hesitation in reminding Conall where his duty lay.

"We need gold and lots of it. That way we can hire men to fight with us." Conall looked around at his friends. After a moment, Mongfhionn rose to offer her thoughts.

"With the right sacrifice to the water gods, the bogs may release their treasures."

Fearghal groaned, "Whose throat do we have to slit?"

A piercing look from Mongfhionn stopped him from saying more, and dissuaded anyone else from adding to that conversation. Irritably, she continued, "Not all sacrifices need blood and well you know it, Fearghal ó Maoilriain." Fearghal winced at the use of his full name, knowing she was angry with him and knowing her capacity for spite.

"So what are you suggesting?"

"Phortaigh na Cullen is about five days walk north-west of here. Maybe a few days more if we stay to the valleys and use teams of oxen to pull the wagons we'll need. I know of a small settlement on the south-east side of the bog. The villagers extract gold from the waters and work it into jewelry. Most of the gold and jewelry goes to Ailill Mac Máta, King of the Connachta, at Ráth Chrúachain, but a good portion also goes to Eochaidh. You can steal his share of the gold. The closest fort, Knockadigeen, is a further day's ride away so we shouldn't face interference from there."

"What's the sacrifice to be?" Conall asked, looking at Mongfhionn with some measure of trepidation.

She laughed, "The water gods will require a full set of armor and all the Roman gold that you have. While you keep the Roman gold, you will not have a full victory – in anything, Conall. It is tainted with deceit and blood. All the Roman gold must be sacrificed or some of your men or women will take its place." As they mulled this over, Mongfhionn looked at Nikandros, "And I mean all the Roman gold."

Fearghal muttered under his breath, "Some plan this. We throw gold into rivers to appease the gods so that they will then permit us to steal gold that is mined from the waters of the bog."

Then out loud he said, "I don't believe that there will be no guard on the gold."

Looking at Mongfhionn and Conall, he continued, "You can be sure that Ailill and Eochaidh will have warriors there. Ailill and Medb will be glad that Eochaidh has sworn allegiance to Chrúachain, especially now that their borders are threatened from the east. But that pair wouldn't trust each other with the gold, let alone Eochaidh Ruad. They'll have their own men garrisoned in that village."

Fearghal paused and Conall took up the conversation, "Cúscraid and Mórrígan will remain at the fort."

Both made to object, but Conall cut them short, "I want to know that the ones left behind are in safe hands. The youngest will remain at the fort, but otherwise choose who you want, Cúscraid. Keep the number low, but not so few that you will not be able to defend the fort. Mórrígan and the hounds will patrol for you."

Conall looked at Mongfhionn, "I'd like you to come with us. You know the land and we'll likely need help with satisfying the goddess."

Mongfhionn hesitated. She had her own loyalties, tasks and duties and was troubled by this interruption of her chosen path. However, it would appear that destiny had taken the choice of her more immediate future from her. She nodded, "This time, Conall, I will, but there is a price for everything – for you and for me."

Eight days later, at dawn, the assembled gold-raiders marched out the gateway leading wagons and oxen, their leather bróga and boots crunching on the still frozen and frost covered ground. Typically for the time of year, it was snowing and a light mist carpeted the ground, yet spirits were high. Including Nikandros and Mongfhionn, there were twenty-seven in the party.

Conall turned to Nikandros, once they were outside the fort. "I don't want any surprises. Range ahead and find the best route. One that avoids contact with anyone – warriors or farmers. The fewer that know we're on the move and away from the fort, the better." Nikandros nodded, leapt into his saddle and rode off.

It was mid-afternoon when Primus Pilus, Spurius Sulpicia Longus, leapt over the side of the Phoenician galley, and into the shallow waters of a sandy cove on the south-east side of the island he knew as Hiberniæ. He flinched, momentarily breathless, as the numbing cold waters rose over his crotch. Splashing quickly to the shore, he stretched, rubbed himself down and thanked his gods for a safe journey. He also cursed the cold weather, so different from his native Rome.

Not being a good sailor, he was glad to be on land again, feeling much better with each step that took him further from the ship. After months at sea, at the mercy of spring storms, his legionnaires happily disembarked from ships that stank of the almost perpetual emptying of their stomachs and bowels. Pytheas, the Greek merchant whose vessels they had hired, had looked upon them with a mixture of condescension and disgust. Especially since his crew now had to clean the Romans' waste before sailing east to pick up other cargo from the larger island.

"Unload the ships. Bring the pack horses and my own. Be careful with mine, he cost me a lot of denarii. We'll get off this beach and find a place to make camp."

A path led them up the shallow cliff face from the cove and onto a meadow concealed under a deep, wet fall of snow. It was a landscape of strewn, huge boulders and rocks, scattered copses of white birch and oak trees, and dense thorn bushes that rose out of the snow to tear at frozen legs. After his scouts had returned, reporting no immediate threats, Spurius called his centurions, Publius and Decimus. "We'll camp here for tonight. In the morning, send the scouts farther to see the lie of the land. Tell your optios to make sure that the camp is well-guarded tonight. I don't want any surprises." The officers nodded affably, saluted and went to issue orders for the men.

The small contingent were part of Marcus Fabius Ambustus' personal guard and therefore much better equipped than would have been expected. More important than weapons, the men quickly donned their winter clothing of heavy cloaks, leg bindings, socks and scarves. Most also wore at least two tunics under their armor.

Like their officers, although less ornate, they wore bronze armor – helmets with cheek guards, greaves and breastplates. The breast and back plates were two solid pieces of bronze, clasped and hinged at the hips and on either side of the neck. For weapons and defense, they each carried a spear, sword and a circular shield. The spear was their weapon of choice, as they preferred to fight in a phalanx formation. Each spear was over a head taller than a man, and was grasped one-handed, with the other hand holding the shield. The spearhead itself was a curved, leaf shape, while the butt of the spear ended with an iron spike. This was normally used to stand the spear in the ground, but could quickly become a weapon in battle.

The shields were of wood, faced in bronze and spanned from chin to knee. They were very heavy; although the dish-like shape allowed the shields to rest on a shoulder, especially important for the men who stood in the rear ranks. While these soldiers continued to help press forward, they did not have the added burden of holding up a shield.

Spurius and his command were used to fighting on relatively flat ground, where a phalanx could be of most use, alongside thousands of comrades. He cursed the terrain, as he gazed around at the mixture of gently sloping hills, valleys carved up into small farms separated by dry stone walls, and mountains cloaked in clouds. He pulled his cloak closer around him, grateful at his foresight in packing heavier clothing and hoping any skirmishes would be on more favorable ground.

The next morning, the scouts brought back news of strangers from a different land who had landed separately and then immediately travelled west along the southern coastline. The Romans took no prisoners, though this was mainly due to potential informants being both tortured for information and then having their throats slit. Indeed, Spurius had given orders that no one was to know of their presence – at least no one who remained alive.

Sadly, Spurius was a victim of timing - and the humor of the fates. He could not have known of the invasion that had taken place further north of his landing. Neither could he have known that raiding parties from Ráthgall, a fort three days ride to his north, were prowling the countryside looking for groups of barbarian invaders or stragglers from their main forces. Spurius was therefore unaware of the warriors well-hidden by the forest cover above his camp and was certainly unaware of the riders that had been sent north to the king at Ráthgall and south-west to the forts at Carn Tigherna, Curraghatoor and Ráth na Conall.

In his ignorance, Spurius put on his helmet, mounted his gray, which stood a full seventeen hands, and formed up his shivering men. They marched south-west, keeping as much as possible to the valleys and fields that followed the coastline. At least, he thought, a forced march would keep his men warm and their minds occupied.

CHAPTER 7

The frozen ground made the journey through the normally wet bog land in the valley east of the hillfort at Curraghatoor easier for the wagons. Centuries of cold weather had dried the bog out in many places, even allowing trees to grow again, but more than enough remained to vex travelers. As Conall's raiding party neared Phortaigh na Cullen, the land became progressively more difficult to travel. Solid, iron-rimmed wheels broke through the frozen surface and into the peaty waters. Muscles strained, and steam rose from men and beasts, as they pushed and pulled the wagons forward. On the edge of the bog, the raiding party made their sacrifices of gold and armor to the water gods.

Nikandros once again rode ahead, scouting for paths to the village which would both keep them hidden and take wagon traffic. He searched for a camp site that would give them shelter and provide a base to launch the attack.

The village sat on an island in the bog and was no more than a scattering of buildings surrounded by a rough wooden stockade. The entrance was reached via a narrow causeway that linked the island to the surrounding land. At the rear of the village, there was a heavily rutted wagon trail that led on to Chrúachain.

As they drew nearer, Conall called Mongfhionn to his side, "If any of us were to go into the village we would raise suspicion. Nikandros will escort you as far as possible and will wait for you until you're ready to leave." Mongfhionn nodded and gathered her cloak around herself, and, staff in hand, departed. Conall marveled at how she appeared to glide effortlessly over the ground, never seeming to hesitate or stumble.

Mongfhionn strode into the village center. As expected, the sight of a Druid's grey cloak was enough to frighten most of its denizens. Hardly anyone dared look at her for fear of being cursed, sacrificed or simply addressed directly. Even the passing guards averted their eyes as she called out, "Who is the leader of this village? Who will give shelter and food to a Druid who serves the Goddess of the woods and the waters? The Goddess who gives gold to this village, and makes it prosperous."

A short, thickset man with a graying beard and thinning hair came shuffling forward and bowed his head, "My name is Seanán, and I'd be honored if you would rest at my home. Our food is not rich or plentiful, but you're welcome to share it with us." Mongfhionn smiled her acceptance and followed the man.

As she sat by the fire, Mongfhionn was grateful for the simple food put before her. The bread was stale and spotted with mold, the stew was mostly vegetables with little meat, but it had the virtue of being hot on a cold night. The beer had been warmed with a hot iron and spices added. All in all, Mongfhionn felt some pity for Fearghal, knowing that he was probably shivering on the hillside. She smiled wickedly to herself - some pity, but not much.

Once Seanán had overcome his nervousness at her presence, he was more than happy to talk about the comings and goings in the village and the pervasive resentment of Medb and Eochaidh's men. He complained of being poorly rewarded for the hard work his people did mining and working the gold and about the rough treatment received at the hands of the soldiers. Mongfhionn became increasingly cross as she heard him describe how young girls were taken to the soldiers' barracks. She was informed that the barracks, a large wooden hall which was in the northern part of the enclosure, also held the stores of gold before they were shipped. Apparently, Conall's timing was good, as a shipment of gold was being readied to leave the settlement. At sunrise, Mongfhionn thanked Seanán, and made her way back down the road towards Conall's camp.

Mongfhionn's long hair reflected the sunrise, glowing as if on fire. It also mirrored her angry mood as she stormed into the camp. Tersely, she described the situation in the village.

There were around thirty soldiers. More than usual, as it was time for a shipment of gold to be moved to the forts of Eochaidh Ruad and Ailill Mac Máta. The warriors were veterans. Neither Eochaidh nor Ailill wanted to take any chances, given the rumors of invaders from the east and given that the Ulaid were not beyond launching a raid even this deep into Connachta lands.

"Well, at least they've packed the gold up for us. We just have to walk in and take it!" Fearghal reflected wryly.

"We'll need a diversion, something to allow us to at least get inside the village gates," Conall said.

"I will provide a distraction." Mongfhionn assured them. "However, these people have suffered greatly under Eochaidh and Ailill's men. I will not see them harmed further. The condition of my help is that no villager is to be injured – even by accident. If you spill the blood of any villager, then for each, you will lose a man. Those are my terms."

Fearghal exhaled in exasperation, "That's bloody ridiculous Mongfhionn, and well you know it. I grow tired of your games with us mere mortals."

"Calm down, Fearghal. Think for a moment," Nikandros interjected. "If we hit the village in a frontal attack without a diversion, we'll probably lose a few men. At least with Mongfhionn's help we might reduce our losses. What worries me is how we attack. The causeway is narrow; we will not have the advantage of the shield wall and once inside the village there will be little room to form ranks."

Nikandros continued, addressing them all, "This will be a bloody, one-on-one brawl and we have some here who are brave, but not experienced."

Brion looked up, irritated, "We'll fight as fiercely as our Cróeb Ruad friends - and yourself, Nikandros." Brocc, Fionnbharr and Labhraidh ó Cuileannáin and Torcán ó Dubhghaill stood up, nodding in agreement.

Conall smiled at his friends, but spoke firmly, "I don't doubt your courage, but you know, as well as I, that we haven't seen as many battles as our friends." Acknowledging the somewhat bitter truth of what Conall had said, they sat down.

"The Cróeb Ruad will lead the frontal attack with Fearghal and Nikandros each taking one group. The rest, led by Brion, will follow the perimeter and attack the rear of the barracks. Since we'll not fight as the shield wall, the choice of weapons will be for each man to decide. Although, we all should carry a javelin, as they may prove useful."

An undulating carpet of white mist floated above the ground in the mid-morning chill as they took up their weapons and set off down the hillside. Intent on the task ahead, none of them took note of Mongfhionn's absence. Conall brushed a flake of snow from his hand, but it was soon followed by another and another. Soon flurries became a dense snowfall.

By the time they reached the causeway, the snow had become a white wall and the village a blurred grey shadow in the distance. Behind them the grey cloaked figure of the sidhe stood chanting, with one hand outstretched to the heavens, and the other pointing the now familiar staff toward the village. The gateway loomed before the group. Veiled by the snowfall in the dim, pre-dawn gloom, two men quickly climbed over the gates and removed the wooden bar that held them shut. Considerably muffled by the falling snow, the gates uttered a low groan as iron hinges, rusted with age, grated as they were forced open.

As planned, they split up into three lines several paces apart. Two columns advanced slowly to the hall; a third, led by Brion, skirted the perimeter and made its way to the rear. The closer they got to the barracks, the lighter the snow became. The band stopped abruptly as the door of the building suddenly opened. In the pale light, a young girl ran naked from the hall, sobbing and shivering, her skinny, milk-white body covered in bruises and bites, the inside of her thighs bloodied. As she caught sight of the raiders in their strange armor, her mouth opened to scream, but Brocc had covered the ground quickly between them and his hand shot out, clamping over her jaw before she could utter a sound. He half-carried, half-dragged her to the nearest dwelling. By chance, it was the village leader, Seanán's, home. Seeing the warriors, he grasped what was happening, pulled the girl quickly inside, and firmly barred the door.

A heavy-set warrior stumbled out of the hall, bleary-eyed and yawning. He stretched, farted, scratched his balls and grabbed his cock to pee. Then it dawned on him that he was not alone. That same instant, he also realized he was about to die. Three javelins thudded into his chest, extinguishing his warning shout to his mates and splattering blood and gore over the entrance behind him. The force of the javelins' impact carried him crashing backwards against the door and into the barracks.

"That should wake them up," commented Fearghal, but as he spoke, there came the razor-pitched scream of the bean-sidhe from the hill-side.

Nikandros looked at Fearghal, "No that will wake them up! You have a strange taste in women, friend, but I'm glad she's on our side." The distinctive wail of the bean-sidhe ensured that none of the villagers would attempt to leave their homes. A wave of stench coming from the barracks meant it had also loosened the bowels and bladders of quite a few warriors.

Inside the hall, Eochaidh and Ailill's veteran men instinctively grabbed their weapons and shields, but prudently held back, as their less experienced and foolish companions made to rush outside. Those unfortunates were met with a volley of javelins. Most fell to the dirt dead or maimed, painting the snow with crimson sprays of blood. Others barreled out from the rear of the building. Whether they had meant to escape or to fight, they met the same end, cut down by javelins from Brion's men.

"I don't think the rest will come out voluntarily," said Conall in the quiet after the initial encounter.

"I'll go to the right inside the door with my men," Fearghal said to Nikandros. "You take the left side with yours." Nikandros drew his xiphos from its baldric and adjusted his shield for balance while Fearghal withdrew his longsword. Conall reached behind him, and gripped the handles of two new, double-headed battle-axes.

Fearghal chuckled, "Would you be looking at him, Nikandros? He must think he's one of your Greek heroes!"

Then, with a great roar, Fearghal and Nikandros simultaneously charged the entrance. Brion heard them and shouted as Torcán and he rushed inside from the back. A volley of daggers and axes from the dimly lit hall met Fearghal and Nikandros. Grunts from behind told Fearghal that a few had been hit and he felt the sting of a blade on his thigh as he strode forward. Nikandros, with the benefit of his shield had immediately started bashing, slashing and stabbing whoever was nearest. There was no finesse about the fight. It was close-quarter slashing, stabbing, hacking, kicking and gouging. Screams, curses and shouts filled the air as more were cut down and more of Conall's warriors pushed and shoved their way into the fray. Men slipped on blood and guts and stumbled over fallen bodies. Soon, there were only fifteen of Eochaidh and Ailill's men left standing – their backs to the wall. Both sides glowered at each other through blood-smeared faces and matted hair.

Conall stepped forward, his battle-axes dripping blood. "Drop your weapons or die where you stand." He knew that these were likely the bravest of the warriors, men who knew how to survive in the melee of close fighting. If they did not surrender, then the next fight would be much bloodier than before and he would lose men that he could ill-afford. "If you drop your weapons, you can leave here alive. Or you can swear allegiance to me - on one condition. If the villagers accuse any of you of wrongdoing, then I'll hang you."

Fearghal, at Conall's shoulder, whispered, "I hope you know what you're doing, son."

There was a heated discussion between the cornered men. In the next moment, three were dead by sword thrusts through their bellies, executed by their former comrades. The leader of the group handed his axe to another and stepped forward to stand before Conall. "I know of you, Conall Mac Gabhann, and of your men. My name is Onchú ó an Cháintigh and my king was Eochaidh Ruad. That may give you cause to hang me but you have my word as a warrior that I and the men I lead, took no part in the slaughter of your families. If you'll have us, then you have our allegiance." Conall gave no immediate acknowledgement, so Onchú continued.

"The others are Ailill's men and you have had no quarrel with them – until now. They also will follow you. You know as well as we, that we are dead men if we go back to our kings." With that, Onchú knelt before Conall and bared his neck. Conall let his breath out; he had not considered that some of these warriors may have been guilty of the murder of his and his friend's families. It would appear that this time he had been spared the breaking of his word and he thanked the goddess.

"On your feet, Onchú ó an Cháintigh. I accept your word, but make no mistake, if you've lied to us, your fate will be much worse than hanging and the crows will feast on you." A sigh of relief went round the hall.

"Get everyone outside, Fearghal. This place stinks of blood, piss and shite."

As Onchú passed him, Conall asked, "Why did you kill those three?"

Caked blood cracked on the warrior's face as he grinned, "They would never have survived the accusations from the villagers."

Outside, breathing in the cold, fresh air, Fearghal remarked, "Before we return to Ráth na Conall we need to rest for a few days to have the wounded attended." Fortunately there was a healer in the village as many of the men had deep cuts and gashes that needed to be sewn. Anxious being away from Mórrígan, Conall reluctantly agreed. Together, the healer and Fionnbharr stitched wounds and applied mud and moss poultices on them to prevent any becoming poisoned.

Brion now sported a long cut that would leave an impressive scar down his left cheek. An axe had narrowly missed cleaving his head in two. Torcán, unburdened by common sense and nicknamed the wild boar, had lived up to his name. The new deep gash across his forehead was from head-butting one of the few warriors who actually had a helmet, but only after he had pushed Brion out of the path of the axe.

The villagers filled barrels of water so that all could wash away the blood and gore. Bowls of steaming hot broth were offered and gratefully received, along with wooden tankards and drinking horns filled with beer. As he sat down on a nearby tree stump to eat and drink, Conall noticed the anxious looks of the villagers and remarked to Fearghal, "Surely, they must know we're not any danger to them."

Mongfhionn snorted derisively. "Are you both that dense? Of course they're afraid, but of Eochaidh Ruad and Ailill Mac Máta, not you. What do you think will happen to these villagers when Eochaidh and Ailill's queen, get news of the raid? Ailill might have some compassion, but neither Medb nor Eochaidh will show mercy."

Fearghal scratched his head, "Aye. That one's a creature of great passions and quick to vengeance, but there's nothing much can be done about it. Maybe they can go hide somewhere for a while."

Three of the villagers approached them nervously. Their leader, Seanán, acknowledged Mongfhionn respectfully before speaking, "We've had a talk among ourselves. We can't stay here. There will be no one to protect us from Ailill and his Queen, or from Eochaidh Ruad." The man gestured towards the small group of inhabitants, "We're tradespeople, not fighters, with no way to defend ourselves or our families. We will go with you - if you will allow us."

A troubled Conall asked the villagers to step back while he consulted with Mongfhionn, Brion, Fearghal and Nikandros. "We put these folk in this situation, but we can't protect them forever. We have our own people to look after at the fort."

"You can't take care of everyone Conall. We'll fight battles in many lands. Are you going to bring them all with you?"

As he spoke, Fearghal looked around, expecting support, but none wanted to voice an opinion on such a difficult decision. Conall considered his friends, the warriors who had fought for him, and the villagers, who had been put in an impossible situation. He thought back to how simple and uncomplicated life had been only a short time ago and wished those times would come again. He was slowly beginning to understand the burden of leadership.

He sighed aloud and slowly stood up, "I know I can't keep everyone safe, but I can give protection to these villagers. That's my decision."

Fearghal acknowledged him, knowing it was a hard choice for the young leader, "You know I'll always be at your side, Conall and I'll defend what you believe. Just beware, there'll come a time when you will have to turn your back on folk like this and leave them to the mercy of the Goddess or the Hag."

"I know, but not this time." Conall strode over to Seanán, "Your people can come with us as far as our fort. After that, it's up to you where you will make your home. We leave at dawn in two days. Make sure everyone is ready. We'll not wait."

On the eighth sunrise from when they had departed Ráth na Conall, the assembled warriors and villagers, accompanied by wagons filled with gold, tools and personal belongings, proceeded from the settlement and crossed the causeway. A few warriors remained behind to fire the barracks and buildings. At least for a while it would not be used as a place to launch an attack on Ráth na Conall. In contrast to their journey to Phortaigh na Cullen, the warriors were in full armor. Alert, they constantly scanned the hillsides as they made their way south-east through territory protected by the fort at Curraghatoor.

A few days out, Nikandros rode ahead to reconnoiter and to ensure there were no surprises. His black cloak and horse contrasted sharply against the snow-covered landscape. Conall watched him and considered that it might be time he learned to ride. He knew Mórrígan would certainly approve.

Fearghal came to his side, interrupting his thoughts, "I think we're being watched."

"Where and who? The hillside is covered in trees, heavy with snow. You could conceal an army in there. Plus there's no other path we can take."

Fearghal scratched his neck, "I'm not sure. I haven't actually seen anyone, but the hairs on the back of my neck are telling me to be watchful."

As they talked, Nikandros cantered towards them. A few paces out, he dismounted and joined them as they tramped on. To anyone watching, there was nothing strange about the scene. Nikandros laughed as if sharing a story with his friends, "On the hillside to your right, four hundred paces ahead, there's a group of about one hundred horsemen in the trees."

Glancing at Fearghal, he continued, "I thought you told me fighting on horse was not the warrior way here. These men are well-armed, and very comfortable on their mounts." Onchú, who, along with Brion and Brocc, overheard the conversation. He spoke without altering his stride.

"They're probably from Curraghatoor. Deda Mac Sin, the king, loves and breeds fine horses. His men are trained to fight on their mounts from when they are very young. Deda's army isn't huge, counted only in the hundreds, but they're brave warriors and very fast when mounted."

"Take your men and without making a fuss, join the villagers. Have them walk slowly, so that they fall back. It is your responsibility to protect them." Onchú smiled in agreement with Conall's instruction.

To Fearghal and Brion, Conall said, "Have the men form up in ranks, but not a tight shield wall, yet. Let's see what our watchers' intentions are." Conall then turned to Nikandros, "I think it's time to show off some of your horsemanship. Maybe that will give them pause to talk with us."

Nikandros smiled, "It will be my pleasure." He removed his cloak, put on his helmet and remounted his black horse. As he trotted forward, the red feather plumes on his helmet flared in the crisp wind, and his bronze armor and shield glowed red and gold reflecting the rising sun.

Alongside Conall, Fearghal chortled, "Well, I don't know about those folk in the hills, but I'm impressed. How he doesn't freeze his balls off wandering about half-naked in this weather amazes me!"

Men and villagers watched and cheered the Spartan. Soon a small group of riders emerged from the cover of the forest and cantered leisurely down the snow-covered hillside to intercept him. At about fifty paces, the group halted and a single rider came forward. The rider held his hands in the air with his palms towards Nikandros as he approached. Conall watched Nikandros sheath his sword, hang his shield on his horse, and remove his helmet. After a short discussion, Nikandros turned his horse around, and rode back at a gallop.

"This looks promising," said Conall, as he watched the tableau play out and the small group of riders continue to approach, albeit at a slower pace.

"At least they don't look hostile." said a very curious Mongfhionn, joining them.

Nikandros leapt from his horse, "Conall, I think the riders are friendly and their leader says he has urgent information for you. The main body of their horsemen will stay in the forest, unless their leader signals that they're welcome."

Conall strode forward, accompanied by Fearghal, Nikandros and Mongfhionn. Brion made to accompany them, but placing a hand on his shoulder, Conall held him back. "They look friendly, and I am sure that Nikandros has the measure of our visitors, but he could be wrong. I want you and Brocc to keep the men alert. Don't do anything that makes it look as if you're preparing to fight. I don't want trouble if it can be avoided. Just keep your eyes open." Brion grinned, turned and walked towards his brother. He put his arm around Brocc, as if sharing some joke or story and then they separated, joining their men.

The leader of the horsemen stopped a cautious ten paces from Conall's party and dismounted, signaling to his men to follow suit. After handing off his weapons and horse, he beckoned another in the group to accompany him.

"Big guy, isn't he?" Fearghal whispered to Conall as the two approached. The rider was at least a head taller than Fearghal, well-built and well-muscled. His face was weathered and most likely he was younger than he looked. Shoulder-length, ginger-colored hair was tied back. He and his men were different from other warriors that Conall had met. They wore leather clothes as protection from the weather and a hard-leather breastplate for additional protection. Pieces of leather had also been stitched onto the thighs of their pants.

As he got closer to Conall, the warrior broke into a great big smile. "I am Íar Mac Dedad, son of Deda Mac Sin, king in the fort of Curraghatoor. My father sends his greetings and apologizes that he was unable to meet with you. He also sends his respects and wants you to know that he mourns for your family, and indeed all at the settlement who were slaughtered. Your father was well known to us and highly respected, Conall Mac Gabhann. We have no love for Eochaidh Ruad, although we're at peace with him and wish that to remain so – at least for a while. My hope is that we will have much more time to get to know one another, as your fame is spreading widely."

Íar paused for a beat before continuing, "For now, I have news that may sit better with a warm and full belly. So I propose we get a good fire going and some food and drink, before we all freeze in this weather that the Hag has blessed us with."

Conall hoped he was a good judge of men, for he found himself drawn to this stranger. He took Íar's hand and clasped it, feeling the vice-like grip of calloused and scarred flesh. As he led Íar towards the center of the encampment, Conall smiled, "Perhaps, your men – all your men that is, would also like some hot food and beer while we talk?"

Roaring with laughter, Íar called to one of his men. "Signal the riders on the hillside to come down and tell them to leave their weapons on their horses. I don't want anyone getting drunk and starting a swordfight." Looking around at Conall's men, he laughed again, "Your men are well trained. They look as if they are totally relaxed, but I'm betting their weapons are oiled and sharpened." He spotted some of the Cróeb Ruad tattoos and drew in a sharp breath, "So it is true that you rescued the northerners from Eochaidh. Whatever happened to that reprobate who was their leader? Eochaidh was furious that he had eluded his clutches."

Fearghal responded with a broad smile, "I'm sure I don't know."

Noticing Mongfhionn, Íar's countenance became troubled. He bowed his head, "My lady, at Curraghatoor we have also heard of a powerful sidhe and queen with no apparent kingdom. I trust you do not have anything, but good intentions towards my father - and my people."

Mongfhionn smiled, "You and your people have nothing to fear from the aes sidhe, Íar Mac Dedad. Your father has always been loyal to us, and constant in his sacrifices and hospitality. Mongfhionn's eyes clouded slightly as she continued, "I think you should state your news before Conall bursts with impatience. However, know this, his queen is waiting for him at Ráth na Conall – and she is soon to be a mother."

Íar sighed unhappily, "Then I'm truly sorry at what you will hear." Looking to the rider he had brought with him, "This messenger is from Ráthgall, a fort in the mid-east. He brings news of a large force of some two hundred men in burnished armor that landed in a cove in the south-east about eight sunrises past. For whatever reason, they made for your fort and besiege it as we speak. I'm sorry, but I have no news of how the siege is going."

Fearghal, Brion and Brocc listened grimly to Íar; Conall's face was ashen. The rider from Ráthgall provided more details about the besiegers, and as he described their clothing, armor and weapons, Mongfhionn and Nikandros in chorus said, "Romans!"

"But why are they here?" Conall asked.

Nikandros spoke dryly, "Romans are a very 'tidy' race, Conall. They do not like 'loose ends'. The master of these soldiers does not want any trace of his past intrigues to return to Rome to embarrass him. To him, you and your people are a loose end." What he did not voice, but thought was, "And so am I."

"We have several things in our favor. These men do not like fighting in rough terrain. Their phalanx is not a good battle formation for these lands. They like large organized battles on open ground. My guess is that they will lay siege to the fort hoping to starve our people into surrender. All may not be lost; our home is well fortified and Cúscraid and Mórrígan are very shrewd leaders.

They will hold out."

"We have been gone eight days, Nikandros. By my reckoning, and from what the rider told us, the Romans would have reached the fort four, possibly five days ago. It will take at least three days at a fast march to reach them." Conall shoulders slumped in despair at the thought of losing Mórrígan and their child.

"Maybe not three days, Conall. Maybe not even two. I am sorry to have brought this news, but I also bring a gift from my father which might help."

Conall looked at Íar questioningly, "I am sure that in other circumstances I would be delighted with a gift from your father, but how can it possibly help us now?"

A big grin wreathed Íar's face, "Oh this is a very practical gift, Conall. The first part of my father's gift is that you should have two of his prized horses – a mare and a stallion so that you may breed your own." Íar waved his hand and one of his men led two superb looking horses to stand in front of them. Conall, though no judge of horseflesh, could see that both were beautiful and powerful animals. The jet black stallion stood a full seventeen hands and pawed the ground as its slightly smaller, golden-coated mate nervously watched its lead.

Conall felt strangely drawn to the stallion. "Does he have a name?"

Íar shook his head, "His name is for you to choose."

"I shall choose at a later date. I am pleased with such a thoughtful gift, but my heart is heavy for my people and queen at Ráth na Conall."

"My father's next gift may lift your spirits. I have brought one hundred horsemen with me. Choose fifty of them to join your army."

There was a stunned silence as Conall and Fearghal considered what had just been offered. Fearghal looked Íar in the eye, "Why? What's the catch? What do you need from us?"

"Such suspicion, Northerner. My father wished to make amends in some small way for Eochaidh Ruad's treachery. As I said before, we have no love for Eochaidh, but are not yet in a position to challenge him. My father knew yours well Conall. The gift has no conditions. Please accept it."

Hope had risen in Conall's eyes and he grasped Íar by the shoulder. "I accept. Please tell the king I am in his debt, and one day I will repay his generosity. But how do I choose fifty from your men?"

As was his habit, Íar roared with laughter again, "There was no shortage of volunteers when they found out that you have gold to pay their wages! I've already chosen for you; they are the best of my men, but all have agreed to swear allegiance to their new king, Conall Mac Gabhann."

Íar paused to warm his hands over the blazing fire, "Night is almost upon us, so I recommend that we get an early night. With your permission, in the morning I'll lead your horsemen and ride for the fort. We will do what we can to help until you arrive. My remaining riders will provide an escort for your villagers and wagons while you force march."

At first light, Conall's new cavalry threw their riding blankets on their horses. Nikandros stood beside Íar as he was preparing his mount, "Be careful, friend. The phalanx is strong and no friend to cavalry, but it is weak on the right flank and to the rear."

As the riders mounted up, Mongfhionn came to Nikandros, "I need your horse, Spartan. I must get to the fort quickly and assess what diversions I can create."

Reluctantly, for his horse was precious to him, Nikandros agreed. "These Romans worship different gods than yours, Mongfhionn. Your undoubted talents may not be as effective against them."

Mongfhionn eyes burned, "Men's hearts can always be made to beat faster - or not at all."

CHAPTER 8

The messenger from Ráthgall stopped briefly en route to Curraghatoor. He reported that a large body of well-armed, foreign warriors appeared to be marching in the direction of Ráth na Conall. Mórrígan and Cúscraid entreated him to remain at the fort, if only to add one more to their small band of defenders, but he declined, stating that it was also his duty to warn Carn Tigherna and Curraghatoor. From his haste to get back on his mount, it was more likely he thought their chances of survival were slim. Disappointed, Mórrígan and Cúscraid gave him food and drink and waved him on. They then turned to inspect their meager forces.

"I wish I had asked for more to remain behind," Cúscraid grumbled.

"You and me both," retorted Mórrígan. "Well, we have ten of your men and fifteen of my friends - although most are very young."

Cúscraid concurred, "Thank the goddess the settlement reinforcements were completed before Conall left. Our defenses are as good as any I have seen in Ériu and our stores of food and water are more than enough to outlast even a long siege."

"How can we possibly hold out? If the rider is to be believed, then there are two hundred men advancing on us. It will be at least another eight days before Conall and the rest return. Even at full strength, we would be outnumbered four to one."

Mórrígan sighed deeply as she looked out over the still frozen land to the east of the fort. The smoke from the campfires in the many shelters, which had sprouted up around the fort, drifted upwards. People thought they were protected by the fort. She pointed them out to Cúscraid, "Perhaps, we can get more men from them, and the closest crofts. I'm sure the soldiers will not be kind to them."

Nodding in agreement, Cúscraid said, "Take the hounds with you. Ride out and warn them. It's the least we can do. Perhaps some will volunteer to join us. Even a few additional bodies will make us appear a more formidable force. While you're away, I'll get the men prepared."

On the fourth day of marching, Spurius Sulpicia Longus spied the silhouette of Ráth na Conall through its usual haze of blue-grey smoke. He had remarked earlier to his centurions that, so far, the only thing he liked about this land was the aromatic smell of the peat fires. His men constantly complained as they marched through rough, snow covered terrain and thorn-covered undergrowth that ripped their leg-bindings tearing flesh from their legs. Spurius mused that the men had spent too long in the comforts of Rome and needed more campaign experience in Gaul.

Spurius had been disturbed by the absence of people in the many small crofts through which they had passed, and was even more troubled by the lack of food. Not being able to forage much more than scraps from the villages and farms, his men were already on short rations. The occasional beast that had ventured out from its hibernation was certainly not sufficient, either to fill his men's bellies or to stop their incessant grumbling.

As they drew closer, Spurius was able to make out the fortifications. He was both impressed and concerned. Its location left him only the option of a frontal attack across open ground and then up a steep incline. He smiled sardonically. At last he had a battlefield where he could deploy the phalanx. The only problem was that his enemy appeared to be in a very secure fortress. His foe was unlikely to come out and fight and Spurius was neither prepared nor equipped for a long siege. He had obviously been badly informed of the strength and resourcefulness of his enemy.

Cúscraid was delighted when Mórrígan brought back news that the nearby communities and farms would be sending their sons to help. He was much less cheerful as he watched long trails of people and carts making their way to the fort. "Where are we going to put them all Mórrígan? And how are we going to feed them?"

Mórrígan shrugged, "There's still room here. We'll do what we can. Most have brought their own food."

Muttering to himself, Cúscraid went to examine his new recruits arriving at the gateway. He pointed to the stacks of weapons in the yard and directed them to their places on the stockade. His men already stood alert, armed with swords, axes and javelins, their shields placed in front of them.

His countenance became less strained when he overheard a group of farmers entering the fort joke about their previous adventures as warriors. In all there were ten men, aged from twenty to thirty summers. These were provided not only with weapons, but also armor and shields.

To Cúscraid's further delight, some farmers brought along their wolfhounds. For many, a pair of wolfhounds was often the only protection they had against bandits, bears or wolves. In all, he now had twelve hounds and Cúscraid was already thinking about how to use them.

"Thirty-five warriors and a pack of hounds against two hundred," he thought, "Fearghal will be pissed he missed this fight!"

At mid-day the gates of Ráth na Conall were closed and barricaded. Shortly thereafter, they heard a shout from Craiftine, "Men marching from the east and they don't look as if they're coming for the craic and a few beers!"

The plain to the east of the fort was about a half day's march in width and length, bounded on the north and north-east sides by tree-covered hills. To the south, the land gently sloped down towards the coast. Spurius' men quickly and efficiently swept the plain clean of anything that could be eaten or used. Shelters were stripped down and homes leveled. Anything that would burn was stored for later use to keep the fires going for heat during the nights and to cook during the day. Trees in the forest were cut down and used to build a stockade just forward from the forest edge. Spurius' plan was to keep as much open ground as possible before them, in the hope of using use his phalanx.

It was late-afternoon when Spurius cantered towards the fort accompanied by the centurions, Decimus and Publius. His intent was to offer the occupants of the fort the chance to surrender and give him any information as to the whereabouts of the depraved idiot, Cassius Fabius Scaeva and the Spartan, Nikandros. As they drew near to the fort, Spurius frowned as he surveyed the stone ramparts, solid stockade and wide ditch. Between the mountains to the west that formed a semi-circle around the fort lay a narrow passage. He was sure the passage would hold a few surprises and it would only take a few men to block anyone trying to get to the rear. When he was within shouting distance, Spurius called out, "I am Spurius Sulpicia Longus, Primus Pilum of the legions of Marcus Fabius Ambustus and of the Republic of Rome. I would speak with your leader."

"So finally we meet some Romans." Cúscraid looked at Mórrígan and innocently said, "I guess he wants to talk to you. As Conall's queen, you outrank me!"

Mórrígan, snorted, "Don't even think for one moment that you're getting away with that one, Cúscraid Mac Conchobar. If I go, you go."

Mórrígan thought for a moment. "However, we can't let them know that Conall isn't here and our strength is reduced. You'll have to play the part of Conall when we talk to them." She smiled mischievously, "Tell him we will talk to him presently. I have to put some paint on."

Cúscraid groaned, "Mórrígan, have you lost your senses? This is no time for dressing up."

Mórrígan laughed. "Calm down, Cúscraid. This is something that Mongfhionn taught me. You can't go to battle without your face on." At that, Mórrígan turned, calling to her two helpers hovering nearby, and disappeared into her home.

"Nothing good will come of this," Cúscraid muttered, "especially if Mongfhionn is involved." To the guard in the gatepost he shouted, "Tell the Roman we'll talk with him in a wee while."

On hearing this, Spurius almost exploded, "Who do these barbarians and peasants think they are, making Romans wait? I'll crucify some of them to teach them respect."

After what seemed a long time, Cúscraid heard whispering and more than a few low whistles from the men on the defenses. He turned round to see Mórrígan walking towards him. She certainly had her face paint on and precious little else! Cúscraid did not know whether to look or avert his eyes. As she walked towards him, her head held high, Mórrígan was totally naked apart from the mysterious swirls and curling symbols in blue and white that covered her entire body. As Mórrígan walked, the symbols seemed to come alive, a tableau of both the sensual and the terrible.

She also appeared to be immune from the cold, although Cúscraid observed that this "magic" did not seem to apply to her prominent nipples. Almost as quickly as they had begun, the whistles from the men faded to be replaced by awe and fear - even from those who knew Mórrígan well. An eerie silence descended on the fort. Cúscraid bowed as she stood by his side, "My lady."

Mórrígan smiled sinisterly, "Let's go greet the Romans," and side by side they walked through the gateway.

Spurius experienced a strange foreboding as he watched the pair of barbarians approach. Both walked confidently, as if unaware of, or indifferent to, the might of Rome that he represented. As they got closer, he saw that one was female, and a great beauty, even though she was clearly quite young. He was to swear later it seemed there was an aura emanating from her as she walked towards him, and that the "clothes" she wore seemed to flow like liquid around her.

It was only when they stopped a few paces from him that

Spurius realized that Mórrígan was naked. He turned to the tall, hard-muscled man beside her who was carefully observing the Romans with both disdain and disapproval. In truth, Spurius had been expecting someone younger, but possibly the tales that he had heard of a young, avenging king had been exaggerated.

"I am Conall Mac Gabhann. This is my queen Mórrígan Ni Cathasaigh. You're trespassing on our lands and in a quite unfriendly manner. Perhaps you're unaware of our hospitality laws. I suggest you state your business and leave."

As Cúscraid spoke, Mórrígan turned her gaze on the centurions accompanying Spurius. She caught and held their eyes with her own - now soulless and black as coal. Publius and Decimus started to sweat in the cold air. Their horses snorted and pawed nervously at the ground. They tried to avert their eyes as their minds were tormented with terrible scenes of destruction and blood. Each saw visions from their worst nightmares, while looking upon a face transformed from a beautiful young woman to a terrible, cruel-faced hag.

Distracted by his own unpleasant thoughts, Spurius sensed the situation was slipping from him. He leant over the neck of his horse and spoke harshly to Cúscraid, "Remove the witch or I will have her cut down."

Mórrígan turned to face him. "Lift a hand, Roman, and my archers will end this conversation." Shocked, Spurius tried to hold his temper as he was outmaneuvered by mere barbarians. His gaze followed Mórrígan's hand as she pointed to the archers in each of the lookout posts. Mounted as they were, Spurius and his centurions presented an almost perfect target.

Fighting to conceal his anger, Spurious responded, "Apologies your highness. I think we may have some "cultural" misunderstandings. I only wish to ask a few questions."

"You have a lot of men with you to ask only a few questions, Roman." Cúscraid replied sarcastically, as he looked to the encampment that had been constructed. "You have displaced my people and seized their goods. How do you propose to compensate them?"

Spurius cleared his throat and tried to clear his mind, "These are but a small honor guard to protect me in foreign lands. They represent a very small part of my Master's armies. However, to my questions, we seek two men – a Roman, Cassius Fabius Scaeva and a Spartan, Nikandros. My Master has business to complete with them and we are to escort them back to Rome."

"We know nothing of these men." Mórrígan replied evenly. "Take your men and return to Rome with my blessing and my greetings to your Master."

"It is almost time for the evening meal. Perhaps, my officers and I could eat with you and discuss our mutual interests." Spurius proposed a meal knowing that barbarian rules of hospitality would protect him from harm. Foolishly, he added, "We would be able to confirm whether the ones we seek are within the fort. Possibly, they may be disguised or known by different names to you."

Cúscraid scowled as he felt his temper rising. He had grown weary of the game they were playing. "Our rules of hospitality are not for those who wish to deceive us. And I don't appreciate my queen being called a liar, Spurius Sulpicia Longus. The men you seek are not here. You have our word. Gather your men and leave."

Spurius bristled, but smiled falsely as he answered, "I will certainly consider your counsel and in the morning will give you my response." At that he bowed and turned his horse around. As they rode away, he snarled, "We attack at dawn. I will not be spoken to in this manner by a barbarian and his whore." The centurions, still unsure about the visions they had seen, returned to the camp and spoke of strange apparitions. This was exactly what Mórrígan had intended. Soon rumors and stories of barbarian witchcraft were rife throughout the camp.

As they walked back to the fort, Cúscraid said, "They will attack at sunrise, Mórrígan."

"I agree. We should prepare for the assault."

She walked ahead of Cúscraid and as he watched her round arse cheeks roll with each step she took, Cúscraid shook his head and called out, "For pity's sake, Mórrígan, put some clothes on or you'll drive the men insane." Then in resignation, he shrugged, "In any event, Conall will probably take my head when he hears of this." As they walked through the gateway, Mórrígan's assistants were waiting with her cloak.

The sound of hounds barking then diverted Cúscraid's attention and made him pause. He chuckled, "Well, why should the Romans have a good night's rest?" He called the wolfhounds' owners to him and after a short conversation they all laughed.

The Romans had a very restless night indeed, as the wolfhound pack, directed by whistles from their masters, constantly prowled around the encampment. The air was filled with howling and barking. Were an unfortunate solder to venture outside to take a piss, the hounds were happy to bite as often as the opportunity was presented.

It was a bone chilling dawn and flurries of snow danced on the wind. As he vigorously rubbed his hands together to get the circulation going, Spurius cursed equally his disturbed sleep, the barbarians and the weather. His breath formed a fine, white, crystalline mist while he briefed his centurions. "We will test their defenses this morning. The fort appears to be defended by farmers with a few barbarian warriors. If the gods are with us, we may be able to breech their defenses and end this charade quickly. Divide the men into four sections. Leave one to guard the camp. I will lead one to attack the gateway; each of you take a section and look for weakness on their north and south flanks. Tell the men that we take no prisoners and we leave no equipment behind." Publius and Decimus saluted and returned to their men.

Cúscraid and Mórrígan had risen early to discuss tactics. "We've no scarcity of water and food and the fort is well located. I doubt that the Romans have provisions for a long siege so my best guess is that they'll try a rapid assault to break us quickly. If their leaders are an example of how they dress for battle then they'll be very well armored. Indeed they'll be as well-equipped as we are."

Mórrígan thought for a moment, "I'll take my brother Bricriu, together with Craiftine and Eirnín. Two will be placed in each of the gate watchtowers. Our bows should be able to hit our targets at two hundred paces and last until our arms tire. We may at least give the

Romans pause for thought."

"We can't afford to lose experienced fighters early in the fight. My advice is that we use the volunteers from farms and villages on the stockade first. They'll be supported by the ten who have fought as warriors before, so that should provide strength and experience. Our own men will be formed behind them and will be ready to fill any potential breech. We've a good supply of javelins, but not enough to waste, and certainly not enough to last many days of battle, so I intend to keep them in reserve. But that means we will have to let the Romans get close on their first assault and we'll take more casualties."

"We should take separate sides of the stockade. If either of us is injured or killed then the other will take command."

As they each turned to prepare for battle, Cúscraid looked at Mórrígan and offered, "The paint on your face and hands suits you, but I am glad you have your armor on this morning!"

The Roman columns, formed up in lines of ten across and five deep, marched towards the settlement. The crunching of boots and sandals reinforced with iron studs echoed in the crisp air. Shields and sheathed swords were borne on the left, leaving their right hands free to carry the siege ladders assembled the previous day. Ropes with grappling hooks were wound around the men's chests and waists.

The archers watched. As the Romans passed the marker arrow, Mórrígan shouted, "Now!" and the four archers sent a flight of arrows towards their attackers. The first volley thudded harmlessly into shields. More followed, finding targets that howled in pain and cursed the archers. Nikandros training had prepared them well, and although the bows were smaller than normal, they were much more powerful. Mórrígan wished she had more archers. A previously skeptical Cúscraid felt the same.

Spurius spat on the frozen dirt and cursed. He was, however, very glad that he counted just four archers and fervently hoped there were not more hidden behind the stockade. There was no doubting

Spurius' bravery as he led from the front, urging, cajoling and shouting at his men to move forward. Within fifty paces of the fort, the columns lead by Decimus and Publius split and jogged to the right and left of the gateway. Realizing that the pathway to the gate was too narrow, Spurius changed the formation to a narrower five-man wide column. A great shout went up as the Romans rushed the gate and ditches. Siege ladders were thrown across the ditch and against the wall.

The thunder of many bodhráns accompanied by shouts of "Mac Gabhann abú, Mac Gabhann abú," filled the air as the defenders took up their battle cry. Now that the Romans were fully engaged, Mórrígan's archers inflicted much more serious injuries. Several soldiers fell to the side with arrow shafts protruding from exposed faces and throats.

The first Romans to cross the ditch and scramble up the rock and dirt ramparts were met by a barrage of rocks. Siege ladders broke under the weight of stones and bodies as too many tried to clamber across. The stakes in the ditch took Roman lives before barbarian swords and axes. With perseverance, enough made it across and having gained a foothold on the ramparts, began to pitch grappling hooks up and over the stockade. Shrieks of pain rose up, as iron hooks found soft flesh, and several unfortunates found themselves helplessly trapped against the wooden fence. Gaps opened up allowing more siege ladders to be raised. Publius, sensing an opportunity, shouted and urged his men on.

Spurius' section faced a constant barrage of stones and arrows, but persevered to reach the gate and heave hard against it. Iron hinges groaned and screamed at the stress, but the gate held, strengthened by logs that had been levered into place as support. As he watched the fight move in favor of the Romans, Cúscraid called for the cooking pots to be dragged onto the stockade. Great iron cauldrons had been filled with hot coals and others with water that had been kept on the boil. Now they were emptied on the Romans.

Screeches of misery and pain from scalded attackers rose

amid the steam. Pots filled with live embers from the blacksmith's forge were tipped over the stockade. Men howled as the coals rained down, burning and adhering to exposed flesh. At the gateway, Spurius swore as boiling water reddened and blistered his arm. He gritted his teeth and shouted, "Keep going, kill the barbarian bastards."

Cúscraid surveyed the battle. He was pleased that the gate was holding even though it was under great stress. The narrowness of the path to the gate had constrained what the Romans could do and he could see that the constant flow of rocks, arrows, boiling water and searing coals, while not causing many fatalities, was certainly frustrating the attackers. His worry was the grappling hooks, which he had not foreseen. The barbed hooks killed several defenders, although more by accident than design. To his right, the defenders on the stockade appeared to be holding their own, and most of the scaling ropes had now been severed.

On his left, however, a substantial gap had opened up where hooks had snagged and pinned defenders against the wooden posts. Romans, with shields on backs and daggers clamped between teeth, clambered over the fence. Inexperienced defenders were cut down as the Romans drew and slashed with their swords, while battering them with bronze shields. Soon, a stretch of the stockade had been cleared and their comrades were now clambering up the ropes in force.

It heartened Cúscraid to see his recent recruits push their way forward through the villagers to block the Romans making further advances. Both sides slashed at each other furiously trying to gain an advantage. Surprised at first that they were facing men with armor equal to their own, the Romans kept up the pressure. Recognizing that he needed to clear the narrow walkway before he had a real battle on his hands inside the fort, Cúscraid shouted to the reserve Cróeb Ruad, "You ten, get off your arses and kill those Romans."

The men laughed and roared, "About time too!" Then, "Kill the bastards," as they sprinted for the parapet.

Now the Romans found themselves trapped between the veterans and the Cróeb Ruad fighters. They were brutally slaughtered and their bodies summarily hurled over the stockade. Those unfortunates, about to clamber over the stockade, were grabbed, kicked and hit with swords, shields and axes, and then thrown down into the fort. As the villagers descended on the badly injured attackers, Cúscraid yelled, "I want them alive. Strip them and shackle them to a post."

A veteran of many campaigns, Centurion Publius knew he had lost this engagement and ordered the retreat sounded. His men disengaged, and made their way back across the ditch. Spurius cursed, knowing he too was not making any significant progress at the gate and was in danger of losing men for no gain. As bronze horns sounded, the entire company of Roman soldiers fell back. Jeers and taunts rang out from the fort as they watched the soldiers retreat. Pale, bare arses were flaunted along the stockade and the bodhráns sounded loud across the valley.

Some badly wounded stragglers, unable to keep up with their companions, fell behind, crawling or dragging themselves towards safety. Cúscraid called to Mórrígan, "Send out the hounds. Let them loose on the laggards. We'll teach the Romans a lesson about fighting in this land." Mórrígan grinned darkly and ran to her horse. Soon she was leading the wolfhounds towards the scattered, disabled Romans. Spurius heard their dying screams and watched with horror, as the huge grey shapes brought the men down and tore their throats out.

Cúscraid was surprised that it was not yet mid-day. He looked at the darkening sky and clouds moving down from the north and heaved a sigh of relief. A storm might bring them some respite. Mórrígan had returned with the hounds, their muzzles covered in blood. She was now busy overseeing the care of the injured and ensuring the dead were made ready for burning. Wailing from the families of the dead and critically injured echoed off the fort's walls, but there was also a surprising sense of satisfaction that their fort had survived its first major battle. The peat and wood fire pits around the fort gave comfort to all and provided hot food.

Most of the men on the stockade were relieved, leaving a

skeleton guard to keep watch on any movements from the Roman camp. A team was sent out to scavenge for weapons, armor and anything of value from the Roman corpses and to stake the heads before darkness fell. Then, there was the matter of the prisoners. The two men were bound naked to wooden railings outside the Great Hall. Cúscraid did not know why he had kept them - they would not be able to tell him anything he did not already know. He just shook his head and wished Fearghal was back. Cúscraid was a warrior and not comfortable with the responsibility and the thinking ahead that went with this leadership role.

He called Mórrígan and some of the village elders together in the Great Hall, "We've survived and hopefully the Romans will take the rest of the day to lick their wounds. Tomorrow, we will man the stockade at full strength with the Cróeb Ruad and our newest recruits, who have shown that they have not forgotten their battle skills. We have but one surprise left, so tomorrow we'll place stacks of javelins on the walkways to greet our Roman friends."

To Mórrígan he said, "I need an archer on each side of the stockade as well as in the lookout post."

She was not happy as both her younger brothers and Conall's were among that small band, but nevertheless acceded, "I will take the left side of the stockade and Craiftine the right."

"I will assign a guard to each as a shield," Cúscraid promised.

"Bricriu and Eirnín will remain in the lookout towers." Cúscraid was uneasy at this as it meant Mórrígan would take up a position on the stockade. Her slightly curved belly was a constant reminder to him that she was carrying Conall's child.

Frustration at their failure to take the fort soon turned into anger in the Roman encampment. Thirteen men had died in the first assault on the fort's defenses and two were missing. Many were wounded and useless for further service. Spurius called Decimus and Publius to talk over tactics for the next day. The men needed rest and the roiling clouds and rippling of thunder promised a storm.

Bitter for having underestimated his enemy, Spurius nevertheless had a newfound respect for these barbarians and understood why his Master was keen to have them as mercenaries. "What have we learned?" he asked aloud.

Publius spoke carefully, "Well sir, we were able to breech their defenses for a short time. With more men we could have held that section of the stockade and got more of our men into the fort."

Spurius agreed, "We did, but their reinforcements cut through our men like a knife through goat's cheese. How many more of that caliber do they have?" He pictured the barbarians inside the walls of the stockade, smug in their temporary victory. "In any event, here's what I have decided. Send the men to cut down trees to bridge that ditch. I make it about two men wide. Also, we need to cut and harden two trees as battering rams. Cut them down and then harden the tips in the fires. We can use the horses to drag the logs and rams to the edge of the perimeter ditch. They only have four archers, a nuisance, but not a major worry. Our main force will attack across the tree-bridges while a smaller section will use the rams on the gate. Replace the injured men with the ones who were on camp guard this morning."

Hail and sleet throughout the night had cloaked the land in a sheet of ice and now, the morning sun burned blood red through the wraith-like mist that hung over Ráth na Conall.

Cúscraid stood beside Mórrígan on the battlement. "I think the Goddess of battle wants a good view this morning. Let's hope she favors the side whose leader bears her name."

Having decided that the queen should be protected at all costs, Cúscraid assigned Urard, a towering Cróeb Ruad warrior who looked as if he was carved out of rock, as her guardian. Urard's orders were simple – to kill anyone who threatened the queen. Ten warriors on each side stood alert along the northern walkway. Five javelins per man, along with their shields, swords and battle axes rested against the stockade. The remaining warriors stood in reserve.

"Here they come," Bricriu announced from his lookout.

Keeping pace to a solitary drum and with the sun glinting off their bronze armor, the Romans marched doggedly towards the fort. Horses strained and puffed out clouds of vapor, dragging heavy logs. Spurius felt confident as he surveyed his soldiers and declared the clear skies and ice-covered ground good omens from the gods. He knew that victory often turned on small details and his men's boots meant that they had an excellent grip on the treacherous ice. At a hundred paces, the soldiers split into two columns. Fifty of the biggest together with the battering rams made for the gate, the remainder marched for the ditch. The men cursed at the grim sight of the heads of their dead friends. "Show these barbarians no mercy," Spurius shouted, "avenge your comrades."

A great roar came from the ranks as they charged forward. It was met by a thundering wall of sound from the bodhráns as once again they took up their insistent drumming. Swarms of arrows flew from the stockade, chiefly towards the attackers' horses. As the Romans reached the edge of the ditch, Cúscraid shouted, "Make the bastards work for their gold." Javelins arced over the stockade. Horses screamed, stumbled and died as the shower of missiles struck. Handlers were crushed and dragged under logs and bashing hooves.

"I wish whoever is in that fort was on my side," Spurius thought grimly. To the men he roared, "Get those logs across that ditch. Cover the men with your shields."

Cúscraid ordered another volley of javelins, "Target the log carriers. Make the ditch their grave."

Huge men, muscles straining within their armor, carried the battering rams to within a few paces of the gate. Volleys of javelins reduced their numbers, yet replacements were at hand. A hissing rain of boiling water and glowing coals fell from the stockade. On each side, soldiers raised shields to cover the rams and protect themselves from the torrent of pain. Shields made cumbersome after being pierced by several javelins were tossed aside and replacements brought forward.

Craiftine and Eirnín focused their shots on the attackers with the rams and other choice targets of opportunity. Black-shafted arrows with distinctive red and white feathers, and tipped with iron felled more attackers. Wooden buckets filled with black pitch, oil and fat were emptied over the wall and accompanied by bales of hay. Indeed, anything that would burn was quickly tossed onto the rams or in their path.

Their hands and wrists shielded from the flames by leather strips, Craiftine and Eirnín switched to fire arrows. Exposed fingers suffered as they drew the arrows back. With clenched teeth, they shot arrow after arrow and watched with satisfaction as the rams slowly caught fire. The Romans, urged on by their centurion, reached the gate and started to slam the rams against it.

A last volley of javelins split flesh and wood as Romans advanced across the ditch using the four bridging logs. Cúscraid appraised the bodies claimed by the ditch and how many lay injured or dying on the other side. They had blunted and slowed the Roman onslaught, but Cúscraid knew that numbers were on the Romans' side. They also appeared much more determined this morning.

The rhythmic thumping of the battering rams against the gate made him flinch. Cúscraid knew it would not hold. The gate had been significantly upgraded from its humble beginnings as the settlement entrance, but no one had envisaged it being subjected to this much force. He looked down at Beacán who, although only eleven summers old, stood resolutely beside his sister Mórrígan. Beacán and his friend Cathán had been appointed messengers during the battle. "Beacán, run to the other side of the gate. Tell them that five are to fall back from the stockade and form the shield wall with the others. Then tell the farmers and villagers that I want anyone who can hold a weapon to fall in behind our men." Beacán nodded and sped away.

"Shields up, javelins ready," Cúscraid bellowed to the men on the left of the stockade, "Make the bastards pay. Show them that a Cróeb Ruad warrior is worth five of them."

The response was quick, resounding along the stockade, "Five? You're just being insulting!"

Spurius watched with admiration and concern as a row of shields suddenly added more height to an already challenging stockade. He shouted orders above the din, "Grappling hooks, throw high and pull those bloody shields down." Many shields were lost, wrenched from arms and hands by the sheer number of hooks thrown, but quickly replaced by the villagers. Siege ladders were raised against the ramparts, and Romans swiftly clambered up them, as well as the ropes. The first to reach the top of the stockade were met with javelins, only their armor saving them from death. Unable to get a purchase on ice-covered dirt and stone, the unlucky fell screaming onto the stakes in the ditch. Unfortunately, the Roman armor and shields trapped many javelins, tearing them from the grip of the defenders.

Surveying the battle, Cúscraid glanced across to Mórrígan and was astonished at how calm she appeared. Her face, swathed with curling blue and white symbols, seemed to glow as she sent arrow after arrow into the Romans. She was clearly the prize target; shouts of "Kill the barbarian witch!" resonated along the Roman ranks. Her guard stood firmly at her side, contemptuously swatting aside any attempt to bring her down.

The fight became signally desperate as more clambered over the fence. Cúscraid's heart sank as he heard a loud crack followed by cheers and shouts, "The gate's down! We're through."

Cúscraid spoke clearly and grimly to Cathán, "Run to the shield wall. Tell them from me that they must hold." As the boy darted off, Cúscraid chuckled to himself, "One less worry on the stockade."

At last, the Goddess, showing disapproval of her land being invaded, decided to intervene and undo the plans of all. At the sound of the gate being breached, the defenders briefly faltered. It was enough time to let a large group of Romans clamber over the northern stockade, splitting Cúscraid's forces.

About to scale the wall, Spurius heard the gate shatter and confidently turned to Decimus, "Join Publius and clear the gate. I will stay here and take command of the stockade. The fort is ours." The centurion saluted, sounded the trumpet to call his men, most of who had not yet crossed the ditch, and led them to reinforce their comrades.

Having done this many times before, Spurius clambered surely up the ropes and was about to leap over the stockade when Mórrígan put three arrows into his cuirass. She had placed them at his heart and had he not been wearing armor, the arrows would certainly have pinned his heart to his spine. Instead, the iron arrowheads slamming into him knocked him back. He gasped, involuntarily clutching at his chest as the barbs punctured his armor and pierced his flesh. As Spurius tried to maintain his grip on the stockade, Urard took a pace forward, bashing an axe head into Spurius' face. The Roman commander fell from the rampart, frantically grasping at rock and icy mud to save himself from the ditch.

With room for no more than three men standing shoulder to shoulder on the stockade's walkway, Cúscraid and two others locked shields, drew swords and pressed forward. On the other side, Urard rumbled, "Sorry," as he unceremoniously lifted Mórrígan out of his way, and set about killing. Gripping the axe two-handed, he scythed through the air at chest height. The razor sharp blades ripped through the bronze shields of the two Romans before him. The savage momentum of the blow almost tore the shields from their arms. Urard swung again, this time bringing the axe down on the nearest shield, splitting it in two and severing a Roman arm. Blood pumped from opened arteries, soaking defender and attacker. Urard's next swing arrested the man's gabbling shriek as it removed head from shoulders. The body spasmed, gouts of blood spurting upwards, before it was kicked aside.

Seeing Urard off-balance, the closest Roman chopped downwards, opening up a long gash along Urard's upper arm. Urard clenched his teeth and heaved the great axe. A black arrow sprouted from the Roman's throat as the huge warrior sliced upwards between the man's legs. The vicious blade split the Roman from his balls to his belly. Urard turned to Mórrígan, grinning broadly through a mask of blood and gore. The Romans were caught, with little room for maneuver, between two pitiless forces. Their comrades were prevented from reinforcing them on the walkway as defenders recovering from their momentary lapse in concentration, and re-entered the battle.

Cúscraid and his companions, legs straining, feet scraping wood, heaved and pushed against the Romans with their shields. In the tight space, their short swords slashed and jabbed while pushing the attackers back onto the bite of Urard's axe and the sting of Mórrígan's bow. The Romans fought bravely, meting out deep wounds on their enemies. With nowhere to go, the choice was to die on the stockade or to scramble back over it, hoping not to roll into the ditch with its vicious stakes. Leaderless, eventually their discipline faded and several opted to jump, leaving their comrades in a weakened position. Sandwiched, the remaining Romans were soon overcome and butchered.

Breathing heavily as he rested on his shield, Cúscraid surveyed the fight at the gate. Its iron hinges had twisted and split under the force of the rams. As the wood splintered, the Romans rushed forward. They were met by three volleys of javelins from the shield wall, which stalled their momentum. It also allowed the wall to move steadily forward to close the gap. As the defenders advanced, injured Romans were quickly dispatched with a sword thrust. When reinforcements under Decimus arrived, they found themselves facing a solid shield wall - not a broken mob of barbarians. In the confines of the narrow entrance, no side had the advantage and a stalemate set in.

Cúscraid strode to the lookout tower and after taking in the situation, shouted, "Romans take your injured and retreat. There's no way for you to move forward. Your companions have died or fled the stockade. Most likely your leader is dead." He took a deep breath and bluffing somewhat, said, "I can call for more men to reinforce my shields and javelins to be brought forward. You'll not break through today. I see no sense in a slow, meaningless slaughter. Where is the honor in that?"

Decimus and Publius exchanged knowing glances and then Decimus, standing aside from his men said, "Agreed. There is no point in continuing this fight today, barbarian." As his men watched warily, Decimus asked, "Will you allow us to gather up our dead?"

"Take your injured, but not your dead. We take the heads of our enemies or their spirits will come back to haunt us. We mean no disrespect, but that is our way. Their bodies will be left for you to collect later, if you wish. Their heads will remain with us."

"It seems today I have no choice, barbarian. We will return for their bodies." Turning to the men, Decimus ordered them to withdraw and led them back towards their encampment.

Cúscraid walked along the blood-stained parapet with Mórrígan, gesturing first at his men, then at the Roman camp. "We will not survive another assault, Mórrígan. We didn't lose any of our warriors, but look at them. Over half are injured; some will take weeks, if not months, to recover their strength. We're short on javelins and arrows. The gateway stands wide open. We can use the discarded rams to partly block the entrance, thank the Goddess, but we're wide-open to attack. We've no more surprises; the Romans know our strengths and weaknesses. Even without the ones we killed today, they are a formidable force."

Mórrígan studied the landscape, recalling how life was so very different only a short time ago. "We will fight – men, women and children, because you know as well as I, that the Romans will show no mercy. They have no understanding of our ways. We are nothing to them. There is no choice for us but to fight and, if the goddess wishes, to die. Blood revenge will be for Conall to deliver."

Resigned to their likely fate, Cúscraid said with a laugh, "At least we can die with full bellies and good beer, which is more than the Romans have. But first, let's see how we can patch-up our defenses."

Spurius Sulpicia Longus was more than grateful for the soldiers who had carried him semi-conscious, to the camp. His chest ached, it hurt to take even short breaths, and the pounding in his head was agony. From his cot, he glanced up at his armor hanging on the tent-pole. The breastplate still had the three arrows lodged in it. The company surgeon had sewn up and bound his gouged chest. He smiled grimly and thanked the gods, knowing that he had been very lucky. At the range the arrows had been delivered, even with his armor, he should have died.

While not normally vain, Spurius' next thought was that his face must look a mess after being hit by the axe head. At least, he mused, the blade edge that had not struck him. He struggled to rise from his bed, but was overcome by dizziness and nausea. "Centurions," he croaked out hoarsely, "Centurions to my tent." The posted guard immediately sent for Decimus and Publius.

"How many did we lose?"

"Eleven dead and another nineteen seriously injured. In total, twenty-four dead and fifty injured," reported Decimus soberly. "One third of the injured will not be fit for duty for weeks. The remainder should be ready for duty after a day's rest. We lost most of the horses."

Spurius pounded his clenched fist against his thigh in disgust. "So we're left with an effective fighting force of one hundred and sixty men," he exclaimed. For a moment he sat thinking. "On the positive side, we've shown we can breech their defenses, we know the strength of their forces, and we know their tricks. They can't repair the gate very quickly; with the men rested we can make a full assault and end this farce. Tell the men to have a good meal and rest up. We will attack again in two days."

Once the centurions had left, Spurius rubbed the stubble on his heavily bruised chin as he reassessed their position. While he had no doubts that his men would eventually take the fort, he also knew it would be costly. He reflected that Marcus Fabius Ambustus and his sons had severely underestimated the resistance that his small force would face on this cold, inhospitable island. As he lay on his bed, something also disturbed him about the barbarian commander at the fort, but he just could not put his finger on the cause of his unease. He was also no closer to finding either the Spartan or the wastrel, Cassius Fabius Scaeva, than the first day he had landed on the island. He hoped that a few crucifixions would loosen tongues at the fort. Exhausted, Spurius passed into a fitful sleep.

At sunrise, Cúscraid and Mórrígan stood in the northern lookout post. It was a huge relief when it became apparent the enemy was not going to attempt another assault on the fort that day. "The Roman forces must have suffered more than we thought. It looks like we have been given some more time to repair our defenses. I'll set the villagers and farmers to do what they can to strengthen the gateway while the warriors rest up."

Slightly irritated, Cúscraid saw that Mórrígan, while gesturing that she had heard him, was only half-listening. She stared intently to the north-west, the direction from where Conall was expected to return. In truth, Mórrígan was both willing and praying for her king and lover to return. Her lips silently offered Mongfhionn's words of incantation to the morning breeze.

Mórrígan turned, "Conall will come. We must hold the fort," she stated with the innocence and confidence of her youth.

Shaking his head, Cúscraid replied, "I hope you're right, my lady. This is not a fight we can hope to survive without help."

That evening, the difference in the two camps could not have been more striking. The Romans prepared their weapons and armor for the next day's battle. On such a still, clear and star-lit night, the scratch and slip sounds of sharpening stones on swords would have carried well to Ráth na Conall. However, the fort's denizens were creating such a racket feasting, drinking and singing, over the pounding bodhráns, they would not have heard the world end.

Spurius, sitting with his centurions, reached for another morsel of meat and gingerly brought it to his bruised lips. His jaw throbbed as he chewed. "What on earth are they doing?"

The men laughed and one commented, "Sounds like they decided to have a final big celebration. They'll be tired with sore heads in the morning. All the better for us, it will make the killing easier."

In the fort, Cúscraid watched as the tempo of the carousing rose and fell. He laughed and shouted encouragement as the revelers drank and ate themselves into exhaustion. He smiled, because he had one more surprise for the Romans. Surveying the revelers, he saw no drunken warriors. After having had a good meal and a few beers, they too, like the Romans, were now single-mindedly sharpening weapons and swapping stories of past glories.

CHAPTER 9

By sunrise, there were again flurries of snow thickening the air and a light breeze swept away smoke from the early morning campfires. In the fort, warriors waited, watching for signs of movement and listening for the crunch of iron-soled Roman shoes on the ice-covered ground. Each rested his shield and javelins against the fence. Mórrígan and her archers stood in the watchtowers and sighted their arrows on the markers. In the yard, villagers recovering from their hangovers bravely grabbed whatever weapons they could find. All were determined that there would be no surrender and that the Romans would pay dearly for each step they took inside the fort.

Spurius rose stiffly, buckled on his armor, sheathed his sword and exited his tent. He walked to the gray tethered nearby and mounted. Once settled on the horse, he was handed his helmet. Slowly and deliberately he adjusted the red crest before setting the helmet firmly on his head. His attendant then lashed his shield to the side of Spurius' mount. It was a routine, well-known by his men and designed to instill confidence.

He cantered forward to the line of men. "We represent Rome in this barbarian land. We have a mission entrusted to us by our Master, Marcus Fabius Ambustus, Pontifex of Rome. So let us make him proud." He paused, his gaze flicking along the ranks before continuing, "These barbarians cannot be allowed to boast that they triumphed over Rome. We will slaughter them to the last man, woman and child, and raze the fort. Arm yourselves. Let us teach them a lesson that will not be forgotten." The men cheered, loudly slapping their weapons against their shields as Spurius led them out of the camp. Once outside, they formed up in their phalanx and with spears pointed towards the fort, steadfastly marched forward.

The tread of leather and iron-clad feet could be heard, long before the soldiers were discernible through the lift and fall of blowing snow. As the Romans came into view, Cúscraid remarked, "They look impressive, don't they?" to the warrior beside him.

To his left, Mórrígan stared towards the north-east. Her eerie song got steadily louder and more intense as she stood, her arms spread wide and uplifted to the sky. Even more unsettling, the early morning sun broke narrowly through the clouds to shine only upon her. The pocket of light was separate from the snow-filled air and radiated a fierce energy that fed the curving symbols on her face. Her aura was both beautiful and frightening.

Mórrígan's straining eyes espied a solitary rider on the horizon. At first she doubted her sight, then she was sure. "Cúscraid," she exclaimed, pointing at the very small silhouette, "Look, a rider approaches."

"Fanciful thinking," was Cúscraid's first reaction. His next was, "What use would one person be?" Fascinated, he watched as a lone figure broke from the trees on the north-eastern hills and galloped along the forest edge towards them at a reckless speed.

The Roman column halted about five hundred paces from the fort. Tearing their eyes away from the aberration of Mórrígan's appearance, all watched the progress of the black horse with its grey-cloaked figure racing towards the settlement. A massive cheer rose up from the fort as the hood fell off and a mane of golden hair streamed back. Spurius laughed, though puzzled, as the horse and rider disappeared behind the fort. "They must be in a bad way if they think one rider, and a woman at that, can help them," he scoffed, for the benefit of his men. Buoyed by Spurius' high spirits, the soldiers resumed their steady advance.

Mongfhionn rode through the narrow gap at the rear of the settlement, dismounted and made her way to the stockade. She quickly took in her surroundings, observing with pleasure that the fort had become a haven for the surrounding villages and farms. She noted the ruined gateway, and the dark red stains and bloody debris that marked recent bloody fights. Inspecting the fighters, she breathed a sigh of relief and sensed that, despite their wounds, they remained determined to stand and fight.

She was relieved to see Mórrígan. Conall's retribution would indeed have been terrible had he lost both queen and unborn child. Mongfhionn feared that the death of another loved one, so soon after the loss of his parents and sisters, would have broken the young man. His current appetite for revenge already whetted, it may have tipped the balance in favor of Conall becoming a coldhearted, revenge-driven tyrant rather than the great leader she hoped he would become.

Finally, feeling some relief, after the days of battle and siege, a misty-eyed Mórrígan clutched Mongfhionn when she reached the walkway. The Sidhe stepped back, holding Mórrígan firmly by the shoulders and out of the line of sight of the people and army. "I see you took my advice on your paintings, Mórrígan. They suit you well and are a fitting mask for a warrior queen." More sternly she continued, "Now gather yourself. This is not the time for tears."

Mongfhionn then addressed Cúscraid, "You have done well. You have my, and you will have Conall's, gratitude many times over for how you have saved his people - and his queen." Cúscraid was shocked that she seemed to know his thoughts when she added, "I'm sure Conall will understand that you saw his queen in a very different disguise the other night." Mórrígan, having regained some of her composure, winked at Mongfhionn.

"Oh, he was disappointingly gallant."

Cúscraid wished the ground would open up and swallow him. Seeking to direct the conversation back to more pressing matters, Cúscraid said, "We badly need reinforcements. The Romans are almost upon us and I fear we will not be able to hold them. Where is Conall?"

"You must and will hold the fort, Cúscraid. That is your duty and you will perform that duty."

Exasperated, Cúscraid said, "You have seen the state of my men. They have fought better than I could have expected and held off two attacks. But the Romans have breached us twice and the gateway is open to them. We have few javelins and fewer archers to keep them at a distance. How can we possibly hold the fort?"

"Conall will not arrive for another three days," said Mongfhionn flatly.

At this, Mórrígan breathed out sharply and instinctively held her belly. Cúscraid's face reflected their shared feeling of hopelessness and dismay.

"Then we will fight bravely and die well, Mongfhionn." He put his hand on the hilt of his sword, and turned to stand with his men.

"Come, come, Cúscraid, surely you don't think I would have ridden here if I did not have some tricks to play. Let us converse with these Romans."

Cúscraid wondered whether Mongfhionn ever spoke plainly, though he held his tongue.

On the stockade, Mongfhionn stood with Mórrígan to her right and Cúscraid on her left. Spurius had halted his men just outside bow range and now dismounted. Flanked by Decimus and Publius, he called out, "Surrender the fort, Conall Mac Gabhann. We will crucify the warriors who have defied the might of Rome, but you have my word that the villagers can go free."

Looking quizzically at Cúscraid, Mongfhionn remarked, "Conall Mac Gabhann? It seems that I am not the only one with a talent for subterfuge." Cúscraid offered a rare and broad grin.

The Sidhe lowered her head to whisper in Mórrígan's ear, "Can you hit any of those three at this range?" Mórrígan nodded. "Then ready your bow. You will know when to strike."

Bricriu, Craiftine and Eirnín, watching the scene intently from their vantage points, saw Mórrígan ready her bow. Instinctively, they did the same.

Impatiently, Spurius called out once more. "What is your answer Conall Mac Gabhann? Will you save your people or subject them to senseless slaughter?"

Mongfhionn stepped up onto a raised platform where she towered over the wooden defenses. The wind rose lifting the Sidhe's hair into a golden cloud about her face. She looked to the sky and prayed that her timing was right.

She called out and deep rolls of thunder echoed her voice, "I know you, Spurius Sulpicia Longus, commander of the guard of Marcus Fabius Ambustus. We were three and now I am one. You have been cursed and well you know why. Now your men will share your fate. You will feed the worms, the wolves, the crows and the ravens in this land. No trace of you will survive. You will be forgotten. Your spirits will have no peace."

The blood drained from the faces of Spurius and his centurions, as they listened to the words echoing from the apparition. Fear slinked into the minds of the men in the phalanx. A single word, "Druidess," escaped from Spurius' lips before he regained control.

To his right, Publius gasped, "How? I thought she was dead, along with her two sisters. How did she escape?"

"Quiet, centurion. The men are alarmed enough without seeing their leaders panic." Spurius turned to the fort and shouted, "I will speak with no witch or whatever you are. I will speak with Conall Mac Gabhann now or I will attack."

A disquieting cackle came from Mongfhionn. Those around her swore that the Hag was again present. "Oh, you will speak with Conall Mac Gabhann, but not now." Turning to the warriors beside her, Mongfhionn ordered, "Bring the prisoners to me. Tie their hands behind their backs and a tight rope around their necks so they cannot struggle." Cúscraid made to protest, suddenly realizing what was about to take place, but a cold stare from Mongfhionn silenced him.

As he watched his soldiers brought forward, and made to stand, naked, on either side of the Druidess, Spurius cursed. He too, had some premonition of what was about to take place. Mesmerized, both sides watched Mongfhionn drop her cloak. She stood naked, save a black ribbon around her throat. The light surrounding her seemed to intensify. Her body the color of alabaster, her skin, save the golden mane on her head, was unblemished and hairless, including the triangle between her legs. Her breasts were magnificent in size; the nipples stood dark, proud and erect. The sidhe's beauty was terrible to look on and in her hands, the curved blades of two knives gleamed.

She stretched her hands to the sky, chanting strange words. Her invocation complete, she glared at Spurius, bared her teeth and snarled, "This is for my sisters."

The blades flashed as Mongfhionn sliced under the soldiers' balls. The small, wet thud as they fell to the wooden platform was drowned by the men's screams of agony. Great gouts of blood drenched her naked form as she alternately screeched and cackled. Drawing the blades slowly, smoothly upwards, she first opened the men's bellies and then their chests. The men were gutted with perverse deliberation and watched as their own entrails spilled onto the walkway before them. The prisoners begged for mercy and death. In answer, the apparition that was Mongfhionn reached into their bloody, gaping chests and tore out their hearts.

Battle-hardened men watched, in silence and dismay, as the hearts of their comrades were held high by the gore-covered Druidess. Her fists closed on the quivering organs, forcing thick blood to trickle down her wrists and arms. For a breath's span, there was silence. Then the apparition's sinister cackling was replaced by the full-throated scream of the bean-sidhe, filling the air. Behind the fort, savage lightning struck the mountain between peels of thunder.

Forcing himself to break the awful spell cast over them, Spurius spun on his heels to face his men. At the moment of his command to attack, he heard several dull thumps and a gurgling sound. Mórrígan, taking the scream of the bean-sidhe as the sign, had loosed an arrow at Decimus. Three more bow strings sang as their arrows were sent to their target.

Mórrígan's arrow plunged through the centurion's throat, emerging bloody from the other side. As his hands came up to clutch at it, arrows from Bricriu, Craiftine and Eirnín took him under his arm. Decimus sank to his knees, blood and froth spewing from his mouth, then fell forward. Immediately, Publius and others sprang in front of an apoplectic Spurius, guarding him with shields as they fell back to join the main body. Spurius again opened his mouth to issue orders, but was curtailed by the sound of Roman and barbarian horns and then shouts, cries and the clash of weapons emanating from the Roman camp.

Mongfhionn's possessed body spasmed in ecstasy before she collapsed, unconscious, onto the walkway. Cúscraid was relieved, though he struggled to keep his gut under control. He regarded a disturbingly calm Mórrígan, "Take the sidhe to the Great Hall and see to whatever she needs." Mórrígan nodded to Urard who effortlessly lifted the bloody Mongfhionn in his arms, and followed his queen.

To break the immobility that had descended on the fort, Cúscraid turned to the nearest man and said loudly, "Can none of our queens wear clothes before a battle?"

First one warrior pulled his eyes from the mangled corpses on the platform and laughed nervously, followed by another and another as the joke rippled around the stockade and in the yard.

In returning to the fort, Mongfhionn had needed speed and had kept to the level, though twisting, valley floors skirting Bohd Carraig, the Cock Rock, affectionately so-named by local denizens due to its resemblance to male genitals. In contrast, Íar Mac Dedad purposefully led his men on a slower but more direct route through the dense wildwood that covered the mountains. Conall and Fearghal had described the area around Ráth na Conall and drawn maps in the dirt to help. While ever ebullient, Íar was no fool. He planned to arrive in the forest north-east of the fort in order to have surprise on his side.

Íar was astonished, but delighted, to find the Roman encampment had been pitched close to the forest edge. The dense forest and snow-covered ground muffled the fall of his horses' hooves allowing his men to traverse the forest without being discovered. He observed the main Roman force march towards the fort, leaving the camp guarded mostly by the injured. This pleased Íar. Nikandros had explained the Romans' favored battle formation. His men were armed with axes, swords and small shields, and not equipped for a frontal attack on a Roman phalanx. Íar had no desire to lose men against the sharp quills of a Roman porcupine.

Before departing, Mongfhionn had given him two pieces of advice, or more accurately two commands. First, he was to wait for a signal before doing anything, and second, no Roman was to be left alive. Non-adherence to the latter, it was emphasized, would lead to ill-fortune for him, the king - his father, and their families. Íar had shivered at the sound of the wailing of the bean-sidhe and gave the command to attack.

Fifty horsemen, swords unsheathed and axes raised, burst from the forest and quickly covered the ground to the Roman camp. The Roman guards, taken by surprise, were dispatched by blades or trampled under the hooves of the horses. There was complete disarray in the camp as injured soldiers found themselves at the mercy of the barbarians. Injured Romans scrambled for their armor and weapons, but it was too late. They were slaughtered, brutally and efficiently, as Íar's men went to work with axes and swords, splitting open heads and disemboweling the injured in their beds. Soon, horses were slipping on the blood, gore and excrement. Contemplating the carnage, Íar conceded, with a tinge of regret, that there was little honor in this type of skirmish.

As they watched dark smoke drift upwards from the distant camp, the population of Ráth na Conall were uncertain as to what was happening, but knew it had contributed to the further vexation of their enemies. Spurius shouted commands to reform the phalanx, with its thick defenses of long spears and shields. In spite of himself, Cúscraid admired how the Roman soldiers, who had moments ago shown every sign of bolting, immediately yielded without question to Spurius' authority. Cúscraid shook his head, "I would not like to face that formation on open ground. Even our shield wall would find it a challenge to combat that fence of shields and spears."

The phalanx wheeled around and steadfastly tramped back towards the burning camp. Spurius, at the center of the front rank, watched, surprised, as a group of riders approached. He had not considered that there might be cavalry in this barbarian land. "Yet another lack of intelligence," he groused. He fervently hoped the barbarians rapidly gaining ground on him would attack and give him the satisfaction of teaching them a lesson. Spurius was to be disappointed. Íar's riders veered off to the right of the column, taunting and shouting curses at his men. A few threw axes as they rode past, but these simply bounced off Roman shields.

Spurius halted the men just short of the camp while he personally inspected the devastation and smoldering wreckage. His nose was assaulted by the cloying odor of blood, shit and burnt and burning flesh. Filled with sadness as well as anger, he shook his head. The aftermath of no battle is pretty. This had not been a good day for Rome. Collecting himself, he called to Publius.

"Set up a new camp and position it five hundred paces from the forest. Have one section of the men prepare our defenses; the rest will remain on guard. Dig a ditch around the camp and fill it with sharpened stakes. Place a double wall of logs around the camp. Make this happen before sunset this evening. Is that clear?"

"Sir," said the centurion before turning to his men and issuing his own orders.

Reassured, Spurius then sent for Decimus' optio. "Congratulations Gaius Aurelius Atella, you are now promoted to centurion. Make sure you keep your men ready or I'll have you executed."

The horsemen arrived at the fort, to loud cheering and the thumping rhythm of the bodhráns. A partially recovered, but still pallid, Mongfhionn gripped her oak staff for strength as she turned to Cúscraid, "I believe I said that Conall would not arrive for several more days. I said nothing about his new recruits."

"Bloody women and their intrigues," Cúscraid growled, before bowing and striding towards the tall horseman with a booming voice and raucous laughter. He was obviously the leader and making short work of the many horns of beer thrust upon him.

That evening, the mood in the fort was much easier. Amid the eating, drinking and singing, many of the women – both young and old, exceedingly grateful at having been rescued, happily spread their thighs to just about any male who could still manage an erection. Privacy was not a high priority and as he made his way to the Great Hall, Cúscraid was subjected to an array of arses, breasts and cocks. Refusing the countless invitations to join in, he laughed, as well as threatening a few barrels of cold water to drench the ardor of the coupling.

Inside the Great Hall, Mongfhionn, Mórrígan, Íar and a few of the village elders had gathered. Íar spoke, "I think we have a stalemate until Conall and the others return. The Romans will have calculated that they cannot take the fort without a massive loss of men. On the other hand, we don't have enough strength to launch a successful attack without equally great losses. My horses cannot prevail against the Roman phalanx, although I can certainly keep them off guard by harassing them. Mercifully, the Romans seem ill-prepared. They have no throwing weapons which would inflict significant damage on my riders."

Looking at Cúscraid, Íar continued "If you can spare some javelins, I'd like to discuss a new tactic with you and get some practice over the next few days." Cúscraid was happy to agree, "There are several villagers who know how to work the forge. They can start to replace the javelins and other weapons lost over the last few days."

Turning to the village elders, he said, "My men will take up their posts on the stockade once more in the morning. Your people will be tasked with rebuilding the main gate and any other repairs that might be necessary. There should be enough wood within the fort's stores." The elders were glad to be considered part of any plan, as such was not the case under Eochaidh Ruad and were delighted to pitch in.

Cúscraid drew a subdued Mongfhionn aside. "We are deeply grateful for the news you brought and your presence clearly unnerved the Romans. You are however, the cause of substantial tension in the fort. If you are willing, I've a humble, but important request for you, a task that may go some way to dispelling that atmosphere." Mongfhionn listened as Cúscraid continued, "It may not seem so from the reveling outside, but many of the men have cuts and gashes. Many have hidden their wounds for fear they would be asked to stand down. We have no healer and without proper attention their injuries will become poisoned. Having survived battle, I have no desire to see men die because of a poorly attended cut. Your gift of healing is well known. I would be grateful if you would use it to tend to the men."

"I can see your diplomatic skills have developed considerably, Cúscraid," Mongfhionn replied. "I will be delighted to help in any way I can. First I must rest and eat to restore my strength. I can begin at first light tomorrow."

Cúscraid was relieved and pleased at the Sidhe's response, "Of course my lady. And thank you."

Spurius pulled his cloak around him as he struggled to get comfortable on the cold, rock-hard ground. Resting his head on a log, he resolutely settled down for the night near one of the blazing campfires. Inwardly, frustration, anger and uncertainty pressed upon Spurius Sulpicia Longus. As of sunset, his defenses had been rebuilt and fortified and his men were on guard and vigilant. The remains of the soldiers who had been slaughtered earlier had been cremated. He knew that the tide had turned against him, leaving him with few good options. Within the new fortifications, his men were safe for the moment and in the open plain, his phalanx was practically unbeatable against horse or man.

However, he was now facing a force twice that of before - and they were fresh men. If the barbarians were to simply use their new men on the stockade, it would make the fort almost impossible to breach. His only consolation was that his enemy was in the same position. They could not attack and deliver a decisive blow without incurring substantial losses. Then there was the presence of the Druidess and the other witch. Both had ably demonstrated their capacity to spread fear among his men.

Negotiation was clearly not an option. Neither did the prospect of a well-managed retreat to the east coast to secure galleys to return to Rome fill him with a sense of wellbeing. In this terrain, they would not be able to use the phalanx and would be ideal targets for barbarian hit-and-run attacks. Even if they made it back to Rome, he did not relish having to explain his failure to Marcus Fabius Ambustus. News that the Druidess lived might be enough to save him from being crucified, yet that was not certain.

His only remaining option appeared to be to journey deeper into the island in the hope of securing the help of friendlier barbarians. The more Spurius considered, the more attractive this idea became. He had a large quantity of gold to bribe or pay for mercenaries and supplies. His mind rested easier and finally he slept.

In Carn Tigherna, Eochaidh Ruad called Faolán and Cassius Fabius Scaeva before his throne. A young, half-naked girl sat on his knee smiling distantly as the king fondled her breasts. Although only thirteen summers, she was wise enough to know that if she persevered for a few more nights, the king would tire of her. She would be given gold to go away and the king would move on to another young girl. She also knew that if her belly swelled, she would receive more gold to look after the king's bastard child; there were many such progeny to be seen around Carn Tigherna.

Eochaidh scratched his crotch and farted. Scowling at Faolán, he asked, "What have your spies told you about the goings-on at Ráth na Conall?" Indeed, Eochaidh had heard many rumors and was not pleased that he seemed to be the only one not fully informed. With each new day, he grew suspicious that Faolán might not be looking after his best interests. The constant snide remarks and sarcasm from Cassius about his second-in-command's ability and loyalties had wormed their way into an already troubled mind.

Faolán, however, was not stupid and discerned what fed the king's increasingly disturbed thoughts. His informants told him of Cassius' remarks, and he had already determined that the Roman was not to enjoy a long life. He also knew that Cassius had bribed several of the king's nobles to send messages to Queen Medb, in Chrúachain, entreating her to provide the Roman with sanctuary. As for Cassius, he well knew who was besieging Ráth na Conall. More to the point, he knew where they would come next and for whom.

There was nothing to gain by keeping Eochaidh in the dark about the siege. "Ráth na Conall is being attacked by a large force of men," Faolán said. "By the description of their armor," and at this he grinned, gloating at Cassius' increasing discomfort, "they're Roman soldiers."

Eochaidh Ruad, though travelling the path to madness, retained his innate cunning. He turned to Cassius and fixing him with a malevolent stare asked, "What are Roman soldiers doing in my kingdom?"

With some relish, Faolán did not wait for Cassius to respond, "There are only two possibilities, my king. Either they've been summoned by Cassius - for whatever reasons he may have. Or they've come for him. There can be no other explanation."

"You piece of shite." Eochaidh Ruad glowered intently at Cassius who tried not to appear too obvious in glancing around. "Which is it?"

The exits from Eochaidh's throne chamber were all guarded, so Cassius kept his voice even, "I don't know what Faolán's talking about. It is impossible for Roman soldiers to be here. He is either mistaken or lying. He wants rid of me."

Faolán moved swiftly to place a knife at Cassius' throat, "No one calls me a liar, let alone a worm like you." Cassius felt the blade bite into his flesh and a trickle of blood left a trail down his neck.

"Enough, Faolán. He's of no use to us dead." Eochaidh beckoned to a guard, "You. Take this bastard and lock him up. We'll see what we can get out of him tomorrow. No. Better still, throw him in with the dogs – and we'll question what's left of him in the morning." Cassius dropped all sense of pretense or pride, pleading his innocence and cursing Faolán, as he was half-walked, half-dragged from the hall.

Frowning, Eochaidh turned to Faolán. "So what do we do about the Romans?"

"That's easy, my king – we do nothing. We let them weaken or even destroy Ráth na Conall and then, if there's anyone left, it will be an easy task to hang them."

Eochaidh stared into space for what seemed a long time; then his face broke into a leering grin. He laughed and shouted for more food and beer, "Maybe you were right after all, Faolán. Let's just hope that that young bastard who calls himself a king is taken alive. I want to make him suffer." His mind more at ease, Eochaidh resumed his fondling of the young girl and soon his big, calloused hand was between her legs. Faolán watched with some disgust as the girl flinched under her king's touch then turned on his heel and left the room.

Had Eochaidh been full-witted, he would have known his suspicions about Faolán's loyalty were groundless. Indeed there was not a truer commander of his forces. However, as Faolán left the throne room and strode towards his own quarters, he now begun to ponder in what direction his future might lie.

Cassius Fabius Scaeva was indeed a serpent and a wily one. As he was being dragged to the dog pens his mind was feverishly reviewing his options. He started to wail and blubber even louder, begging for mercy and offering the guard gold to release him, none of which had a drop of impact on the guard's actions or demeanor.

Left with little choice, Cassius pissed and, for good measure, shit himself. His guard hesitated for an instant when the warm stream sprayed his bare legs and the smell of shite hit his nostrils. At that moment, Cassius thrust the dagger, which had been hidden in a sheath strapped to his thigh, up into the soft flesh under the guard's chin. The blade slid into the man's brain. Cassius twisted it a few times to make sure and the guard slumped to the ground, dead in a few short heartbeats.

Cassius' shoes crunched in the frozen dirt as he ran to the rear gates of Carn Tigherna. He had paid substantially for two horses to always be ready for him. Tonight, as he mounted up, he congratulated himself on his wise investment. He rode east, beyond the hills that protected the fort, then turned north to Chrúachain. On his way, he paused at a clump of trees to change his soiled clothes, but more importantly to dig up two small chests filled with gold. He placed one on each flank of his spare mount.

In the north, lived the Ulaid, a people famed across the island for their ferocity in battle. It had long been agreed between the three Ulaid kings, Aedh Ruad, Dithorba and Cimbáeth that they should each reign as Ard-Righ - or High King, for seven years, until each had enjoyed the royal power three times. They were then to be succeeded by their sons who were to maintain this agreement. Unfortunately, Aedh Ruad had drowned after producing only one offspring – a girl.

It was nearing the end of Cimbáeth's reign, and according to the agreement, the next in line was to be the son of Aedh Ruad. His heir and daughter, Macha Mong-Ruad was determined to claim her right to reign as High Queen, or Ard-Righan, despite the fact all knew Dithorba and his sons would never cede power to a woman. A battle was coming and Macha needed to marshal her forces.

As she rested in her quarters, Macha smiled at the strange creature sitting in the cage before her happily nibbling on the nuts and fruit she fed it. She had been told by a trader that the animal was from a distant land. Of more interest was who had gifted the beast. Wistfully, she thought of the Cróeb Ruad warrior and noble, Fearghal Ruad, and soon the lips between her legs became quite moist. She grew angry when she thought how her father and that repulsive creature, Mongfhionn, had conspired to exile Fearghal. Now, she needed her protector again. With her father dead, there was no reason why Fearghal should not return.

There was always fighting in Ériu and Macha's spies kept her informed of the various battles and invasions. Though young, Macha was astute. She had heard rumors of strange happenings taking place south of the territory of the Connachta and her instincts told her that Fearghal was involved. Macha called for her army's commander, Cearbhall ó Domhnaill, along with Aengus Ruad, captain of her royal guard and Fearghal's younger brother.

"I want three hundred of the Cróeb Ruad sent south. They are to stay hidden as far as possible and to stay out of trouble." To Aengus, she said, "Emphasize to those unruly bastards that I will have the head of anyone who disobeys my command. Your mission is to search for Fearghal, to inform him that his exile is over and that his queen awaits his return."

Cearbhall shook his head disapprovingly, "Three hundred from the Cróeb Ruad will be missed my queen."

Macha cut him off, "Nonsense! Three hundred will hardly be missed from the ranks of thirty thousand. See to it that my orders are carried out - or perhaps you would like to retire?" Wisely, the commander bowed, "As you wish my queen."

At the next full moon, Aengus led three hundred men, six chariots and ten horses out of the gates of Emain Macha. The detachment moved south to the Black Pig's Dyke and on into the land of the Laighi.

Minor skirmishes, training and preparation continued at Ráth na Conall, as the opposing forces fell into an uneasy stalemate. Spurius decided he would march west, hoping to find other forces he could befriend or hire to complete his mission. His men's experiences had made them much more vigilant and wary and they were determined not to be surprised by the barbarians again. They also had sworn to avenge the deaths of their friends whose heads remained staked along the ditch.

Mórrígan had been pleased when some of the farmers' sons and daughters had come to her inquiring about increasing their skills with a bow. Like her, they had basic hunting talents that, with discipline, could be honed and used for battle. Mórrígan set about showing them how to make their own bows and to drill with a series of practice targets.

Behind Íar Mac Dedad's blustering and jovial nature, there dwelled a shrewd and tactical mind. Having seen the Roman phalanx, Íar was deeply concerned that his men would be at a considerable disadvantage in future battles. Apart from some throwing axes, which bounced harmlessly off the Roman shields, Íar had no answer to Roman tactics. This caused him great frustration. When Cúscraid had described how effectively his men used javelins against the Romans, Íar began to wonder whether javelins could be thrown from horseback. Soon, Cúscraid and he had devised training exercises suited to his mounted warriors, but there was the practical matter of how his men could carry a supply of javelins. In this, they were helped by village leather-workers who designed a leather sheath which held three javelins and could be secured to the flank of the horse, without restricting maneuverability.

Meanwhile, Conall had finally reached the end of Bohd Carraig, and was less than a day's march from the fort. Before them was the narrow river valley running south-west of the mountains that protected Ráth na Conall. He called Brion, Fearghal and Nikandros to him, "Tomorrow we will join with our people at the fort. Hopefully, the goddess has been merciful and we have a home to return to." Conall's words sounded hollow even to his own ears and he bent to more concrete matters.

"Nikandros, we will rest here for the night, but I want you to take my horse and ride to the fort. Íar's men will be there, but we don't know how many of ours have survived. If Cúscraid is alive, tell him to move his men out south-east of the gate before dawn and to hold them at the bottom of the hill. Íar's riders will protect their right flank; we will join on the left. Íar and Cúscraid should have information on how strong the Romans are. Once we know this, we can decide on our final battle plan. Get some sleep friends. I think we are in for a long day tomorrow."

Nikandros threw a blanket over Conall's black stallion and departed for the fort. Like Mongfhionn, he fervently prayed to his gods that the defenders – and that one in particular had survived, for Conall's sake. The rest, looking solemn as they remembered their friends and family at the fort ate, sharpened their weapons and tried to get some sleep.

It was full dark as Nikandros cantered along the ditch of Ráth na Conall. A line of torches burned brightly along the stockade. "At least someone survived," he thought. The outlines of guards came and went, as the evening breeze played with the flames. A shiver went down his spine and he prayed that he was not seeing the spirits of the dead. His train of thought was interrupted by low growls several paces ahead. Instinctively, his hand reached for his bow, until a voice from the stockade called out, "I would not be advising you continue that action, if you want to live, Roman."

"I am no Roman. Get Cúscraid or Mórrígan," Nikandros threw back rather testily, "Tell them Nikandros, the Spartan, is here."

"Spartan? What's a Spartan? You look like a Roman to me in that armor. I should know. I've killed a few recently." In the chill of the evening breeze, Nikandros grew hot with indignation as he heard the whispered conversations on the fence. Then came peals of laughter and a mischievous voice. "You'd better come around the back, Nikandros; there are traps and stakes in the path. The hounds will guide you in."

Nikandros and his horse snorted simultaneously, "You're not too old to have the flat blade of my sword laid across your arse, Bricriu ó Cathasaigh."

More laughter echoed from the tower, "Awww. Can Spartans not take a wee joke? Besides, I just saved your life. These new men don't know you. I've spared you from a javelin that would most certainly have spoiled that nice armor you wear."

"Póg ma thoin – kiss my arse! Tell your sister and Cúscraid, if they still live, that I need to talk to them immediately."

"What language! You've been around Fearghal too much. And yes, my sister lives, as does Cúscraid." Nikandros breathed a great sigh of relief as he followed the dark grey shapes of the wolf-hounds to the rear of the fort.

Spurius' scouts had returned with news of two possible routes. They could travel south, passing the fort, and then west through a wide valley. However, they would also have to pass through a narrow river gorge at the coast before turning west and would be vulnerable to attack. The other option was to travel north over the hills until they met a river, then follow the river north-east to a large plain. Both had advantages and disadvantages, but none appeared to be more difficult than the other.

After deliberations with his centurions, Spurius decided on the route that took them within sight of Ráth na Conall. He had decided that a final flourish of Roman power, while unlikely to make much of an impact on the defenders, might restore some pride to his men. At dawn, they broke camp and began their march. It was a decision that Spurius would regret.

At the same time, the stakes were removed from the pathway leading up to Ráth na Conall and Íar led his horsemen down the sloping pathway. A great cheer went up and the bodhráns once again took up the beat. He turned left at the bottom and stopped about one hundred paces away. The riders were arrayed in two rows along the edge of the ditch with Íar in front of his men. Each rider now carried three javelins in new leather sheaths.

Cúscraid's men followed taking up position on Íar's left. Nikandros rode out from the fort, leading Conall's black stallion, and halted beside Cúscraid. The men, in full armor, stood behind their shields in two rows. Behind them, dog-handlers struggled with the taut ropes that held back the baying wolfhounds. Cúscraid smiled fiercely and looked back to the stockade where Mórrígan and Mongfhionn stood. The rest of the fort's inhabitants crowded along the battlements, straining to see what might take place. The air crackled with expectation.

The Roman soldiers had intended to march past the fort in defiance, but as they drew closer, Spurius knew that his withdrawal was not going to proceed as planned. At five hundred paces out he halted his men, and rode forward with Publius and Gaius to assess the situation. On the face of it, it appeared that the barbarians had decided to come out and meet him. On this terrain, he firmly believed the advantage was with his phalanx; at a rough count, his forces still outnumbered the barbarians two to one. Spurious allowed himself a brief smile.

That said, Spurius' newfound respect for the barbarians as fierce and unforgiving warriors made him more cautious. As he turned to rejoin his men, a great roar went up from the fort. Startled, Spurius looked to his right, and observed a body of men emerge from behind the wooded hills and jog along the northern ditch.

With disquiet, Spurius observed the arrival of the small group of reinforcements. Yet, he remained confident that his men in open battle would be victorious. A young warrior strode forward and embraced the one Spurius knew as Conall. The warrior turned around and waved to someone on the stockade and then shouted to the other men. More orders were relayed, and the warriors divided into two groups. In the center there was now a body with two rows of twenty men; to their left another group of about twenty men stood. The cavalry remained on the far right flank.

CHAPTER 10

Conall could see that the fort had taken a lot of damage, but was relieved to find Mórrígan and his people were safe. He, strode forward, and clasped Cúscraid by the shoulders. Finding it almost impossible to hold back the deep emotions he felt, he simply said, "Thanks Cúscraid, I will die before I ever forget what you have done. Many stories will be told of your defense of Ráth na Conall." Then with a glint of steel in his eyes, he said, "Now, how about you introduce me to our Roman friends?"

Nikandros brought Conall's horse to him. To the amazement of the fort, who had never seen their leader on a horse – let alone one as magnificent, he mounted.

Tongue-in-cheek, Fearghal called out, "No fancy riding and don't fall off. You, on your arse in the dirt is not the impression we want to give."

Conall laughed and looked at Nikandros, "Well, if I make a fool of myself, it's because I had a poor teacher! Let's go greet our adversary." Conall, Íar and Nikandros trotted slowly forward with Fearghal and Cúscraid walking at their side.

Spurius and his centurions watched the group approach. He soon recognized Nikandros. Turning to his centurions, he said, "Well, it seems we have at least found one of our missing people." The small band halted five paces from the Romans. Spurius looked at each in turn, disturbed at the confident and assured way they held themselves. His instincts told him that these were men not to be underestimated. Cold gazes and fresh scars bore witness that they were no strangers to battle.

Hoping to seize the initiative, Spurius spoke slowly and firmly to Cúscraid, "I see you have brought me the Spartan, Conall Mac Gabhann. Rome will be thankful. You may hand him over so that we may all part peacefully. In this field, your warriors, although very brave, cannot prevail against mine – as I am sure the Spartan has informed you."

To Spurius' consternation, a roar of laughter came from Fearghal, "Maybe you're not quite as clever as we thought, Roman. So far you've made two mistakes. We've got quite used to Nikandros and I think he likes us too. It wouldn't be very hospitable of us to hand him over to you. He may have some strange ways, but he is a friend and will stay with us until he chooses to go." Fearghal paused and grinned at Conall before turning back to Spurius.

"As for your next error, may I formally present the king of this territory and lord of Ráth na Conall?" Fearghal bowed to Conall. "I think this Roman would like to speak to you." Conall edged his black stallion forward.

Taken aback at this unexpected turn of events, Spurius cursed himself for having been so easily deceived. His earlier misgivings about the age of Cúscraid compared to the stories of the young avenging warrior returned to haunt him. Quickly regaining his composure, he said, "My compliments to your men, Conall Mac Gabhann, king of Ráth na Conall. They played a good game and fought well in your absence. You can be proud of them."

Pausing, and with a flourish of his hand, Spurius directed their attention to his phalanx, "However, if you think you can best my soldiers on this day and on this field, you are mistaken. This is a battle we have won many times." Pausing to gauge the response to his words and seeing a reaction that did nothing to lower his misgivings, Spurius continued, "All I ask is that you hand over the Spartan. He is wanted by my Master, indeed, his former Master, to resolve some matters between them. If you do this, no further blood will be spilled."

A hard-faced Conall leaned forward, his steel-gray eyes holding

Spurius' gaze, "You have attacked my fort. You have attacked my queen who carries my child. You have attacked and killed my friends and people. You have destroyed the homes and property of ones I protect. Now, you insult me further by demanding that I hand over a friend.

You should never have come to Ériu, Spurius Sulpicia Longus, for you and your men will not leave this land alive. Today, the ravens, the wolves and the worms will feast on your flesh. Your heads will decorate my stockade until the bone is bleached white. As for your phalanx, we know of your great battles. But, you have less than two hundred men and not the many hundreds that usually stand in such ranks." Conall paused and then spat out his final words, "Go, tell your men to make peace with their gods. It is time to die."

White-faced, Spurius wheeled his horse around and rode back to his men. Conall turned to Fearghal, who rolled his eyes, "I still think we have some work to do on the diplomacy aspect of being a king, Conall!"

Conall watched the Roman phalanx quickly consolidate – three cruel rows of spears and shields that hurled defiance at his men. "They look impressive, Nikandros. I hope you're right about their weaknesses or we'll lose many good men."

As they cantered back to their own men, a somewhat downcast Nikandros remarked, "I would prefer to fight alongside Íar, and his riders, but I don't have my doru. I'll join Brion's company."

From behind, came a mocking exclamation, "The Goddess preserve me, Conall, but is that man ever going to stop complaining about leaving a bloody spear behind? He'd complain less if it was a woman." Fearghal's hazel eyes flashed a golden-brown, as he watched Nikandros color in discomfort. He called to Brion, "Do you have it?"

Brion shouted, "Aye Fearghal, I got it when you were all talking to the Romans."

"Well, I suppose if it will stop him moaning we should give

him it now." Confused at the direction and tone of the conversation, Nikandros watched Brion stride towards him and bring a spear up to rest on its butt spike. The spear was fully half as tall again as Brion. The flat, leaf-shaped spearhead glinted ominously in the morning sun and the shaft was of black ash. As Brion offered the doru to Nikandros, Fearghal laughed, "That's one bloody big spear. I hope you know how to use it."

Nikandros was speechless as he gripped the weapon, feeling its perfect balance and smooth polished shaft. He smiled broadly, "You're a bastard Fearghal ó Maoilriain, but a good friend." Looking at Conall, he said, "I have a doru to blood and we have a battle to win. With your permission, I'll join Íar."

Conall dismounted, took his shield from Beacán and handed over the reins of his black stallion. He took his place in the front rank of the shield wall alongside Cúscraid and Fearghal. Brion jogged over to take command of the left section with his friends Fionnbharr, Labhraidh, Torcán and Uallachán. They stood with the recruits from the villages. He nodded to them before putting on his helmet and waited for the signal to march.

Raising his sword in the air, Conall shouted "Mac Gabhann abú, Mac Gabhann abú." A roar, accompanied by the thunderous drumming of bodhráns came from the fort. It was well matched by the sound of hunting horns from Íar's riders. The sections advanced.

Spurius had fought barbarians many times, as had many of his men. They fully expected Conall's men to act no differently. The phalanx took up a firm footing and waited patiently for the barbarians to charge and throw themselves against the formation's shields and spears. Spurius was confident his men would set about slaughtering their enemy, after the barbarians had exhausted themselves in a futile attack.

Conall was aware of Spurius' expectations. With Fearghal, Íar and Nikandros, he had devised a different strategy, relying on diversion and timing. At five hundred paces, Íar's riders broke to the right and galloped on a wide arc that would take them around the Roman phalanx. At the same time, Brion's section jogged to the left side, until they were opposite the right flank of the phalanx. Conall's division, formed mostly of Cróeb Ruad warriors, tightened up their formation and continued forward at a faster pace. At their heels were the wolfhounds.

The Roman formation, bristling with long spears in the hands of stone-faced soldiers, waited. Spurius was impressed with the barbarians' creative tactics, although not worried. To his way of thinking, Conall had made his work easier by dividing his forces. The central group of barbarians was only twenty men wide and two deep. He could not see how this could threaten the phalanx. Spurius also knew that the barbarian cavalry had been reluctant to engage the phalanx, since they lacked weapons to cause significant damage. However, as a precaution, he ordered the rear rank to turn and face the cavalry.

As for the small force closing on his right, he acknowledged that his enemy had deduced correctly where his weakness might be. However, his men had never been defeated in the phalanx, so he was not unduly perturbed. "Hold your ground men," Spurius spoke confidently and calmly. "Today we avenge our friends and show these barbarians that Rome is not to be trifled with."

As the two formations closed, Íar's horsemen rode into position behind the phalanx. Conall bellowed, "Loose the hounds," and a dozen grey brutes leaped forward. The memory of what these beasts could do was fresh in each Roman soldier's mind. On hind legs, each hound was taller than and as heavy as a full-grown man. Used to fighting bears and wolves, their jaws were more than capable of ripping out a man's throat or crushing bones. They sought weakness in their prey and fought as a pack. The thuds of the warm-blooded projectiles crashing against Roman shields echoed across the plain. The line wavered as the men fought off the slavering beasts. Spears were lowered to fend the dogs off, only managing to stop a few. Soon the dogs were in among the ranks, biting and snapping at exposed legs, hands and arms.

Conall's forces continued their advance. At a hundred paces, he shouted for the shield wall to pick up speed. Keeping their tight formation, the highly disciplined Cróeb Ruad warriors built up momentum. Whistles called off the remaining hounds. Conall shouted for javelins. The wall halted and twenty missiles arced through the air, striking the Roman formation. The first flight lodged mostly in Roman shields making them unwieldy. The second killed or injured those who dropped their guard. Under the force of the missiles, the Roman center wavered, but the centurions and Spurius quickly restored order as the barbarian wall closed the space.

Prominent iron bosses on the barbarian shields punched into bronze Roman shields. Loud grunts were heard as spears snapped, shield grips were strained, arms wrenched aside and tendons torn. The opponents then began the bloody business of stabbing with spears, javelins and swords. Conall wrestled to gain ground while Spurius fought to hold it. Curses filled the crisp spring air as flesh was torn and gouged. Conall's front row stabbed low at the feet and legs of the enemy, while the rear targeted Roman chests and heads.

When Íar saw Conall release the first flight of javelins, his riders reached for their new weapons and closed with the enemy, charging in behind the phalanx. Three volleys of fifty javelins ripped into the largely undefended rear of the phalanx. It was totally unexpected and the shock to the Roman ranks was profound. Shouts and cries of pain filled the air as they were cut down by the vicious spikes. In that one assault, Spurius lost almost a quarter of his men.

Íar's horsemen, their javelins exhausted, reverted to their natural fighting style with their longer swords and axes, harassing the rear rows. Their height gave them a decided advantage, as they hacked and slashed downwards. Horses screamed, kicked with bone-hard hooves against shields, and bit anything within reach of their big, yellow teeth. Nikandros, now on familiar ground, set about killing the Romans in the rear rank. His doru gave him more reach than the Roman spears. Its wicked edge sliced across exposed faces and throats. The tempered point easily punched through the Roman armor. Soon the doru was well baptized in the blood that splattered his horse's chest.

Spurius remained calm, but struggled to steady his men and keep order under the intensive assault. Substantial gaps had appeared in his rear ranks and his once solid formation was now looking weak.

Brion had been ordered to harass the Roman's right flank and his men engaged the clearly out of position Roman soldiers in a bloody fight. Axes and swords sliced through the end of the Roman line and the soldiers struggled to bring their shields around for protection. Under the onslaught, the right end of the phalanx was beginning to fray and unravel.

The barbarian tactics and sustained ferocity surprised the Romans who were equally dismayed to find that the barbarians wore armor. These were not the half-naked Gauls they were used to fighting on the borders of the Republic. By now, Spurius realized that his beloved phalanx was being well out-maneuvered and that his right flank was almost useless. The phalanx center was greatly weakened under the relentless attacks of the cavalry. In contrast, the barbarian shield wall held firm and pushed the Roman formation to the point of breaking. The phalanx took on the shape of a crescent and was about to fold in on itself. Spurius decided he would preempt being forced to adopt another defensive position and gave the command to form a circle.

Timing and luck deserted Spurius, for as he was giving the order to form circle, Conall shouted for one more push. The Roman front rank, reduced in numbers and slipping on blood and gore, broke. Before Spurius could issue new orders, the shield wall had carved his phalanx in two. The barbarian wall, also reduced in numbers, turned so that its two ranks were now back-to-back facing both fragments of the Roman formation. In a reversal of fortunes, the shield wall now found itself being rushed by the Roman soldiers.

"Hold steady, men, hold steady," roared a hoarse Conall, his face covered in blood and his hands a mass of cuts. "They'll break without the strength of their phalanx. Loose javelins and switch to swords." The remaining javelins were hurled at the Romans, inflicting minor damage, yet curbing them long enough for Conall's men to unsheathe their swords. As the Romans advanced, they thrust forward with their spears, but these were largely deflected by barbarian shields. Conall's men slashed down on the wooden spear shafts, forcing the Romans to abandon their spears, and switch to their own swords.

Spurius knew the battle was going badly. The barbarian wall showed no sign of weakness. Indeed, they seemed to relish each attack by his men, so that they could throw them back and show how superior they were. Conall, fighting at the center of the shield wall, was clearly in command and knew his men's strengths well. The pretender, Cúscraid, fought solid as a rock beside him and the one they called Fearghal was at Conall's back, making sure his rank held. Spurius and others had witnessed Conall take several spear hits to the chest, but apparently without serious injury. This increased the apprehension of his men, who remembered the witches in the fort and now believed they were fighting an immortal. Spurius grimaced and wished he had Conall's chain-mail.

Íar's men had now moved in on the left flank, slashing at any Roman that came within range. Without their solid phalanx, the Romans were reduced to fighting man-to-man. Even with the length of their spears, they could not keep the barbarian cavalry at bay. The howling barbarians' blood lust had risen and skulls were split open as axe blades rained down. Sword blades slashed backs, arms and faces, opening wide, red grins in vulnerable flesh.

Dismounted, with his shield on his left arm and doru in his right hand, Nikandros carved a bloody path through the hapless Romans. The brutal spearhead in the hands of the Spartan terrified men drilled to fight in formation. As Nikandros plunged on, Publius brushed aside his men to stand in front, his own spear painted a dark crimson and his shield marked with many deep indentations. "Try someone who can fight, Spartan," the centurion growled, crouching as he thrust forward. Nikandros' shield deflected the spearhead off to the left and he immediately lunged forward, feigning a strike to the centurion's shield. Changing at the last moment, he delivered a downward stroke to Publius' calves.

Publius grunted in pain as the Spartan's blade sliced along the outside of his leg. He pushed the doru away with his shield and sprang forward, battering Nikandros; then quickly reversed his spear, aiming the butt spike at the Spartan's feet. Nikandros jumped backwards and stepped to his right as the spike slammed into the frosty ground. The Roman regained his grip, but Nikandros aimed his own spearhead under the centurion's arm. A roar of pain told him he had timed his strike perfectly. The blade had slipped between the centurion's ribs and pierced his lung before the point was halted by his spine. Blood flowed from Publius' mouth and the centurion dropped to his knees. Pulling the doru free, Nikandros thrust the blade through the centurion's throat.

On what had been the Roman right flank, Brion's men sustained their assault with axes and swords crashing against shields and slashing across flesh. True to form, Torcán fought like a wild boar, roaring and swinging his axe at the nearest soldiers, using his shield to parry spear thrusts. His younger brother, Uallachán, equally reckless, but not quite as accomplished, rushed in believing he was immune from Roman spears and swords. His reward was a spearhead that sliced through his shoulder; dragged to the side, his participation in the battle was over.

Spurius surveyed his ranks. He knew his position was perilous and getting worse. He was outnumbered by a ruthless and fierce enemy who fought with a passion his men could not match. Yet, the leaders of this barbarian pack made sure their men fought with purpose and a clear focus. Glancing around, as he fought off several barbarians, he saw that the remainder of his men would only have a chance if they could retreat to the camp and hold off the barbarians from behind the double-walled stockade and ditch. The irony of this was not lost on Spurius.

He called to Gaius, his remaining centurion, "Sound the retreat. Form a square with the remaining soldiers. We will fall back to the camp." Gaius nodded. Those that were able disengaged from the fight and ran to form the square formation, quickly locking their shields. As they slowly shuffled away from the battle, the cries of the wounded rose to fill the air. The cries turned to curses as Conall's men sought them out and stilled their voices. Of the original two hundred Romans who had landed on the shores of Ériu, just sixty survived.

Íar's men continued to harass the formation, yet were unable to break it as it made its way slowly and surely, to the camp. Those left with Spurius had proven themselves the best of the company and were in no mood to give up any more men to barbarian weapons. Íar considered whether to place his men between the Roman remnant and their camp, but ruled this out as impractical. The Romans would simply have continued walking while hacking at his men and horses. He would lose good men and horses for no gain.

When the last of the Roman injured had been finished off, Conall called his leaders together. "Today, we have dealt a blow against these Romans. They now retreat to their camp. We will allow them time to eat and rest – and to consider their fate. Tonight we shall feast, attend to our wounded and decide how to rid us of the vermin remaining." To his commanders he said, "Gather the men. Let's go home."

CHAPTER 11

The crowds on the battlements cheered raucously as Conall led his men through the entrance to the fort, their armor splattered, and each face encrusted with blood. Conall smiled thinly and bowed to Mórrígan and Mongfhionn on the stockade, noting with some curiosity the strange markings on Mórrígan's face and arms.

Joined by his commanders as well as Mórrígan and Mongfhionn Conall dismounted and walked to the Great Hall. He spoke bluntly to Mongfhionn, "I have heard disturbing stories about what happened in my absence. Make no mistake, I am very grateful for your part in saving my people, but when this is over, I'll have an explanation for your behavior, or we'll part company."

Mongfhionn looked to Fearghal, who had joined the trio and then back to Conall, whose grey-blue eyes held her stare without flinching. "It is not wise to question the aes sidhe. You will have your explanation at a time of my choosing. I will leave it to you how you act upon that knowledge. In the meantime my healing gifts are required by your men." She turned and walked away.

Drawing Cúscraid aside, Conall said, "Take men and return to the battleground. Íar will send horsemen with you just in case the Romans try any surprises. If any of our men remain there – dead or alive, bring them back so we can say our farewells or tend their wounds. As for the Romans, stake their heads so that those remaining can see them. Let them watch the crows and ravens feed on them. Burn the bodies and anything they brought with them.

Nothing is to remain but ashes."

As Cúscraid nodded and turned to walk away, Conall's hand on his shoulder interrupted his stride. With a sparkle in his eyes and a voice loud enough to carry to Mórrígan, he said, "You too, will not escape the need for explanations, friend." Nervously Cúscraid glanced towards Mórrígan whose cheeks now burned pink. She hastily averted her eyes and was thankfully rescued as Conall continued with more urgent matters.

"To business. What's the state of my forces? How many did we lose? How many are injured and can't fight?"

"Six dead in total, we lost three horsemen and three of Cúscraid's new recruits. Another fifteen are injured, including that young eejit Uallachán ó Dubhghaill. If he hasn't learned his lesson today then that boy's pride will be his downfall. Oh, and we lost five horses, which seems to annoy Íar more than the loss of his men!"

"We need to end this quickly, Fearghal. We've more warriors than Spurius, but he's behind his stockade with probably his best men. It could get very bloody to pry him out of there. With summer coming and the possibility of an attack by Eochaidh Ruad, I don't want to lose men if I can avoid it."

Fearghal ran his fingers through his hair and scratched his head, "We could always just let them starve. They can't have much food and water and we can stop them from getting more. At some stage, they would have to make a run for it. Weakened they would make easy prey."

"Depending on what they have in the camp, that could take two or three cycles of the moon. That's too long. The spring rains will be with us soon and will turn this plain into mud. After that, we will be at the start of the summer season. I don't think Eochaidh will wait longer before making some mischief for us. You can be sure his spies are reporting back everything that's happening here. Let's join the others. We can discuss tactics over hot food and beer."

The Roman camp was subdued. Spurius called Gaius to his tent,

"How many men do we have and what is their physical state?"

Gaius said, "Not counting ourselves, we have sixty. All are in good shape and are probably the best men that we have. They will fight and fight well."

"Assuming half-rations, what are our supplies and how long will they last?"

Gaius coughed to clear his throat, "We have enough food to last two weeks on half-rations, and could stretch this further if we went to third or quarter rations. But we only have water for five days, even at third rations. If it rains, we may be able to collect rainwater and stretch the supplies longer."

After a few moments spent thinking, Spurius said, "Well we can be assured that the barbarians will not allow us to hunt for more food or to get water. They could simply starve us and when we are sufficiently enfeebled, walk in and slaughter us. On the other hand if they choose to attack us now, our position is strong. Unfortunately, I do not see that young, barbarian leader making such a poor choice. It appears that he has surrounded himself with wise heads." Spurius paused as he mulled his predicament.

"I will consider our options and let you know my decision in the morning. In the meantime, keep the men busy. Drill them the rest of the day if need be. Just keep their minds off that abomination of heads."

Gaius Aurelius Atella saluted and exited the tent. Alone, Gaius contemplated their misfortune to himself, "It would appear that the gods are the only ones who can save us. Sadly, it appears that gods do not cross seas and, without a doubt, the gods of this land have shown us neither favor nor mercy."

At times, the discussion flared as hot as the embers in the cooking pit. Cúscraid and Íar proposed that since the Romans had fought with honor, they should be offered the opportunity to leave and find a ship to their home. Mongfhionn and Mórrígan vented their wrath on the unfortunate men, saying that the Romans should be shown no mercy. Conall watched and listened to the merits of the arguments on both sides. He was deep in thought when Fearghal nudged him, "You had better lance this boil before things go too far and weapons are drawn."

Slamming his mug on the table Conall said, "Quiet! This is a discussion between friends and fellow warriors, not a competition in name-calling and spite. If I cannot hear both sides of an argument from my friends and advisors, in this hall, and without any being accused of cowardice or treachery, then maybe I should find new counselors." Scowling at the irate faces before him, he continued, "I will not have a leader of my people who feels he or she cannot speak openly. This is only the beginning of our journey. Each of you may grow to lead hundreds – maybe thousands of men." Conall gazed at each in turn as he said, "The bravery of no one in this room is ever to be questioned. Have I made myself clear?"

Shamed by Conall's words, Mórrígan spoke first. "Cúscraid, I owe you my life and that of my unborn child. Forgive the words of one who is still young and has much to learn."

Cúscraid bowed and smiled, "Forgiveness is not needed. You know that I will always be at your side."

Mumbled apologies and refilled mugs restored a more convivial atmosphere as they grappled with the challenge of the Romans.

Conall spoke, "There are two imperatives. The first is that no Roman should be left alive. My childhood friends and our people would not countenance freeing them after what they have done. The second is that we're still a small and weak force. We can't afford to lose warriors foolishly."

"Let the Romans starve, Conall. At least for one cycle of the moon," Fearghal said. "The rest of the folk from Phortaigh na Cullen will arrive in two or three sunrises and that will add Onchú's men to ours."

Cúscraid looked quizzically at Fearghal and then Conall, "Perhaps you should tell us what we're to expect in a few days."

After hearing the story of the Phortaigh na Cullen raid, Cúscraid looked concerned, "I will be delighted to see reinforcements, especially if they're experienced warriors, but what will we do with the villagers? There is barely enough room in the fort now. As you can tell by the smell, the conditions are not healthy. Sickness will spread among us and we, as well as the Romans, will soon start to run out of food."

"That shouldn't be a difficulty," said Fearghal. "The folk from Phortaigh na Cullen will remain in the forest valley to the northeast until we resolve the Roman problem. They have enough food with them without burdening the fort. However, even the additional warriors will not make a big difference as to how we remove the Romans," Fearghal finished, emptying his horn of beer.

The discussion rambled on into the early hours of the morning. Finally, Conall rose, "I see no option. We'll wait seven sunsets. They can't thrive without water. If the weather is favorable, then on the eighth sunrise we will use fire to drive them out of their camp and onto the iron of our javelins and swords." Looking to Mongfhionn he added. "In the meantime we'll offer sacrifices to the gods and pray it doesn't rain."

On the eighth day, Spurius looked out over the stockade towards Ráth na Conall. His view was blighted by the skulls of the fallen. Thankfully, the clouds of ravens and crows had finished picking the heads clean and he did not have to listen to the incessant, loud *kraa kraa* of ravens or the *caw caw* of crows. Now, during the day, the ivory white skulls simply stared accusingly at the camp while at night the wind made them shriek and rattle eerily.

Gaius had reported that the supply of drinking water was finished. Even careful rationing and the men drinking their own piss had not forestalled this moment. Men sucked on small stones to stimulate saliva, but dry, rasping voices and coughing could be heard all around the defenses. The rationing of food and water had left them with a gaunt, grey appearance and it was becoming increasingly difficult to keep them motivated and alert. Spurius sometimes wished the barbarians would attack, as this at least would propel the men to action. Instead, Conall's forces restricted their actions to a few patrols, ensuring Spurius was not resupplied with food or water.

At the fort, fire wagons were prepared. Each was filled with bales of straw, jugs of oil and fat and carried a cauldron containing burning coals. As teams of oxen pulled on their yokes, the wagons trundled towards the Roman camp.

Conall's men walked or rode to either side of the wagons. Mórrígan rode proudly alongside Conall on her new horse. She had been delighted to see that Conall could ride, although not very well, and hoped that there would be times for them to ride together away from the duties that now bound them to their people. A few paces back, Mongfhionn rode with Íar and Nikandros.

Gaius was relieved in a sense, but also had dreaded this moment. He called out to his optio, "Inform our commander that the barbarians are approaching." Then he called his men to arms, "Man the stockade, and stay alert. Show no mercy and expect none."

He was joined shortly by Spurius. "A good strategist, this Conall Mac Gabhann has turned out to be. From the smoke coming from those wagons, I expect we are to be burned out." Smiling wryly, he continued, "I would have done exactly the same. We have no water to douse fires, but at least the wood is not fully dried out and so should burn slowly."

"Should we try to stop them before they reach the gates?" Gaius asked.

"No point. We would simply lose the men to their javelins. It is better that we stay behind our defenses and fight them inside when they burst through." Lowering his voice, he said, "This was an ill-advised venture, Gaius, and we are about to pay a very high price." Turning to the soldiers manning his defenses, Spurius called out, "Romans, the barbarians will soon be among us. I know you will make Rome proud this day. You are my best men. Make them pay in blood for each step they take." A defiant, if hoarse, cheer went up around the stockade and weapons were slapped against shields – a little more feebly than before.

"It would seem the Romans want to fight," Conall looked down at Fearghal who was striding alongside.

"You've got to give them credit, Conall. They're not afraid of a fight. Pity we're enemies, as we could be doing with warriors like that."

Conall nodded, "Aye, but it seems that the gods will have their amusement at our expense."

He called Íar over, "Have your riders escort two wagons to the rear gates. Take Onchú's men with you, as well as Eirnín and Craiftine. When the wagons are against the gate, have Eirnín shoot an arrow in the air to let us know you're in place. Then set the wagon alight. When the gate is burned, you know what to do." Íar nodded and rode back to his men.

At the front gate, Conall's men halted a few paces back from the ditch. Both sides glowered at each other and exchanged insults and curses. The Romans watched, helpless as the fire wagons were unhitched, then pushed and rolled into place hard against the gate. The bales of straw were split and tossed into the ditches on either side.

Conall watched the sky and saw an arrow rise from the rear of the camp. He nodded at Mórrígan who, along with Bricriu, shot arrows into the wagon. It was not long before the oil-soaked wagon burst into flames. Then the archers turned their attention to the straw in the ditch, firing arrows until it too, was ablaze. Thick smoke soon curled up into the air around the stockade as the green wood resisted the flames. At the gate, the intense heat and flames soon forced the nearest Roman soldiers back from the gateway.

Spurius did not see many good options, but knew that having his men spread out on the stockade while it and the gate burned was not a particularly promising plan. To Gaius he said, "They will rush us from both gateways once they burn through, but the entrance will still be narrow and we may be able to hold them. I will take half the men and hold the front entrance, you take the remainder and secure the rear. Make sure the men keep their shields high. The barbarians are bound to have a supply of javelins with them." Gaius saluted and ordered his cohort from the stockade.

Inevitably, the charred remains of the wagons collapsed, leaving a mound of burning embers at the gate. "Hope you're wearing a good pair of bróga today or you'll get your feet singed." Fearghal grimaced and began to walk towards the camp. He was roughly pushed aside by Urard, who, without hesitation, walked through the embers and began to hack at the charred gate with his huge axe. The air rang with the sound of the blows of the axe and the wood splintering. At the rear of the camp, Onchú's men attacked the smoldering gate.

Both gates groaned, but the rear was the first to crash inwards. Much as Íar wished for a fair and honorable fight, he reluctantly agreed with Conall that they could little afford to lose men. He looked sadly on the Romans standing before him, resolute expressions set on their ash-blackened faces and shouted, "Javelins!" Each man hurled his missiles. Even with their shields, the Romans fell, under the sheer numbers of javelins. Soon Gaius was left with a remnant of his force to face the screaming barbarians that charged or rode through the gateway, their axes and swords swinging. Surrounded, he fought hard and bravely, with spear, sword and shield, until a glancing blow to the back of his head sent him into blackness.

Glancing behind him, Spurius knew that his slim thread of hope had broken and the barbarian cavalry would soon be upon him. To his men he said, "As soon as the gate is brought down we will rush the barbarians. Fight well for Rome and if the gods allow, we will all eat, drink and sleep with virgins in the Elysium Fields." Dust and sparks rose from the flattened front gate. Spurius shouted, "Advance, kill the barbarian bastards."

His men bellowed curses as they pushed forward, but their cries were cut short as volley after volley of iron struck them. Spurius strode forward defiantly, challenging his enemy to fight, even as his shield was wrenched from his arm by the impact of several javelins. His helmet was torn from his head by a missile, its iron spike having first taken a fragment of bone and flesh from his cheek. Another punctured his shoulder. Soon, he fell backwards, unconscious.

Conall left behind a camp in flames. Brion remained, with orders to raze the entire enclosure and leave nothing. The Roman fallen were beheaded and their bodies tossed onto the many fires. Their heads joined those of their companions and were immediately enjoyed by the crows and ravens. Behind Conall and guarded on all sides, Roman prisoners either walked or lay in one of the wagons brought from the fort. In total, fourteen Romans had survived the battle. This included the newly promoted centurion, Gaius Aurelius Atella, and his commander Spurius Sulpicia Longus, although both were suffering from severe wounds.

Mongfhionn strode towards them as they approached the fort. Seeing Spurius, she made to speak, but was interrupted by Conall. "Bring healers to these men and have their wounds dressed." To Cúscraid he said, "Have the villagers bring food and drink for them."

A startled Cúscraid asked, "Why? Surely they will all be executed."

"Yes they will, but they fought well. They should meet their gods on a full stomach and be able to stand like a warrior when they face their executioner."

Fearghal smiled approvingly and then turned to Mongfhionn. The Druidess looked stricken - an unaccustomed countenance for her. He could see that she was fighting hard to reconcile her hatred for the Romans with Conall's command to dispense mercy. It had come as a complete surprise to Fearghal when Mongfhionn revealed she had sisters who had died at the hands of the Romans. He was disappointed that she had kept her story from him and looked forward to hearing her reasons.

Having been on short rations, the prisoners were appreciative of their captor's generosity, but under no illusion as to the brevity of their future on this world. Some accepted their fate stoically, as soldiers who both dispensed death and received it; others attempted to trade pieces of information in the hope of gaining some sympathy – or at least a sharp blade edge.

A very feeble Spurius and Gaius had been separated from their men, and now sat with Conall, his advisors and commanders. Opposite them glowered the plainly hostile Mongfhionn and Mórrígan. Even attended by the best of healers, Spurius would have been unlikely to survive, yet his mind remained sharp. He deftly parried the various questions about his master, Marcus Fabius Ambustus, and the mission on which he had been sent.

Spurius knew he was going to die, either by a barbarian blade or more likely at the hands of the Druidess. His intent therefore, was to save Gaius so he could return to Rome and tell their story. In this, Conall was likeminded, as he wished the young soldier, who had fought bravely, to return to Rome with a message. However, Conall was mindful of the promise he had made that no Roman would leave Ériu alive. Mongfhionn and Mórrígan looked on suspiciously as the men conversed with Spurius.

Finally, Conall threw up his hands in frustration, "I see no resolution to this problem. Gaius is a Roman and by my oath all Romans must die."

Gaius bent his head to Spurius and whispered something. Spurius nodded and said to Conall, "Gaius Aurelius Atella is no more Roman than the Spartan." The statement stilled the room.

"Explain yourself, but it had better be good. There are ones seated who would should no mercy – and for good reason."

"Gaius is not a Roman. He is from Velitrae, a town in the territory of Rome's ancient enemy, the Volsci, in the south of Latium. We conquered his people. He was given a choice of enlisting or slavery. What choice would you have made?" Spurius stopped, the pain in his head making him lightheaded and then added, "His name is from his sponsor's family." He struggled to keep his thoughts in order while he studied the looks on his captors' faces.

Relieved, Conall slapped his thighs and thumped the table, "It seems we have a solution that suits all of our purposes. Gaius will return to Rome bearing our messages for Marcus Fabius Ambustus. Now let us eat and drink, for tomorrow will not be happy for some."

With one voice Mongfhionn and Mórrígan screeched, "No!" Daggers in their hands, they flung themselves at Spurius and Gaius. Fortunately for the startled Romans, the women were intercepted, disarmed roughly and restrained by Fearghal and Cúscraid as they cried out, "He should die with the rest. We want justice. We want revenge for our families. They must die."

A furious Conall reached for an axe and slammed it into the table, splitting the wood in front of them. "You dare to challenge my oath of safety. No man shall be harmed under my roof, if he eats with me without deceit." Mórrígan suddenly realized the peril she was in; Conall would stubbornly defend his values – no matter the cost. Her hand went to her belly as she saw the anger burning in Conall's eyes and the axe handle quivering before her. She scrambled to her knees, "Forgive me Conall, my passions overcame my senses. Please think of our child. Forgive my foolishness."

Conall ignored her and regarded Mongfhionn coldly. Even with her ancient powers, the Sidhe flinched under his steel-grey gaze. "You, my lady, are fast outliving your welcome. I begin to disapprove of your influence on my queen. Control your hunger and thirst for revenge or leave. I believe this man is not a Roman by birth. I have given my word that he will be returned to Rome to deliver a message from me. Do you or anyone else have a problem with my decision?"

Mongfhionn stared at the dirt for what seemed a long time. In Conall, she saw a great power developing and found it alluring. Drawing herself up to her full stature, she answered, "I will trust you, Conall Mac Gabhann. Your word is good enough for me — this time."

"Well that was a bit tense. Would anyone like some of my special brew?" The gloomy atmosphere in the room was relieved by Fearghal. He frowned and pointed at the ruined table, "Anyone know a good carpenter?"

Laughing, Conall gripped his axe, pulled it from the table, and pushed his bronze mug forward. As Mongfhionn took her place beside Fearghal, Conall bent over and whispered, "Tomorrow you may have the Roman. He is aware that this is part of our deal. But I'll have no repeat of the scene on the stockade. Consider what is appropriate." Mongfhionn nodded and took comfort from Fearghal's strength as she rested against him.

At sunrise, the prisoners, dressed in full armor, were lined up alongside the perimeter ditch. Separately, Spurius was taken to a stake and secured to it. He was not armored, wearing only a red woolen tunic; he leaned heavily against the wood, shivering in the morning breeze. The stake was about ten paces from his men, but his face displayed no sign of emotion. On the stockade, villagers craned their necks to get a good view of the executions. Gaius observed from the side, supported by two warriors.

"Let's get this over with, Fearghal," Conall murmured as they walked towards the prisoners.

"Why don't you leave this to me and the other volunteers? There's no need for you to do anything. Just give the command." Brion, Cúscraid, Nikandros, Onchú and Urard nodded in agreement with Fearghal.

"I'll not order the men to do something I'm not willing to do myself." Conall turned to the prisoners, "You fought bravely, if for a poor cause. I pray that your gods will take you to a better place. Kneel and it will be over quickly for you." The men knelt as one, their necks bared as they prayed for a sharp blade. Taking a deep breath, Conall swung his axe. He was glad, both for the prisoner and himself, when the blade cleaved the soldier's head from his shoulders. As the head rolled to the side, blood gushed onto the frost covered ground and the body slumped forward.

As he prepared to strike the next prisoner, Conall was moved aside by the giant, bare-chested Urard, who simply said, "No, now it's my job." His great axe glinted red in the morning sun, as Urard walked down the line of prisoners, striking one after the other. By the time Urard had finished, the dirt in front of the men was a dark and sodden crimson. Conall was amazed and thankful at the speed and efficiency with which Urard had dispatched the remainder of the Romans.

Spurius watched expressionless, but he too was grateful that the huge barbarian was obviously accomplished at this work. His men would have felt little pain as they were sent on their journey to the Elysian Fields. He, on the other hand, did not feel the same level of comfort at his imminent fate. His wounds throbbed even in the numbing cold, but he was grateful for the pain and hoped that what he was already suffering might balance what was to come. He watched as Mongfhionn approached in her gray cloak. She handed her oak staff to Fearghal and stood before him – knife in hand.

"What, no naked body to send me on my way to the Elysian Fields, Druidess?" Spurius mocked.

"There will be no Elysian Fields for you, Spurius Sulpicia Longus - or for your master and his sons. Your fate lies in the abyss of Tartarus." As she spoke, Mongfhionn tore Spurius' tunic, exposing his chest. "Thank your gods for Conall Mac Gabhann. Without his intervention it would have taken days for you to die and your suffering would have been beyond your imagination." Mongfhionn lifted her hands to the skies and sang her strange incantations.

The last words that Spurius heard were "Do mo dheirfiúracha – for my sisters."

The knife was first drawn slowly across his throat opening up a deep crimson gash that spurted blood. Then it was plunged into his chest, cracking ribs. Moments later Mongfhionn turned around. In her hand was the still warm and pulsing heart of Spurius Sulpicia Longus, Primus Pilus of Rome. Reaching into her cloak, she brought out a red leather pouch and placed the heart inside. She walked up to Gaius and put the warm pouch firmly in his hand. "Give this to Marcus Fabius Ambustus. Tell him I have pouches for him and his sons."

Mongfhionn looked thoughtfully at Conall and smiled at Fearghal, then turned and walked towards the sunrise. Moments later, she was gone.

"Damn woman or Sidhe or whatever. Will I ever understand her? She has more hidden rooms and locked doors in her soul than there are caves in the gleannta of the Ulaid," Fearghal shook his head in frustration. Then took a deep breath and slapped Conall on the back,

"Well, where do we find this Cassius Fabius Scaeva and who do we have to kill?"

Troubled thoughts played on her mind as she combed her long red hair by the roaring fire. Since the incident in the Great Hall, she had been nervous and, for the first time in her life, very afraid of Conall. They had grown up quickly since the death of their parents and friends and now she hoped in her heart that they were not growing apart. She knew she had let him down, but was unsure how to put things right.

She heard Conall enter the dwelling and his sigh of relief as he removed his armor. Her heart beat rapidly, and her breasts heaved under her nightgown as she first heard and then felt him stand behind her. His hands untied the thongs on her nightdress and it slid to the floor. Soon Mórrígan felt his strong hands cup and squeeze her breasts. She let her comb fall and clasped his hands firmly to her, loving the warmth. Then she rose and turned around, her jade-green eyes not daring to look into his.

She felt her chin softly tilted upwards and soon his lips were on hers. Feeling the urgency and passion in his kisses, she smiled inside, and then she guided his hand between her legs. A gentle tug at her red bush made her moan and then his long fingers were deep inside, feeling her wetness. They fell onto the straw and skins, and she groaned as she felt him enter her. He took her over and over as she gripped and scratched his back. An intense sensation of pleasure flowed through her body when she heard him gasp, his final thrusts filling her.

As she lay on her back, purring with pleasure, her skin flushed pink, Conall smiled at her. "Since when does my queen not look me in the eye?" Mórrígan tried to answer, but could not find the words. She was rescued by a gentle finger on her swollen lips. "We'll always be together my love and you should never fear me or feel you can't speak honestly. But, there is one thing that troubles me greatly."

Anxious, Mórrígan gulped and spoke hoarsely, "Tell me my king. As you say, there can be no secrets between us. No matter how difficult it may be to put words to them."

The flames in the fire were liquid reflections in Conall's eyes as he looked upon her, "When do I get to see this fancy body paint that my men tell me you wore to frighten the Romans? I've never seen Cúscraid so embarrassed as when I was told my queen had been flaunting her considerable talents to the whole fort."

Conall lay back roaring with laughter as Mórrígan beat his chest with flame-scarred fists.

"You bastard, you've known all along and said nothing." Then she tossed her hair back and laughed, "Well, Conall Mac Gabhann, I may not have my paint on this evening, but I can still work a spell on you."

With that she straddled him, arched her back, to show her breasts off in the firelight and then lifted her bottom up and slid down on his hardness. As she rocked back and forward she treasured hearing Conall moan, while she enjoyed his hardness in the warmth and wetness between her thighs.

CHAPTER 12

414 B.C.

The blessing of spring rains came a full cycle of the moon following the executions. Many thought it Mongfhionn's parting gift, as if the rain had been sent to cleanse the land of the blood that had been spilled. The land smelled fresh and clean and this heartened the residents of Ráth na Conall. Yet, the rains became incessant and after weeks of storms, the land around the fort had turned into a morass of mud and ponds – some quite large. It made it difficult for the villagers and farmers to rebuild their homes, plant crops or move cattle onto pasture.

Conall and his trusted friends and commanders had been given the title of an Chomhairle – the Council, by all at Ráth na Conall and the neighboring lands. They met regularly to plan and to resolve disputes. The first Chomhairle included Conall, Mórrígan, Fearghal, Brion, Nikandros, Cúscraid, and Onchú. Íar and Mongfhionn were included, if present.

After supervising the building of the stables and corral, Íar said his farewells and rode back to Curraghatoor. With him, he took messages from Conall including a promise that he and Mórrígan would visit during the summer. At Íar's suggestion, Conall put Nikandros in command of the horsemen. It was a proposal that Conall keenly agreed with and one which delighted Nikandros. The riders also approved and while not able to match the high, red plumes that crowned the Spartan's helmet, quite a few foxes in the neighboring forests met an unhappy end so that the riders could sport the bushy, red tails now hanging from the crests of their newly forged helmets.

It amused Conall that wherever his queen went, so followed her protector - the giant Urard. He had remarked to Mórrígan that, at night, he sometimes expected to see Urard rush in to rescue her, since she was quite loud in the throes of passion. Mórrígan's group of archers had grown to ten, male and female, who continued to practice daily. She supervised the crafting of bows and arrows, as well as their training program. Several of the villagers soon developed into skilled bowyers and arrowsmiths. The arrowsmiths spent long hours perfecting what was to become their signature arrow – a black shaft tipped with an iron head and using a mix of white and dyed red feathers as the flight.

The archers' dedication was remarkable. Mórrígan, Eirnín, Bricriu and Craiftine proudly bore the scars on their hands from the fire-arrows. They were the center of curiosity and attraction for many not used to seeing bows used in battle. Even a skeptical Conall and Fearghal soon recognized that the range and power of the bows could be useful.

The blacksmiths and leather-workers were kept busy producing weapons, armor and shields to build up the fort's stock, and to replace weapons damaged from the over-enthusiastic daily drills. Even in practice, Conall's men gave no quarter and expected none to be given and so the continuous line of warriors looking for healing herbs and dressings from Fionnbharr and the other healers.

A few days following the execution of the Romans, it dawned on Fearghal that Mongfhionn had truly gone. He tried to pick up her trail, but failed, returning dejected and melancholic by the time another full moon had appeared. To keep Fearghal's mind off his companion's absence, Conall suggested that Nikandros and he take some men and scout the valley east of the fort that led to Carn Tigherna. This was the quickest route between the forts and for most of its length the valley was wide and level, but mid-way through lay Carraig na Caillí. Here a steep cliff face of black rock narrowed the valley considerably; Conall wanted an assessment of how easy it would be to defend this pass against Eochaidh Ruad's men.

Fearghal protested at first. Not at the task, but because Nikandros made it plain that he would only be taking mounted men with him, which meant Fearghal would have to learn to ride. Conall informed him that they would practice together and for a few weeks the fort was treated to the sight of their leaders repeatedly falling off their chosen mounts. It became obvious that Fearghal would be competent, but never comfortable, on a horse. He would always prefer to have his feet on solid ground – especially in battle. However, Conall soon became a very proficient rider and grew to love the black stallion, which he had named Toirneach.

Conall consulted with Cúscraid about sending scouts along the river north of the fort. They were to seek high ground, and establish a lookout post at the mouth of the Bohd Carraig. Although they both thought it unlikely that Eochaidh would attack from the direction of Bohd Carraig, this would be the best route south for the Connachta, should Ailill and Medb decide that the young king in the south needed to be taught a lesson for stealing their gold.

After distributing what he considered a fair proportion of the gold from the raid on Phortaigh na Cullen to his men, the rest was stored in the cellars beneath the fort. Since they now had a good supply of gold, the Chomhairle discussed where they could recruit more warriors. Onchú was delegated to travel north-east towards Ráthgall to see if more could be persuaded to join. He was also tasked with escorting Gaius Aurelius Atella, now restored to full health, to the coast to secure passage on a galley that would return him to Rome.

It seemed to Conall that he spent an endless amount of time in the Great Hall, some with the elders from the people of the land around the fort, people who had farmed and lived there for generations and some with the elders from Phortaigh na Cullen. Eventually, it was agreed that the new people could settle the land two days walk to the east of Ráth na Cullen. Conall had hunted and fished near this land, knew it was good ground and encouraged the acceptance of this proposal. During the negotiations, Seanán emerged as an astute negotiator and civic leader, respected by both communities.

A group of artisans, workers of precious metals, jewelry and leather from Phortaigh na Cullen, asked if they could remain within the fort to practice their trade. Once Conall had given his consent, they were never idle. He often laughed at the vanity of his men. Their new wealth now evidenced in arm rings, wristlets and torcs, as well as quite ornate broaches and belt buckles. Shields, sword hilts and helmets became colorful and distinctive as the warriors displayed their personality with intricate designs. The women of Ráth na Conall were not excluded. Soon those that had bonded with a warrior were proudly wearing gold and silver pins, broaches, anklets and earrings. Those remaining were not neglected, being well-rewarded by the men for having friendly thighs.

At Carn Tigherna, Faolán Ó Floinn was angry and disappointed that the sniveling piece of dog-shite, Cassius Fabius Scaeva, had escaped. He had hoped to personally slit the Roman's throat. Thus, it was fortunate that the guard who escorted Cassius had died from his wounds, otherwise Faolán would have gutted him. Despite many days of questioning, none of the men who guarded the gate through which Cassius had escaped admitted to having taken the Roman's gold. In the end, Faolán had all six, together with their wives and children, stripped, hung, and their bodies thrown into the ditch that surrounded the fort. Their corpses impaled on blackthorn bushes provided a garish display near the entrance to Carn Tigherna.

It was late summer and raining heavily as Faolán sloshed his way through the mud to the king's throne room. Faolán knew he faced another challenge. While he had thought the young Conall Mac Gabhann brave, he had been totally surprised at his resourcefulness with the raid on Phortaigh na Cullen. He was also angry that additional experienced warriors had been persuaded to join Conall's growing warband – it could hardly be called an army. Now, the news that Conall's men had first held off and then slaughtered two hundred Roman soldiers was spreading quickly among the peasants. There was also a rumor that Conall had horse warriors. Faolán found this hard to believe, since the only horsemen in the region were from Curraghatoor and Deda Mac Sin was loyal to Eochaidh Ruad.

Perhaps Eochaidh had been right and they should have attacked Conall sooner. Given his king's degenerate and disturbed, almost mad behavior, it momentarily crossed his mind that he should attempt to negotiate with Conall to give up Eochaidh and ensure his own safety. However, since Faolán had led the original attack on the settlement, he could expect to be shown no mercy by Conall.

He pushed open the door to the throne room and was met with the usual stale smells of vomit, shit, piss, sweat and sex, together with rotting food and beer. As usual, the king sat on his throne with a young girl on his lap. This one could not have been more than twelve summers, although Faolán had to admit that, for her age, she had good-sized breasts, which were being pawed and sucked on by the king.

"Well, do you have any news that I might like to hear? Anyone else escaped from your custody? Maybe there's another upstart king challenging me?" Eochaidh spoke, his eyes heavy and his voice laden with sarcasm.

Faolán bowed, "No news my king, but I think now is the time to make plans for when the rains end. I hear the Sidhe, Mongfhionn, is not presently among them, so that should remove one complication from our plans. Although, I hear rumors that the one called Mórrígan, Conall's queen, appears to have developed dark powers under Mongfhionn's guidance."

At this, Eochaidh exploded and stood up, throwing the young girl to the dirt floor. His fur-trimmed and finely-decorated robe was wide open displaying his limp cock. "Queen! She's no more than a striapach. After I've opened her thighs, I'll give her to the men. Then we'll let the dogs do what they want with her."

Looking at the pathetic manhood before him, Faolán thought that the likelihood of his king being able to get an erection was not high, but diplomatically responded, "We should send messengers to your nobles to start mustering the army. Conall Mac Gabhann, although young, has shown himself to be both brave and astute. He has surrounded himself with strong advisors and many of his men are elite fighters. Our task may not be without risk."

Eochaidh sat down and for a moment looked to have forgotten

whether he need respond. Eventually, he nodded wearily, "Do what needs to be done. We will march on Ráth na Conall in the spring of next year when the ground is firmer. You can tell me what your battle plan is closer to the time. Now leave me, I have urgent matters to consider."

Faolán bowed, "Yes lord." As he was walking away the 'urgent matter' was made to kneel between Eochaidh's legs. The retching of the poor girl rang in Faolán's ears, as she took her king's foul-smelling cock in her mouth.

Summer was almost at an end and the temperature, although not hot, was pleasantly warm. The sun shimmered in a cloudless blue sky as the party cantered through the lush grassland and forests to Curraghatoor. Conall and Mórrígan rode out front, followed by Brion, Fearghal and Nikandros, and a guard of ten horsemen. As they had departed Ráth na Conall, Cúscraid was heard to complain, half-heartedly, that he never got to go anywhere. The party moved at a leisurely pace, because of Mórrígan. Even the most unobservant could see that her belly and breasts were huge, and her time was close. Conall had tried to persuade her to stay at the fort, or to rest in one of the wagons, but she simply refused to listen.

As they neared the fort of Curraghatoor, three riders came towards them accompanied by a guard of twenty horsemen. Even at a distance, it was easy to recognize the large shape of Íar Mac Dedad. He rode to the right side of an older man who galloped erect and with ease on a chestnut stallion. He was smaller than Íar, but then everyone looked small beside Íar. As they drew closer, Conall saw a man who, although having long, red-streaked grey hair and being quite old, clearly was still in his prime. Íar roared a greeting as the two groups met and his father's face broke into a huge, if slightly embarrassed, smile at his son's behavior. The third rider was a beautiful, pale-skinned young woman with long hair, black as raven's feathers and eyes a deep shade of blue.

"Father, may I present Conall Mac Gabhann and his queen, Mórrígan Ní Cathasaigh? Conall, Mórrígan, this is my father and king at Curraghatoor, Deda Mac Sin." Íar was silent for a few moments and was abruptly stung on the cheek by a horse whip. He laughed, "Oh, and I suppose I should introduce this unfortunate girl. This is my sister Áine."

Noting that Brion had not taken his eyes off Áine, Íar winked mischievously, "We're looking for a man for Áine. At seventeen summers she's getting old and I hear she's still a virgin." At that, the lightly built Áine gave her brother a furious look and struck him with near enough force to knock him from his horse.

Before riding off in mock anger, she smiled at a red-faced Brion, "Welcome to Curraghatoor."

Íar pointed to Fearghal and Nikandros, "As for these troublemakers, the best I can say about them, Father, is that I count them as my friends."

Deda Mac Sin looked at Conall with piercing blue eyes, knowing that few could hold his stare. He was both surprised and delighted that the young man before him did not flinch. As he reached forward, hand outstretched, he said, "I apologize for the behavior of my children. Perhaps I did not beat them enough when they were young." Conall laughed appreciatively.

"I knew your father well, Conall Mac Gabhann, and for that alone you and your queen are welcome in my home. That my son counts you as friends makes you doubly welcome. I see Mórrígan is with child, so enough of this talk. Let us go to my home where we can all be comfortable."

Conall took Deda's hand, holding it firmly. "I thank you for your greetings and hospitality, sir. The road has been hard on Mórrígan. I'm sure she would appreciate something softer to sit on other than the fine horse that you gave her."

That evening, the feasting hall rang with the sounds of men and women drinking and eating and telling stories. In the hall, it was difficult to distinguish who told or sang the tallest tale or drank the most beer. Roaring fires lit up the building with their red and yellow flickering light, and soon everyone's faces matched the glow of the flames. The food, roasted pig, lamb, chicken and deer was served along with great mugs of beer and ale by what seemed an army of females of all ages. The atmosphere was loud, good humored and relaxed, with many of the women lingering to entertain the men.

Deda Mac Sin drank less than most and studied each of his visitors in turn, assessing their manner and bearing. Mórrígan was indeed beautiful and plainly struggling with the child she was carrying. Something in her eyes troubled Deda, but he passed this off as too much beer. He could see that Fearghal and Nikandros were seasoned warriors and laughed at the good natured craic that they swapped. In his opinion, the Spartan's clothing was a bit strange and somewhat inadequate. The strong bond between Mórrígan and her brother Brion was evident. The young man had obviously survived a few recent fights, given the fresh scars on his face and hands. Deda could also see that Brion was quite taken with Áine. Given how closely they were sitting, he was sure that those affections were reciprocated.

He perceived Conall was indeed a born leader, and by all accounts becoming a wise and prudent one, willing to take risks when needed, but not foolish with his men's lives. When Íar described how Conall had executed the first Roman soldier himself, Deda approved. Even though he was young, Conall commanded and was freely given the respect of experienced warriors, such as Fearghal and Nikandros. His thoughts were interrupted as his eyes made contact with Conall's. They both smiled before breaking the glance and rejoining the many conversations. Like, Deda, Conall was intently observing all that was taking place rather than simply getting drunk like everyone else.

Deda considered the true reason that the young warrior had chosen to visit. Although in abiding by the rules of hospitality, Conall had not spoken of serious matters at the feast, Deda could see in the young man's eyes that he was troubled. Deda knew that in the next few days, Conall would ask for his help against Eochaidh Ruad. He also knew his own son, Íar, would support Conall with his plea.

A few days earlier, a messenger had arrived from Eochaidh commanding Deda to assemble his horsemen and bring them to

Carn Tigherna to prepare for a battle with Conall Mac Gabhann. At fifty-five seasons, Deda had hoped that he could gracefully slide into his old age, see Áine with a good partner, and pass on his crown to Íar. It appeared that fate would not give him his desire.

The peacefulness of the morning was shattered by piercing screams from Conall and Mórrígan's quarters. Fearghal almost took the door off its hinges as he burst inside, followed by Nikandros, Brion and Íar – all with swords drawn or axes in hand. They were greeted with a screeching Mórrígan, and a very confused and pale Conall, who looked at them beseechingly. "I think the travel, and feasting may have been too much for Mórrígan. If anyone knows how to deliver a baby, now would be a good time to volunteer!" Faster than they had entered, the brave warriors retreated. Fortunately, Áine had heard the uproar, and followed her brother. Immediately, she sent for her assistants.

In the Great Hall, the king scratched the salt and pepper stubble on his chin and pondered this turn of events. It had been a long time since there had been a noble birth at Curraghatoor. Deda, with amused remembrance, watched Conall wear a deep track in the dirt floor as he paced up and down. The well-intentioned, but feeble attempts by Conall's friends to comfort or distract him did nothing to relieve the young man's anxiety. The king wondered if this birth was a sign from the goddess.

His fate seemed to be getting more and more entangled with the young warrior, but he was king, and like Conall had to make prudent choices for his people. Eochaidh Ruad could call on at least three thousand nobles and warriors who had sworn loyalty to him. Conall had perhaps a hundred fighting men, so what chance would he have – even with Deda's horsemen? He certainly had an excuse to break his oath to Eochaidh. Conall's father, although not a noble, had been a good friend. The slaughter of the settlement was a vile act that deserved punishment. Furthermore, the rumors he had heard from Carn Tigherna, about the growing depravity and madness of Eochaidh did not sit well with him.

There was the not inconsequential influence of the Sidhe to consider as well. Mongfhionn had cursed Eochaidh and all who would

Conall: The Place of Blood - Rinn-Iru 163

help him. Deda had never had cause to bring the wrath of the aes sidhe down upon himself, his family or his people. It was something he was very reluctant to do, even for his oath king.

Several hours, and a few beers later, Deda's musings were brought to a close by cries a pleasant kind, as the lungs of a newborn were filled. Conall rushed to his room and met Áine with a smile on her face as broad as any her brother could have displayed, "Well my lord, it would seem that Mórrígan has a surprise for you." Chortling at what she knew, Áine hurried down to the Great Hall to spread the news.

Taking a deep breath, Conall strode into the room and quickly lost his composure. On the thick bed of clean straw, rushes and furs, sat an exhausted, but smiling Mórrígan, her cheeks flushed with the exertions of the past few hours. Her robe had slipped down from her shoulders, exposing her pale, milk-laden breasts, where two babies were happily suckling.

"What? How?" Conall stammered.

Mórrígan smiled at him, "I don't think the how is much in doubt - unless you want to make a striapach of your queen. As for the what, I am proud to introduce you to your daughters - Danu and Brighid."

Conall steadied himself and crossed the room to sit beside Mórrígan. "I take it that I have no choice in the names of my daughters." He spoke softly as he put his arms around the mother of his children. Mórrígan was silent for a while and then said, "You will have to trust me on their names. An explanation for my choice will be given and at that time you may choose to accept or reject the names."

"May I hold my daughters? Or would I be interrupting their feasting?"

Mórrígan smiled, "I hope you will always want to hold your daughters, my love and king."

As Conall relaxed, he had a fleeting regret that he did not have a son. This was quickly replaced by relief that he did not have to fear the words of the geis of which Mongfhionn had spoken, that his sons would not inherit their father's throne. The door opened; Áine had ordered food and drinks brought to the room. She felt a warm pleasure at what she witnessed.

The childbirth had exhausted Mórrígan. She remained in her room until she had regained her strength and was very grateful for Áine, who made sure she was well attended. From their conversations it became very clear that Áine had more than a passing interest in Brion and that she was hoping to recruit Mórrígan to her side. In truth, Mórrígan had been lonely since Mongfhionn had departed and was glad to have a new friend. Since Áine was of similar age, they had much in common.

The king inquired daily about Mórrígan's health and when informed that the new mother was almost at full strength, called for a feast to celebrate the birth of the twins. At the full moon, Conall led Mórrígan to the seat of honor at the king's side. Each carried one of the twins proudly in their arms. They were met with raucous cheering, the clanging of swords and axes against shields and the drumming of many bodhráns. As the cheering died down, Deda rose from his throne. "I am pleased to welcome Danu and Brighid to our home. They will always be welcome here and will have the protection of my armies should they ever be in danger." At that, the assembled warriors from Curraghatoor and Ráth na Conall shouted their agreement with the king.

Many gifts were brought for the twins. As they were in the company of warriors, the gifts tended to reflect the nature of the giver. Two shining daggers, each with a dark ruby in the hilt, from Fearghal; two small bows and quivers of arrows from Nikandros; and two tiny sets of armor from their uncle, Brion.

"I think our daughters had better grow up to be warriors or else our friends will be disappointed," Conall remarked to Mórrígan, as he thanked each of the givers.

Áine and Íar brought two torcs of gold, inlaid with rubies and emeralds. Íar grumbled that he had wanted to bring two small shields rather than jewelry. As the cheering subsided, the rear doors of the hall swung open, and two ponies were led into the room, gifts from Deda Mac Sin. The ponies were perfect miniature versions of Conall and Mórrígan's horses, and both had ornately decorated and bejeweled leather reins and bridals. The celebrations went into the small hours of the morning and many remarked that it was a good omen that, in all the noise, the girls slept soundly. Others pointed out that whenever the babies appeared to get restless, they were presented with their mother's ample breasts.

CHAPTER 13

Days later, after the headaches had subsided from the feasting and drinking, the leaders of Ráth na Conall met with Deda Mac Sin and his council.

"You put me in a difficult place, Conall. Frankly, I see no way you can defeat Eochaidh. Even without my riders he will be able to raise at least five thousand men to march on Ráth na Conall. You have great warriors, led by the best commanders anyone could wish for, but you have no more than one hundred and twenty men. Even with my riders on your side, we would be hopelessly outnumbered. This is impossible."

"It does look a challenge, my lord, but then no one expected a clutch of children to survive the first attack. No one expected us to raid the gold village at Phortaigh na Cullen. And no one expected us to defeat the Romans. We seem to make a habit of doing the unexpected and now we have gold to hire more warriors. I've sent men east towards Ráthgall to find fighters willing to join us." Deda shook his head and scratched at his beard as Conall continued.

"Most likely, Eochaidh will attack us either this coming autumn or the spring of next year when the ground is firmer. I've look-outs positioned to warn us of that attack. I may not be strong enough to attack Eochaidh this year, but for the sake of my people, I have to be able to at least hold him. Indeed, I don't have a choice." Conall drank slowly from his wooden jug, and looked at Mórrígan, Fearghal, Nikandros, and Brion "For the sake of my own children, I have no choice but to fight and win."

The Great Hall, that had been filled just a short time ago with loud singing, shouts and music, now was quiet and somber, as each brooded over the enormity of the task before them. Exasperated, Íar spoke up, "Father, we can't in all conscience leave Conall to the mercy of Eochaidh. The man is both mad and dissolute. He should not be the ruiri. He has no honor."

"Son, do not misunderstand, the fates have decided our path. I have no intention of leaving Conall and his people to the mercy of that madman. Conall's father was a good friend. Conall's daughters were born under my own roof and are under my protection. If I am not mistaken," he turned to Brion and Áine, "our families may be drawn even closer together in the future. But we need a plan that at least gives us a fighting chance. We also need to consider what happens after Eochaidh is defeated. Who will rule as ruiri and prevent the tribes and nobles reverting to fighting among themselves?" There was a tangible sigh of relief at Deda Mac Sin's words, and it seemed as if the huge log fires had started to throw out more light and warmth as well as the rich aroma of peat.

"I can answer your last question easier than your first, my lord," Conall spoke, as he stood up to carve a slice of pork from the carcass on the platter. "I have no interest in becoming ruiri or even Ard-Righ. My own destiny, it would appear, lies far from these shores." Looking Deda in the eyes, Conall said, "I would hope that you would be the ruiri of this region. I know you would rule justly and with strength."

Íar beamed at his father, and slapped Conall on the back, "Good words, Conall."

Deda was somewhat surprised, but also pleased. He nodded, "Well, we still need a plan to survive first. Has anyone come up with any good ideas?"

Conall looked to Fearghal, who rose. "We've scouted the paths that Eochaidh might consider. I don't think he'll send his forces past Curraghatoor and down the Bohd Carraig valley. The valley is wide, flat and bordered by thick forests. Once he knows that your horsemen are not on his side, he'll not want to risk his army being attacked from the cover of the trees or on ground that is ideal for mounted warriors. Also, Íar can train all the riders to carry and use javelins which should provide an unpleasant surprise for Eochaidh."

Fearghal paused, and seeing he had the attention of all, continued. "My best guess is that the attack will come along the most direct route, the valley that runs east to west beside the mountain. The valley is narrow at the western entrance, and widens as it gets closer to our fort in the east. A well-organized army would take two days to get from Carn Tigherna to Ráth na Cullen. I do not believe that Eochaidh's men will be well disciplined so I suspect we may have four days before they traverse the valley.

The valley narrows at Carraig na Caillí, and a small river runs across the land at that point. The river is not deep, but will be an obstacle that we can use. That is where we hold them. I've discussed this with Nikandros and Íar. The valley isn't narrow enough to allow us to block it. So, instead, we place the shield wall, two deep, in the center of the valley, on the east bank of the river. Horsemen will be positioned behind the wall on the two flanks. Their role is to stop any warriors that try to bypass the wall. The key to this is discipline. Neither the shield wall nor the cavalry can move out of position."

Murmurs of agreement flowed around the table. "A good plan, but one with considerable risk. They will sing great songs about us - if we pull this off." Deda looked at his son, "How many horsemen can we field and how many foot warriors do we have?"

"Not counting the younger trainees, we have seven hundred mounted and one hundred fifty men on foot, Father."

"When the time comes, five hundred horsemen will go with Conall, under your leadership. The rest will remain here. I do not believe that Eochaidh Ruad will leave Curraghatoor alone once he hears about our change of allegiance. He may attack here first, if only to teach a lesson to less loyal nobles." Looking to his own council, Deda said, "There is much to prepare. Get the blacksmiths' forges heated; we will need weapons and armor." To Íar and Nikandros, "You have five hundred horsemen to train. Get some rest. In the months that remain before winter, you will be well-occupied."

As they all reached for the mugs of beer and more food, a gentle cough was heard from beside Conall. "What of my archers? Where will we be placed?" Mórrígan looked around the table, as the conversation paused, her deep green eyes searching each face.

It was Brion, who broke the awkward silence. "You can't be serious, Mórrígan. You've just given birth and now you want to go to battle. Besides, you have just ten archers. Conall, tell my sister to cease her foolishness."

Conall shifted uncomfortably on the wooden bench as brother and sister glared at each other. He looked at Brion and then Fearghal and Nikandros and finally, Mórrígan. "I have considered this and strange as it may seem, I only wish I had more archers. The scars on Mórrígan's hands testify that she has the right to stand with us, but that decision is hers to make."

Brion banged his tankard on the wooden table, splashing its contents. "This is madness. My sister and her archers will be slaughtered."

Mórrígan walked around the table to her brother, and placed her scarred hands against his scarred cheek, "Better we die together on the same field, brother, if that is to be our fate."

"Enough talk of dying," Conall snapped, "I have discussed this with Fearghal and Nikandros. Mórrígan and her archers will take up positions behind the shield wall. They will fight until their last arrow is shot, and then withdraw behind the cavalry. That is my command. Is it understood?"

Deda Mac Sin was somewhat perplexed at Mórrígan's insistence and Conall's consent to her joining the battle. He too, had heard the rumors of the two witches at Ráth na Conall. "I may be able to increase the strength of your archers," he offered. "I have some good hunters who could be persuaded to join the battle. I expect we could find another ten volunteers if Mórrígan agrees and can train them in the time that we have."

Pleased, both Conall and Mórrígan acknowledged the king's offer. Nikandros laughed, "With twenty archers, we may be able to do some damage. We'll need to inform the bowyers and arrowsmiths that we're going to need a lot more equipment."

With the tense atmosphere dispersed, everyone started to talk and the sound rose into a loud din. Above the noise, another voice rang out clearly, "Father, you of course are aware of who is the best archer in Curraghatoor."

Íar groaned, "I should have seen this coming."

A hush descended as Áine stood up from her seat beside Brion, "If Mórrígan will have me, I will stand with her archers. I have as much right to join this fight as any."

All eyes turned to the king. Deda knew his daughter well. Once she had decided on a course of action, she would not be moved. The king sighed, "You have my blessing, Áine. You make an already proud father even more so."

Putting his head in his hands, Brian muttered into his beer. He looked at Fearghal sitting across from him, "Can none of our women be normal?"

Fearghal laughed,. Standing up, he walked round to Brion and slapped him on the back. "Does it matter? We'll all be dead soon, anyway!" He headed for the door, "I need a piss after all this beer."

Mórrígan and her daughters thrived, but after two new moons had passed Conall thought it was time they returned home to Ráth na Conall to prepare for battle. It had been decided that Áine, along with the other archers who had been recruited, would accompany them. It pleased Conall to see Mórrígan with a friend other than the enigmatic, sometimes dark and terrible, Mongfhionn. It also pleased Brion who, in trying to hide his feelings for Áine, only made them more obvious. Íar was to remain at Curraghatoor to train his father's horsemen to fight with javelins.

On the morning before Conall was due to depart, he and Deda were walking the stockade. They saw a lone rider gallop from the north-east towards the fort. The gates of the fort swung open. Once inside the rider immediately leapt from his sweating mount and dashed up the wooden steps to where Conall and Deda stood. Breathlessly, the man fell to his knees, "My king, I'm sorry for this interruption, but there's a large force – hundreds of men – warriors and chariots – rounding the head of Bohd Carraig. They are moving in this direction. At the rate they are walking, they will be here by tomorrow morning – if not sooner."

"Damn that bastard, Eochaidh. He has sent for men from Ailill and Medb. They must be Connachta, coming from that direction." Deda turned to his aide-de-camp, "Sound the alarm, I want the stockade manned, and inform Íar that I want our horsemen assembled. Send out riders to call them in." To Conall, Deda said, "Fortunately the riders are close, having already been summoned for training. Well it looks as if the battle is about to start sooner rather than later, and from a different direction. So much for planning. The Goddess must be laughing at us."

The next morning, over seven hundred horsemen, including Conall's riders, assembled on the densely forested hills to the west of the fort. Deda had expressly forbidden that anyone should ever cut down that forest and now he was very grateful for the cover it provided. Inside the fort, Deda and Conall's men waited. An early morning mist hovered over the ground giving the scene an ethereal feeling. Fearghal nudged Conall and pointed west to the nose of the mountain range on which Curraghatoor stood. The warriors of whom the messenger had spoken were marching in a tight disciplined formation around the outcrop. They were led by six chariots, the iron rimmed wheels of which rumbled over the dry and rocky landscape at the mountains' edge.

Standing in the lead chariot, Aengus Ruad scanned the landscape. He thought he spied a flash of metal from the tree-lined hillside about a thousand paces out and brought his men to a halt. Bearing in mind his queen's command to avoid a fight - at least until he had found Fearghal, Aengus continued alone towards the hillside. As he reached the bottom of the slope he called out, "I am Aengus Ruad of the Ulaid. I have no quarrel with anyone in this land. My queen, Macha Mong Ruad, has sent me on a mission to find her champion, Fearghal Ruad who was exiled long ago. I am commanded not to start any battles on our quest, but we will defend ourselves if needed."

After what seemed like a long time, a single horse cantered out from the trees and down the slope. Mounted on his equally large horse was one of the biggest warriors that Aengus had ever seen, yet he appeared perfectly balanced and graceful. The rider called out in a deep, booming voice, "I am Íar Mac Dedad, son of Deda Mac Sin, king in Curraghatoor. I think that you and I should go alone to the fort and speak with my father. We know of no one called Fearghal Ruad, but there are others who bear the same mark as you in the fort. Our men can remain here until we decide if battle or friendship rules this day."

"Agreed Íar Mac Dedad. I accept your invitation and look forward to speaking with your father, the king." Aengus then grinned broadly, "Although, while you most certainly wear the armor and look to be an impressive warrior, I see no other men that my comrades should fear. Perhaps you are bluffing?"

Íar laughed in response, turned around and waved to the trees. There was an astonishingly loud rustling and cracking of branches and wood as Íar's horsemen emerged from the forest. "I think we can give you a good fight, northerner, if that is what the goddess wills, but first, let's you and me go take a meal and beer with my father."

Aengus called out, "It would be a fine battle indeed, but maybe not today. Will you share my chariot? There is room – even for a warrior as big as you and rings on the back where you can hitch your horse."

Íar scratched his chin and dismounted, "Why not? It will give the ones in the fort something to talk about."

The king eyes were as sharp as in his youth and he watched the proceedings with a growing perplexity. Conall, Fearghal, Nikandros and Brion were equally bemused by the actions of Íar, though not exactly surprised. Íar had demonstrated many times that his bluff and hearty exterior masked a shrewd and nimble mind. A movement to his right caught Conall's eye. He turned to see Mórrígan, her gowns shed and replaced with armor. She had retrieved her bow, an arrow nocked and drawn back in readiness; the muscles in her slender right arm were hard and taut as she held the stance. It amused Conall that beside her stood the faithful Urard, his hands resting on his giant axe. The giant had had a terrible time on the journey to Curraghatoor falling from his mount so often that, in the end, he angrily strode ahead rather than remount.

Fearghal watched closely as Aengus and Íar approached the gates. Then, to everyone's surprise, he exploded in anger, "Damn that woman. Damn all women. Shite!" He ran down the steps towards the gateway roaring at the top of his voice, "Open the bloody gate!" The gatekeepers were frightened to obey, yet frightened to ignore the red-faced northerner and looked to Deda. The king waved to them and the gates swung wide just as Fearghal reached them. He stomped over to the chariot. Ignoring Íar, he growled, "Get down off that bloody chariot, you young idiot, before I trail you off it. I might just beat you to a pulp, in any case."

The chariot rocked on its iron-rimmed wheels, as Aengus grabbed the rail of the cret and leapt over it, landing neatly beside Fearghal. In a broad northern accent, nearly unintelligible to anyone listening he said, "How's about ye, brother?"

Íar, still in the chariot, slapped his hand against his forehead, "I should have known." Something about Aengus had piqued his curiosity. Now, seeing the two standing face-to-face, he could plainly see the family resemblance. Aengus was indeed, in every way, a younger version of Fearghal. Íar also saw the anger and anguish that swept over his friend's face before it relaxed into one of delight at seeing his younger brother.

Gripping his brother's shoulders, Fearghal embraced him, "It is good to see you Aengus, but this is foolishness. You know the geis that is upon us – if two brothers cross the Dyke then only one can cross back."

"Life is short, Fearghal. Introduce me to your friends, tell me what you have been doing in exile these past years." As he looked around the stockade and saw the warriors lined along it, Aengus laughed, "I guess you haven't been sitting comfortably by the fireside with a few young women." Glancing up, he spied Mórrígan, and called out, "My lady, I would appreciate if you would loosen the arrow from that bow. Your muscles are undoubtedly strong, but I would prefer not to be the victim of a lapse in your concentration."

Conall nodded to Mórrígan and the bow was laid aside.

Before escorting Aengus to the Great Hall, Fearghal spoke quietly with Íar, "You have my word that the men you see are not your enemy. They are Cróeb Ruad warriors. I would appreciate if you would send food and drink to them, as a sign that they are welcome at Curraghatoor. Send a messenger with my ring. Tell them that Fearghal Ruad commands them to stand down and make camp."

Íar nodded in agreement and his demeanor switched to amusement. "It would seem that Mongfhionn is not the only one with deep secrets," Íar smirked. "Who would this woman be that you were plainly blaming this on? I sense you were not speaking of Mongfhionn."

Pretending not to hear Íar's last words Fearghal led his brother through the gathered crowds. He moaned, "It's only after sunrise and I feel the need to get drunk."

The air in the Great Hall was filled with expectation and the smells of peat fires and bread baking on giant iron griddles. To everyone's astonishment, Aengus was introduced as Fearghal's brother. The young warrior was made to feel welcome and asked to explain why he had travelled so far beyond the Black Pig's Dyke. That Aengus had travelled with his men through the lands of the Midi and the Connachta without engaging in major battles spoke volumes about his capabilities.

To the amusement of all and the embarrassment of Fearghal, Aengus related how Macha Mong Ruad had been responsible for his brother's exile, but now wanted him back to ensure her coronation as Ard-Righan. Fearghal's friends roared with laughter at the not so subtle inference that this future queen had spread her thighs for Fearghal and that he had not refused the offer.

Fearghal muttered, "I was much younger then," and kept drinking throughout the tale. He was very thankful that Mongfhionn was not present. As Aengus spoke, it became very clear that Fearghal was not just a great warrior, but also a noble of the Ulaid, with considerable authority.

Deda Mac Sin was a man of simple tastes and desires. Therefore, the past few weeks of feasting and drinking had taken its toll on him. Drinking from such an early hour of the morning, he thought, was something that should be left to younger men. Standing unsteady on his feet, he announced, "I will retire, but it is proper that we should give Fearghal Ruad - or Fearghal ó Maoilriain, his proper place as a noble in our company. So again, I welcome you, Fearghal Ruad, to Curraghatoor, but as a king from the North. Tomorrow we shall talk about how, or if, this changes our plans." As he finished, two of the prettier serving maidens stood either side of Deda and taking his arms, accompanied him from the hall.

Aengus said to Íar, "Your father has good taste in women."

"My father loved our mother deeply, but she died in childbirth many years ago. It is good that he has companions to warm his bed."

The conversation became more thoughtful as they described recent events to Aengus. Conall quietly asked, "How many men did you bring?"

"Three hundred men and six chariots."

"Will they fight with us?"

"No, they cannot. They are Macha Mong Ruad's men. Their duty is to protect Fearghal and ensure his safe return to Emain Macha."

Fearghal, displeased at Aengus' words and his voice slurred by the beer said, "Aengus, you understand little of these matters. I am your and their commander - and king. I have given my oath to Conall. The men you brought are mine and I will use them as I see fit. They will fight with me alongside Conall and if necessary, they will die."

A frown darkened Aengus' face and his chin set stubbornly as he spoke, "This cannot be, brother. I gave an oath to Macha to escort you back to the North and I will not break that oath."

Not wanting to see the brothers fight, Conall intervened, "Such an oath cannot be so easily set aside, Fearghal, or else you'll anger the Goddess."

Turning to Aengus, he continued, "However, your presence at this time does suggest that the goddess of battle has a hand in your fate. Perhaps our destinies may lie along the same path." Aengus' anger subsided as he considered Conall words. "Today we will celebrate the re-uniting of two brothers. We will eat, tell many stories and drink ourselves to sleep. Tomorrow, we shall make sacrifices to the gods and seek guidance."

"I begin to understand why my brother has given his allegiance to you, Conall. You have a wise soul. Let's drink and eat. As for the stories, I have many that my brother will probably not want told." Looking at Nikandros, Aengus said, "In truth, I am much more interested to hear stories from this warrior, who is most certainly not from this island."

At sunrise, Deda and Conall carried gifts of gold and armor to the water's edge and tossed them into the flowing waters of the river south of the fort. Following the ceremony, they made their way to the warriors' camp. Conall gasped as they approached, "What on earth has happened?"

The camp was in disarray, with equipment scattered everywhere. Bodies lay on the ground in odd, relaxed positions. Many appeared to be missing articles of clothing. A closer look revealed that a good few of the men had apparently acquired impressive breasts.

A great roar of laughter burst from Íar, "Our men have been getting acquainted and I think the women from the fort have been making our visitors feel at home."

Deda turned to Íar, "Do you still carry that old hunting horn with you? And can you still blow it loud enough to wake the dead? Our men need reminding that they are warriors."

Íar lifted the bronze hunting horn to his lips and, taking a deep breath, sent out several long blasts into the morning air. The effect was immediate. Those with bare arses and tits scrambled to find clothing. Those with bare arses and cocks dived into tents or behind barriers, hoping to find weapons. Íar bellowed, pointing to a makeshift corral, where horses patiently waited to be fed and watered, "Men from Curraghatoor, you neglect your horses and shame your king who stands before you."

Deda remarked to Conall, "You will note Íar's priorities. He has always cared more for his horses than his father!"

Ignoring his father's comments, Íar continued, "You have your duties, men. See to your mounts." Cursing their headaches, the horsemen made their way towards the corral. "As for you, women of Curraghatoor, your chores and duties await." Unable to resist, he said, "And make sure you have nothing between your legs that doesn't belong there!"

Attempting to keep a straight face, Aengus eased his chariot forward and called out, "Men of the Cróeb Ruad, you shame Macha Mong Ruad, you shame me… and you shame your king and commander, Fearghal Ruad." The disorganized scurrying of the former revelers came to a halt as Fearghal walked forward. To a man, they bowed their heads and dropped onto one knee. The effect on the remainder of those accompanying Fearghal was just as stark as they realized the full stature of the man and warrior they had known as Fearghal ó Maoilriain.

The solemn atmosphere was soon broken when, from the rear, a broad northern voice spoke irreverently, "Are ye going to make us kneel all day with no clothes to cover our arses? It's bloody cold at this time of the morning."

Unable to stop himself, Fearghal burst out laughing. "It's a good job that you can fight, otherwise I'd have no use for a bunch of no-good bastards like you. Put some clothes on and line up. We have important matters to discuss."

As the warriors assembled, Conall remarked to Brion that each of them had found a weapon and shield first, before clothes. Fearghal introduced each of the members of his party. As he announced Mórrígan and Áine, there were long whistles of admiration.

Brion remarked to Nikandros, "The Hag help any of them if they get on the wrong side of either of those women."

Fearghal introduced Nikandros who, sitting astride his black horse, in full battle armor and with his crimson cloak flapping in the morning breeze provoked the usual range of comments. Their ribaldry was cut short when he shouted, "Póg ma thoin!"

The irreverent voice dared add, "Well, yer arse is hangin' out for all to see," provoking more laughter.

Describing the current situation and the imminent battle, Fearghal concluded by saying, "The decision is yours. You are all free men and at least some of you are old enough to piss on your own. I will return to the North to fulfill the oath my brother, Aengus, made to Macha, but it may not be this year or the next. If I die in battle, it will be my shade that crosses the Black Pig's Dyke. You may go back North now and you will go as my comrades and with my blessing. Or you can join me and fight with me for Conall Mac Gabhann."

The men fell silent as they pondered the unexpected turn of events. Then the irreverent voice from the rear was heard once more. "So you're telling us that if we stay here, we'll probably piss off the future Ard-Righan; we'll soon be in a battle where we're outnumbered; and we'll most likely have to fight our way home. Would that be accurate?"

Bemused, Fearghal nodded, "That's about right."

Then the voice continued, "I have another question. Do we get paid or are we fighting for fun?"

At this, Conall stepped forward to answer. "Any man who fights with me will be paid and will have his fair share of the spoils. You have my word."

"That's a better deal than you ever gave us, Fearghal Ruad. A good fight and we get paid as well. Sign me up. Now, if you don't mind, I have one final question. Are the women at Ráth na Conall as friendly as the ones here?" The men burst out laughing and roared their decision,

"For Fearghal Ruad, and for Conall Mac Gabhann!"

Deda Mac Sin turned to Conall, "It seems that the goddess continues to be with you. You now have a good start to an army."

Conall nodded, "We need to review our plans. In a few days I'll take my men back to Ráth na Conall. With your permission, I'd like your horsemen to accompany us."

Deda took only a moment to reply, "Granted. Íar will have his men ready to ride in two days."

CHAPTER 14

The gold and yellow hues of the morning sun formed a fitting background as, sitting astride Toirneach, Conall led his army out of Curraghatoor and eastwards along the Bohd Carraig valley. Mórrígan rode beside him: behind them were Fearghal, perched uncomfortably on his horse, Nikandros, Brion, Íar and Áine. Aengus led the chariots next, their wheels rumbling over the hard ground. The mounted contingent was completed by the cavalry riding in columns of one hundred.

In the wake of the horses, wagons filled with supplies, armor and weapons, trundled along the trail. Whips cracked, encouraging the oxen to maintain a steady pace. Walking at the side of the wagons was a sizeable group of women who had decided to continue their friendly relations with the northern warriors. Bringing up the rear were the Cróeb Ruad warriors, throwing coarse and lecherous comments at those in front. In this, they were not discouraged by the women, who quite happily flashed pale tits and arses.

The messenger from Curraghatoor lay on the filthy dirt floor. He had a deep red gash across his throat and blood pooled beside him as his heart pumped its last few beats. Although the poor wretch may not have appreciated it, Faolán reckoned he had done him a huge kindness. The messenger had brought news that Deda Mac Sin would not be sending men for the battle against Ráth na Conall.

On hearing this, Eochaidh flew into a rage and ordered the poor man flayed and his skin removed piece by piece. The intervention of Faolán's knife across the courier's throat had thus saved him an excruciating fate.

As Faolán appraised the assembled nobles in the Great Hall, he observed that they fell largely into two groups. There were those who would do anything to curry favor with Eochaidh, happy to indulge his depravity, satiating their own lusts by abusing the young girls culled from nearby villages. The other group, while smaller, was nonetheless significant. They watched with open distaste at the debauchery around them. Ironically, they were present by force as much as the young maidens. They either feared the king's retribution or their sons and daughters were held as Eochaidh's "guests." Given the opportunity, these nobles would turn their spears and swords on Eochaidh in an instant.

The rage that drove Eochaidh to demand the torture of his own messenger was understandable. Madness had not totally deprived him of his cunning. He knew that the revolt by Deda Mac Sin would encourage wavering nobles, if not to rebel, then to be unenthusiastic about the imminent battle.

"When will all the men be assembled and how many will we have?" Eochaidh asked.

"The winter will soon be on us. Your army will be ready when spring comes. You'll have over five thousand men – even without Deda's horsemen," Faolán responded. He cautiously continued, "We should be wary. I've heard rumors of warriors from the north seen near Curraghatoor."

"You talk like an old man, Faolán. Rumors! Next you'll be telling me you had dreams and visions. If you're afraid to fight that young bastard, I'll have someone else lead the army and you can stay with the women. I want this army marching on the first full moon of spring. Surely, you can defeat slaves and children, with five thousand warriors?"

Stung, Faolán snarled, "I'll kill anyone who dares to take my place as your commander. I'll bring you the boy's head." Turning on his heels, he stormed from the hall.

It was mid-day. Conall smiled as he caught sight of his fort and gestured at the huge red banners, fluttering in the breeze. "Someone has been busy while we were away!" As they approached, the gates opened. Cúscraid and Onchú marched out, followed by forty horsemen and over a hundred and fifty warriors.

"Looks like Onchú was successful in the east," Fearghal said. "That lump of shite, Eochaidh, is in for a nasty shock."

Cúscraid walked alongside Conall as the leaders and captains entered the fort to loud cheers, the thundering of the bodhráns and the sound of many hunting horns. "Welcome home, Conall. We're delighted at the news of Mórrígan and your good fortune. Mind you, with three females against one poor man it would be best if you found a lot of excuses to stay away," Cúscraid laughed. Looking beyond Conall, to the men, chariots and horses, he continued, "I thought Onchú was doing well with his recruiting, but you have put us to shame."

"We had some very good fortune. The horsemen are from Deda. The birth of my girls at Curraghatoor tipped the balance for Íar's father and he agreed to join with us against Eochaidh. As for the rest, they're friends of Fearghal from the North who were looking for him – and a good fight, I think! Their captain is Fearghal's brother, Aengus." Seeing the bemused look on Cúscraid's face, Conall laughed, "We'll catch up and celebrate tonight. From tomorrow, we train and prepare for battle. I don't think we'll see Eochaidh before the winter, although he may send some warriors to test our defenses. My guess is we'll fight in the spring."

Brion called to Onchú loud enough for Conall to hear, "I see from the banners and the shields we have a new emblem and sign to fight under."

"The men wanted something that would unite them under one banner," Cúscraid said. "The artisans came up with the idea of a fiach – a black raven, embroidered on a field of red." Looking to Conall, "We hope you approve. If you're offended, the fault is mine and they will be removed."

"Not in the least, Cúscraid. It's a rare compliment. Although, I'm taken aback at the speed with which it has been done." Then with a wide grin Conall said, "Now, tell me how you propose to decorate and paint another three hundred shields before we fight Eochaidh? And five hundred smaller shields for the horsemen!"

As he started to stammer a response, Cúscraid was rescued by the approaching crowd of villagers bringing gifts for the baby girls. Conall and Mórrígan dismounted and had the twin girls brought forward to loud cheering. The throng parted, allowing a delegation of village elders and artisans to come forward with gifts of fine jewelry and leather. When the girls' gifts had been accepted, two craftsmen stepped forward, each carrying an ornately designed bronze, iron and gold helmet. Each was crowned with a small golden fiach crested with trailing black plumes. The men bowed to Conall and Mórrígan. "A king should have a helmet worthy of him and so should his queen."

Humbled at the generosity shown, Conall thanked the men and shouted his thanks to the crowds. "Tonight we'll feast, drink and tell stories of brave warriors. Tomorrow we begin the preparations for our revenge on Eochaidh Ruad."

Fearghal caught up with Conall as he made his way through the crowds. "That's a very pretty helmet. Worth a year's wages I'd guess. I might be tempted to kill you on the battlefield for that prize, or Nikandros may kill you from jealousy at not having the best helmet anymore!" Laughing, Fearghal clapped his hands on Conall's and Nikandros' shoulders and propelled them forward to the Great Hall.

The plain to the south-east of the fort was ideal to practice new strategies. Before the winter storms arrived, the ever-shortening days were spent in readying warriors for battle. Healers at the fort were fully occupied treating cuts, bruises and egos as the men took their instruction very seriously. Fortunately, the discipline and previous training of the Cróeb Ruad warriors lent itself to the tactics of the shield wall. They took to it and their new armor enthusiastically - especially when it was explained that the role of the wall was like a battering ram to break apart their enemies, leaving them open to slaughter and plunder.

Íar's riders perfected the use of javelins and as Conall watched the training, he could see that the riders were becoming more comfortable and accurate with their throwing style. They had also realized how the javelin could be used at close range alongside their swords and axes.

Mórrígan's archers had all been fitted with the new style of bow. They learned to appreciate the power and distance their arrows could be propelled and with a high degree of accuracy. Their speed had also improved so that an arrow could be drawn and loosed at every count of twenty. Arm and shoulder muscles ached at the end of each practice session and the archers paid regular visits to the healers and to their Cróeb Ruad colleagues for advice on building muscles.

The advent of winter snows and storms all but finished any training and Ráth na Conall slumbered, covered in a thick blanket of cloud, ice and snow. The residents wrapped themselves in furs and hibernated like the animals in the nearby forests, only coming out of their communal dwellings for food, drink and to relieve themselves. The women who did not have families to stay with soon found they were made welcome under the furs of the warriors. By mid-winter, the dwellings took on a strong, heady and musky atmosphere of unwashed bodies and sex.

By early spring, an edge of frustration and impatience permeated the fort as they waited on news of Eochaidh Ruad. Adding to a growing level of discontent, the mock battles designed to occupy the men had to be discontinued as they were producing too many casualties. Even the recreational visits of the many camp followers did little to lessen the grumbling. Indeed, many of the young women now complained of disinterest and neglect from their formerly eager lovers. The steady rasping of sharpening stones against metal could be heard in the still of the evening.

Several nights after the yellow orb of a new spring full-moon appeared on the horizon, a rider came galloping to the fort. Breathlessly, he reported the message they all wanted to hear, "Eochaidh Ruad has left Carn Tigherna. He approaches with a force of about five thousand men." Previous frustrations dissipated like the morning mist on a hot summer day.

CHAPTER 15

413 B.C.

After much discussion, Conall and the Chomhairle settled on a simple strategy over some of the more exotic options suggested. It was a philosophy that Conall was to repeat many times in the future.

The cavalry and chariots under Íar, Nikandros and Aengus were dispatched immediately, to secure the ground behind the river at Carraig na Caillí. Led by Conall, the rest of the army marched resolutely to the valley.

Later in the day, as they approached the river, Conall was glad he did not have to rely on it as a barrier. The shallow river was frozen solid. While it would prove little obstacle for horses and chariots, it would slow the enemy down once the ice had been cracked. With only a few hours of daylight remaining, supplies were quickly unloaded from the wagons and camp set up. Soon dozens of fires were burning. In the dark, cold night, the sounds of horses neighing and softly nickering in their makeshift corral were as comforting to the men as the warmth and light from the fires.

The following morning, Conall's men ate, had a beer, checked armor and weapons, and reported to their ceannairí céad – the leaders of a hundred. All were thankful that the blacksmiths and leather workers at Ráth na Conall and Curraghatoor had worked all the hours of the day and night during the winter to ensure they were well-equipped.

The wall, now around two hundred and fifty men wide and two

deep, stood twenty paces back from the river bed. The rows were staggered to allow the men row room to throw their javelins and to be resupplied quickly. Once engaged in battle, the wall would close and shields lock. Behind the wall, Mórrígan and Áine's archers broke the frozen earth with daggers, each stabbing their supply of arrows into the dirt. If more were needed, Cathán and Beacán stood ready to run to the wagons.

The horses, divided into two divisions, each led by Íar and Nikandros, were positioned on the left and right flanks of the wall. In front of them, rocking back and forward, were Aengus' chariots, three on each flank. The chariots, drawn by four horses for speed, were equipped for battle. Each wheel hub now sported a vicious long knife.

Conall, Fearghal, Brion, Cúscraid and Onchú used the height of their horses to survey the valley before them. As they waited for Eochaidh, Conall heard the sound of hoof-beats on the hard ground behind them. A party of eleven horsemen drew up, their horses snorting and sweating from a hard ride. One detached from the party, removed his helmet and walked his mount around to Conall. Deda Mac Sin, with a smile rivaling his son's looked at Conall and said, "With all that is at stake did you really think I was going to miss this battle?" Pointing to a small grassy mound, "However, I will stay behind your archers and leave the battle to younger men. That piece of dirt should give me a good view."

The contrast between the two armies was stark. Though well outnumbering Conall, Eochaidh's forces were largely a mob of the reluctant, the recalcitrant, the sullen and the drunk. By and large, Eochaidh's men expected to be facing a bunch of upstarts who had got above themselves and needed to be taught a lesson. The army was a mass of bodies trudging along the valley without form or grace. However, at its heart strode two thousand, battle-proven warriors that Faolán knew he could count on. The rest of the nobles and warbands he considered expendable. Faolán, deep in thought, rode until his nose wrinkled as an unwashed Eochaidh maneuvered his chariot alongside.

"I don't trust those nobles and their warbands at the rear. Why haven't you put them at the front? Let their bastards get killed first and save the ones that are loyal to me."

"I could do that, my lord, but the nobles you are referring to would as likely join Conall mac Gabhann as fight him. Also, if they fought and won, they would claim that the victory was theirs, not yours. Either way, the omens would not be good for you. Better to have them in the rear. When the battle is going well, they will join in for the plunder."

Coughing harshly, Eochaidh spat a mixture of blood and phlegm onto the ground. Over the winter he had found it increasingly hard to breathe. Most days his wracking cough was accompanied by bloody spit that sprayed anyone unfortunate enough to be close. "I suppose that makes sense, but mark my words, Faolán, your neck will be stretched and your flesh food for the worms if Conall Mac Gabhann is not in my hands this day."

Íar's scout trotted over to Conall, "Eochaidh is about two thousand paces away. The sun is on the rise and blinds them. They are unaware of our position."

Conall nodded and turned to face his men, "It seems that the battle will soon begin. At Ráth na Conall, the Romans expected us to fight like barbarians - we didn't. Today, Eochaidh Ruad's men will fight as Spurius thought we would. They will fight like barbarians and die on our shield wall." The men roared and started to slap weapons against shields.

The clamor was heard along the valley. Faolán knew a small warband could not make that much noise and cursed the angle of the sun. It had disturbed Faolán that his normally excellent spy network had been quite lacking in information over the winter, although, he had put this down to the bad weather conditions. Furthermore, his scouts had not returned this morning and thus he was truly blind. But at five hundred paces, Faolán understood everything. So, Deda

Mac Sin has ambitions and has chosen his side, he thought. Surveying the red wall on the opposite bank of the river and the flanking horsemen, Faolán knew that this was not to be an easy battle.

Raging, a purple-faced Eochaidh struck Faolán's charioteer as a substitute for Faolán. "Why didn't you tell me that young bastard had this many men? Is that Deda Mac Sin's horsemen? I'll strip the skin off his flesh and feed his daughter to the dogs."

Holding his temper, Faolán suggested that they go forward and inspect their enemy's forces. Eochaidh was reluctant to put himself so close to danger, but knowing his army watched, had little choice. Both chariots moved forward until they came to the west bank of the river. Conall cantered forward on his black stallion, accompanied by Fearghal and Brion. Removing his helmet, he glared fiercely at Eochaidh. Unable to hold his gaze, Eochaidh cursed and spat on the ground.

"Tell your men to go, Eochaidh Ruad. They will not pass and we will fill this river bed with their blood. Fight me. Let us settle our differences – king to king." Conall spoke knowing Eochaidh would likely not take up his challenge, but it would please the goddess that the offer had been made.

Eochaidh spat his response. "You are no king, you insolent young bastard. I'll gut you like your father. My men will have your so-called queen - like they did your mother."

Conall's eyes flared in anger, and it was with great restraint that he did not cross the river bed. "Prepare for battle then, for by the end of this day you will not be the ruiri of this or any land."

While Conall and Eochaidh spoke, Faolán carefully measured the forces before him, swearing as he recognized the marks on the arms of the men that stood behind the young king. Faolán cursed the day the bastard Cassius Fabius Scaeva with his Roman gold, had come to Carn Tigherna, convincing Eochaidh to slaughter a previously useful and trouble-free settlement.

The exchange over, both parties turned around. As they did, a wail came from above Carraig na Caillí. Across the valley, horses reared up, snorted and squealed. Again, the terrible high-pitched screeching that almost burst ear drums rent the air. All looked to the rock. No one could miss the grey-cloaked figure, her arms stretched to the sky, or the huge black cloud of ravens circling, their cries of *kraa kraa* filling the air. Then there came an abrupt silence and a voice of anger and dread spoke.

"Judgment is at hand for Eochaidh Ruad and those who fight with him. You are cursed by this land, by the waters and by the trees. Your geis is now due, for as it was spoken, 'The ravens will strike you down and will feast on your flesh.'"

Equally terrified and enraged, Eochaidh drove his chariot back to his men, screaming, "Kill them. Kill them all. Kill the witch." Confused and unnerved by the king and the Sidhe, the men began to move forward under the prodding and cajoling of their leaders. Gradually, they moved faster and gathered momentum. Shouting war cries and curses at the enemy, they banged weapons against shields as they charged forward.

As Conall's men prepared for the onslaught, a familiar insolent voice was heard, "Fearghal, if that's who I think it is, you're in deep shite when she finds out who wants you back." The men laughed as Conall and Fearghal dismounted and joined the front row.

To Fearghal's right Brion grinned, "Great timing the Sidhe has, as always."

Shouting over the growing din, Conall commanded, "Stand firm. Hold the wall. Break them on it. Archers, draw your arrows. Let loose when they are within range."

Behind the wall, archers nocked black arrows and grunted as they drew bowstrings back. Mórrígan took measure and as Eochaidh's horde crossed her markers yelled, "Loose arrows." Flight after flight of lethal black shafts rose high in the mid-day sky and dropped on the approaching warriors. Even in the cold spring weather, many were almost naked. Most wore no armor. Their cries filled the air as iron arrowheads bit deep into soft flesh. The fallen trampled underfoot by their comrades.

By the time Eochaidh's men had reached the west bank of the river, and stepped onto the ice, over a thousand arrows had done their damage. Each of the archers had been assigned a guard whose duty was to be their shield. As always, the faithful Urard kept watch over Mórrígan. The queen called for more arrows to be brought and gave her orders, "Spread along the wall. Choose your targets. Keep safe. Stay with and be guided by your protector."

The river bed was no more than fifteen paces wide. As the screaming warriors reached the mid-point, Conall bellowed, "Javelins." The front ranks of Eochaidh's army shuddered, staggered as if drunk, and then fell on the stone-like ice as they were struck by hundreds of iron-tipped missiles. More javelins were passed forward as men grunted and strained to keep up their constant onslaught. Soon the river bed was a mass of bodies, some dead, others writhing in agony as blood ran from broken flesh or spurted from torn arteries. Scrambling over former friends, those remaining threw themselves in fury at the wall of red and black shields.

Seething with rage, Eochaidh watched impotently as his army's charge was blunted and bled to death on the ice. Eochaidh screamed at Faolán from his chariot, "Do something, you bastard. What sort of an incompetent commander are you? You'll hang for this." Incensed at the ranting of the unhinged and slavering king, Faolán wished he had traded his loyalty more wisely. He vowed that when the battle was over that he would personally cut Eochaidh's throat.

As he surveyed the growing slaughter, Faolán estimated he had lost nigh five hundred men, dead or injured, in the first onslaught against the wall. He also was aware, at no great surprise, that the less loyal nobles had held their men back. A gap had now opened up between these nobles' men and those fighting. To win, Faolán knew he had to break the shield wall. He also hoped that Conall's stock of missiles had been spent and the battle would move to tactics he understood.

He needed a diversion and called Sleibhin to him. "Send messengers to the battle leaders. Tell them to fall back from the river and attack on the right and left flanks. But tell our own men to fall back to the higher ground with me. We need better ground to fight on than that slick of ice. Conall thirsts for revenge. He'll not let us walk from this field without giving chase." Sleibhin grunted and shambled off to relay the orders.

Conall watched as the attackers broke off, streaming left and right towards his chariots and horses. The front row of the wall heaved a collective sigh of relief as the screaming mob ebbed away, hoping to find an easier fight elsewhere. Splattered in blood and gore, as were all those in the front rank, Conall turned to Fearghal, "If you were Eochaidh's commander what would you do?"

"Don't underestimate Faolán. He's shrewd, but he needs time to reform and control his men." Shrugging at the river of the dead and dying before them, "These were mostly drunken assholes, too dumb to know they were being used. Faolán will have kept his best men behind, hoping to weaken us with these bastards. Now he'll want to fight on a field of his own choosing. If it were me, I'd retreat back to that higher ground and wait for you to attack. The attacks on the flanks are a diversion to gain him time to organize his main force."

On the left flank, Aengus watched hundreds of screaming warriors run towards him. He turned to Íar, "I think it's our turn."

Íar simply grinned, "And about time too, I was getting bored. Just keep those damn chariot knives away from my horses or I'll use one to skin you alive!"

On the right, Nikandros, rubbed the soft, velvet neck of his horse, and gave the order to advance. On both flanks, chariots moved forward, slowly at first, but quickly gaining momentum as horse teams strained and pulled against their harnesses. The role of a chariot was simple – create terror and disorder. This they did very effectively as few warriors would willingly choose to stand in the path of a speeding war chariot with its slashing knives and thundering hooves. As the chariots scythed through Eochaidh's men, bones were crushed, flesh torn from limbs, and limbs torn from bodies.

Close behind, Conall's cavalry charged into the midst of the attackers. Bone-hard hooves and great yellow teeth did as much damage as the slashing, hacking and stabbing of their riders. To the right, swinging his doru in a wide arc, Nikandros cleaved a path of destruction, slicing and thrusting into unprotected flesh. He admired the bravery of these fierce warriors, but most fought without armor, making his work much easier. On the other flank,

Íar's men continued their bloody harvest and soon the maimed and the dead lay scattered over the valley floor.

A few of the more astute warband leaders, comprehending the dire situation to which they had been sacrificed, spotted a gap between the shield wall and the cavalry. It was a path that would lead them to the archers and the small group of horsemen that guarded Deda Mac Sin. Ignoring the slaughter around them, the leader of each band drove their men towards the gap. The warbands, each containing around a hundred men, made for Deda Mac Sin and Mórrígan, easily identified by her fine helmet and familiar battle markings. Hoping for glory, the warriors screamed themselves into frenzy as they charged.

Suddenly alert to the danger streaming towards them, Deda shouted to his guards, "Attack the warbands. Protect the archers." As his horsemen charged towards the screaming enemy, Deda dismounted and stood beside his daughter. Turning to Áine and Mórrígan, he drew his sword and said grimly, "I hope your archers are well-trained. Make each arrow count. Pick your targets well." To Urard he said, "Take ten men. Guard the left flank. I'll take the rest and hold the right." Urard nodded and stood at the center of his men, balancing his battle axe in his hands.

Mórrígan surveyed her archers. Her stomach knotted when she saw that each had just a handful of arrows. "Aim for the leaders. When you exhaust your arrows, draw your weapons. Be guided by your guard – and pray to the goddess." As she feared, the arrows were shot rapidly. The oncoming fighters hesitated for a moment, then quickly regained their momentum. Urard's first swing whipped downwards, slicing through the leading warrior's shoulder. The severed stump sprayed those around him with hot, dark blood. The warrior shrieked in pain and fell to the dirt, only to be trampled by those behind.

Desperately, they slashed and hacked at the screaming mob, but were pushed back into an increasingly compressed area on the mound. Deda breathed harshly as he used his shield to push back on the foul smelling, broken-teethed warriors yelling and spitting at him. He slashed at exposed flesh, hearing men cry out as limbs were severed and flesh torn. Deda's riders were taking a toll, with swords and axes, but the momentum of the attack had carried many of the warbands' warriors past this line of defense.

As a group of warriors approached, Mórrígan sent her last arrow into the eye of the closest. He fell, clutching his face as blood streamed from the socket. Urard, realizing her danger, swung around and sent his axe deep into the back of a trailing warrior, splitting his spine in two. The body fell jerking to the ground as life ebbed away. Urard dispatched another attacker, as his axe bit into the muscle and tendons in the man's neck, nearly severing his head.

Crouching and armed with daggers in both hands, Mórrígan watched as two warriors advanced on her. As one jabbed at her with a spear, she rolled to the side and then forward, slashing at the man's calves. He grunted in pain as he felt the blades open up deep wounds in his legs, then swung around to thrust at her again. Rolling to the side again, Mórrígan slashed the thick tendon at the back of his ankle and saw him stumble as his maimed leg failed him. Seizing her chance she leapt forward, plunging her blades into his back and neck. Blood poured from his wounds as he fell forward.

Swinging around Mórrígan turned to face the second warrior as he crouched, ready to strike. Áine had seen his approach and swung her own short sword. The edge of the blade sliced through the warrior's threadbare clothes and ripped along his left side, yet did little more than make him briefly pause and grunt. It was, however, enough time for Mórrígan to leap forward and efficiently slash his throat. The warrior fell forward, clutching at his torn neck, his life seeping into the dirt.

In the rear row of the shield wall, engrossed in what was happening to his front, Torcán ó Dubhghaill, now promoted to ceannaire céad, heard shrieking and yelling behind him and glanced back over his shoulder. He was horrified to see the skirmish taking place and bellowed at his cohort, "Turn. Protect the queen!" A hundred warriors turned as one. Seeing Mórrígan and Deda about to be overrun, they sprinted towards the melee roaring curses, hoping to distract the enemy warriors.

To Torcán, it seemed an agonizingly long time before he had covered the gap and was able to bring his axe to bear on the first warrior. The warrior's skull split open, splattering blood and brain gore. As he retrieved his axe Torcán grunted at a sharp stab of pain in his left side. His eyes looked down at the spearhead being withdrawn from his armor and followed the shaft to a crazed and barechested warrior. The man readied to spit Torcán with his next thrust.

Enraged with pain, Torcán dropped his shield and seized the spear shaft with his left hand. Then, to the attacker's surprise, Torcán swung his axe across the warrior's chest. The blade ripped a deep gash from nipple to nipple. Bellowing, the warrior reached for the dagger in his belt. Before he could throw the knife, the Cróeb Ruad warrior who had stood beside Torcán in the wall, opened up his side with a sword thrust. Torcán mouthed, "Go raibh maith agat," to the warrior, and finished the unfortunate attacker off with a swinging blade to the head.

The warbands, now caught between Mórrígan and Deda's group and the reinforcements, were quickly slaughtered. Deda mused that it was sad that the men and their leaders had thrown their lives away foolishly for a worthless king. "They would have made a good addition to our forces," he thought.

For Faolán, the diversion had worked better than he had expected and like Deda, he considered it unfortunate that several warbands had proven themselves as brave fighters, but to no purpose. His chosen men, now assembled on the high ground, waited for Conall. Truthfully, he doubted his men's ability to defend a position. It was his hope that Conall would be angry and foolish enough to attack him on the hill. However, given that Conall Mac Gabhann so far had shown an inordinate amount of common sense and focus, Faolán had little confidence in him making such an obvious error.

Squeals of rage diverted Faolán's attention, and he cursed the coward who now wheeled to and fro along the rows of his men. Shaking his head, Faolán strode towards his king's chariot. As it made to pass him, he seized the reins, bringing the team of horses to an abrupt halt. Ignoring the threats and the lash from the horse whip, Faolán rounded the back of the chariot and jumped into the cret. His patience now exhausted, he grabbed the king by the throat and pulled him closer until their noses almost touched.

"Hit me with that whip again and I'll slit your throat, you miserable bastard. These men have enough to think about without hearing your ravings. Now, either grow some balls and fight alongside your men or get out of my sight."

Eochaidh spluttered, meaning to strike back at Faolán, but refrained as he saw Faolán's hand move to the hilt of his sword. As Faolán jumped down from the chariot, Eochaidh whipped his horses and wheeled his chariot around.

Conall moved his men to the other side of the river bed and now looked to the forces assembled on the far hill. Mórrígan stood beside him as he called Fearghal, Nikandros, Íar, Cúscraid, Brion and Onchú to him. Wiping blood from his face Deda Mac Sin also joined them.

"I thought you were only here to observe the fight - not to join in," Conall remarked.

"It would appear the goddess had a different view," Deda growled, "and if it wasn't for that young Torcán, more than a few of us would have been watching the rest of the battle from Mag Mell."

"Torcán will be thanked properly later. Right now, there's a force of two thousand men on the high ground. I'm open to suggestions as to how we dislodge them."

"Eochaidh's men are attackers not defenders. Give them a good target and they'll not be able to resist it. His commander will not be able to hold them back." Everyone turned around at the voice of Mongfhionn as she strode into the circle of friends and leaders.

"Can you not just summon a thunderstorm or something as a diversion? The ravens were pretty effective earlier." Fearghal's eyes glinted mischievously as he smiled at Mongfhionn. She slipped her hood off and shook her long hair loose. "Water, earth and forests are my kingdoms. Take a look at the sky you big oaf. It's a perfect day. Not a cloud in the sky. I have nothing to work with – yet."

"Well, if your curse on Eochaidh is to come true, that force on the hill has to be defeated. So who'll be bait for the trap?" Fearghal looked around.

It was Deda who spoke up first, "Well that's not too difficult to work out – Conall, Mongfhionn, myself," he looked at Conall as he hesitated, "and Mórrígan."

Fearghal made to object, but was halted by Mongfhionn's hand on his arm, "I agree with Deda."

Conall breathed deeply and looked to Mórrígan who nodded in solidarity, "We four, with a hundred men, will lead the army. As we get closer to the hill, we'll break away from the main force. It will look as if we are eager to be the first to battle – something Eochaidh's men will understand. The rest, led by Fearghal, Cúscraid, Brion and Onchú will let us get far enough away that we look an easy target for Eochaidh." Looking at a pensive Íar, Conall continued, "Íar and Nikandros will go left and right as if they mean to go around to the back of the hill. They will keep a good distance away, but remain in line with us. Remember, the only way this works is if we look like an easy target."

When he called for volunteers to make up the foolish hundred, Conall was faced with five hundred men. A smiling and proud Fearghal made the final selection, amid loud grumbles from those who were not chosen. The smart-arse was chosen last and grinned widely as he quipped, "Good selection Fearghal - for once!"

Fearghal looked to Brion, "You do know that we're going to have to kill that bastard ourselves or promote him if he survives!"

Since his duty to Mórrígan was now his life's purpose, Urard would not countenance a no and probably would have gone even if ordered otherwise.

Mid-afternoon Conall's forces marched or trotted forward.

On the high ground, Faolán watched Conall's men march towards his position. He laughed and thumped Sleibhin on the back. At last, something seemed to be going right for him and as he had predicted. Conall, filled with a lust for revenge, could not resist attacking. Another good omen was that the afternoon sun was now in his enemy's eyes. He turned to his men and bellowed out his orders, "The young bastard is coming to us. No man is to attack until I say so. I'll kill anyone who disobeys me." Faolán's mood brightened further as he watched Deda Mac Sin's horsemen go wide to his left and right, "The fools think they can outflank me."

Conall strode forward, his shield slung over his back, and constantly altering the grip on his axes. To his right, Deda Mac Sin matched his stride and cursed about being too old for this sort of thing. The king settled his shield comfortably on his left arm. A well-used sword, whose edge glinted gold in the sun, rested naturally in his hand. Conall smiled and hoped that, should he live as long, he would look as good as Deda.

On Deda's right, Mongfhionn stared purposely forward, her long pace enabling her to stay alongside the others. The Sidhe's eyes constantly scanned the land, the skies and the forests looking for any means to take advantage of her natural and considerable powers. In her hands, she balanced her oak staff. At least she knew how to wield the staff as a weapon. Finally, on Conall's left, Mórrígan tested the tension of her bow, adjusted the arrows in the quiver that hung on her belt, selected one and nocked it. She would be the first to strike, but had a limited supply of arrows. Her life could depend, once more, on the two blades that hung from her belt. She smiled in the knowledge that her shadow, in the form of the huge frame of Urard, walked behind her.

His gut told him it was too good to be true, but Faolán's feverish hope refused to let him consider that it was he who was being lured into a trap. He would destroy Conall and Deda Mac Sin in one battle and then he would turn his attention to Eochaidh. Faolán had decided that it was time for Eochaidh's reign to come to a close. A knife across Eochaidh's scrawny throat would send him into the next world and put Faolán on the throne as ruiri. None of the nobles in the south-east would stand against him.

He studied the black, raven-feather plumes on their gold-decorated helmets as Conall and his witch, Mórrígan came closer. "Look. The arrogant bastard Conall Mac Gabhann and his striapach insult us with their arrogance and fancy armor," he shouted to his men who, in reply, roared curses and slapped spears and swords against their shields.

The noise from the high ground reached Conall's group. "It seems that Eochaidh's men are looking forward to welcoming us," he remarked to Deda, before turning around and shouting to Fearghal, "Don't be late!" To the chosen hundred, he called out, "Pick up the pace. Let's bait the trap." The men roared in response and increased their pace. They looked forward to being first to fight, but were well-aware their mission was to make sure Conall, Deda, Mórrígan and Mongfhionn were protected until their comrades joined them.

Faolán and Eochaidh watching from the hilltop, discerned that slowly, but steadily, Conall and a small band were pulling ahead of the rest. "The young hothead has finally made a mistake," Faolán muttered to himself. Behind him, his men had also seen the smaller group separate from the main body. As a result, they were becoming restless to take advantage of what they saw as a gift from the goddess. "Not until I say," growled Faolán toward the nearest rumblings. The tone in his voice assured them that punishment would be swift and harsh for those who disobeyed.

Moments later, Eochaidh, in a moment of lucidness and from the vantage of his chariot, realized that Conall's front row was well apart from the main forces and that they had almost reached the hill. Seizing the reins, he rode up and down the rows of warriors shouting, "A hundred gold pieces for the heads of Conall Mac Gabhann and his whore; a hundred gold pieces for the heads of Deda Mac Sin and the witch Mongfhionn; and ten gold pieces for the heads of the rest of the bastards who follow Conall Mac Gabhann." There was a moment of silence. Then, as one, the men ignored the furious cursing of Faolán and ran screaming down the slope to meet their enemy.

Conall couldn't believe his luck as he watched the horde stream off the hilltop and down the slope. His own men were still on level ground which was much better than fighting on a slope. However, the sheer momentum of Eochaidh's warriors was going to be a grave test. He called out, "Form two ranks. Mongfhionn and Mórrígan to the rear. Now!" Mórrígan let loose flight after flight as they ran to their positions behind the warriors.

On the left, Íar watched as Eochaidh's men rushed down the hill. When he judged that the mass was not going to be stopped or recalled, he shouted orders for his horsemen to gallop towards his father and Conall. On the right flank, Nikandros had, like Íar, judged that Eochaidh's warriors were fully committed to the assault and gave the order to close on Conall's group. Now well distanced from Conall, Fearghal bellowed orders to increase the pace of the main body, praying that he could reach Conall before the small band were overrun.

As he stood on the hilltop, fuming at Eochaidh, Faolán was ideally positioned to observe Deda's horsemen change direction and to see that they were rapidly closing the gap with Conall. Chariots, previously obscured by the main force, now wheeled around the warriors with their drivers encouraging their teams forward with whip cracks. Faolán watched as the main body of Conall's army steadily closed the space behind Conall's group.

"Shite!" he exploded, now understanding the trap that was about to be sprung. Encouraged by Eochaidh's gold, his men were about to recklessly throw themselves at the bait. Faolán realized there was only one way to save his men and regain the advantage. His men had to reach and kill Conall's band before the supporting forces linked up with him. Turning to Eochaidh, in fury, he shoved the man aside and then dashed to catch up with his men, shouting and bellowing, "Faster you bastards, faster."

Fortunately, only the leading wedge of about five hundred of Eochaidh's men crashed into the small shield wall. The force drove Conall's men back four paces before they were able to get a solid footing. The front row's javelins stabbed at the snarling, foul-smelling, sour-breathed warriors. Spit flecked beards and drool flowed down chins, as the frenzied attackers battered the wall with bodies and shields, slashing and hacking with swords and axes. The rear row of the wall, having steadied, pressed shields against the front row then took up their javelins and stabbed high. Screams of pain and rage rose from Eochaidh's men as cruel iron spikes pierced flesh and bone. The attack faltered, then was reinforced as the slower-paced warriors arrived. Once again the shield wall was slowly pushed back, but stayed solid under the unrelenting pressure.

Along the wall, the grunts of men resonated as they strained to hold their position. Breathing hard and pushing against the mass of attackers, Conall and Deda stabbed high and low at exposed flesh. Soon shields and faces were covered in sweat and blood. Howls of pain punctured the still afternoon air as blades and spikes found targets. It was not long before Conall's front row was as bloody from seeping cuts as from the gore of their assailants. Fighting desperately, but slowly losing men to injuries, the formation was forced back and compressed as the attackers surrounded the beleaguered band.

Above the battle sounds, Conall shouted, "Turn!" Shields locked, the men closed the circle and faced the determined enemy baying for their blood. Mórrígan and Mongfhionn were drawn into the center along with the growing number of wounded. Gritting his teeth, Conall, his ears numbed to the unceasing clamor of battle, thrust a javelin into yet another warrior. His leather wrist bands, slashed and torn from the constant blade strikes, were now held to his wrist by blood. Arms ached from the endless need to defend and attack.

"I hope my son gets here soon," breathed Deda thrusting his sword into yet another torso. "The young ladies would miss me this evening."

Conall spat and said hoarsely, "Do you not think you're getting a bit old for that? You need a quiet life."

Deda snorted and laughed aloud, and not for the first time Conall was reminded from whom Íar had inherited his great laugh and strength. "After this battle, I'll need a lot of care and attention to be able to do my lady friends justice."

In the ragged circle, the small band fought hard and viciously, but soon the number of wounded and dead approached those still able to fight. Mórrígan, her arrows long exhausted, slashed at the legs of any warrior within reach of her short blades. Those unfortunates who came close to her fell to the bloody axe of Urard. The oak staff of Mongfhionn, thrust into the faces of many warriors, smashed noses and blinded eyes. The sigils carved into the staff glowed eerily as it became soaked in blood.

Faolán pushed, shoved and in some cases killed his way to the front of his men. He cajoled, kicked and shouted in desperation for them to reform and face the coming onslaught, but his efforts fell largely on deaf ears. His men were wild and irrational with battle fever.; fixed on securing their reward from Eochaidh with the heads of Conall's band.

In frustration and resignation, Faolán launched himself at the small circle of shields battering his nearest opponent with the boss on his round shield and lashing out with his battle axe. His furious attack pushed his adversary back a pace, opening up a space in the circle, but as Faolán made to take advantage of the gap his face met the solid oak head of Mongfhionn's staff. Temporarily stunned, his nose broken and gushing blood, Faolán staggered back into the mass of bodies.

The sound of hunting horn blasts confirmed Faolán's fears. His men having pushed back and encircled Conall's group, had left a track wide enough for a chariot to pass through between them and the hillside. It was a gift that Aengus' chariots did not refuse. Shouting curses at Eochaidh's men they drove their chariots at a furious pace behind the attackers. The sharp blades on the wheels carved a bloody swathe through human flesh. Shards of white bone and lumps of meat spun into the air. Having reached the outer edge of Eochaidh's men, the chariots wheeled around and made their horrific run again and again.

Soon Íar and Nikandros' riders arrived and immediately launched a hail of missiles that decimated the flanks of Faolán's warriors. Before long Fearghal's men closed the gap hacking a path through to link up with the beleaguered Conall. Under shouted commands, Fearghal's four hundred warriors fanned out, forming a protective wall for Conall's group. Relieved that he had been reinforced, Conall shouted, "Bog ar aghaidh - forward!" and the combined ranks started to push forward, slashing and stabbing at

Eochaidh's warriors.

At last it dawned on Eochaidh's men that the jaws of an iron-toothed trap had snapped shut on them. Faced with fresh warriors, Deda's horsemen on their flanks, and Aengus' chariots cutting a bloody track across their rear, the men panicked and scattered in all directions, searching for a path of escape. Seeing his enemy's disarray, a reinvigorated Conall yelled, "Ionsaí!" With a roar of victory, his men charged into the midst of the fleeing rabble.

The archers supplied Mórrígan with a refreshed quiver of arrows and she began to pick her targets. The men's lack of armor made them vulnerable to the powerful bows and iron arrowheads. Meanwhile, Mongfhionn, her striking blonde hair appearing afire, used staff and dagger to cripple and kill her chosen prey. Her swirling, great, grey cloak caught by the wind made her slim body an almost impossible target for those brave enough to stand and face her.

A bloody scythe harvested the ranks of Eochaidh's warriors. If they ran, they were struck down by the long swords of the cavalry or trampled and dismembered by the battle chariots. Those brave enough to turn and stand fought courageously, but were overpowered by the fresh Cróeb Ruad warriors, who slashed and hacked without mercy. With the advantage of their armor, the Cróeb Ruad soon dominated the battlefield, littering the ground with twisted, broken and bloodied corpses.

Realizing that his army was in tatters, Eochaidh screeched the foulest of curses at Conall. Then he wheeled his chariot around, whipped his horses and rode off to the west. As he passed the nobles who had been reluctant to fight, Eochaidh, bloody saliva and spit dripping from his mouth, spat venomous words, "I will have my revenge on you bastards. I'll flay every one of you and your sons and daughters. I am your rightful king. I am your king."

The nobles looked on with a mixture of disgust and disinterest. Their scouts had reported how the battle had gone and their present concern was how the young king and victor would treat them after the battle.

Faolán's nose was twisted and broken from Mongfhionn's staff and his face was encrusted with blood, but he had recovered and slashed his way towards Conall. Finally, spotting the distinctive helmet of the young king, he used his anger and shield to bludgeon his way closer.

Conall swinging his axe blade across another warrior's throat, once more felt the splash of warm blood on his face and arms. His arms ached and his body felt battered and bruised from the numerous blows he had taken. He was more than grateful for the weighty chainmail he wore. Without it, his body would be a mass of cuts and torn flesh rather than a collage of multicolored bruises. He also had thanked the goddess for the helmet; the ringing in his ears told him of the many axe and sword blows from which it had saved him.

As he wiped the blood-smeared back of his hand across his eyes in a vain attempt to clear away the salty sweat that made them sting, Conall saw Faolán standing before him. The two circled each other warily, each balancing on the balls of their feet and altering the grip on their weapons so that they rested more comfortably in their hands. Faolán adjusted his shield and swept the air between them with his axe. Conall's bloodstained axes flowed in a smooth diagonal movement across his chest. The area around the combatants fell silent. A corona of space appearing around them as both sides fell back to watch the duel.

"Your head on a spike will look good as a trophy, Conall Mac Gabhann," Faolán exclaimed, his voice raspy from shouting commands and his mouth thick with the dust and blood of battle. He circled his opponent, looking for weakness, remembering that many, including his brother Olcán, had misjudged this young man and died.

Laughing grimly, Conall spat to clear his mouth. "Your confidence is futile. You are dead, no matter how this fight plays out, Faolán Ó Floinn." As Conall moved to his right, Faolán saw a hostile-faced Mórrígan, an arrow already nocked in her bow. Behind her, Urard waited, his bloody axe at the ready.

"So much for honor in battle," Faolán spoke through gritted teeth.

"Honor, you have no honor, you bastard. You slaughtered our mothers, our fathers, our infant brothers and sisters. Mag Mell is too good for you, but this day, the worms will have their fill and that is where you will go. Tell me where Cassius Fabius Scaeva is and I'll make your end swift," Conall kept circling to his right as he spoke, holding Faolán's gaze.

Faolán snorted through a bloody nose, "That piece of shite. He fled to Chrúachain to seek sanctuary with Ailill and Medb. That one has more lives than a cat."

Conall nodded and changed direction, hoping to catch Faolán off guard. Instead, Faolán stepped forward, and slammed his shield into Conall's chest. Grunting, Conall twisted aside. An axe blow to his shoulder that should have taken his arm off, glanced off his chain mail leaving a numbing ache. He swung the axe in his left hand towards Faolán's right side, while bringing the other axe to strike his shield. Faolán snarled as he felt the axe blade slide along his side, and was forced to step back from the blow to his shield.

Again and again, they circled, trading and fending off blows. Both were breathing hard and sweating heavily. Conall was faster, but Faolán was stronger and not easily fooled by Conall's feints. Faolán cursed Conall's armor, which forced him to focus on the harder targets of exposed arms and legs. Conall continually stepped beyond Faolán's reach, and then sprang forward to land axe blows on the wooden shield, hoping to crack Faolán defenses.

While battles are won by good strategy or overwhelming force, duels are won by fate. A single minor distraction or stumble will turn a contest between two equally matched warriors into death for one, victory for the other. After this contest, the songs that were sung told of how the war goddess herself appeared and gave Conall the victory. The truth was less dramatic, but just as deadly.

The throbbing in his arms and shoulders from the weight of the axes and the thumping headache from the strain of combat were slowly undermining Conall's concentration. As he fought his own mental battle, a lone raven flew overhead, its *kraa kraa* shattering the silence that had descended on the battleground. Faolán's attention faltered, his eyes flickering upward for the briefest of moments. Seizing the opening, Conall sprang forward with a loud cry, "For my father and mother." The axe in his right hand came down on Faolán's left shoulder, its dulled blade biting deeply through leather and into flesh and bone. Faolán stumbled, and slouched, under the impact and agonizing pain. He felt his shield slip as he lost the use of his arm. Concentrating on holding his shield up, Faolán left himself open. Conall's other axe swung towards Faolán's side laying open a huge gash as it tore through flesh and muscle, and cracked ribs.

All knew the fight was over. As Conall stepped backwards, Faolán fell to one knee gripping his shield as support. Blood gushed from his side and a grey pallor settled on his face. He grew light-headed as he struggled to remain conscious. In his heart, Faolán knew he was dead. He cursed himself for having served Eochaidh, and then cursed Eochaidh to have a painful and lingering death. The last memory he registered was of a bloody axe arcing through the air to split his head and splatter his brains over the dirt. As if to seal his fate, two black arrows pierced his heart.

Conall looked at Mórrígan and nodded in approval. The first step in their journey now completed.

The remaining warriors, hoping for mercy, threw down their weapons at the sight of their leader's bloody corpse. They were quickly restrained and guards were set to watch over them. The Chomhairle sent patrols across the battlefield to retrieve the wounded and dead for healing or the flames of the burial pyres. The enemy's dead and living were stripped of anything of value. The dead were decapitated; the injured dispatched to Mag Mell with a blade to the throat - and then beheaded.

"That was a most advantageous time for a raven to appear out of nowhere." Fearghal commented through a mask of congealed blood.

Mongfhionn, smiled, "Destiny uses many messengers. It was how Conall took advantage of the moment that set him apart, not the appearance of the bird."

It was the first time, since she had left, that Fearghal had examined Mongfhionn's face. He reached out a bloodstained hand caressing the blue paint above her right eye.

"I'm not the most observant, but that strikes me as being new, somewhat attractive – and permanent."

Sadness fleetingly clouded Mongfhionn's bright eyes, then she spoke,

"It is a reminder from the Ancient ones of where I should not tread."

Fearghal held her hand tenderly and firmly, "Should or will not?"

She winked, kissed him lightly on his encrusted lips and walked away to her healing duties.

CHAPTER 16

The army set up a temporary camp away from the stench of the battlefield. Still, the acrid smell of wood smoke mingled with charred flesh, from the funeral pyres burning throughout the night, could not be avoided. Of Eochaidh's warriors, less than half had survived the battle. The remainder sat in groups, guarded by Cróeb Ruad fighters. They were exhausted and shocked by the outcome of the battle. Few had considered the possibility of defeat. Now even fewer thought about escaping. Those foolish enough to entertain the idea reconsidered as they watched their guards sharpening swords and axes, almost willing them to try. Disconsolate, they knew if they escaped their guards, it was unlikely they could outrun the black arrows of the archers or the horsemen who patrolled the perimeter of the camp.

At dawn, Cúscraid informed Conall, "Íar's scouts report a small group of men coming from the west. Several chariots and the rest on foot. They should be here around mid-day."

Conall nodded, "What's the state of the army? Do you have a reckoning of our injured and dead?"

"We were lucky, not many dead – maybe fifty depending on whether the worst injured recover. A few of the horsemen broke their necks when their horses stumbled in rabbit holes. We've many injured, especially from the warriors that fought alongside you. I'd say there are around a hundred, maybe more, too badly injured to fight. It will take many cycles of the moon for them to recover fully."

"Make sure all are well taken care off. If the dead have families, we should make sure they are provided for. In the meantime, let's prepare for our guests. Ask the Chomhairle to assemble and invite Deda to join us. Have the commanders gather our men; we will appear to be prepared for battle." As an afterthought he added, "Line the prisoners up as well."

As the small band of nobles and chieftains approached, they could clearly see the ranks of red and black shields as well as the chariots and horsemen. Much to his chagrin, but thinking his character and age would give them the best hearing, the group had nominated Aodh Mac Eochaidh Fionn from the fort at Clárach as their spokesman.

In truth, Aodh was a striking man. He had seen over sixty summers, yet stood tall and straight in his chariot, his flowing, almost white hair matched by a long silver-grey beard. A moss green cloak, embroidered in gold thread with swirling symbols, whipped in the wind covering his leather tunic and leggings. He bore all the markings of a wealthy noble with his broach, fine jewelry, and ornately designed belt and sword scabbard. As Aodh drew closer, he saw what he took to be the leaders of the army before him. He presumed that the young man at the center of the group was Conall Mac Gabhann. With a sigh of relief, he recognized his old friend, Deda Mac Sin, standing next to Conall.

The party halted a cautious and respectful fifty paces from Conall. Those on chariots dismounted and fell in behind Aodh as he strode purposefully towards Conall's group. Aodh bowed first to Deda Mac Sin and then to Conall. Looking at Deda he spoke clearly, "Perhaps, my old friend, you would introduce me to the king of Ráth na Conall and the conqueror of Eochaidh Ruad."

Smiling at the older man's reserve, Deda turned to Conall, "Conall Mac Gabhann, king of Ráth na Conall, I present Aodh Mac Eochaidh Fionn, king of Clárach – and a friend?" He paused briefly and then added, "I also present Conall's queen, Mórrígan Ni Cathasaigh. These other good men and the lady Mongfhionn are his Chomhairle." For the first time, Aodh's reserve slipped and he looked unsure as he regarded the Sidhe.

Aodh cleared his throat, "I and the nobles that accompany me have over two thousand men beyond the hilltop. We had no wish to join this ill-advised venture, but many had sons, daughters and grandchildren held hostage by Eochaidh. We have no wish to do battle. If you will allow, we will withdraw to our forts." Behind Aodh, the rest of the nobles signified their agreement. Up close, the ranks of Conall's army were intimidating and the nobles thought their chances of surviving a new battle were slim.

Conall rubbed his chin, taking his time to consider the proposal. His silence made the delegation even more nervous, although, in truth, he had no intention of starting another battle if at all possible. However, he also knew that he had to make sure the nobles were fully aware of what they could expect if they deceived him.

Taking several paces forward, he bowed in deference to the older king and reached out to grasp Aodh's hand, "I agree. There will be no fighting. You will take food with us at our camp, but before that, we have some business to take care of which you should witness." The nobles were relieved, yet uncertain as to Conall's meaning. They followed as he walked through the ranks of warriors until they stood before the prisoners.

Conall mounted his black horse so that all the prisoners could see him. He called out, "I am Conall Mac Gabhann. Surrender the cowards among you who attacked and slaughtered the innocent settlement at Ráth na Conall. Do this and you will be set free." Letting his words sink in, he then added ominously, "Refuse me and one man in every ten will be executed and you will be tarnished with disgrace until you die." An increasingly loud rumbling of angry voices and pronounced local brogues swept through the prisoners as heated arguments erupted and blows were traded. Over the growing din, Conall added to their distress, "Know this also, try to deceive me and I will hunt you down like a mad dog. I will leave your body for the worms, the wolves and the ravens to feast on."

One theme became stronger as one after another declared, "Give them up. Why should we die for these bastards?"

Soon, men were seized and thrown at Conall's feet. Within a short time, over fifty terrified warriors stood or prostrated themselves, begging and groveling for mercy before him. Conall and Mórrígan walked along the line of prisoners, looking upon them with a mixture of disgust, rage and pain. Turning to his men, Conall nodded curtly. An equal number stepped forward, weapons in hand. Almost immediately, the grass was covered in blood as swords were thrust into bellies or axes cleaved heads. It was a harsh, uncivilized execution. The bodies were beheaded and tossed at the forest edge for the beasts to feed on.

Following the executions, Conall turned to a white-faced Aodh and the nobles who accompanied him. "I keep my word to my friends – and to my enemies." Then with a more benign demeanor, he said "Come, let us eat and put these events behind us."

The nobles had little choice, but to agree to the elevation of Deda Mac Sin as ruiri. Conall proposed that an óenach - or gathering of the kings and nobles, should be convened in the summer. At this time Deda would be formally crowned ruiri. The question of who would rule Carn Tigherna, now that Eochaidh had fled, was settled, in the short-term, by necessity rather than negotiation.

Deda had increased his earlier gift to Conall by a further two hundred men and horses. Many from the conquered army had asked to join Conall and after being assessed by the Chomhairle, about three hundred warriors had finally been selected. Then there were Aengus' chariot teams and the growing band of archers led by Áine and Mórrígan. All agreed that Ráth na Conall simply was too small to house all these men as well as their women and children. Without much argument, Conall was given command over Carn Tigherna.

Later, Conall was to learn that Eochaidh had fled to the coastal fortress of Caher Conri, five days march to the west, where he still had a small force of loyal warriors. The fort, although small, was formidable, remote and almost inaccessible. It stood on a shoulder of rock projecting from the summit of an isolated mountain. It had but one narrow entrance guarded by massive walls. Forbidding sheer cliffs on the north and south protected its other two sides. Eochaidh Ruad had chosen his refuge well.

Clouds of pollen danced on the fresh summer breeze as the party made their way to Curraghatoor for the óenach. Lost in his thoughts, Conall was comforted by the steady pace of his horse and the presence of Mórrígan riding alongside. The screams, cries and giggling of his daughters, who demanded attention from anyone who came within range of their already sharp eyes, made him grin broadly.

The good natured banter from his caomhnóirí – his guard, added to his good humor. His caomhnóirí consisted of the men who had chosen to fought beside him at Carraig na Caillí. From that day they had grown fiercely loyal to their king. Not all the caomhnóirí travelled on this day. Many had been injured and it would take a long time, together with Mongfhionn's healing herbs and chants, before they would fully recover.

Conall was troubled that Eochaidh had not been captured at the battle of Carraig na Caillí or Rinn-Iru - the place of blood as it had been renamed by the local population. His concern was the price he may have to pay to prize the mad king from the fortress of Caher Conri. Although not a quick solution, so far the best option appeared to be to lay siege to the fort, and starve the king and his men into surrender. One of the fort's strengths was that it had only one entrance, which would prove costly to attack. On the other hand, there was only one path to supply the fort with food or anything else. Stores would be quickly devoured, especially if it was a harsh winter.

Word was sent out to the local villages and nobles that anyone who supplied or provided help to Caher Conri would face the wrath of Conall and his army. In the end, few objected. A camp was constructed in the valley that ran along the mountain edge to the north east of the fort. It was manned by fifty warriors and twenty horsemen. Enough to dissuade the residents of the fort from attempting an escape. While it was a pleasant summer now, conditions would be very different during the coming autumn and winter. Therefore, Conall ordered that the warriors and horsemen should be regularly relieved and at least one of the Chomhairle be present at the camp.

The óenach went well with much of its success attributed to Deda Mac Sin's hospitality and the seemingly never-ending series of feasts. Spit-roasted animals of all shapes and sizes were available from breakfast to midnight and, of course, beer was equally abundant. Fortunately, Deda had the foresight to have Íar organize contests with prizes for strength, stamina, sword and axe-play, horsemanship and archery. Otherwise, as Brion remarked to Conall, "We'd have lost more men to burst bellies or failed hearts than to the swords of Eochaidh."

After a week of celebration, even the most reluctant of the nobles conceded that Deda was by far a better prospect than Eochaidh and were persuaded to swear allegiance to him. Conall sensed that many were equally happy to know that, once Eochaidh had been either been captured or killed, he and his army would travel north in pursuit of the Roman, Cassius Fabius Scaeva. While many sympathized with Conall's quest, they also longed for the days of cattle raids and minor skirmishes rather than full-scale warfare.

Following the óenach, Conall divided his forces. Along with Fearghal, Nikandros, Brion, Aengus and Mongfhionn, he remained at Ráth na Conall together with his caomhnóirí, a hundred horsemen and fifty archers.

Íar returned to Curraghatoor to brood through the winter. He had a tough decision to make. Should he travel north with Conall, where he was assured of a warrior's life of plunder and glory and more than likely a warrior's death in a distant land or should he remain at Curraghatoor where it was almost certain he would succeed his father as ruiri of the southern lands of Ériu? His sister, Áine, he mused, had a much simpler choice to make. With her father and Íar's blessing she had accompanied Brion to Ráth na Conall.

Cúscraid, now commander of Carn Tigherna, with Onchú as his second-in-command and the remaining men and horsemen, were given the task of cleansing the fort of the legacy of Eochaidh. The first reports Conall received were filled with graphic descriptions of the squalor, the rank-smelling pits and cages filled with nearly dead souls and rotting corpses, rat-infested living quarters and the filth of the fort's non-military residents. Cúscraid painted a picture of depravity and squalor that put Conall off his food for several days.

More offensive, were the reports of how the cowed residents

remained willing to hand over their young daughters to their new masters, as they had with Eochaidh. Cúscraid quickly disabused them of this by declaring, "There are enough young girls with swollen bellies and Eochaidh's bastards running about without more being added." He bluntly informed his men that anyone taking advantage of any female under the age of thirteen summers would find his head on a stake.

Even as the winter rains, snow and biting cold winds encroached, the majority of Cúscraid's men chose to live in tents. Until the fort was purified by sacrifices to the gods and fire, and new barracks and eating halls were built for them, they had little stomach for Carn Tigherna.

CHAPTER 17

412 B.C.

The winter was bitter cold. Heavy snowfalls and storms battered the land and its people. Men and women exhaled clouds of ice crystals. Noses glowed red from the constant rubbing to relieve frozen nose-hairs and encrusted snot. Even the thick wood and solid stone walls of the forts, could not keep out the sharp talons of winter as it tore at took the lives of the elderly, the weak and the very young.

Nikandros had finally acquiesced to wearing a bearskin over his tunic, as his bones chilled to a level he had never experienced in his native Sparta. He smiled at the good natured craic of the men and their shouts of, "About time too. Wouldn't want to see your balls fall off, son," as he strode by. The lucky shared their beds with a woman; in some cases, several shared the same one. Swollen bellies from the winter rutting would produce a harvest of new life in the fall.

More pleasingly, the air was filled with the comforting familiarity of the smoke and aromatic smells from the peat fires and the birch and oak logs on the cooking pits. Feast or famine, the fires of the forges roared and the clanging of hammers against anvils as glowing metal was beaten and shaped into armor and weapons continued day and night. In the cold depths of the winter, the smiths worked almost naked, protecting their crotches with leather aprons, their bodies perpetually scorched red and gleaming with sweat.

The cold winter did little to cool Eochaidh Ruad's rage or to stem his further descent into madness. He constantly roamed Caher

Conri, cursing and bellowing orders that were mostly disregarded. In misguided loyalty, several hundred men chose to stay. Fortunately their foolishness did not extend to their families, who were quietly shepherded to safety in the confusion of the king's arrival. Upon discovering that the residents of the fort did not include any females to satiate his lusts, Eochaidh's disposition became even more sullen and resentful. His men heaved a sigh of relief whenever the king drank himself into one of his many stupors, which often lasted for days at a time.

By mid-winter, the fort's stores of food had been greatly depleted. True to form, the king noticed anything that decreased his comfort, including the diminishing portions of meat on his plate. His men ignored his ranting to go to the nearby villages and requisition supplies by threat of death if needed. For a start, the fort, being on the highest ground, was quickly snowed in. As well, not far from the fort, lay a camp full of warriors eager to punish any who might consider following such orders.

For the fort's residents, the days were long and dismal. More than a few drifted away during the night, preferring to take their chances with the winter storms or the mercy of Conall's men. By spring, the fort was down to almost half of its original strength. Those remaining did so for greed, succumbing to the king's constant lies and promises of gold and power once he was restored to his throne.

The fact that the patriarch of his family, Marcus Fabius Ambustus, had, in all likelihood, sent the Roman force to ensure his demise, gnawed at Cassius. While he pined for his previous lifestyle and the comforts of Rome, Cassius also knew he needed to obtain vast wealth to ensure his own survival.

To his new hosts, Cassius Fabius Scaeva was a figure of amusement – a curiosity. This grated on the Roman who considered himself vastly superior and more intelligent than the barbarians on the island they knew as Ériu. A generous gift of gold eased his way into the good graces of Ailill Mac Máta and fleetingly into the bed of queen Medb. Widely and proudly known as Medb na pluide cairdiúil – Medb of the friendly thighs, the queen's insatiable lust required constant servicing. Cassius' novelty and stamina lasted only a short time, before he was cast aside and ridiculed for his poor performance. This greatly amused Ailill, who was both well aware of his queen's desires, and not beyond taking a few young women to bed each night.

While he remained in the sanctuary of Chrúachain, Cassius was safe. He paid generously for information and for women to keep his bed warm. Yet he was in the wrong location to secure a means to travel back to Rome. Ideally, he should travel east to the coast and find a Phoenician trading galley. Unfortunately, that option was inadvisable due to the fierce fighting that was ongoing in the kingdom of the Laighi. He knew this, as Ailill and Medb were constantly in conference with their commanders to ensure their borders were secure.

Cassius was left with journeying to the north. This was not a very promising choice. He understood from Medb that the Ulaid were longstanding enemies of the Connachta. Grudgingly acknowledged as the best warriors in the island, the Ulaid also had a reputation for not being overly friendly to strangers. Cassius' only glimmer of hope appeared to be rumors of the ambitions of a new northern queen who wished to be crowned as Ard-Righan. Reportedly, she had many enemies equally determined that she should never be crowned. It was a situation that suited Cassius' talents.

Gaius Aurelius Atella finally reached Rome in the early spring. It then took him weeks to gain an audience with Marcus Fabius Ambustus and his son, Quintus. As expected, his welcome was cold. Gaius dutifully related all that had transpired, informing Marcus that his best soldiers had been slaughtered to a man by barbarians led by a young leader called Conall Mac Gabhann.

He opined that a high degree of fault for the events that had taken place should be placed at the feet of Cassius Fabius Scaeva. His greed had inflamed a whole region and he appeared to be still at large and fomenting trouble. On hearing this, Marcus swore and spoke to Quintus, "I should have had that dissolute idiot's throat cut. If there are any members of his immediate family alive, make sure they do not live another day."

The grim expression on Marcus' face hardened as the leather pouch containing the heart of Spurius Sulpicia Longus was handed over. Gaius, with some satisfaction, as in this brief conversation he found little to like about Marcus, observed a fleeting look of fear when he described how the heart had been ripped out of the living Spurius by a Druidess called Mongfhionn. Quintus exclaimed, "No, she is dead. She and her two sisters were executed many years ago. You are mistaken, centurion." Quintus' countenance lost its color, however, as Gaius stood his ground and described Mongfhionn in detail.

Finally, Gaius delivered to Marcus the message from Conall Mac Gabhann that he would have his revenge even if this was to be at the gates of Rome. Marcus was dismissive, "A young, and possibly brave, hothead who most likely will meet his death at the sword of another barbarian." Gaius did not share Marcus' confidence, but decided to keep his own counsel.

As Gaius was dismissed, Marcus spoke with a clear warning in his voice, "You will say nothing of this to anyone, Gaius Aurelius Atella, or any family and friends you may have in Rome will not enjoy a long life. For your troubles, you will be paid a generous amount of gold, which will allow you to live a much better life than you could have expected. Your rank as centurion will be confirmed and you will join my guard." Gaius saluted Marcus and Quintus and exited the room.

The blazing peat and log fires filled Ráth na Conall's Great Hall with warmth and a blue haze. Cooking pits spattered burning fat at anyone unlucky enough to get too close. It was the last defiance of the animal, before its carcass nourished the bodies of its slayers. Craiftine ó Cuileannáin played the harp and his brother, the poet Tadhg, crafted songs of battles, heroes and duels as they entertained the rowdy, largely drunk, but appreciative audience who were more than happy to suggest additions to their repertoire. The sounds of the harp and the many bodhráns made warrior hearts and souls happy to be alive as they drank to fallen friends.

It was on one such night that Mongfhionn rose from her seat at the high table and spoke, "It is time for me to share that which has been hidden in my heart and my soul for many years. Hidden," she continued, as she looked on the flushed face of Fearghal, "even from my dearest and closest of friends."

"With my two younger sisters, Danu and Brighid, I lived ..." Mongfhionn paused as she heard the sharp intake of breath from Conall. His eyes narrowed in anger at Mórrígan who wilted under his stare shrinking back into her seat. "Yes Conall, I asked that Mórrígan name your daughters after my sisters. When you have heard my tale, you can decide if they should keep the names."

Mongfhionn spoke with passion, wringing her hands in remembered grief. "My sisters and I lived one of our lives in a colony on the Pomentine Plains, in what is now Roman territory." To Nikandros she said softly, "The colony was called Foronia."

It was Nikandros now, whose passion was barely contained. "By the Gods of Sparta," he rose abruptly, knocking aside tankards, platters of food and those nearest him. "This cannot be." His normally tanned face was pale and his coal-black eyes searched Mongfhionn's for any sign of deceit.

Fearghal, totally confused, said, "I know I've been drinking, but in the name of the Hag, will someone please explain what is going on here?"

Nikandros first looked at Fearghal, and then Conall. "Mongfhionn is Spartan."

Fearghal grunted, "Well that goes some way to explain her belligerence and temper... and her clothes sense!"

As Nikandros slumped down on his seat, Mongfhionn resumed her story. "My years are longer than yours. I have no nation of birth, but yes, in one life my sisters and I were Spartan." The Sidhe now had everyone's attention, wondering what other surprises would be unveiled. "We were very young. I was no more than ten summers and my sisters seven and five when our family travelled north from

Foronia to a small village in the Apeninos Mountains called Nursia.

Following my first bleedings, my gifts and powers began to develop rapidly. Forewarned by dreams, our parents had chosen the isolation of the mountains for our safety. The village was on the borders of Gaul, and in an area the Senones considered as their territory. The Senones were envious of the land and there were skirmishes, as the Republic's armies and barbarian warriors tested each other's strength. We often had visitors who were trading or spying or both."

"One day, an elderly Gaul priest, a Druid, came to the village and took us from our parents. Strangely, neither of our parents objected. Over many years, it was he who taught us who and what we were and guided us in the development and use of our gifts. My gift was for healing and for the air and skies; Danu loved the forests and land and Brighid the waters. We all could look into the future. We knew of the imminent arrival of death and sometimes could hasten it. Our curses and geis were final - they could not be broken. On the day I reached my eighteenth summer, the Druid brought us together, blessed us and told us that we would be tested by blood and fire and that only one would rise. Then he turned and walked away. We never saw him again and we returned to our home."

Mongfhionn paused, lifting a drinking cup to her lips with trembling hands as she gathered her thoughts. "With the use of our gifts, our village became quite prosperous. Our reputations grew and travelled as far as Rome. In hindsight, we were foolish to think that our good deeds would go unquestioned – or unnoticed.

Marcus Fabius Ambustus was, indeed still is, Pontifex Maximus in Rome. He has three sons, Quintus, Numerius and Caeso. The Pontifex Maximus is not simply a priest. His title confers on him both political and religious authority. With Marcus, it was religious fervor that drove him. He knew of the Druids, hated what they represented and loathed our rituals. When he heard of the miracles in Nursia, he sent a division of his men to search us out. The mission, disguised as fostering friendships with the tribes that bordered the Republic, was led by his son Quintus. Quintus' true orders were to find and execute us."

Conall: The Place of Blood - Rinn-Iru 219

Now, not only her hands were trembling, but her entire frame. Mongfhionn reached deep into her inner well of strength, plainly in anguish at what was to come next, "The villagers were farmers and tradespeople. They could not resist the force that entered Nursia one autumn day and most fled to the hills to wait until the soldiers departed. Quintus' men entered our home, slaughtered our parents, and dragged us naked and screaming to the village square. The bodies and powers of my sisters and me were pure. We were virgins. In the square we were raped – over and over."

Tears flowed down Mongfhionn's cheeks as she remembered. She choked on her words as she continued, "At sunset, after the soldiers had had their fun with us, they bound us to three stakes. I begged and cried for mercy for my sisters. Quintus just laughed and nodded to his two centurions – one of whom you have met – Spurius Sulpicia Longus. They slit my sisters' throats. I watched my sisters' life blood stream down their naked bodies and soak into the ground. I heard their cries as death took them. In the night, I still hear their cries."

"As Quintus approached," Mongfhionn sobbed raggedly as she looked around the table, her eyes now burning with sorrow and rage, "with all my being and powers I cursed the village and all who lived there. I cursed the centurions and the soldiers. I cursed Quintus, his father and all his family and all future generations of his family.

To Quintus I said, 'Your spear will bring death and destruction upon your family and upon Rome and you will be cursed by all. Justice for my sisters and I will come from the west. Ravens in a sky of blood will feast on your flesh.'

He just laughed, then slowly and deliberately, with sadistic pleasure, drew the serrated edge of his dagger across my throat. I felt agonizing pain as my neck opened up and my own warm blood flowed down my breasts while my heart continued to beat. As my life's force ebbed from me, curses - as dark as you will ever hear, flowed from my blood-stained mouth. My final memory was of loud peals of thunder and a burning flash of lightning. When I was awakened, I was being tended by the Ancient ones of this island."

Brion looked at Conall, "How can this be? The tale is terrible and I'm sure Mongfhionn has suffered greatly, but how can this be?"

"I believe her," said Fearghal. "She has always been more than one of us and her powers are not like anyone I've ever known. Her vessel may be flesh and bone, but she is also aes sidhe." Mournfully he looked at Mongfhionn, "I'm just sorry you couldn't have told me."

"Fearghal we are close, and will always be close, but we all have our geis. Mine prevented me, until this moment, from telling my story. I had to go away and seek permission from the Ancients."

To Brion, she spoke softly, "My hair was pure gold, the color of the summer sun on corn until my sisters' deaths, when it turned as you see it now. Perhaps this may also help you understand." Reaching to the black ribbon that always circled her neck, Mongfhionn tugged on its clasp until the band fell away. The hushed audience grew even quieter, and motionless, as they looked on the ugly red scar. Conall rose and quickly took up the ribbon, replacing it gently around the Sidhe's pale neck.

"We need see and hear no more, my lady. I can't express my sorrow for your loss and don't understand how or what took place. As for all of us, we need to temper our thirst for revenge with mercy or else we will become as those that we seek out."

Glancing at Mórrígan, he continued, "My final word on this is that from henceforth I will be proud for my daughters to be called Danu and Brighid. The Lady Mongfhionn, if she accepts, will watch over and guide them and will always be welcome in my home."

A thoughtful Conall looked at Fearghal. "While I am wary of suggesting advice to my elders, I would think that Mongfhionn might appreciate your company now, but not ours." Fearghal nodded, and taking Mongfhionn's arm, led her towards the wooden doors. A dark hand was laid on Mongfhionn's pale shoulder. She stopped and turned to see Nikandros.

"Wear this, I doubt you need it to keep you safe, but perhaps it will bring memories of kinder times." Nikandros slipped over her head his wolf's tooth amulet. "Take good care of her, Fearghal; from now on she is my sister."

Conall rode into the camp near Cahir Conri under a spring sun. Timing his journey to coincide with Cúscraid's rotation he brought with him fifty horsemen, a hundred foot warriors and Mórrígan's fifty archers. Nikandros and Mongfhionn also accompanied him. They gathered around a blazing campfire sharing a breakfast of oatmeal, bread and goats cheese. Beer, heated with a hot iron poker, kept the dawn chill from their bones and bellies.

"What's your guess of the strength of the fort now that winter is past, Cúscraid?" Conall asked as he bit into a large slice of bread.

"About a hundred men. Roughly the same number drifted away during the winter. The ones who came this way were very talkative and eager to be useful." Cúscraid laughed, "They thought if they weren't cooperative we would cut their throats or open their bellies." In a more serious tone he went on, "The ones that remain are there for the gold and power that Eochaidh has promised them. The fools actually believe that bastard's word. I don't think they will be persuaded to leave and, unfortunately, even a handful of men could hold Caher Conri. The good news is our reports suggest they have run out of food. It turns out that the fort was not well stocked before Eochaidh's arrival. No one expected a siege and it has been a harsh winter."

Rubbing his hand through his winter beard, about which he was undecided whether to keep or scrape off, Conall said, "We'll go the gates this afternoon and make a plea for the men to give up Eochaidh. I don't hold out much hope. If and when that fails, Mórrígan's archers will take the lead. The fort has many wooden buildings which will burn, her archers will use fire arrows until the fort is ablaze. With the buildings ablaze, the fort's defenders will have little option, but to attempt to flee.

Fifty men will stand in front of the archers. If any try to attack or escape from the fort, kill them, even if they show signs of surrender. Take no chances. I'll not lose another man or woman to this king and the vermin with him. Nikandros will hold the horsemen in reserve. To Mongfhionn he said, "I will not advise where you should place yourself, but high ground would likely be good."

Mongfhionn looked to the sky before answering, "I see clouds on the horizon, Conall. Perhaps I might be able to add some theatre to your strategy."

Conall nodded, "Well friends, eat up and let's go speak with Eochaidh."

With his warriors and archers in place, Conall strode with Cúscraid to within hailing distance of the fort's gates. "Eochaidh Ruad, act one last time like a king and surrender. Save your men from the call of the bean-sidhe, from the worms and the ravens."

A cackling, screeching voice came from the stockade and the head and shoulders of a grimy and disheveled Eochaidh appeared, "Never! Never will I surrender and you will not take me from Caher Conri. This fort is impregnable. Not once has it been taken."

Conall looked along the stockade at the row of gaunt, grey faces, "Men, you can't win. We'll take this fort by fire and by iron. Give up this hopeless cause. You can't trust this bastard. He is no longer a king in this land." His answer was a hail of rocks that fell short. In response, a shower of arrows sunk into the wasted flesh of those on the stockade foolish enough to present a target. Shrieks of agony echoed in the brittle morning air as Conall turned away. Bitterly he said to Mórrígan, "You know what to do."

Arrows were dipped into the flames of a dozen braziers, nocked and bowstrings drawn back. The smoky trails of arrows went skywards and then dropped like stones into the fort. They were followed by another and then another flight. At first, nothing appeared to happen, apart from more yelps from those unfortunate enough to have been caught by a flaming missile. Then, random wisps of smoke ascended into the still air. The smell of burning wood grew stronger as hungry flames gained a foothold on the wooden buildings. Soon they gathered strength, bursting into a seething, devouring cauldron of fire.

On a nearby rocky outcrop, the awful scream of the bean-sidhe shredded the air. The sound of thunder boomed across the darkening skies that gathered over the fort. Soon the sky alternated between day and night as great flashes of lightning appeared to glance off Mongfhionn's staff before striking the fort's ancient gates. The gates exploded, sending showers of charred, splintered wood into the air. Fingers of lightning struck the high towers, cracking and dislodging rocks and stones. The roar of flames, rolls of thunder and lightning flashes overwhelmed the cries of suffering within the fort. Conall's forces shuddered at the onslaught, but stood resolute.

Eochaidh's skeletal warriors burst from the fort's entrance, hurling curses at their tormentors with hoarse voices and lungs filled with smoke. Their eyes were blood-red and streaming with tears, their skin blackened by smoke and scorched by fires. Later, Conall was to ponder whether the remaining defenders were so cursed by greed and rage that they were no longer human. They were cut down by arrows and javelins before they were more than a few paces from the fort. As the last of them gasped his final breath, Conall's men searched the bodies for Eochaidh.

"He's not among the dead, Conall," Cúscraid called out as his men reported back to him, "so, either he's burned in the flames or is hiding in the ruins."

"We'll wait here until the flames die down before searching the fort." As if on cue, the dark clouds that had hovered over the fort burst, and icy rain curtained down. The roaring flames hissed in disappointment as they retreated. A short time later, Conall and Cúscraid led the men into the smoldering rubble.

Eochaidh Ruad was discovered cowering in a storage room under the fort. He was dragged out screaming and kicking, and thrown at Conall's feet. Conall looked down on Eochaidh in disgust. Faced with imminent death, Eochaidh stood up. First he raged, spewing curses at his captors; then he tried to bribe, with promises of great wealth and power; finally he threw himself on the ground, begging for mercy and forgiveness. Conall's judgment was swift, "There will be no forgiveness and no mercy." Conall gave his orders, "Bind him. We will take him to Ráth na Conall where justice will be delivered."

As they journeyed back, messengers were sent to Deda Mac Sin and the nobles in the southern lands, informing them of Eochaidh's capture and his destination. As Eochaidh was led in chains to the fort, his former subjects were not shy in showing their true feelings about the depraved king. By the time he reached the gates of

Ráth na Conall, Eochaidh's clothes were in shreds. He was bleeding and bruised from a constant barrage of rocks and stones and stank from the human and animal shite that adhered to him. Conall was convinced, from the look in Eochaidh's eyes, that the madness that formerly protected the king from reality was slipping away, and that he was now very aware of his circumstances.

It was late afternoon when they had arrived back at Ráth na Conall. "He will not set foot in our home." Conall said. "Strip and bind him. Stake him before the fort so all may see his humiliation. Let him have time to consider how he arrived at this hopeless place. Set a guard to ensure no beast feasts on him tonight."

The following day, the Chomhairle joined with Deda Mac Sin, Aodh Mac Eochaidh Fionn and several nobles, as well as those remaining who had lost their families at the settlement. They stood before Eochaidh in judgment.

"I will not dwell long on the heinous wrongdoings of Eochaidh Ruad, for his depravity is known far beyond our villages and forts," Conall exclaimed to all gathered on the stockade as well as the party outside the fort. "The Law gives us the right to blood vengeance, but Eochaidh will not be slain by any human hand for this is not his geis." There was a hush, since no one could really understand how the king would be punished. Conall continued, "Those from the beginning shall have blood, but my command is that no man shall take this king's life."

Leaving them with these puzzling words, Conall strode to the bound king and took out his knife. Fear filled the king's eyes as he watched. Then he cried out as the blade was drawn diagonally across his chest. Conall walked away and Mórrígan took her place before Eochaidh. "For my parents and for the children you violated." Mórrígan's blade, deliberately dulled for this moment tore through the king's balls and cock. Pitiful shrieks and whimpers escaped from Eochaidh. Following Conall and Mórrígan's example, one after another, the survivors from the settlement cut Eochaidh's body until it was little more than a bloody slab of raw meat.

Finally, Fearghal approached. Eochaidh looked on the tall warrior hoping and beseeching with his eyes, that at last he would be put out of his misery. It was not to be. Fearghal spat on him, "It would give me the greatest of pleasure to rip your heart out, you bastard, but I've given my word." Fearghal took the king's long hair in his hand, pulled it tight to stretch his skull skin and sliced off his scalp. He tossed the lank tresses and attached skin into the ditch, wiping his hand of the filth as he strode back. In excruciating pain, with no relief, no escape or respite from the many cuts, the king writhed against his binds, whimpering and crying.

Conall looked at Mongfhionn who nodded approvingly, "For the remainder of this day we will stay within our fort ... our home. No man or woman shall look upon the king, for the goddesses have their own justice to dispense."

The gates of Ráth na Conall closed once again on Eochaidh Ruad. It was not long before the *kraa kraa* of ravens was heard, as a great flock gathered over the helpless king. His screams echoed long into the night as the birds fed on his flesh. At sunrise, an eerie silence settled on the plain, and it was taken that Eochaidh's soul had passed on to be judged.

Conall ordered that the king's carcass be cut down and beheaded. The king was buried not burned, so that the worms could have their fill of the remaining flesh.

In this, Eochaidh Ruad died according to his geis.

PART 3: THE TRAIL NORTH

411 – 410 B.C.

CHAPTER 18

Lugnasad proved a timely celebration. As the flames of huge bonfires rose up into a balmy, midsummer sky, Conall looked around the feasting tables, laden with platters of food and horns of beer that were continuously refilled. He smiled as he recalled the earlier handfasting ceremony for Brion and Áine and pondered the four years of fighting that had transformed childhood friends into warriors. Whether this was to their good, would be for the goddess to decide.

The feast had one somber piece of business. For Conall, although it was tempting to settle down at Ráth na Conall with Mórrígan and his daughters, he knew his destiny was to journey north in pursuit of Cassius Fabius Scaeva. Yet, this was now a personal quest. Could he expect his friends – new or old to follow? For many, their search for justice had been satisfied with the death of Eochaidh Ruad.

So Conall rose and raised his horn. "To good friends - old and new. Slántu." Raucous cheering accompanied by the banging of mugs, weapons and platters on wooden tables was the response.

"In the spring of next year, I will travel north to Chrúachain and the land of the Connachta, and then to the Ulaid beyond the Black Pig's Dyke. The journey will be full of risk. Only the goddess knows if we will survive against new foes that will likely far outnumber our army. During the summer and autumn we'll prepare supplies of food, clothing, armor and weapons. Scouts and envoys will be sent north to gather intelligence.

My friends, and leaders of Ráth na Conall and our community, you do not have to follow. I will not think badly of you for staying in the land where you were born. Ráth na Conall will always be my home. I will not leave it undefended. Those of you who remain will have enough men to ensure your safety."

Conall paused to wet his throat and continued with a smile, "To my friends from the North. Well, it would seem we are stuck with each other, at least until you fulfill your oaths to Macha Mong Ruad."

Then to Brion and Áine, Conall spoke soberly, "Brion, you are my dearest friend and a brave warrior. And, I can see that my daughters will soon have a cousin." Conall waited until the cheering settled down, before continuing, "Consider carefully the harsh road that lies ahead if you choose to march alongside me."

As he sat down, Conall gripped Mórrígan's hand tightly and waited for his friends to respond. Fearghal was first, "My decision is simple. I go north not because of any oath, but because you're my king, my friend – and my family."

Mongfhionn stood, "So far, you have proven to be a wise leader, Conall. I intend to see that you continue on that path." Glancing at Fearghal she mocked, "And I'm looking forward to this oaf's explanations of his dealings with Macha Mong Ruad ... and Medb."

"I will travel with Conall." Unsteady on his feet, having imbibed too many mugs of Fearghal's special brew, Nikandros then pointed to him, "Who else will protect my sister from that eejit?"

"Póg ma thoin, you half-naked foreigner," Fearghal laughed and cuffed Nikandros roughly on the arm and spilling beer over the nearest guests.

Uallachán ó Dubhghaill, his left arm permanently weakened from the wounds received in fighting the Romans arose. A proud and bitter warrior, his arrogance was not restrained, "The ó Dubhghaills will remain. We will take charge of Ráth na Conall."

Conall's eyes narrowed and he was about to speak when Torcán rose, "Brother, we discussed this. You know my decision. I will go with my king."

Tight-lipped at being corrected, Uallachán stood up once more, "My apologies brother, it was my hope that you would change your mind. Nuadha and I will remain to oversee Ráth na Conall."

"No!" Conall's tone was sharp and reprimanding, "Ráth na Conall is my family's home. My daughters, if not my sons, may choose to return one day. If they do, then they shall rule. The fort will be managed by the Council of the Elders, under the protection of Curraghatoor. You, Uallachán, and your brother can see to the rebuilding of Caher Conri. Be thankful or serve another."

Scowling, an ungracious Uallachán muttered, "Yes, my king," and sat down. He sulked the rest of the evening.

Brion broke the tense atmosphere, "I speak on behalf of the ó Cathasaighs and now Áine Nic Dedad. We will follow you to the North - and wherever you travel after that." Brion beamed at his sister, Mórrígan, his long scar making his smile look lopsided and quirky instead of ferocious, "From this day, the ó Cathasaighs and the Mac Gabhanns are one family."

At the mention of his family name, Eirnín Mac Gabhann, flushed and reeling a little from too much beer, stood up and slurred, "I go where my brother goes." He thumped back down on his seat to loud cheering.

Fionnbharr ó Cuileannáin rose, "My brothers Craiftine, Tadhg and Labhraidh are much more eloquent than I, but this evening I speak for our family. We stand with Conall."

Of the original families, one voice remained - the youngest of all, Cathán ó Bric. Now fourteen summers, he stood up and nervously addressed the table, "My parents were slaughtered by Eochaidh. My brothers all died bravely in battle. There is nothing for me here. I will march with Conall – if he will have me."

A stool scraped across the dirt floor, pushed away as Nikandros got up, "My parents are dead, my brothers killed in battle. I have no sons or daughters. I would be proud, Cathán, if you would allow me to adopt you as my son."

The room was silent until Cathán choked out an emotional, "Yes," then erupted into loud cheering as he and Nikandros embraced.

"Sadly, I will not march with my friends and fellow warriors," said Onchú Ó an Cháintigh. "With Conall, and Deda's, permission I will remain at Carn Tigherna - as commander." Conall's discomfort at this request showed as he scratched and rubbed the stubble on his chin. He looked, first to Cúscraid, currently commander at Carn Tigherna and then to Deda. He was rescued by Cúscraid.

"I see no reason to refuse Onchú's request. He is a brave warrior and will make a worthy leader. I have served as commander both at Ráth na Conall and Carn Tigherna, but as with Fearghal, my place is with Conall. He is my king and has my allegiance until death."

Thinking all was finished, Conall rose from his chair and raised his tankard, "I thank you all for your words and allegiance. I could not ask for better commanders or counselors." A loud cough from his right interrupted Conall, as Íar stretched and got up from his seat. His emerald green eyes twinkled as he began to speak.

"My guess is you're all assuming that I will remain at Curraghatoor. Or possibly you're just reluctant to beg the best warrior of this disreputable band to ride with you!"

From the opposite table Fearghal slammed his well-dented bronze mug on the table and shouted out, "Best warrior! In yer dreams big man! And scrape your face. Do you call that arse-fluff a beard?"

"I'll ignore the drunken rabble at the lower end of table!" Íar took a large mouthful of beer most of which flowed down his newly grown beard and onto his chest. "This has been a difficult decision and I've talked at length with my father and sister. My choice is to fight at my friends' sides.

"My father has assured me that he has enough bastards running around Curraghatoor who can take my place until I return, wealthy and renowned - or strapped to my horse."

The entire audience erupted in loud cheers, banging their tankards on wooden tables. Conall smiled knowing he was better prepared to face the future now than at the start of the evening.

CHAPTER 19

411 B.C.

Bidding a nostalgic farewell to Ráth na Conall, the army journeyed east to Bohd Carraig. From there they tracked west towards Curraghatoor, where Íar waited, then north-west to Phortaigh na Cullen. The hounds ran ahead, barking and chasing rabbits, sheep and any other poor animal that crossed their path.

The army, now over a thousand strong, was led by the Chomhairle and a full strength caomhnóirí. The contingent of horsemen together with ten chariots guarded the army's flanks and scouted ahead. Bringing up the rear were the supply wagons, livestock, spare horses and over a thousand followers. This was not a force that could easily go unnoticed even in the dense woods and forests of Ériu.

Bogs covered the width of Ériu and stretched northwards almost to the earthworks of the Black Pig's Dyke. This was a menacing land of myths, superstitions and spirits; a land of reeds, deep stagnant pools and mats of trembling mosses waiting to suck the unwary traveler into its dark, damp heart. It was a land of mists, mysterious lights and strange noises. The dense forests surrounding the bogs provided refuge for brigands always watching and waiting to prey on the weak. The southern edge of the bogland was marked by the now deserted village at Phortaigh na Cullen. It was a land that no one was particularly looking forward to traversing.

The scouts reported no significant forces in Phortaigh na

Cullen. Any bands of outcasts, outlaws or raiders melted away when they saw the body of well-armed men moving steadily towards the village. Conall's caomhnóirí crossed the narrow causeway and entered first to make sure any possible dangers were dealt with swiftly. A few families of an trua, near starvation and clothed in rags, now eked out a miserable existence in the deserted village. Later, these vulnerables offered up sacrifices to the goddess for their rescue from a slow and almost certain death. Few had expected to survive the coming winter.

"I guess we shouldn't have done such a good job of burning the buildings the last time we were here!" Conall remarked to Fearghal, as they surveyed the ruins.

Fearghal grunted, "The stockade appears to be intact, although it wasn't in great shape to begin with."

"Ask Cúscraid to set up a guard around the perimeter. Make use of the hounds. Tell their handlers to set patrols from sunset to sunrise – no matter where we are. Tomorrow, the men can scavenge materials to reinforce the defenses. After we have eaten this evening, I want the Chomhairle to meet. Now the journey has started, we need to review our plans. We can't afford to lose too many warriors as we travel north. I don't think we'll find many Connachta volunteering as replacements."

The path to the north was guarded by two great forts, Knockadigeen and the coastal fort at Mooghaun. The strategy was to make a camp at Phortaigh na Cullen and use the village as a base of operations. Fearghal, Aengus and Cúscraid had convinced Conall that the best route north would be to strike west from the fort at Knockadigeen until they met the Abha na Sionainne - the great river that flowed to the borders of the north. On reaching the river, they would make sacrifices to the goddess of the river in the hope of ensuring a peaceful journey to the land of the Ulaid. It provided little solace that the river goddess was rumored to protect her kingdom with a terrible river monster.

The first challenge would be Knockadigeen. The fort guarded the two entrances to the Abha na Sionainne. It sat on the edge of a mountain overlooking the narrow valley that ran south-west to north-east. There was little chance that Conall's forces could reach the river unseen by the occupants of the fort.

Built on a large sprawling site, Knockadigeen had at least two lines of staggered ramparts and ditches for defense. This was the fort of Sláine Ulfhada who, according to Deda Mac Sin, was loyal to Chrúachain. Sláine was reputed to be quite eccentric. His name suited him well since, by all accounts, he had not shaved since he was a young man. Now his braided beard was long enough to cover his crotch. This was somewhat of a blessing since another of his peculiarities was that he preferred to go unclothed. According to Deda, Sláine encouraged his people – male and female - to follow his example. However, Deda warned Conall not to mistake Sláine's ways for stupidity. Nothing could be farther from the truth.

"How long will it take to reach the northern territory?" Brion asked as he gnawed on a rib and wiped grease from his chin.

"That depends on the track we take," said Fearghal, "or are forced to take, and whether we have to fight along the way. With all the camp followers that we have with us, we can't just fight and run.

The best route would be along the Abha na Sionainne valley. Most of the river is no more than waist high; it's an easier route for the wagons and chariots; and there's good feed for the animals. The river is full of eels and large, pink-fleshed fish so there's a good supply of food."

Cúscraid added, "If we are forced into the heart of the bogland it will take a lot longer. No matter how many sacrifices are made, we'll lose wagons and people. We need to cross the dyke before the winter sets in. Northern winters are much harsher than what you've been used to."

"Agreed. We'll also need to send delegations to the forts of Chrúachain and Emain Macha to gather intelligence and negotiate or buy safe passage. At least one member of the Chomhairle will have to travel with each delegation," said Fearghal.

"Macha Mong Ruad will, of course, need to be informed that her hero is riding to meet her," Conall said unable to resist a sly smirk at his battle commander.

"Póg ma thoin," Fearghal growled, as his friends roared with laughter at his discomfort. Mongfhionn simply sat stone-faced, which made him even more ill-at-ease.

"The envoy to Emain Macha is the least of our challenges, although the ride north may not be without hazard. I propose that Aengus ride to the Ulaid with a bodyguard of ten men. He will seek advice from the queen as to where we cross the dyke. Fearghal and Cúscraid can agree with Aengus on a suitable location for us to rendezvous after his negotiations." Conall paused for anyone to add or dissent to his proposal.

When none was offered, he continued. As was now his habit when deep in thought, he scratched the stubble on his chin, "Chrúachain is the biggest challenge. I suspect that Ailill and Medb will not be welcoming hosts. There's the slight issue that we stole their gold!" After the laughter had died down Conall continued, "The size of our force is much smaller than any army Ailill or Medb could gather, but we are still big enough to cause them grief. My hope is that they'll not want to be distracted overlong from securing the defense of their border with the Laighi. Rather than provoke a battle, we should make the effort to negotiate passage through Connachta lands. We also need information on the whereabouts of Cassius Fabius Scaeva."

"Fearghal will not be going to Chrúachain as an envoy or spy under any circumstances," Mongfhionn interrupted. "The big eejit doesn't have a devious bone in his body and would be instantly discovered and beheaded. And he will not be alone with that striapach – ever again!" A miserable Fearghal stared at his feet, as Mongfhionn continued, although now with a mischievous twinkle in her eye.

"I suggest that you send Nikandros to negotiate with Medb. Though Ailill is king, Medb wields substantial influence at Chrúachain. Her renowned appetites for the exotic will make

Nikandros irresistible." Looking directly at Nikandros, she said sweetly, "Brother, if all those campfire stories you have regaled us with are in any way true, then I am certain you will be able to satisfy Medb's lusts, at least long enough to get the information we need." Feigning embarrassment, Nikandros looked away, although he didn't raise any major objection to his proposed task.

"Conall, I suggest that you also send Craiftine, Tadhg and Labhraidh ó Cuileannáin with Nikandros. Ailill is well known for his interest and respect for musicians, poets and seanachaí. He will most certainly enjoy and value their undeniable talents." Finished, Mongfhionn sat down with a satisfied smile.

"We're just pawns in a game we'll never understand, Nikandros," Fearghal slapped his friend on the back and called for his horn to be refilled. "but, the plan has merit and deserves serious consideration."

"I agree," said Conall. In a few days, Nikandros can set out for Chrúachain with a guard of ten men plus the ó Cuileannáins. Aengus and Nikandros can travel together until they reach the lake that lies south-east of Chrúachain."

"What about Knockadigeen?" Brion asked.

"With Knockadigeen, I think a small demonstration of force may avert the need for battle. You, Fearghal, Íar and I, together with Mongfhionn, Áine and Mórrígan, will take my caomhnóirí and a hundred horsemen. We will ride to the fort to speak with Sláine Ulfhada. The rank of our party should please Sláine and the size of our honor guard will give him pause to think."

"I guess I'm left back at the fort. Alone as usual," said Cúscraid pretending to be hurt, but knowing that Conall had entrusted him with not only the rest of the army and their followers, but also his daughters.

"Alone! Don't give me that, Cúscraid," teased Íar.. I've seen your woman, the one with the auburn hair and cute nose. Oh and yes, she also has the biggest tits in the camp!"

The delegations led by Nikandros and Aengus rode north

following the Abha na Sionainne to Chrúachain and the dyke. The remainder turned east and made their way to the trail that wound its way to the gates of Knockadigeen. When they were within shouting distance of the entrance, Conall, Fearghal, Íar and Brion rode forward and waited.

Within the fort, Sláine Ulfhada and his commander, Breácan, watched the warriors approach.

"A pretty sight in their fancy armor and shields."

Sláine growled at his commander. Breácan was a great warrior and well-liked by his men, but he was as thick as two short planks when it came to strategy or planning.

"You're a bloody eejit, Breácan. No brains at all in that head of yours. They may be pretty, but they're dangerous. This Conall Mac Gabhann fought and slaughtered Eochaidh Ruad's army and then executed Eochaidh himself. Look at the way they carry themselves. Some may be young, but they bear the look of seasoned fighters to a man. And don't forget they have the Druidess with them.

Hear me well, it will be a bad day for all of us if we ever have to fight them. We'll treat them honorably as guests while they are with us and we'll fight them honorably if we have to. Now take a few men that don't look as if they just crawled out of a pigsty and greet our guests. Ask them if they would have food with me this evening - and send food and beer down to their men."

As Breácan walked towards the group, they removed their helmets and dismounted. A smile flickered across Conall's face as his commanders now sported similar style helmets, though not quite as ornate. Breácan, it had to be said. was an arresting sight with his shock of bright – almost orange, hair and a very impressive beard. His face, arms and legs were so covered in a mass of coarse red hair, freckles and scars that he appeared to be wearing some sort of animal hide. He was as well-built, if not quite as tall, as Íar and walked with an easy, balanced stride.

Fearghal turned to Conall, "He'd be a tough one to kill."

"My lord, Sláine Ulfhada, welcomes you to Knockadigeen and asks if you, and the ladies, will join him in the Great Hall for food and drink. If your men will set up camp on the plain, we will have food and beer brought to them. We live simply at Knockadigeen and do not have the same accommodations as Curraghatoor or Carn Tigherna, but several shelters have been set aside for you. They're dry, with new bedding materials and will keep the cold wind from you." Breácan spoke clearly and while not shouting his voice carried well.

"Please tell the king that we will be delighted to share his hospitality."

Once camp had been established, Conall led his party and their small guard into the fort where they were shown their rooms. A servant then guided them to the largest building. Located at the center of the fort, the Great Hall was an impressive circular hall built of cut stone and wood, and had a thick thatched roof. Inside several hundred men sat eating and drinking around long wooden tables. As they made for the high table, several guards blocked their way. One grunted, "No weapons," and looked at each of the party in turn.

Fearghal's hand went to the hilt of his longsword, "And who is going to take my sword from me?"

Noticing the commotion at the door, Breácan walked briskly over to Conall, "My apologies, but no weapons are permitted in the eating hall. We've had a few attempts to murder the king. You may of course keep your personal daggers so you may eat."

Conall looked to Fearghal and then to Breácan, "Not a problem. Do theach do rialacha."

As they approached, Brion gripped Conall's shoulder, making him wince as Sláine rose. For indeed the king had a magnificent, braided long red beard. Seeing this and the looks on the faces of the rest of the party, Sláine howled with laughter and looked at Íar, "I detect that your father still enjoys a joke. Has he been spinning tall tales about me? Did you really expect that I would greet my guests half-naked?" Indeed, Sláine wore a loose green tunic over a pair of well-worn brown leather pants. "Welcome to Knockadigeen. Come join me, there are seats for you at my table."

He continued, "Mind you, if any of you - especially the women, feel the need to remove your clothing, don't let me stop you. We're quite tolerant at Knockadigeen."

Laughing, Conall took the hand that was outstretched and shook it firmly. The hall was filled with the smells of burning peat, roasted food, beer and sweat. While they ate and drank, the increasing din from many conversations at times made it difficult for Conall to hold anything but the lightest conversation with his host. There was little doubt in Conall's mind that the shrewd eyes of Sláine Ulfhada were taking the measure of each of his guests.

"I'm glad to see the son and daughter of my dear friend, Deda Mac Sin. It has been a long time since I bounced Áine on my knee or watched Íar mount and fall from his first horse. Now that my friend is ruiri I must travel to Curraghatoor to give him my best wishes – and support." Looking at Conall directly, Sláine remarked, "Being ruiri means you are cursed to make decisions based on politics not battles."

Sláine's eyes inspected Mórrígan and Mongfhionn. He noted the strange markings on Mórrígan's arms and face and how her appearance seemed to glow strangely in the fire and candlelight. Her constant scanning of the hall disturbed him. As for Mongfhionn, he knew of the Sidhe by reputation. A stunningly beautiful woman, obviously enjoying and encouraging the attention from Fearghal Ruad who was seemingly a rogue, but also one of the best warriors in Ériu. As Sláine was studying Mongfhionn, her eyes caught his and for a moment a searing warning seized his thoughts, before she smiled at him and laughed at some tale or joke.

As he leant over to speak to Conall, Sláine smiled thinly and spoke just loud enough to be understood by those at the table, "My instructions are that no weapons are allowed in this Hall." Pausing he glanced pointedly at Mórrígan and Mongfhionn, "I did not foresee that weapons other than those made of iron or bronze would not only walk through my gates but look quite so beautiful."

The words troubled Conall, as it reminded him of a darker side to Mórrígan, which he usually chose to ignore. He often teased her about her body designs and markings – and on more than one occasion she had covered herself in them before they gave in to their, at times, rough and passionate desires. Sometimes, as he entered her glowing body, he wondered who or what she was becoming. Sláine took note that Conall hesitated before responding with a loud laugh, "There is no deceit, no harm, and no weapons in your home this evening. The good ladies are what they appear to be – beautiful and enchanting."

Somewhat pacified, Sláine called for more beer, "This evening we join as friends. Tomorrow we will talk as kings."

Throbbing heads had become bearable by mid-day as Conall led his team to Sláine's Great Hall. The stale smell of beer, sweat and puke assaulted their noses as the debris of the night's feasting was being raked into the dirt floor by an assortment of female servants. As they walked over the freshly turned floor, they could feel and hear the crunching and cracking of animal bones under their feet. The king sat with Breácan and several other chieftains, a mound of fresh bread and cheese lay before them together with pitchers of water and milk.

"I think we need clear heads today." Sláine said pointing to the ample, if simple, food and drink.

"That's good for us. Too much feasting makes my throat burn and I have to exercise harder to work the food and beer off." Conall sat down opposite the king, "You know why we're here, of course?"

"Yes, my scouts tell me that you have a sizeable army and followers camped at the old gold village at Phortaigh na Cullen. The same village a young warband leader raided several years ago." Sláine smiled and his thick ginger eyebrows bunched, "You didn't make too many friends at Chrúachain with that raid."

"We needed the gold and it was relatively close," Conall answered wiping a trickle of milk from his chin. "I'll apologize to Ailill Mac Máta and Queen Medb, when we meet."

"So that's where you're hoping to go; you intend to meet the king and queen of the Connachta. I hear tales of a young avenging warrior on the trail of a stranger from another land and of a stranger who is guest of the queen – although not a terribly well-liked guest, if my sources are truthful."

The king paused to bite into a lump of cheese. "Frankly, I cannot allow you to use the paths to the Abha na Sionainne. My fort sits on the meeting place of three kingdoms – the Connachta, the Laighi and that which used to be overseen by Eochaidh Ruad."

"The great river marks the border of the kingdom of the Connachta to its east. I, while not part of that kingdom, do have to be pragmatic. I cannot be seen by Medb to be openly assisting you." Glancing at Mongfhionn, Sláine continued, "Also, if my spies are worthy of their gold, the invaders of the Laighi may be known to the lady Druidess who graces our gathering."

Mongfhionn smiled, "Be careful Sláine Ulfhada, your spies may tell you only what they think you need to hear. It may not be wise to know the truth - and my sisters lose patience with the kings of Ériu."

"Bloody politics and words that have many shades of meaning. Give me a good fight any day." Fearghal banged the table with his mug, "Do we pass or not, Sláine?"

Sláine tugged on his great beard, "I have no wish to fight you. Our forces are matched in numbers and a battle would only serve our enemies. However, I can't let you use the paths to the Abha na Sionainne that are on my land." Conall, started to rise, but Sláine waved him to take his seat again. "Stay, Conall, and consider my offer. I cannot let you use the paths to the river, for if I did, then the might of the Connachta would descend on me. My men would be beheaded and staked and my people slaughtered or sold into slavery. So my men will block the two approaches. If need be they will die to stop anyone who tries to go past."

"However, a few days travel north-east of Knockadigeen there is a path to the waters we call the Nathair. The Nathair links with the great river a short distance from that approach. I will allow your army and people to cross my land without interference to reach the Nathair. That is my offer. I think it gives us both what we need if not what we want."

"I think it a fair offer Conall," Mongfhionn said, gazing around the table to gauge the reaction of the others. The affirming voices and nodding heads suggested that it was also the view of those present, but in the end it was Conall's choice.

Standing up, Conall offered his hand to Sláine, "It is good to deal with an honorable man. We will accept your proposal of safe passage. Perhaps you would be good enough to describe in detail all you know about the Nathair and the river beyond it."

The king beamed with pleasure, and there was obvious relief on both sides that a costly fight had been averted, "I can do better. Breácan knows more about the Nathair and the great river than anyone. He will travel with as your guide."

Mongfhionn spoke as they were about to take their leave, "There is an oak tree that can be seen from the gates of Knockadigeen, Sláine Ulfhada. As long as there is honor in your dealings, it will flourish and will be a sign to the ones from the east that an honorable king rules here."

Several weeks later, the army, supply wagons and followers left Phortaigh na Cullen. They first travelled north-west along the mountainside that bordered the bog, then north as they made for the entrance to the narrow valley that led to Knockadigeen. Although the army had made offerings to the goddess, the mists rising from the dark bogs joined with the late spring rains to make the journey unpleasant and dangerous. The ground had become softer as the winter frosts receded and the rains descended, making it difficult for the heavy-laden wagons to make steady progress. The sounds emanating from the bogs and intermittent fires that exploded suddenly and then vanished, served to keep everyone on edge.

Horsemen rode several hundred paces ahead. While Conall did not expect any problems from Sláine, there was always the possibility that a rogue warband or outlaws might use the cover of the forests to mount an attack. Mórrígan and Áine, together with the best of the archers, rode with the cavalry, providing a long-range option to discourage attacks. The mounted archers were Mórrígan's idea and this time she did not receive any objection or ridicule. The wagons and followers had been placed between the foot troops for added protection.

Sláine Ulfhada observed from the walls of Knockadigeen as Conall's men passed the fort. He watched Breácan and a guard of ten men stride down the pathway towards the head of the column. Adjacent to Sláine, a tall, almost skeletal and sallow-faced man surveyed the passing army and supply wagons. His fingers flicked over several pieces of rope, forming knots as he counted the army and resources.

Fachtna was disliked throughout the kingdom. His crooked body and odd gait, was an unwelcome sight at any fort or village. His face bore a long scar from scalp to chin. Reputedly it was earned not in battle, but from a striapach's sharp blade when he refused to pay for her services. The absence of hair on the left side of his scalp, save for a few lank strings of auburn locks, added to the discomfiting appearance of this thoroughly disagreeable man. Nevertheless, Fachtna was, above all, a faithful servant and the eyes of Ailill and Medb.

His words hissed through several broken teeth and his rancid breath made the juices in Sláine's stomach sour. "Medb will be thankful for this information, Sláine Ulfhada. You will be well rewarded. The queen does not take lightly, or forget, that this upstart not only stole her gold, but also executed her servant Eochaidh Ruad. She has lost influence in the south, influence she had built up over many years, and she does not like to see her plans thwarted."

"I am glad to be of service to the queen," Sláine replied in a somber monotone. As he spoke, he was looking not at Fachtna, but at a tall figure cloaked in grey, her flowing blonde hair caught by the wind. He watched as she rode her black horse alongside Conall, paused for a moment, turned in her saddle as if looking towards him. Then she cantered around to Mórrígan, conversed briefly and pointed to the oak tree with her staff. A bow was unsheathed and soon a black arrow had pierced the oak.

Later, after Conall's army had passed heading northwards, a troubled Sláine watched his unpleasant guest mount a pale grey horse nearly as lean as its rider. Fachtna would be at Chrúachain long before Conall had made the arduous journey through bog, forest and valley.

As he turned to walk to the Great Hall, Sláine glanced towards the oak and cursed as he remembered Mongfhionn's words. Weeks later, he observed that the tree's leaves had started to discolor. By autumn the tree had become leafless and black - as if struck by lightning. It was a constant and foreboding reminder of a broken geis.

The following spring, Knockadigeen was besieged and taken by the invaders from the east. The headless body of Sláine Ulfhada was found crucified on the oak. The body of his faithful servant Breácan lay broken at the foot of the tree.

By midsummer, the great tree was flourishing once again.

CHAPTER 20

SUMMER 411 B.C.

Armor and clothes were soaked by the persistent mizzling rain as Nikandros and Aengus parted company at the head of the waters south-east of Chrúachain. Aengus rode north for the widest stretch of the Black Pig's Dyke. His small band of warriors forged a path through the bogs, their horses snorting and breathing heavily as they plunged through the sodden black earth that threatened to suck them deep into its oozy grasp. They were relieved only by the infrequent paths and small islands of land forced from the bog by centuries of cold weather. On the largest of these islands small settlements barely survived a precarious existence.

The grey skies of the north beckoned to Aengus as he gazed on the massive earthworks of the Dyke in the distance. He never failed to be amazed at its construction. Legend had it that the dyke had been gouged out of the earth by the tusks of a large black boar. "More like the sweat of a lot of men and slaves," Aengus thought to himself. Contrary to what was often told, he knew that the dyke was not a continuous wall, but a series of earthworks that linked natural barriers of mountains, rivers, bogs and forests. The dyke plugged the gaps that might lead an enemy into the land of the Ulaid. For all that, it was no less impressive.

The dyke consisted of a massive wooden palisade for most of its length with an internal ditch facing north. In front of the palisade, earthworks sloped down from a height of two or three tall men. It was comprised of a double bank separated by a ditch that was the width of four men laid head to foot. From the palisade to the bottom of the earthworks was the length of ten to fifteen men. Carved into each of the larger sections of the dyke were narrow passages, which allowed access and could be defended by a few warriors. This honor and responsibility was the duty of the Cróeb Ruad.

As he approached the guard post, Aengus was troubled. For a start, it was more than two years since he had been given his mission by Macha Mong Ruad. Quite possibly she was imprisoned or dead. The destinies of the kings and queens of Ériu often swiftly changed with politics or a vengeful relative's blade.

Then there were the disturbing activities around Portach an Choirr, an area of bogland a day's ride north east of Chrúachain. Finally, Macha's temper was as fiery as the color of her long red tresses. Because of Fearghal, there was no love lost between her and Mongfhionn. Aengus wondered if Macha could control herself sufficiently so as not to provoke the ire of the Sidhe.

After satisfying the Cróeb Ruad guards, Aengus' party travelled a few more days north-east through the valleys to Emain Macha. The stronghold sat atop a hill that overlooked rolling drumlins with their clusters of narrow ridges and the lush green countryside. It would make a fine fort, Aengus thought, if and when it was ever completed. The site showed great promise, but its design reflected the rough, utilitarian nature of the Ulaid people. It would need a lot of work if it was to take preeminence over Tara or Chrúachain.

Macha was clearly agitated as she paced up and down in her throne room. She was a young woman of twenty-four summers. Yet worry lines had started to make an unwelcome appearance between her flame-red eyebrows. Macha was not unattractive, but neither was she was a beauty like Mongfhionn or the whore queen of the Connachta. However, she did radiate an aura of sensuality. Not tall, her body made up for its lack of stature with an endowment of lush curves. Allied with Macha's very sharp mind, it made her a force not to be taken for granted.

The time for Cimbáeth, the current Ard-Righ, to relinquish his position was almost at hand. Thus, at the turn of the year, Macha would have to formally stake her claim to rule as Ard-Righan. With persistence, Macha had finally overcome Cimbáeth's initial reticence to a High Queen, and an understanding had been agreed between herself and the Ard-Righ. She knew he would not oppose her. In fact, Cimbáeth had openly discussed making their partnership permanent. Being ambitious, Macha had little intention of giving up power at the end of her allocated seven-year term as Ard-Righan. Thus, Cimbáeth's offer was one potential means to ensure her continued grip on the throne.

In the meantime, Macha's rival for the throne, Dithorba, together his five sons were strident in their opposition to any woman becoming High Queen, and had actively recruited nobles and warriors to support their position. Rumor also had it that Dithorba was being advised on strategy by a stranger from across the seas.

Therefore, Macha was relieved to hear that Aengus had returned, but less happy to learn he was accompanied by only ten men – and none of them her former lover. Her eyes had teared and glistened at the thought of Fearghal's presence. Indeed, her eyes were not the only part of her that became damp. When Aengus entered her throne room, Macha stormed towards him yelling, "Where is that bastard Fearghal Ruad? And where are my three hundred warriors?"

Taken aback by the stormy reception, Aengus tried to remain calm. Deciding that offering some good news might defuse the intensity of the encounter, he said, "Fearghal sent me ahead, my lady, to inform you that he is marching north with an army of a thousand men and horsemen. He should be here before the winter snows return."

Her volcanic temper subsided almost as quickly as it had erupted. Now a smiling and gracious Macha looked at Aengus, "My apologies, captain. Please sit down. Have some food and refreshment. You must be tired from the journey." The change in tone made Aengus more nervous than before and he pictured himself as a fly trapped in the spider's web. In this he was both right and wrong. Macha, recalling past and imagining future pleasures when her lover returned, continued, "Wonderful. How is Fearghal? Why did it take you two years to find the brave king? Our Ériu is not overly big. Surely it can be travelled in less than a year?"

Aengus chose to speak plainly, "Fearghal does not lead the army, my lady. He has sworn allegiance to a king of the South, Conall Mac Gabhann, who was once his ward. It is he who leads and is marching north to help his friend and battle commander fulfill his oath to you. I bring greetings and presents of gold from the ruiri, Conall Mac Gabhann. They travel through the land of the Connachta as we speak."

They rode through bogland and along the west bank of the Abha na Sionainne. Now caked in mud and slime, and stinking of sweat from themselves and their horses, Nikandros' band surveyed the land before them. Surrounded by limestone mountains, bogs and forests, Chrúachain rose up from one of the rare green swathes of land in the region. The site was built on two levels. On great earthworks, the height of two men, sat Ráth Chrúachain – the fort and residence of Ailill Mac Tata and his queen Medb.

On raised dirt banks, which sprouted from the fort's earthworks like the spokes on a chariot wheel, were located the long halls and barracks. Between the outer edges of each spoke sat a smaller ringfort. A variety of other enclosures and burial mounds were scattered throughout the great complex. Finally, tall, oblong standing stones weaved a strange pattern throughout the complex and legend had it that they signposted the way to the Oweynagat and the under-world. Both the fort and the complex were ringed by a strong wooden stockade and deep internal and external trenches.

Nikandros looked at the ó Cuileannáin brothers - Fionnbharr, Craiftine, Labhraidh and Tadhg. It only now crossed his mind that if their mission went terribly wrong then this young, talented family would be lost from the earth. He dismounted and guided his horse to the edge of a small river that guarded the narrow approach to the fort. "We should look our best for the king and queen of the Connachta. We will make camp here for tonight. Get some rest, clean up – and sharpen your weapons. Tomorrow morning we will ride for Ráth Chrúachain."

Sunrise found them cantering towards the fort with their armor cleaned and weapons glinting in the sunshine. The great wooden gates of Chrúachain swung open as they approached.

"Well, that was easy," Craiftine remarked.

"Too easy," Nikandros said as he scanned his surroundings for possible escape routes. There appeared to be none, save the way they entered. Several men strode towards them as they slowed to a walk. The largest was striking, by virtue of the fact he had only one arm and yet carried a large axe on his back.

He stood before Nikandros' black horse and stroked its neck, "As good a beast as I've seen in a long time. Would you care to sell him?"

Nikandros removed his helmet, smiled and shook his head, "Sorry friend, I've had him for too long. He's family."

Noting Nikandros' color and accent, the warrior stood back a pace, surveying the group more closely. He noted their armor and the red shields with a black raven. His experienced eyes quickly took in their weapons: the swords in their leather scabbards on well-crafted belts or baldrics, the javelins in their leather sheaths and a range of other weapons that were slung on their backs or strapped to legs. He had not missed that many bore the sign of the Cróeb Ruad, whom he had fought many times.

He laughed, "Well since you're all so finely dressed, you must be the entertainment for the feast. Maybe you're the dancers in your short tunics."

Chuckling, Nikandros responded, "Dancers no." Then pointing to the ó Cuileannáins he continued, "But you'll not find a better harpist, poet and seanachaí in this island or beyond, than these. We come from Ráth na Conall, which is many days ride to the south of here and bring greetings and presents from our king, Conall Mac Gabhann. At their pleasure, we would like to speak with the king and queen of the Connachta on matters of some urgency."

"I will pass your greetings and request on to the king's Chomhairle. Now please, dismount and I'll take you to shelter. It's nothing fancier than a wind break with a roof to keep the rain off, but there's clean straw for bedding. The boys will feed and take care of your horses. Don't worry, they know what they're doing. For as long as you stay as a guest, the women will keep you supplied with food and drink. Or you can join with us in the eating halls."

As they proceeded towards a small roundhouse, one of their guides coughed and spat on the ground. Fionnbharr's sharp eyes widened observing flecks of blood in the man's spit. He also now noticed that many of the men, women and children had flushed faces, hacking coughs and streaming noses and eyes.

Once inside their accommodation, Fionnbharr reached inside his leather healers' bag and handed out small cloth pouches filled with a fragrant mix of herbs. He looked at Nikandros, "We should keep these with us at all times. If possible keep your mouths and noses covered. There's a sickness here."

It was several days before Cathal, their one-armed friend, returned. "Who's the healer?"

Since their arrival, rumors had spread around Chrúachain of a new healer. The talk began after Fionnbharr had taken pity on some children and offered them his own cures. His strange mix of herbs and chants appeared to be quite successful and soon he had a stream of men, women and children offering gifts in exchange for his medicines. The people did not look wealthy, so he rarely took the gifts unless they were herbs and grasses that he could use to make more potions.

Nikandros stood up, placing himself between Cathal and Fionnbharr. "Is there a problem?"

"No, quite the contrary, seems whoever it is has become well liked."

At this, Fionnbharr stood up and stretched to his full height. Now twenty summers old, he still had a wiry body topped with a shock of straw-colored hair, but the taut leg and arm muscles were certainly not those of a callow youth. Fresh scarring on exposed flesh testified that he was no stranger to battle. Yet, Fionnbharr was painfully shy unless he was at his healing – or in battle. His face blushed red as he acknowledged that he was the healer.

Cathal laughed, "Oh, she'll love you."

"And who would she be?" asked Nikandros.

"Why, the queen, of course. Your young friend's reputation has reached her ears. Medb has been ill for many days with this cursed sickness. Our healers are a useless pack of blood-letting charlatans, so she wants to see the new one." Cathal looked Fionnbharr up and down, his eyes glinting as he winked at Nikandros, "He's a skinny one. Maybe he should have a hearty meal before he meets the queen. If he cures her, then most likely he'll need all the strength he can muster!"

Roaring with laughter at his own jest, Cathal accompanied Fionnbharr to the queen's quarters in the main fort.

Upon hearing of Fearghal's new allegiance, the atmosphere in the throne room chilled, becoming tense once again as Macha retorted, "Fearghal's allegiance is to me and the Ulaid, not some upstart southern king. I'll have to remind him where his loyalties lie. If it were not for that jealous witch, Mongfhionn and her plotting with my father, Fearghal and I would be joined and ruling Ériu. They exiled Fearghal in the first place." Seeing Aengus' left eyebrow twitch several times at the mention of Mongfhionn, Macha inquired artfully, "Is there anything else I should know, Aengus?"

A disconsolate Aengus wished he had not been the messenger. "Mongfhionn travels with Conall Mac Gabhann," he said. "And she appears to spend a lot of her time with Fearghal," he added with an uneasy cough.

Macha's face at first grew pale and then turned the color of her red tresses as she exploded, "I'll hang the witch. I'll hang Fearghal. And I'll hang the southern king."

Deciding he had little to lose – other than his head, Aengus spoke slowly, but with determination, "It is not my place to counsel you, my queen, but perhaps it would be wise to temper your anger. The Sidhe, Mongfhionn, was powerful when you knew her many years ago. Believe me when I tell you she is much more powerful today. Confront her openly or fight her and you will surely lose everything – your life and soul included."

Seeing Macha's rage diminish to a simmer, Aengus seized the moment to add, "Also, believe me when I tell you that you need Conall Mac Gabhann more than you realize. On the journey north, I passed through the Connachta lands near Portach an Choirr. Ailill and Medb are building a road, wide enough to take two war chariots, across the bog. If the road continues, it will end at the Black Pig's dyke. The bogs that lead to the dyke will no longer be a barrier for the armies of Chrúachain. Conall Mac Gabhann's army is the only ally and significant force you can rely on in the land of the Connachta."

A sharp intake of breath met Aengus' words and he saw the look of concern and worry on Macha's face. "Remain here," she commanded, then went to the door and dispatched a servant. A short time later Cimbáeth and Cearbhall ó Domhnaill, the commander of Macha's forces, entered the room. At Macha's insistence, Aengus repeated the story of the road through the bogs. When he had finished, Macha said, "You may leave us for now, Aengus. I will send for you when we have considered your report."

"This could be the perfect foil against Dithorba," Cimbáeth commented, "the future Ard-Righan preventing an invasion and war with the Connachta – and at little or no cost to us. We use this Conall Mac Gabhann as our weapon. If he and his men are killed then that is no loss to us. A force of Cróeb Ruad can also be dispatched to the bog with instructions to provide support and ensure the battle is won and the road destroyed."

"I agree," said Macha. Then after mulling the options over in her head, she continued, "Our commanders will be instructed only to enter the battle if the road has not been destroyed. With luck, the witch Mongfhionn will be killed in the battle also."

Seeing the somewhat startled looks of Cimbáeth and Cearbhall, Macha declared, "None of this is to be told to Aengus. He is fiercely loyal to Fearghal and any indication of delay or deception would not sit well with him. He will return him to Conall and Fearghal with warm greetings and an appeal for their help. Tell them we are also sending Cróeb Ruad reinforcements – hopefully that will make them overconfident." Macha dismissed her two advisors. Left alone in her throne room, she regretted that her royal scheming meant that she was not quite as moist between her thighs.

Outside Macha's room, Cimbáeth spoke in urgent and quiet tones to Cearbhall, "This is not precisely what I had in mind. I have no problem with Conall Mac Gabhann's men being killed, but to send our men and deliberately hold them back. That is doubtful tactics and has little honor. We had better hope that not only Conall and Fearghal fall in the battle, but that Mongfhionn is also slain – that is if the Sidhe can be killed. If Mongfhionn ever finds out about the queen's plan, we will have a short and very painful journey to Mag Mell."

Several days later, Aengus and his men were given orders from Macha and commanded to return to Conall's army.

Exquisitely embroidered tapestries lined the walls of Medb's bedroom, but their impact was somewhat reduced by the room's ambience. A musky odor with pungent accents of stale piss. Medb reclined naked on a raised bed made of straw, rushes, skins and furs. Her lack of attire disturbed Fionnbharr much more than the other attendants - both men and women. They snickered at the high red glow that suddenly appeared in his cheeks. It was well-known, although apparently not to Fionnbharr, that the queen enjoyed flaunting her superb body and the admiration of men and women that naturally followed. She reveled in her reputation as "she who makes men drunk" or "Medb of the friendly thighs" and it was said that no man could ever hope to satisfy her.

Fionnbharr could not begin to guess her years. To him, she appeared almost ageless. Long, thick red curls draped over full breasts; full red lips and deep green eyes sat like jewels in a face as pale as alabaster. Today, Medb had no need for paint as a constant wracking cough had brought a natural rose-pink coloring to her high cheekbones. Even in sickness, the queen succeeded in stirring men's loins. When she coughed her ample breasts heaved and bounced, brushing her hair aside to reveal glimpses of dark, erect nipples set in an even darker and expansive field. Fionnbharr was unable to stop his eyes from travelling down the queen's firm belly to the thick red bush between her legs.

Medb rested on her elbow as Fionnbharr approached. A hoarse, seductive voice flowed from Medb's lips, "Are you going to gawk at me all day or cure me? Come, sit by me and see what you can do to relieve this awful sickness. Succeed and you will be well-rewarded. Fail, and you and your friends' compensation will not be as pleasant." Turning to the rest of the attendants, Medb spoke, "Get out. Tell the king I will have no visitors until I am recovered."

Fionnbharr attended to Medb day and night for three days. Thankfully, his herbs made her drowsy and he was able to get some rest from the queen's never-ending recounting of her exploits with multiple partners. It also turned out the queen was an appalling name-dropper. During the course of his stay he was forced to listen to descriptions of her play with a certain Ulaid king, Fearghal Ruad – in graphic detail.

While she slept, Fionnbharr enjoyed the freedom of Ráth Chrúachain and made good use of the opportunity. After listening to conversations and gossip, he had a good grasp of the strength of Ailill and Medb's armies and where they were located. Medb alone had a personal guard of two thousand men, not counting her mercenaries or the massive forces inherited from her father. Ailill's forces were even greater. Fionnbharr also learned that Cassius Fabius Scaeva was no longer at Chrúachain. Having outstayed his welcome, Cassius had fled north in the hope of reaching the east coast and finding a galley to return him to Rome.

On the fourth day, Medb again called for Fionnbharr. To his eyes and initial relief, there appeared to be nothing much wrong with her. She glowed with good health and was more foul-mouthed than before. As he entered the room, the doors were closed firmly behind him as Medb's attendants sniggered and left. Fionnbharr felt like a lamb facing a wolf. She looked on him with her jade green eyes and in a deep languorous voice she said, "Well healer, it is time for your reward." Spreading her thighs and drawing her legs back, she exposed the glistening pinkness previously hidden by her thick bush.

Several days later, a haggard, dog-tired Fionnbharr returned to his companions. He winced noticeably as he walked and rubbed his crotch as if making sure everything was still in place. Even from a distance, the bites and bruises that covered the exposed areas around his neck and shoulders were plain to see.

Nikandros slapped Fionnbharr on the back remarking, "You look worse than if you'd been in battle," as he led him inside the shelter. He was greeted by the raucous laughter of his friends and endless questions about what it was like to mount the queen. After satisfying some portion of their lecherous curiosity, Fionnbharr said, "In two days, there's a feast to celebrate the victory over the sickness. We're all invited." He then added, drawing another round of laughter, "I'll be sitting as far away from that woman as possible!"

Led by Nikandros, the party walked through the entrance of the Great Hall. While not armed, the group of warriors looked impressive. All were in full armor apart from Nikandros, who had decided to wear only his red tunic. Normally short, the tunic barely covered his crotch and, as he strode forward, little was left to the imagination. Dense, billowing blue smoke from the cooking pits enveloped them, along with the musky smell of sweat mixed with cooking grease, peat and beer; the din of hundreds of loud male voices having countless conversations and arguments assaulted their ears.

Crossing the room, they were greeted by good-natured whistles and taunts ranging from the ribald to the obscene. As usual, Nikandros was the main target of the shouts because of his strange looks and dress. However, Nikandros now had an impressive repertoire of local curses and happily threw them back at the warriors. The mob of warriors soon roared with laughter along with the black-haired, olive-skinned stranger who cursed them in their own tongue. As the group approached the head table, King Ailill rose and bellowed for quiet.

"Welcome, to our guests from the South." He then added to appreciative laughter, "We'll even welcome the bastards from the North." Looking at Nikandros, Ailill continued, "And we have a visitor from even much further afield I think. We seem to be getting a lot of those recently. Come, sit down with us. We're grateful for the help you gave to our sick, although I think my queen has already thanked the healer – quite a few times." Ailill roared with laughter while Medb looked at Fionnbharr and winked with her long, auburn eyelashes. Fionnbharr need not have worried. Medb's interest was already diverted as she watched the Spartan make for a seat at the end of the table.

She spoke in deep, smoky tones, "No, stranger. Not so far away. I want to hear tales of distant lands. Come, sit by my side." Nikandros bowed a gracious acceptance and strode to the seat beside the queen. He lifted his leg over the wooden bench making sure that Medb had a good view of what was under his tunic before sitting down. The gesture did not escape Medb's notice as evidenced by the pleasant, luxurious wetness between her legs.

"Perhaps the king, and queen, would enjoy our harpists and seanachaí. They are brothers of the healer. Even a stranger to this land, such as me, appreciates their outstanding skills in music and the singing of odes of heroes and gods." At Nikandros' words, Craiftine, Labhraidh and Tadhg were quickly given permission to play and jumped upon the table. As they played, sang and recounted many stories, even the drunkest in the hall could appreciate their talents. Soon the brothers had their audience alternately in tears or laughter with their blend of high and low tales.

Before they finished, Medb leaned over to Nikandros, laid her hand on his firm, muscled thigh and murmured, "You're clever, Spartan. You bewitch us with healing, music and poetry. And, of course, the healer provided a pleasant diversion for me. However, you and I have business to conduct. You are the emissary of a king, a king who has stolen my gold and executed my ally in the southern lands. So, Spartan, shall we withdraw and negotiate?" As she finished, her hand now stroked the hardness between his legs. "I think our discussions may not be without their pleasures."

Conall and his men said their goodbyes to Breácan at the head of the Nathair. The journey through the bogs had been torturous and slow, although fortunately no people or baggage had been lost to the deep, black murky waters. As they emerged from the bogs, Conall was glad to see that the river valley before them appeared to be friendlier for man and beast. Looking over his tired, foul-smelling and mud-encrusted army, Conall and his Chomhairle suspected that their friend, Breácan, may not have taken either the most direct route or the path over the best ground.

However, they were in no real position to confront their guide and, in the end, Breácan had led them to the location that Sláine Ulfhada had promised. Before he departed, Breácan was seen deep in conversation with Mongfhionn and it was a very ashen-faced and subdued warrior who started the trek back to Knockadigeen.

It was now mid-summer as the army and followers journeyed north along an Abha na Sionainne. The weather was not overly warm, but the skies were a deep blue, spotted with clouds shaped like wisps of pulled sheep's wool that scurried across the expanse. The sun brought out the men's craic and at least for a while the incessant rain had decided to go elsewhere. The valley had good pasture for the animals, and the river was sufficiently inviting that it encouraged most of the army to have their annual bath. This alone made the atmosphere in the camps infinitely more bearable.

Unfortunately, the more pleasant path along the river valley was balanced by an increasing number of skirmishes and raids as they crossed territories to which local warbands claimed ownership. Their presence was mostly an irritant, although at times the raiders got close enough to injure the lightly armored camp followers. For the most part their impact was to slow the progress of the army; for many, their reward was the iron point of a javelin or arrowhead.

It was Cúscraid who first opined that the raiders seemed both too numerous and too well organized for ordinary warbands looking for an easy opportunity or target to plunder. Noting this, Conall asked his scouts to watch for anything strange. Soon he heard about sightings of a tall, crooked and thin man that seemed to presage an attack. The description of the man appeared to fit with one that Conall had seen in conversation with Sláine Ulfhada.

After several days, Medb and Nikandros emerged from their "negotiations". The Spartan had a distinct pallor to his face and was walking quite stiffly. Medb, for once, also looked tired and drawn from their excesses. From her room, she watched Nikandros' unsteady gait as he made his way back to join his friends and ran her fingers and tongue across bruised and swollen lips. Almost unconsciously, her fingers weaved curls in the patch of red hair between her legs.

On seeing the state of his queen, Ailill snorted, "Maybe you've met your match in the dark stranger."

His queen's smile darkened, "Perhaps. It is such a pity that he, his men and his upstart king will have to die. Has Fachtna returned with his report on their strength?"

Ailill, with some disdain at the mention of Fachtna said, "He arrived back yesterday and has rested. He waits for an audience."

Nikandros winced and swore as he sat astride his black horse, but received little sympathy from his comrades. Despite his protests, there was a marked skepticism and a barrage of lewd jokes about his bargaining strategy. Still, his grim look and insistence that they should leave Chrúachain immediately was a good indicator that the more formal negotiations had not gone well. Quickly, they donned armor and weapons, retrieved their horses, and rode for the main gates. In the distance, Nikandros saw Cathal speak to the guards and the great wooden gates began to swing shut.

"Faster! Death awaits if we're trapped in this fort." Nikandros grasped his bow firmly and guiding his horse with his knees, sent his first arrow to the feet of Cathal. A second and third thudded into the wooden gate, close to the faces of the guards. The act was just enough to make them pause as fourteen horses thundered past.

As they rode by Cathal, was heard to swear, "Bastards." Although it seemed to Nikandros that the huge grin on Cathal's face meant he was not unduly worried by their escape. Away from Chrúachain, the group rode south-east towards an Abha na Sionainne, and then to the agreed rendezvous point at the head waters leading to Portach an Choirr.

It was just after the fourth new moon of their journey when Nikandros and Aengus rejoined the main army. Now mid-autumn, the air had started to take on its winter chill and the odd flurry of snow was a reminder to Conall of the need to get his army and people to a safe haven for the winter. They set up camp several days ride from Chrúachain on the east bank of Abha na Sionainne. Once the encampment had been secured and guards and scouts posted, Conall called the Chomhairle together to hear the reports from Nikandros and Aengus.

Speaking first, the youthful Aengus enthused about his meeting with Macha Mon Ruad. Taking little time to breathe, he recounted how Macha would welcome them to the North. In return for this welcome, she asked for their help to secure the borders of the Ulaid by destroying the new roadworks at Portach an Choirr. To support this, she had promised a thousand Cróeb Ruad warriors would cross the northern borders. He was much less enthusiastic at the persistent questioning from Fearghal about the queen's mannerisms, her tone and precisely what she had promised. Frustrated, Aengus glared at his brother, bowed to Conall and stormed from the meeting.

There was a much more sober assessment from Nikandros concerning the likelihood of the army being allowed to complete their journey across Connachta territory. While he made no mention of the details on how his negotiations with Queen Medb were conducted, as he gazed around the Chomhairle, the wide grins on the faces of his friends told him that he had few secrets.

"Ailill and Medb can raise an army of ten thousand against us now. With time they could increase this to thirty thousand." Looking at Conall, Nikandros confirmed, "The queen seeks revenge. She means to make you pay for stealing her gold and killing Eochaidh Ruad."

"Well it seems that we are to fight the Connachta, either to help the queen of the Ulaid or to defend ourselves from the queen of the Connachta," Conall said.

"The bogs are no place for horses, Conall," Íar spoke up. "We'll have no advantage if we fight on that ground. It will be the same with the chariots. They will not be of any use in a battle in the marshes."

"If we give them a bloody nose, will they stand and fight or withdraw?" Cúscraid asked.

Nikandros considered for a moment before responding, "What are you thinking, Cúscraid? Of all of us, you're the one who prefers not to take big gambles."

"The people who follow us need to be clear of the battlefields. Most are unarmed and there are women and children. So we need to make sure they have enough time to cross this new road through the bog. Once past the road they can wait for the army on the island of land north of the roadway. Nikandros and Fionnbharr have described, in good detail, the fortifications of Chrúachain and the surrounding land. It strikes me that the land to the north-east of Chrúachain is the ground we should be fighting on – and with all our forces. We have better weapons, better armor and we have horses and archers. Make them fight on our chosen field, give them a bloody nose and then retreat to An Portach an Choirr while they are licking their wounds."

There was silence after Cúscraid had finished talking. It was broken by a loud smack as Fearghal thumped Cúscraid on the back, "Longest speech you've made in a while. It makes sense to me."

Conall nodded, "I agree. If we have to fight, and it does appear we have little choice, then as Cúscraid says, let us choose the battlefield."

"Maybe we can also sow a little confusion before the battle Conall." All eyes turned to Mongfhionn who had been listening intently. "You should seek an audience with Medb and Ailill. Mórrígan and I will make some special preparations that just might put the Connachta royalty off their guard." Trepidation was evident among the men at what Mongfhionn might be thinking.

"Make your preparations," Conall said with some resignation to both Mongfhionn and Mórrígan. "I'll take any advantage I can get."

"You have to admit, they look impressive. They would make great mercenaries. Perhaps you should reconsider," said Ailill as he stood with Medb and Fachtna on the massive stockade that ringed Chrúachain and they surveyed the army standing defiantly a thousand paces from the fortifications. At its heart were two rows each with almost four hundred warriors. They stood firm, a pace apart, their red and black shields in front and three javelins stuck in the ground beside each warrior. Before them stood Mórrígan's archers and in front of the archers, ten chariots rocked back and forward on spoked, iron-rimmed wheels, as their horses paced, tossed their heads and snorted impatiently. To their left were three hundred horsemen, each carrying javelins as well as axes and swords. Red and black tails hung from the crests of their helmets.

"Huh! They look pretty, but can they fight? Can't you see they're taunting us?" Medb spat at what she perceived was another insult by Conall Mac Gabhann.

Ailill watched, admittedly with some satisfaction, the discomfort on his queen's face, "Well, my dear, if they all have the stamina of the Spartan, I suspect we will have a fight on our hands. But look, it appears as if they want to speak with us." To Cathal he shouted, "When they get close, open the gates and invite them in. Escort them to the Great Hall. I am curious to meet this young king and we're not barbarians. We can at least eat and drink before we kill each other!"

As the Chomhairle trotted forward, the gates opened up and Cathal strode out. "King Ailill, and his Queen, Medb, invite you to eat with them. We will take good care of your horses, as your Spartan friend can attest."

Conall dismounted and removed his helmet, "Please, tell the king and queen that we are most grateful for their hospitality."

Fearghal spoke quietly as he matched Conall's stride, "I'm not sure which makes me more uneasy. Walking into that female bear's cave or…" and he glanced at the two grey-hooded and cloaked women, "or what those two have cooked up." Conall smiled uncomfortably.

With Conall at their head, Fearghal, Brion, Íar, Nikandros,

Cúscraid, Áine, Mongfhionn and Mórrígan walked resolutely across the dirt floor towards Ailill and Medb's table. They were accompanied by Urard who once more steadfastly refused to leave Mórrígan's side and glowered at the Connachta nobles as he marched forward. Jeers, taunts and the banging of swords and axes on tables followed their footsteps. The shrewd among the Connachta measured the confidence in the party's steps and demeanor, looked at their well-honed weapons and at the red shields with the black raven. They also took note of the scars on their hands, arms and faces.

A livid, white-faced Medb sat stiffly beside Ailill. As the party reached the king's table, Ailill stood up, "Please sit at my table. Let us eat and take the measure of each other."

"I can't say it is good to see you, Fearghal Ruad, though you didn't appear to dislike my company on your last visit," Medb hissed. She rose and made a show of peering over his shoulder at Mongfhionn. "So where's the striapach for which you deserted me?"

Fearghal fumed inwardly, "She never did learn to control her tongue. Now we'll have trouble."

"I hope you're not referring to me, sister. For whore is a much more appropriate description of you." Mongfhionn's voice brought an eerie silence to the Great Hall.

As she spoke, Mongfhionn and Mórrígan's grey cloaks fell to the dirt floor. Conall did not dare look behind him, but his suspicions were confirmed when he heard Cúscraid groan, "Not the two of them this time." Apart from the intricate blue and white designs that covered their bodies and faces, and which shimmered in the firelight, Mongfhionn and Mórrígan were indeed naked.

Shocked, Medb stumbled back onto her seat. "Leave my halls and my lands," she gasped. Then, taking a deep breath, she recovered her composure somewhat and rose to confront Mongfhionn, "You cannot harm me in my home and lands. You know the laws of the aes sidhe. Leave now and do not return."

"The Ancient ones are not pleased with you, Medb. They have tolerated your depravity and appetites for a long time, but that is coming to an end."

"Your threats mean nothing. No harm can come to me. I am immortal. I am Sidhe." Medb had now recovered and angrily glared at Mongfhionn.

Mongfhionn spoke slowly and harshly as Mórrígan swept the room with intense black eyes, chanting and singing strange words that chilled the ears, souls and hearts of the Connachta. "My power is greater than yours and more ancient. Do not speak to me as you would one of your thralls. Your body can be broken and burned. Your immortality is a gift from the Ancient ones.

Be warned Medb, queen of the Connachta. Not on this day, and not while this generation nor the next lives, but because of you, a hound from the North will slaughter the might of the Connachta and you will return to the Oweynagat."

Mongfhionn and Medb's exchanged threats hung like a pall in the silence, the Great Hall completely still.

"I guess we're not staying for supper," Fearghal said.

Conall turned quickly and nodded, "Women in the center, you and me in front, Íar, Brion and Urard to the rear and Nikandros and Cúscraid on the flanks. Weapons ready."

A hand was placed on his arm and Mongfhionn spoke softly, but firmly, "I am grateful for your concern, Conall, but this time the women will lead or none will survive the night. Take your leave of Ailill, then follow."

Conall made a calculated bow to Ailill and Medb. A faint rising of his hand signaled that Ailill acknowledged their regrets and imminent departure. Led by Mongfhionn and Mórrígan, the group walked purposefully toward the great wooden doorway. The Connachta warriors were silent and brooding as the group walked through the doors to their horses. As they rode for their camp, they could hear the screeching of Medb as she vented her fury and anger on anyone who crossed her path.

"I fear we have upset the queen," Fearghal exclaimed with mock concern. "The Hag help the poor man who lies between her legs tonight." The party roared with laughter as they rode for the camp.

CHAPTER 21

The valley, north-east of Chrúachain, was flanked by steep limestone cliffs on one side and rolling hills and thick forests on the other. A broad and clear path led to the marshes and the newly constructed roadway. Mid-way between the fort and the path to the bog, a lone hill rose up. It was here that Conall decided to make a stand. His warriors waited, shivering in the morning air, the hairs on their arms standing on end as cold breezes flowed through the valley. Positioned on the large hummock of land, the men gazed to where in the distance, a massive Connachta force steadily marched towards them.

The occasional snort of horses and clinking of chariot chains signaled the location of their more mobile comrades, concealed in the forests to their right. Mórrígan's archers stood in front of the shield wall, a supply of arrows stabbed into the dirt at their feet. A similar supply was placed in the dirt behind the wall and more remained in the weapons wagons several hundred paces behind. Mongfhionn took up a solitary position on the cliffs overlooking the battlefield.

"The scouts say ten thousand Connachta are marching towards us. They should be with us before mid-day," Fearghal said as he adjusted the grip on his shield and made sure his favorite longsword could be drawn smoothly from its sheath.

"Just ten thousand, are they trying to insult us? Sure, we're worth ten of any Connachta." The voice from the back row sparked off a ripple of laughter along the shield wall, which soon gained volume until the roar was carried to the front ranks of the opposing force.

Behind the wall, a group of young boys beat a rhythm on their bodhráns. The boys had pleaded with Conall to be allowed to accompany the army. He had agreed, but only if they ran as if the bean-sidhe was chasing them if the enemy broke through the wall.

"Let's hope that Nikandros' assessment is right, Conall." Brion's finger traced the long scar that parted the stubble of his beard. It seemed to grow whiter as he thought about the battle and gave the normally good-natured warrior a sinister look.

Conall nodded, "I hope so."

Nikandros was convinced that Medb's pride and anger was the Connachta's weakness. He argued that she would send the best of her warriors to battle first as she wanted to gain a quick and bloody revenge. If the shield wall and mounted warriors could break Medb's elite warriors, she would be weakened and, in the chaos, Conall's forces could make good their retreat to Portach an Choirr.

Medb and Ailill rode at the head of their army with Fachtna following a few paces behind. The previous evening Ailill had counseled against attacking Conall's army. He saw no profit or glory in it and disagreed vehemently with Fachtna's groveling assessment that the Medb's forces would easily rout the upstart king's forces. This army had proven over and over that they were fierce and stubborn fighters and had prevailed against seemingly overwhelming odds.

Ailill bristled when Medb asserted that he was afraid to fight, but finally conceded to Fachtna's argument that Conall's forces could not be allowed to go north with news of the road in the bog. Ailill was certain the Ulaid were aware of the road, but not how much it had progressed. He was neither prepared for nor willing to risk, a war with the Ulaid when his eastern border was under threat.

Hence, it was a somewhat unenthusiastic Ailill that rode at the head of the Connachta. His consolation was the insistence of Medb, because she had been insulted, that her own elite warriors should have the privilege of slaughtering the rabble on the hill. At least, Ailill thought, this would conserve his men. If Conall's forces fought as well as their reputation, Medb might lose a few of her favored chieftains, which would weaken her political influence in Chrúachain. The more he considered this, the more Ailill relaxed. This was somewhat to the consternation of Medb and Fachtna who wondered why the king's face had broken into a broad smile.

At a thousand paces, the Connachta army divided into two sections. The larger section halted while about two thousand of Medb's warriors picked up the pace. Slowly the gap between Medb's elite and the rest of Ailill's forces widened.

"Shite. Nikandros was right. How could Medb be so rash?" Fearghal adjusted the leather chin-strap until his helmet sat comfortably on his head.

"This will not be easy, Fearghal. And it will not be pretty or glorious." Conall tightened his own chin-strap and turned to the men behind him. "We will stand firm. The wall will not break. Anyone who breaks from the wall puts his neighbor in danger and will face me after – if he is still alive. Let's show the Connachta how to fight." As he took his place in the wall, Conall's ears rang with the roars of hundreds of voices and the incessant pounding of the bodhráns.

At five hundred paces, with swords and axes held high, Medb's men broke into a charge, screaming their war cries at the enemy. The chariots that led them broke away and raced for the wall, their drivers whipping their horses and adding their own shouts to the din. At that moment, Mongfhionn made her presence felt as the Hag within her loosed a terrible cry as if from the depths of the Other-world. For a moment, Medb's forces faltered, remembering the dread that the presence of the Sidhe had spread among them. However, their captains regained composure quickly and drove forward.

At two hundred paces, the autumn skies became dark and foreboding, sheets of lightning turned the battleground into a nightmarish scene of light and darkness. It rained - but not water. A stormcloud of iron fell from the skies. Bone, wood and muscles strained, and bowstrings hummed as hundreds of arrows were fed to them. Men and horses screamed as the iron barbs bit deep into soft flesh. At fifty paces Mórrígan commanded, "Fall back!" The archers ran through gaps in the shield wall to their new supply of missiles. As the screaming horde bore down on them, the shield wall held steady and launched volleys of javelins. Then they closed ranks and waited – a solid line bristling with iron spikes.

When he saw the wide gap in the Connachta army, Íar shook his head in disbelief. At the sound of his battle horn, the forest edge suddenly came alive as horses and chariots thundered down the slopes. Medb's warriors had taken on the semblance of a falling star - a densely packed mass at the front followed by a long tail of men at the rear who were not quite as fast as their comrades. The tail was the target for Aengus' chariots. The creta shuddered as spinning blades left the debris of blood, bones and limbs in their wake. As they carved through the Connachta, flashes of lightning revealed the glistening red blood that now painted the chariots.

Hearing the sounds of horses and wheels, the Connachta chariots wheeled around. The two sets of chariots raced for each other, but as they got closer, Aengus' drivers swung their chariots sharply around letting their warriors throw their javelins. Horses screamed as iron spikes crippled them. Drivers, entangled in the reins, were pulled out of the creta and under the wheels and blades. Several chariots flipped over killing or maiming their occupants. Those remaining closed in on Aengus. As the chariots clashed, spinning knives snapped, flinging shards of iron and bronze into the air, and crippling horses and men.

Íar and Nikandros' horsemen reached the edge of the charging men and launched volley after volley of javelins into the charging horde. Then, tramping over the bodies of the dead and the dying, the cavalry began a brutal harvest, hacking and chopping downwards with swords and axes. The war cries of Íar and Nikandros rose over the noise of the battle urging their men to show their enemy no mercy.

There was a resounding grunt as Medb's men smashed into the shield wall. Along the wall, javelins were torn from hands as the impaled fell back or were pushed aside by the next fighter. Swords were quickly drawn from scabbards and the front rank began the bloody process of stabbing and slashing. The second row complained loudly about not being in the fight, but pushed hard with their shields making sure the wall did not give ground. Meanwhile Mórrígan's bowmen kept up a steady stream of missiles, showering the largely unarmored attackers.

Medb's battle commanders readily understood the perilous position in which they had been placed. On their flanks, they were assaulted by fast moving horses and chariots and they were making no headway against the wall. Even when struck, their opponents' armor turned blades aside causing little more than superficial wounds. The javelins and arrows had caused a high level of carnage. Therefore, the leaders issued the only sensible command, "Retreat."

The orderly withdrawal impressed Conall. There was little sign of panic among Medb's men. He called to Cúscraid, "Signal Íar, Nikandros and Aengus to join us. They hold no surprise for the Connachta now."

"They'll regroup and come again Conall. Their honor demands it. Besides, Medb will have their heads if they don't." Conall acknowledged Fearghal's observation, while surveying the slaughter before him.

"Sadly, I think you're right." He shook his head, "What a waste of good men. Have the rear rank change places with the front. It will mean fresh arms for the next attack."

A white-faced Medb railed against Ailill and Fachtna. She glowered at Fachtna, "So much for your military assessment. If your eyes are that poor then maybe I should relieve you of them." Fachtna flinched, but wisely said nothing. He too, was visibly shocked at what was unfolding.

Medb next rounded on Ailill, her eyes flashing in anger and her breasts heaving and pushing against her gown. "As for you, why do you smile while the elite of Connachta are humiliated? I demand that you commit the rest of our army now. Our honor is at stake."

"My honor is not at stake, my queen, but yours is. This battle was ill-advised. I will not send my men to be slaughtered by that meat-grinder on the hill. Conall Mac Gabhann chose his ground and tactics well. I will not blindly throw good warriors to their death to satisfy your passion for vengeance."

"So you're going to let that bastard escape to the north. Others will see that as a sign of weakness - and you know what happens to weak kings." Medb smiled thinly as she spoke, her usually full red lips now drawn tight.

"No, Medb, Conall will not escape me. When he has concluded this battle my guess is the young king will make his escape through the hills behind him to the bogland. His horses and chariots will be of little use in the water-soaked ground of the bogs and my men will hunt him down. We know the land and paths much better than he does." Ailill smiled allowing himself a measure of satisfaction in anticipation of success.

It was not Medb's nature to let anyone have the last word. "You forget one thing. The Sidhe of air, earth and water travels with them. She is mistress of the bogs." The frown that fleetingly clouded Ailill's countenance improved Medb's humor.

The hill where they had made their stand was no more than a great mound of dirt and rock covered in grass and moss. As Conall watched and waited, an involuntary shiver rippled through him. No longer warmed by the heat of battle, he like his men, shivered as the cold air chilled the sweat-soaked tunics worn as under-armor. The masks of blood and sweat that covered faces, arms and legs hardened and cracked, scattering dull red flakes into the air around them and dusting the ground.

The horses and chariots divided and cantered to the level ground on the left and right of the hill. Suddenly a great roar came from Medb's warriors and once more they hurtled towards the hill. The shield wall almost heaved a sigh of relief as they locked shields, adjusted their stance and waited for the initial crash of bodies. To their surprise, as they closed on the hill, Medb's men divided into two groups running towards the chariots and horses on both flanks.

"Clever bastards," said Brion. "They have no stomach for the wall. Our chariots and horsemen make an easier target."

Fearghal spat on the blood-soaked dirt in disgust, "Íar and Nikandros will never hold against that many warriors and it's too late to have them retreat."

Conall, sorely regretted having split his horses and chariots. His forefinger rubbed in a circular motion against the grain of the stubble on his chin. "Divide our men into three. Cúscraid will be our reserve and remain on the mound together with the archers. Fearghal, you and I will each take a section and advance down the slope to attack Medb's forces on their flanks. Keep the wall together. Since Medb's men still outnumber us our strength will be in the discipline of our shields."

"Mórrígan, do the archers have any arrows left?"

"We have some, but not many."

"Divide your archers into two groups. Stay on the slopes with Cúscraid. Target the Connachta leaders."

Their position meant that they were unsighted, reliant on signals from the hilltop. So, the first thing that gave Nikandros a clue to what was about to descend on him was the smell of battle sweat, blood and the pungent odor of unwashed bodies. The smell, carried on the breezes that flowed over him, assaulted his senses making him grimace.

"They're pretty ripe aren't they?" came a voice from behind him.

Another retorted, "Yeah, not like us clean folk with our horse piss and shite." The troop erupted in laughter.

Nikandros looked at Aengus, "We don't have any choice, but to attack. Drive your chariots into the front of the pack. Hopefully we can scatter them. My horses will be behind you. Pray that our gods are with us." Aengus leapt into his chariot, shouting orders to his men and drove his chariot forward. Within a short distance, the chariots were moving at full speed towards their enemy. The thunder of hooves on the ground behind him told Aengus that Nikandros' men were not far behind.

On the other side, Íar had assessed the situation and, like

Nikandros, came to the same conclusion. They had to attack and blunt the charge. Although well outnumbered, Íar was confident that the height and weight of his horses together with their fierce snapping teeth and hard hooves could prevent a disaster. Íar had no doubt that his men were the best on the island and he turned to them, "No room for fancy tactics, men. This is a good, old-fashioned charge. Kill anyone who gets in your way. Chariots lead out and make sure your blades keep away from my horses or you'll be the first to die!" The sound of Íar's battle horn let Conall know that the mounted forces were about to engage the enemy.

The bodhráns, accompanied by thunder and flashes of lightning crawling across the horizon, thumped out their loud and incessant beat as Conall and Fearghal's units tramped steadily down the slope.

With an almost suicidal fervor, Aengus' chariots slammed into the apex of the attackers. Mayhem spread as teams of horses were whipped and forced to continue their path. Kicking and biting, they vented their own fury on anyone within range. Several chariots upended, throwing driver and warrior into the attackers, while horses, creta and wheels crushed anyone underneath. The remaining chariots churned through the mass, splattering blood and gore widely.

Horses charged through the enemy, their riders slashing downwards with axe and sword. Those who still had javelins skewered hapless warriors before switching to other weapons. The broad chests and solid, muscular shoulders of the horses knocked men aside and trampled those who fell beneath their hooves. The sheer momentum of the charge meant that the cavalry were more than half-way through their frenzied opponents before they were slowed and surrounded. Soon the horsemen, hemmed in by the furious onslaught of Medb's warriors, were forced into a circle. Horses snorted and squealed as their flesh was slashed by axes, spears and swords. They needed no goading from their riders to retaliate with teeth and hooves.

Conall urged his men forward. He was frustrated at their lack of haste, but knew that they had to keep the discipline of the shield wall to break through to the beleaguered horsemen. As they tramped down the hillside, they shouted themselves hoarse hoping to attract the attention of Medb's men.

On the mound, Cúscraid looked on helplessly as the cavalries were crammed into ever shrinking circles. He paced up and down the ranks of his men cursing and swearing at the agonizingly slow pace of Conall and Fearghal's approach while praying to the goddess for battle mercies. Cúscraid watched exhausted horses, slathering with sweat, collapse from the stress and merciless blows. He saw the long, black doru of Nikandros hefted up and slicing through lightly armored heads and torsos. On the other side, the huge battle axe of Íar cracked open skulls and ripped through bloody torsos. The remaining chariots that had escaped the seething mass of warriors now drove along the edges of the attackers, their blades maiming warriors as they passed.

Arrows descended like a cloud of midges on a hot summer's day. Hands cramped from gripping the bow constantly; arm muscles burned and screamed for relief as arrow after arrow was nocked, bowstrings were drawn back and the barbs loosed. Mórrígan prayed that they would distract Medb's warriors, if only for a short time. In battle, only the briefest moment was needed for a blade-edge to lay open a face or an arm. The archers kept up a steady stream of arrows until their supply was exhausted. Then she called her band together and stood behind Cúscraid's men.

Medb was ecstatic. Sneering at her younger partner, she exclaimed, "Look! See how my warriors are punishing that upstart. The battle is mine. I'll have the glory."

"Your men fight well Medb, but the day is far from over. Conall's horsemen have battled ably and they still resist, although fewer in number. His chariots continue to harass and strike down those who stumble into their path. However, that is not what should really concern you. Look to the slopes. The red and black shields of Conall's main force are almost upon your men."

Derisively, Medb tossed her long, braided red hair and spat on the ground. "My men will crush Conall Mac Gabhann. And you will beg your queen's forgiveness - or you will not lie between my thighs for a long time." Medb's scorn was soon doused by shivers of fear along her spine. As Conall's men came within reach of the Connachta forces, once more the blood-curdling scream of the bean-sidhe was heard above the battlefield.

Cúscraid prided himself on being a fairly sensible, practical man with a high degree of skepticism for the realm of gods or other ethereal creatures. Mongfhionn had upended his pragmatism. She was beautiful, had great timing and a presence that made the queen of the Connachta tremble in her own fort and the normally bold Fearghal retreat. The lady was also terrible and scared the living shite out of him with her air-slicing screeches. As loathe as he was to admit it, Cúscraid knew no earthbound creature could make such a nightmarish sound, and one that was, without exception, accompanied by death and destruction. He was very thankful that she was on their side.

For a fleeting moment, the bean-sidhe's shrill voice caused the battle to pause, opening up the Connachta's souls to a fearful dread. It allowed Conall and Fearghal's men to bridge the last few steps unchallenged. The few who turned to face the threat were cut down by vicious blades and iron-tipped javelins.

The Connachta were focused solely on the horsemen. They had achieved their goal of encircling Conall's horsemen, but in doing so had weakened themselves. At their strongest points they were now only four or five deep and most were facing in the wrong direction. Howling for blood, they pressed forward towards the crush of horsemen, and had little warning when the red and black shields slammed into the backs of those at the outer edges. Iron bosses pierced, broke and crippled unprotected spines. For many, relief from the excruciating pain was a sharp sword edge.

Conall and Fearghal's sections hacked, slashed, and pummeled their way through the melee of Connachta men until they reached the struggling horsemen. It was a grim-faced Íar who greeted Conall, as his blood-stained axe cleaved another skull open and even more blood splattered onto his encrusted beard and long red hair. "Glad you could make it. I think we sent out too many invitations for the céili!" He bellowed, "Kill that bastard," as a mountain of a warrior sporting a shock of stiff white hair, was pushing forward intent on adding more gore to his already blood-stained axe.

The broken Connachta circle became a semi-circle of battle-rage possessed warriors. They continued their ferocious assault and more men and horses fell under the onslaught.

"The bastards are killing my horses, Conall. I'll not have that."

Conall saw great tears of anger and grief leave trails of white down Íar's blood-encrusted face as he surveyed dead and dying horses. Then he shouted, "Open the wall. Let the riders fall back through our ranks." There was a moment of pandemonium as the wall relaxed to let the horses pass. Warriors on both sides hacked and hurled curses at each other – Medb's men trying to follow the riders while Conall's blocked their path. When the last of the horsemen were through, Conall roared, "Close ranks. Push them back hard. When they break, finish them off."

Slowly the wall reformed and locked shields. While the opposing sides were roughly even in numbers, Conall's men were fresh to this fight and their strength prevailed. The wall began its relentless and bloody push forward. Soon, their strength galvanized Íar's men who formed up and brought their mounts forward with renewed determination.

Much the same took place on the other side of the hill – with one exception. In the chaos of battle, Nikandros had thought he was being attacked by new forces and ordered half of his remaining cavalry to turn and face the new threat. It was only a bellow of, "You bloody Spartan eejit!" from Fearghal, which prevented a disaster. It did not, however, save the red and black plumes that adorned Fearghal's helmet as Nikandros' doru sliced through them.

The repost was a volley of Spartan curses, and then a huge grin, as Nikandros realized what was happening. "Póg ma thoin, you big lug. What kept you?"

From his vantage point, Cúscraid watched Medb's forces crumble as the shield walls literally broke their backs. There was a brief moment of furious fighting as her remaining chieftains cajoled and swore at their men to stand firm. But as soon as their courageous leaders fell, the men turned tail and scattered. The unfortunate, who were not quick enough, fell to the dulled blades of Íar and Nikandros' horsemen as they took their revenge for fallen friends. The remnant who escaped the slaughter fled into the hills and forests knowing that to return to Medb would risk almost certain death.

Medb was fit to be tied as she saw her men first appear to gain the advantage and then watched them slaughtered. She turned to vent her rage on Ailill, but he sternly said, "It was a small part of the army. You underestimated the enemy. Learn your lesson for the next time. In the morning, my men will hunt Conall Mac Gabhann and his men in the boglands and leave their bodies to swell and feed the creatures of the dark waters." Ailill swung his horse around and made for Chrúachain.

Praying that he was not in Medb's mind, Fachtna hoped to escape to sanctuary and make himself scarce for a few days. The queen's temper would subside and would inevitably be redirected to feeding her carnal lusts. While normally a sound strategy, Fachtna's timing was poor. As he turned, he first felt a sharp pain in his back followed by a push to his left shoulder making him fall from his mount. His last moments of sensibility were of the queen's voice saying, "Throw the useless dog into the ditch. The crows can have him."

CHAPTER 22

Conall stood on the hilltop with the Chomhairle. As each took off their helmets, they revealed striking white marks imprinted on a background of blood, sweat and dirt. In another situation the picture would have been amusing. However, as he surveyed the battlefield, Conall saw only tragedy and felt a deep sadness at the dead and the broken bodies that littered the ground. Those who had fought well might find a place in a poem or song, but the rest would be forgotten by all but their families. By the next moon, the autumn rain would have cleansed the blood spilt; the carcasses carried away by wolves, bears and birds.

"Sound the recall, Íar. The men have had enough time to strip anything of worth from the bodies. Stack the reclaimed weapons on the wagons. If there's any room left they can add their plunder. Otherwise they carry it themselves."

Íar nodded, he knew the men would not object. Chrúachain was a very wealthy center and many of those who had died had ornate brooches or wore armbands and torcs of gold and silver. After several blasts of his horn, the men made their way back to the hilltop.

"How many did we lose? What's the state of those left?" As was his habit, Conall looked to Cúscraid for an answer, but Nikandros spoke first.

"We lost about fifty horses." He paused as a great sigh escaped from Íar, and then continued, "But they can be replaced from the herd at the camp. The cavalry took heavy punishment with thirty dead and almost half injured. We'll need lots of healing support from Mongfhionn and Fionnbharr. We lost three chariots, although we can salvage some parts."

Fearghal asked about Aengus, whom he had not seen since the battle had begun. Nikandros said, "Aengus is good, Fearghal. He's taken a beating like many, but will be fine with some rest."

"The men?" Conall again looked anxiously to Cúscraid.

"A few dead, but mostly battle injuries that can be fixed with a needle and thread and lots of beer. The biggest risk is sickness if they don't see the healers quickly."

"Make sure the injured are treated, even those with minor wounds. We're not out of the land of the Connachta yet and we'll need every man on the journey north. Tell the ceannairí na céad that this is their responsibility. I'll have no one shirk this duty."

Fearghal started to speak again, but his mouth was dry and coated with battle dust and debris. He coughed and hacked for a bit before spitting a disgusting mix on the dirt. "What's the plan?"

Íar handed Fearghal a horn of beer as he spoke, "Here drink this, you disgusting Northerner. I don't want you spitting that crap on my bróga. They'll get abused enough in the bogs."

"My guess is that Ailill will come after us at first light. So, we'll move as soon as it is dark. We'll light fires on and around the hilltop to make it appear as if we are still camped here. Mongfhionn has predicted a moonlit night so hopefully we will have enough light to see where we're going. The horsemen will walk their mounts. The badly wounded can ride or be strapped to the horses. We'll have a good start on Ailill, although that gap could quickly disappear in the bogs."

"Are you sure, Conall? I know it was decided, but travelling by night seems a huge risk with such a large band of men, horses and equipment. We're liable to lose more men and beasts from broken legs and ankles than we did in battle."

"We have little choice and few options, Íar. We'll be slow in the bog without a guide, but we have a few tricks and surprises that might just slow Ailill down. And there's solid ground a thousand paces from the end of the road that Ailill is building."

Later that night, as the last men vacated the hillside, Conall looked back across the battleground. Bathed in the moon's spectral silver light, the empty shells that once were men made an eerie spectacle. Blood once crimson now looked black. There were dark, low shapes moving among the fallen as packs of wolves trotted in from the forests to tear apart and feast on the remains. Sporadic shrieks from the nearly dead, their last memories now of blood-soaked jaws and hot panting breaths, rent the night. The howling of beasts had replaced the war cries of men. In the morning what was left would be picked over by flocks of crows and ravens.

The route wove a ragged path along the valley floor. Thus, progress was painfully slow as the army picked its way to the roadway. The snickering of horses mixed with muttered curses from the men as they struggled to choose a safe path forward. As they got closer to the bog, chariot and wagon wheels sunk into the soft ground. Already aching and tired muscles were put to use to free them.

Fortunately, their way was lit up by torches, yellow flames smoking and flapping in the moonlight breezes. The lights had been staked out by the men, women and children not involved in the fighting. The ground on either side of the pathway had been sown with iron caltrops, wooden stakes planted and holes, deep enough to snap a man or horse's ankle, dug. Íar had not been pleased with this, but was placated when reminded that, apart from their commanders and chieftains, the majority of Ailill's force would be on foot. Hence, it would likely only be men, not horses that would fall victim to the traps.

The army reached about mid-way to the new roadway at Portach an Choirr as the first light of dawn tinted the skies red and pink. Avoiding the deep, black waters of the bogs, weary legs trudged through cloying mud and slime that resisted efforts to release the feet it had seized. Some relief was provided in the few small areas which were elevated and dry, but these were all too few. The men ate and drank as they walked, driven by the sound of distant horns and encouraged by the Chomhairle. The armor, so favored by the men, had become an affliction that many would gladly have sacrificed to the goddess of the bog, but stubbornness won over temptation.

By mid-day, the scouts had returned. "There's a force of about a thousand Ulaid on the far side of the pathway. They've made camp on the island," one reported. He was greeted by cheers from the weary men.

Aengus glowing with pride looked at Fearghal, "See. I told you Macha would send support. The queen has kept her word."

Still unconvinced, Fearghal nodded, "So it would appear."

The news from the other scouts, although not unexpected, was far less comforting. "Ten thousand men are closing fast. They are using paths that we never knew about and have split into three columns. One is coming directly at us; the other two columns are moving to flank and cut us off. The traps we set only slowed them a little. It is the nature of these men to walk carefully and to be watchful of new ways that the bogs might deceive them."

"It would seem that Ailill is not as rash as his queen." Conall tossed away a bone from which he had gnawed the last shred of meat. His legs and shoulders ached from the battle, the march and from wearing the heavy chainmail. His skin was chafed raw where several stretches of his inner tunic had torn, allowing the metal rings to abrade his skin. His arm ached from carrying the heavy shield and his head pounded from the weight of the helmet, but he gritted his teeth, set his jaw firm and shouted encouragement to the men.

"Medb's political influence ensured that Ailill became king of the Connachta, but he is no fool and is known to be fearless in battle," Mongfhionn spoke as she matched Conall pace for pace as they made their way to the roadway. "It was fortunate that you fought Medb otherwise the outcome may have been a lot less satisfactory."

"We'll still have to face Ailill and very soon."

Fearghal gulped down some beer from the horn he carried. "Luckily, it will be dusk by the time we reach the new road. I doubt Ailill will fight at night. It gives him no advantage, so the battle will begin in the morning, which is better for us. We will be on the road and solid ground, the men will have had a good night's rest and our followers will have reached the safety of the island"

"We'll also have the warriors from the north to add to our men. Surely that will make a difference and we can give Ailill a bloody nose like we did Medb," Brion looked hopefully at Conall, and then at Fearghal who shook his head.

"Learn this. You can count on no one unless they are standing at your side. Look to your friends and comrades, the men who have fought by your side and who you trust to guard your back. We have to be able to stand and survive with what we have here. If the reinforcements from Ulaid join the fight, then that's a bonus, but don't count on it. If I was their commander, I'd probably stand by and watch both sides grind each other down. Then I'd enter the battlefield with fresh troops and take the victory. By that time we wouldn't care; as likely we'd be in Mag Mell."

"No Fearghal, if you were their commander, you would honor your warrior code," Mongfhionn smiled and then looked to Brion, "Unfortunately, Brion, Fearghal is not their commander."

Conall walked along the new roadway, kicking, pulling and probing with a javelin. He beckoned Urard temporarily away from Mórrígan's side, "Pull or push one of these logs out of place. I want to see what lies underneath and how easy it is to move." Urard set his weapons and shield down and moved to where two logs butted against each other. Back straight and bending his knees, he steadied himself, and took a good grip on one log. With no more than an extended grunt, the log was lifted and pushed aside. Conall nodded and examined the road's foundation.

Glancing up, Conall spied Torcán, who had been watching the scene with some curiosity, and called him over. "You saw what Urard did?"

Torcán, wishing he had not been quite as inquisitive muttered, "Yes."

Grinning, Conall pointed to the roadway, "Pick another log. See if you can do the same."

Somewhat relieved at the request, Torcán walked a few paces

from where Urard had lifted his log and set on one he liked. He handed his weapons, shield and armor to a friend. Then, after stretching his muscles, he bent his knees and took hold of the end of a log. It was obvious, from his grunting, that Torcán was having more difficulty than Urard, but he was not about to give in. His muscles tensed and strained as he pulled and rocked the log to start its movement. Snarling at the piece of wood, he smiled as he finally felt it lift. Once pried from its setting, the log was quickly rolled aside to the cheers of Torcán's supporters.

"Are you going to let us know what you're thinking?" Fearghal and most of the members of the Chomhairle had gathered to watch.

"The road is new and the oak logs that form the surface have yet to fully settle," said Conall. "The cracks and spaces between them have not filled with sufficient dirt or moss to bind them together. The foundation of the road is made from birch and, from what I can see, the birchwood has been protected by the oak logs and is relatively dry. My father taught me which woods burn best. This birch with the oils in its bark will burn well – wet or dry." Conall paused while everyone pondered his words.

Suddenly, and for the first time in many days, Íar loosed a great gust of laughter, "You're going to destroy the road, aren't you?"

"Here's the plan," Conall continued, now animated as he thought aloud. "We pull up and roll the logs off the road onto the dirt between the roadway and the bog. There are perhaps four thousand logs. We've a thousand men plus the horses. You've seen the time it took Urard and Torcán. We should be able to achieve this well before dawn. When the logs are off the road, and if we've time, then we can pile some on top of each other to create a barrier for Ailill's men. Even if they are just scattered around, they'll cause Ailill's men to stumble and will disrupt his attack.

Seanán can organize the villagers to fire up braziers along the path and light torches along the roadway so we have better light. Once the road is clear of enough logs, we'll torch the birch foundation and burn it as we go. That way we reduce the length of road that we have to defend. We will fight as a shield wall to the island of dry land where the Ulaid are camped. Íar's men will form the rear of the

Conall: The Place of Blood - Rinn-Iru

column. The villagers can take the horses and chariots back to the camp on the island to wait for us."

A murmur of approval rippled outwards from the members of the Chomhairle to the rest of the men. From the ranks a voice shouted, "Well let's get stripped, we have work to do before we sleep." Weapons and armor thudded to the ground as the men set about leveraging the massive oak logs onto the dirt under the pale moonlight and smoky flames of the torches.

Once the first one hundred paces of roadway had been stripped of logs, Conall looked to the group of villagers waiting with unlit torches. They dipped their torches in the braziers and proceeded to flame the wood. At first nothing appeared to happen, and then the smell of wood burning drifted back to the men on the road. With satisfaction, Conall watched as flames of blue, green and yellow took hold of the wood. Soon one stretch of the path was burning well. Heaving a sigh of relief, Conall said, "Well at least now we know it will burn!"

To the front of the road and on each of its sides, hundreds of fires twinkled like the stars in the skies. These were the campfires of Ailill's men. As he looked towards Portach an Choirr, Ailill wondered at the strangely colored lights lifting into the night sky. Lights in the bogs were fairly common, but not of these tones. He pointed it out to his commanders, "There's something strange happening out there."

After a while, one spoke up, "Birch burns that color my lord."

"The bastards! They're burning the road," Ailill exploded, "and there's not a thing we can do about it." The muscles in his jaw clenched in a tense scowl, but after a moment the king laughed, "Oh how I wish that Conall Mac Gabhann was on my side."

With more seriousness he said, "My informant at Emain Macha tells me the Cróeb Ruad reinforcements have orders not to fight until Conall Mac Gabhann is defeated. Make sure they do not escape; I will not be humiliated like the queen. When we've dealt with the upstart and his people we'll chase the Ulaid back across the dyke."

Conall's army was roused from their all too short slumbers. To the accompaniment of yawning, farting and stretching they stood around the braziers warming themselves and eating a simple breakfast of oats, bread, cheese and milk. Their mood was somber, interspersed with the occasional joke or description of how they would teach the Connachta another lesson. As the morning mists lifted off the bogland waters, they donned their armor and prepared their blades for battle; each resolving not to let their friends down.

Conall and the Chomhairle walked the road, speaking to the men, sharing the craic and letting them know what was expected. They then made their way to a deep stretch of water where armor and gold gifts were lowered into the cold, murky waters as sacrifices to the goddess for battle mercies.

"Fearghal, Nikandros and I will be positioned with the caomhnóirí at the southern end of the road. Our job will be to hold off Ailill's forces as our main body retreats towards the dry land. At our backs will be the archers. Brion, Cúscraid and Torcán will command the centre of the column and fend off attacks on the flanks. Íar and his horsemen with Aengus and the charioteers will form at the northern end of the column." Looking to Íar, Conall continued, "Your priority is to prevent the Connachta from cutting us off."

Conall paused, breathed deeply and turned to Mongfhionn, "The army would appreciate your assistance in evening up the odds. If that can only be that they see you stand with them, then that will be enough. As for me, I would very much like to see my daughters again, but if that is not my fate then I would like your promise to ensure their safety."

The sigil above Mongfhionn's eyebrow seemed to glow in the moonlight as she smiled at Conall, "My sisters in the east will surely banish me from Ériu for meddling in the affairs of men. Medb is not the only Sidhe who has drawn sharp comment lately.

The smell of rain is in the air. Rain will make the solid ground that the Connachta now use to their advantage wet and difficult to cross. However, the rain will douse the fires that are now destroying the road."

"A large section of the roadway has been destroyed and scattered into the dirt or the bog," he said. "I'm satisfied that we've kept our pledge to Macha Mong Ruad. It is true that wet oak will not burn, but the oils in the birch bark will resist the rain. I'll take the rain and be very grateful."

Mongfhionn nodded, "Then I'll go prepare for the battle." She paused, "and of course, your daughters will always be protected as if they were my own."

Deaglán ó Neill was exasperated. His face was now a ruddy red to match his mop of hair. "What do you mean we stay here and watch? Look around you. We can't just leave these folk to be slaughtered by the Connachta. From what I hear, the army on the road has just about destroyed the path through the bog. I don't know who they are, but they've done us a good turn and now you're telling me to sit on my arse and do nothing. The Hag protect me, but that's just shite. There's no honor in watching brave men die for nothing."

"You'll follow orders," said Odhrán Mac Seáin, who at thirty-two, was six summers older than his young captain. "The future Ard-Righan has given us our orders. We're to watch and make sure the roadway is destroyed. We are not to fight unless that has not been accomplished. If you want a long career in the queen's army, you'll follow orders."

"It's not right, Odhrán, and you know it. Besides, who are these men? And why are they doing us a good turn?

Impatiently, Odhrán said, "I don't know who they are and I don't care. We have our orders. We'll do what Macha Mong Ruad wants and then return to Emain Macha. Is that clear? Or would you like me to replace you?"

Shaking his head in disgust, Deaglán muttered, "Bastard," under his breath and stormed off to find better company. Watching him stride away, Odhrán's face was pensive. He did know who was on the road and he fervently hoped that Fearghal and Aengus Ruad died in the battle.

Ailill led the main Connachta force of five thousand men towards the southern stretch of the roadway. If his orders were being followed, the other columns were approaching the flanks of Conall Mac Gabhann's army to cut off their path north. He would then squeeze the life out of his problem. Grimacing at the blue-green glow from the road he knew it was likely that his roadway now lay in ruins. "Such wasted effort," he thought.

A large water droplet splashed on Ailill's hand as he dismounted and handed his reins to his young attendant. Ailill paused for a moment. He was rewarded with another droplet, then another and another. Soon, the light shower had developed into a curtain of cold autumn rain soaking his men – and the ground. Ailill recalled Medb gloating as she reminded him that Mongfhionn was Sidhe of water, air and land. He swore, but gave the command to move forward.

One hundred paces from his opponent, Ailill discovered his next challenge. Clouds of steam rose up from the burning birch, obscuring his view, but giving him glimpses of a shimmering, wall of interlocked red and black shields bristling with javelins. The width of the road, the wall stretched back until obscured by the rain. He surveyed the ground in front of him and cursed again as he spotted marker arrows. Bows had never been a favorite weapon for warriors in Ériu, but he mused that this could change.

From their helmets, he recognized Conall, Fearghal and the dark-skinned Spartan. True leaders, he thought, not afraid to fight in the front row. The king of the Connachta sorely regretted that they were not part of his army, but what really pissed him off was that on this narrow road, his numbers meant little. Once again his opponent had chosen his battlefield shrewdly. Breathing deep, Ailill roared, "Ionsaí!" Battle horns took up the refrain encouraging the men forward.

Barely able to see, as the rain hammered down under the darkening sky, Fearghal groaned, "To think I had a bath recently! Well, you asked for Mongfhionn's help. You might have known she doesn't do anything by half."

Conall laughed and was about to retort when he heard the Connachta horns. Instead he called out to his caomhnóirí, "First two rows hold steady and brace yourselves. The next two, launch javelins on my shout. Archers shoot as soon as you can see anything."

Their enemy's roars were soon accompanied by shouts, curses and yelps of pain as the first of the Connachta reached the roadway and found it was a track of smoldering wood and red hot cinders. The embers burned through leather bróga and boots. By the time the first wave reached the shield wall, their pace was broken and they quickly fell to javelins, arrows and swords. The odor of burnt flesh and clothing filled the air as bodies lay on the roadway and were slowly consumed by the remaining fires.

Brion and Torcán looked to the west as ghostly shapes appeared out of the curtain of rain. The Connachta stumbled over scattered oak logs, skinning elbows and knees as they closed on their enemy. They approached from several paths spreading out along what had been the dirt track along the road, but which was now an expanse of stinking, glutinous mud. Brion shouted, "Javelins." Along the rows of men was heard the scrape of hundreds of lethal spikes as they were tugged from the wooden road. The closing, rain-sodden warriors were met with several volleys and the unfortunate, dead or injured, were brusquely pulled aside or stomped on by their former comrades not wanting to break the pace. "They're a determined lot," Brion called, as he secured his helmet, balanced his shield and took a firm grip on his javelin. "We hold until Conall gives the word to retreat." A roar of defiance rippled along the wall as shields were locked into place and they braced for the first assault.

On the east side of the road, Cúscraid squinted through the rain. At his side stood Fionnbharr, looking like a drenched rat. The first volleys of javelins had slowed, but not halted the advance of the Connachta. Cúscraid observed, as well as he could, the paths taken. Then he shook his head and cursed, "Bloody stupid, I am." Fionnbharr looked at him questioningly. "Look, look at the pattern of the attack."

The blank look on Fionnbharr's face exasperated Cúscraid

even more and he said, "Thank the Hag you're a healer, son! The Connachta are attacking from pathways they know in the bogs, but those paths are narrow – maybe ten or fifteen men wide. If we block those paths, we will only have to fight a small force at a time. Pass the order to the ceannairí na céad to have the men advance and clear a way to the pathways. Form up at each one and block it. Leave a few gangs on the road in case we miss one."

Along the wall, Cúscraid's men broke into smaller gangs and waded into the sea of mud. As they made their way to the Connachta pathways, the bog sucked at their feet until they were up to their calves in the dark slurry. "I hope you're replacing my new boots," hollered a voice along the ranks. In truth, that day saw the biggest loss of boots and bróga ever to be experienced by Conall's men. The Connachta commanders, taken by surprise, cursed the storm that had turned the battle into a slog through foul smelling mud. Their routes to the roadway blocked, the Connachta were reduced to flailing against solid walls of shields. Both sides set to hacking, stabbing and slashing.

During a lull in the flow of men across the mud, Torcán spotted how Cúscraid had reorganized his men into small groups. "Look at Cúscraid's division, Brion. They've split up." It took Brion a moment to understand, but then he howled in laughter and roared orders to his ceannairí na céad, "Thick, that's what we are, Torcán. We're fighting along the road when we can stop before they reach us. Have the men form up and clear the way to the pathways the Connachta are using. We defend the paths."

Torcán nodded, "This will be dreary."

"Yes, but we might just make it out of here alive. We're used to standing in formation, the Connachta are not. With a bit of luck, in this weather, they'll get fed up and drift away."

On the northern end of the road, Íar watched helplessly as the horns of the Connachta came together, cutting the army off from the island. The island, no more than a thousand paces away, may as well have been on the other side of the world. Beside him, a perturbed Aengus scanned for a glimpse of the Cróeb Ruad men he knew were camped on the island.

"I don't see we have much choice, Aengus. We'll have to force our way through, but we're horsemen, not trained for the shield wall," he sighed, "Back to the old scream and slash tactics. At least the rain should slow everyone down."

Aengus unsheathed his sword from its ornately decorated scabbard and gripped it firmly. Íar turned to face his men, "When you get in range, throw your javelins and then run like the Hag was chasing you! Our aim is to break through and get to Macha's men." The men, their clothing soaked through, hefted their javelins and stared through the grey curtain of rain, resolutely waiting for the first sign of the enemy.

The sloping island rose up out of the bog to the height of several men. On a clear day it normally afforded a good view of the roadway. Today, the rain made it difficult to see beyond the hill's boundary. Scouts had returned to Deaglán with news of how the battle was proceeding and how the men closest to them had been cut off. Overhearing this, Deaglán's men grew restless. Fuming, Deaglán once again approached Odhrán and pleaded with him to at least allow Deaglán's brigade to enter the battle. His pleadings fell on deaf ears as Odhrán ignored him and continued to eat and trade jokes with his own clique of captains.

Outside the tent, murmurs of discontent rippled through Conall's people as it became obvious that these warriors had no intention of fighting. Soon this reached a crescendo of hisses, jeers and shouts of "Cowards!" As their leaders disregarded the growing clamor, the main body of Ulaid men stood shamefaced and watched women, children and old men start to strap on weapons.

Whether by surprise or good luck, the volley of javelins from Íar's men followed by the screaming charge disconcerted the Connachta and their wavering allowed a small group to break through their ranks. Íar later reflected that perhaps the Connachta were genuinely surprised as, instead of facing a disciplined shield wall, they were met by a pack of screaming eejits. In any event, their captains soon recovered and closed the arc once again, cutting off Conall's main force from any help. The horsemen left behind were soon fighting a vicious retreat, heavily outnumbered by the Connachta.

The small band charged up the slope of the island. Cheers from their people greeted them, and food and drink was pushed into their hands. Íar and Aengus quickly made their way to the command tent and accosted Odhrán. A furious Aengus snarled, "Get off your arse, you bastard. Get these men into the battle. Macha Mong Ruad will have your head for this cowardice."

Odhrán looked up and laughed derisively, "I'll kill you later, you insolent pup. Our orders from Macha Mong Ruad are to stand down. There will be no support for this pack of bandits and outlaws. Whether they live or die is of no consequence to the queen or to me. My orders are to make sure the road has been destroyed, and your friends seem to have done a good job on that. We'll not engage Ailill's men unless attacked."

Aengus glowered pointedly around at the other captains. Some of whom stared at their boots, while others, following Odhrán's example, laughed or scoffed at his frustration. Aengus' hand went to his sword, but Íar restrained him, "These men have no honor, Aengus. Let's grab what we can and go back to help our friends."

Spitting at Odhrán's feet before leaving, Aengus spoke one more time, "You had better pray that Fearghal Ruad or Mongfhionn do not survive this battle. The Sidhe's vengeance will be terrible - in this world and the next."

Odhrán's face lost its color at Aengus' words. He had no love for Fearghal Ruad, but he had no doubt that a merciless Sidhe could preclude a long and prosperous life. The fact that Macha had not shared this piece of information annoyed him.

As they strode away from the tent, a shout was heard, "Aengus, hold up a moment." Deaglán ó Neill rushed to their side, breathless. "Look, Aengus, none of the men knew about this treachery. We thought we were coming to help. Most are disgusted, but are unwilling to go against orders from the queen. You know as well as I that's a sure way to an execution."

"A promise was made and a promise has been broken, Deaglán. Fearghal Ruad will not forgive any of this." Íar and Aengus turned once more and began to walk down the hill.

"Wait, Aengus. We weren't told that Fearghal was with you. That could change things. Most of the men are from Fearghal's former command. Stay a little longer. I have an idea, but I may need your swords to give me the time I need."

Guarded by Íar and Aengus, Deaglán strode to where the majority of the Ulaid were resting, "Men of Ulaid. Honorable warriors of the Cróeb Ruad, friends. We have been betrayed for on the battlefield, fighting the Connachta to keep our land safe, is your former commander, Fearghal Ruad. Odhrán and his captains say you cannot fight. Not even to save the ruiri who fought by your side. What say you?"

As he was finishing, a raging Odhrán, accompanied by his commanders and over a hundred men with swords drawn, descended on Deaglán, Íar and Aengus, "Lay down your weapons, traitors. In the name of Macha Mong Ruad, lay your weapons down or be killed."

"Some greeting this," murmured Íar as he balanced his great axe in his hands.

"Odhrán Mac Seáin," a shout came from the main body of men, "is what Deaglán says true? Is Fearghal Ruad fighting on the road?"

Not expecting this resistance, Odhrán said tightly, "That is of no consequence. The queen commands that we stay here."

"She may be queen, but she is not Ard-Righan. She is not High Queen yet, Odhrán Mac Seáin. Answer us truthfully. Is Fearghal Ruad among the fighters in the battle below?"

Resignedly, Odhrán admitted, "He is."

Deaglán stepped up close to Odhrán's face, "Stand aside, Odhrán Mac Seáin." Turning to the men, he said, "Any man who wishes to fight for Fearghal Ruad, take up your weapons and follow me. We have some Connachta to send to Mag Mell."

There was a brief moment of silence as Deaglán marched towards the road. Then there was a great roar as hundreds of Cróeb Ruad warriors plunged down the hillside through the heavy rain. On the island, Odhrán waited with a remnant of his own men, amid the jeers, curses and spit of Conall's people.

Íar and his men managed to find their horses. The people had made them ready with full weapons and javelins and handed over the reins as they passed. In the driving rain they might not be much of an advantage, but they all preferred fighting from horseback. Aengus located a mount and rode alongside Íar with the screaming mob of Northerners fast bearing down on the Connachta warriors.

The Connachta lines shattered under the onslaught of horses and new men. Even in the rain, hurtling across muddy ground they had gained considerable momentum as they stormed down the hillside. Bravely, the Connachta turned to face the fresh wave of Cróeb Ruad warriors, who by reputation had no equal in Ériu. Shouts of, "For Fearghal Ruad," were matched by shouts of "For Conall Mac Gabhann," as the northern warriors broke through, linking up with the main body of Íar's horsemen. Íar's men were exhausted, yet determined to fight to the last breath.

As the two forces combined, Aengus shouted to the northerners, "The ones with the red and black tails on their helmets are friends!"

His voice was down to a weak rasp when one northern voice shouted back, "We're not blind. They're the only ones on the road with helmets!" Aengus gave himself pause to laugh and wheeled his horse around. Then he gasped, as he felt a sharp pain in his back that spread deeper and wider. His vision blurred as pain stabbed upwards into his head and then, beginning to lose consciousness, he slumped forward.

It was a lucky throw by a fleeing Connachta warrior, but the axe blade was sharp and buried itself deep between Aengus' shoulder blades. As he dropped the reins and fell forward over the neck of his horse, Aengus was only dimly aware of the Connachta spear that finished him off and, of the muddy waters that took his body.

Watching his men flounder in the rain and mud, Ailill growled, "This is no way to fight a battle." The rain had thwarted his battle plan and reduced to ashes his vision of a glorious victory over the younger king. While his men had weathered the initial onslaught of arrows and javelins, the battle had descended into a vicious cycle of hacking and slashing fought in a filthy quagmire. There were few deaths, but many injuries. His men, sunk to their ankles in mud, had little answer to the wall of shields they faced.

He smiled grimly in the knowledge that his opponent's position wasn't much better. They could neither attack nor retreat. To cap it all, his messengers had informed him that the Ulaid warriors had joined the battle at the far end of the road, "So much for my spies. Useless bastards." He looked to the skies, but saw no break in the dark clouds. At this time of the year, the rain could continue for weeks. "Dammed Sidhe," he snarled in frustration. He owed his kingship to one and now was losing this battle to another.

Unlike Medb, Ailill was no hard-headed fool and not one to waste his men's lives to spare his embarrassment. Common sense took over and he summoned his battle commander. "Sound the retreat. The only thing we're accomplishing here is giving the gods a good laugh. Then bring my guard and follow me. I'm going to speak with Conall Mac Gabhann." Horns sounded across the battlefield and slowly the Connachta disengaged from their skirmishes.

"What's going on?" a mud-splattered Fearghal asked warily.

"They're probably rethinking tactics." Conall replied. He scraped a layer of mud from his face and then hacked up a glob of mud, blood and phlegm. "We're going to need the healers after this battle to stop sickness spreading. I expect we'll lose more men to illness and rotting flesh than from the battle itself."

Nikandros interrupted Conall's musings, "We have visitors."

Out of the rain, strode Ailill and his bodyguards. Arrows were put to bows and the remaining few javelins lifted, but Conall raised his hand, "No. Let's hear what they have to say." He removed his helmet and walked towards Ailill. In the midst of a battlefield filled with muddy, half-drowned men, Ailill and Conall still managed to maintain the bearing of kings.

They took the measure of each other in silence for a moment before Ailill opened the conversation with a forthright, "This is bloody stupid. Neither of us can win. All we are doing is providing carrion for the scavengers and spirits for Mag Mell. I'm pulling my men back."

Relieved, Conall nodded, "Agreed, your decision is wise and brave. In your place, I hope that I would do the same." As Conall bowed and turned to walk back, Ailill spoke again.

"One piece of counsel, Conall Mac Gabhann. Don't return to the lands of the Connachta during my lifetime. The rains may not be there for you the next time. Look for a kingdom elsewhere. With your growing army, you are no longer an annoyance, but a threat to any ruiri. And you can be sure that ambitious northern bitseach knows this well. The Goddess go with you and give you luck – as long as you're not in my lands!"

Ailill turned and walked back along the remains of his road. As he kicked the ashes, he shook his head at its folly.

CHAPTER 23

"Pass the word. The battle's over. It's on to the Black Pig's Dyke, the North, and a well-earned rest." Weary cheers followed by the sounds of men freeing themselves from the mud greeted the news. Conall, Fearghal and Nikandros, helmets under their arms, strode back along the road. As they did, a solitary figure came to meet them.

"If I'm not mistaken, that's young Deaglán ó Neill. I used to bounce him on my knee. He was a tough and stubborn wee lad. Appears to have grown up a bit since then," Fearghal bellowed out a greeting to Deaglán and was taken aback at the young man's distinctly somber manner.

"The battle's over Deaglán. Put a smile on your face. Tell me, how is your family doing? I've missed the ó Neill hospitality."

The young warrior took a deep breath and bowed his head, "I'm sorry, my king." When he spoke, he glanced toward the huge frame of Íar trudging doggedly behind him. Íar was not smiling either, for in his arms he carried the body of Aengus.

The howl of anguish was heard along the broken roadway. Many claimed that it reached Odhrán's men on the island. Macha Mong Ruad, years later, was to confess of the terrible nightmare that had disrupted her sleep. Fearghal fell to the ground, holding his brother. Great tears of pain splashed on the muddy, lifeless face of Aengus. Conall and Nikandros stood on either side of their friend, their strong hands on his shoulders in support, yet helpless, knowing little could be said to ease his pain. Soon, a grief-stricken and ashen-faced Mongfhionn knelt by her lover. She fervently hoped that the blame would not be placed at her feet. Fearghal looked at her and simply said, "Damned geis. Why wasn't it me?"

After a time, Fearghal rose. The rain had eased and a stiff northerly wind was blowing across Portach an Choirr. He looked around him and asked, "How did this happen? How did my brother die?"

Observant as ever, Conall noticed the glances exchanged between Íar and Deaglán, "What have we not been told? There's no reason to hold your words. The truth will come out either this day or another. Speak."

Íar looked to Deaglán, "You'd better tell them." With a heavyheart, a hesitant Deaglán related the story of how Odhrán Mac Seáin, under the orders of Macha, would not support Conall and had held his men back.

Fearghal exploded, "You're telling me if that bastard, Odhrán, had committed the men as promised, then Aengus would be alive?" Miserably, Deaglán nodded.

"Well, this battle is not over. I'll kill the bastard. Then we go north and I'll kill the bitseach in Emain Macha. She will never be Ard-Righan." Fearghal grabbed his helmet and shield, pushed through the assembled crowd of men, and stormed up the road towards the island.

Cúscraid groaned as he, Brion and Torcán made their way to join Conall, "Is there anyone in this island who we're not going to fight?"

Knowing it was useless to persuade his friend of another course of action, Conall gave orders to the Chomhairle and his caomhnóirí to fall in and support Fearghal. It was Conall's intent that the rest of the army would remain behind. However, that was not in the minds of the men. Weary as they were, they quickly tightened armor straps, donned helmets, took up their shields and swords, and followed.

Not willing to be left behind, the Cróeb Ruad who had previously served Fearghal saw that their time as members of the Cróeb Ruad was drawing to a close. Having disobeyed Macha's orders, they knew her revenge would be swift and brutal. Once more they put their trust in Fearghal and a force of almost two thousand men assembled at the bottom of the island.

As he strode up the hill, Fearghal called out, "I am Fearghal Ruad, ruiri and commander of the Cróeb Ruad. Stand aside or die. My fight is with the scum called Odhrán Mac Seáin."

Around two hundred and fifty men stood on the crest of the hilltop. They looked both grim and nervous, for their fate was not at all certain. They had supported Odhrán as their commander, but now faced not only the southern warriors, but their former comrades as well. They knew they were heavily outnumbered. The baying and close proximity of a large pack of wolfhounds, restrained only by the ropes of their handlers, did little to reduce their anxiety.

Had the balance of forces been more even, Odhrán Mac Seáin would have had no problem using his men as a buffer and letting them die while he made his escape to Emain Macha. As things stood, he cursed his bad fortune knowing the force before him would quickly overwhelm his men. Once his men were defeated, the horsemen would have access to their mounts and would quickly run him down if he tried to get to the Dyke.

So, affecting confidence, Odhrán called for his shield and sword and shoved his way through the ranks of his men. His only hope was to challenge Fearghal. Assuring himself that he knew how Fearghal Ruad fought with that famous longsword, Odhrán believed he had a good chance of killing him.

"The queen demands that all Ulaid lay down their arms, go back to Emain Macha and face her justice. She may be merciful even though you have disobeyed her commands. As for the traitor, Fearghal Ruad, the time for his justice is now." Odhrán strode in front of his men, "If you're not a coward, fight me, Fearghal Ruad."

Turning to Conall, Fearghal spoke quietly, "This could be a toss-up as to who wins. He's a bastard with no conscience, but he's as good a swordsman as me. He and I trained together, so he has a good idea of how I fight." Fearghal thought for a moment, his hesitation bringing a smile to Odhrán's face. He then unsheathed his favored longsword and handed it to Conall, "Maybe I have a trick or two. Take care of this for me. May I borrow one of your axes?"

Conall smiled as he handed over his axe, "The blade is sharp and the balance true. Kill the bastard."

Balancing the weapon in his right hand, Fearghal turned and walked purposefully up the hillside. It annoyed Odhrán to see his assumptions had been wrong, even before the fight had begun. As the shadows of dusk began to lengthen, he took several quick paces and then charged. Fearghal halted, raised his shield and set his feet firmly on the dirt of the well-drained slope as Odhrán slammed into him. The crack of shields resounded across the island. The impact pushed Fearghal back several paces; he exhaled explosively and his head jerked backwards as Odhrán's sword banged viciously against his helmet.

The fetid breath of Odhrán filled Fearghal's nostrils as he mocked him through yellowed teeth, "You look like a striapach with that nice shiny helmet and armor. Does your witch or your master dress you before battle?"

Fearghal shoved him away, "Are you going to talk me to death or fight? Maybe you're hoping your sour breath will dull my senses enough for you to stab me in the back."

He saw that the clash of shields had left his opponent's smaller, wooden shield with a sizeable dent. In the dimming light, he spied the beginning of a crack. A flurry of axe strokes pounded Odhrán's shield, their speed a blur to those watching the duel. Odhrán was not without experience in fighting and feigned a stumble as his shield took another hit. When Fearghal moved in, Odhrán rebalanced his weight and swung his blade across his enemy's thighs, slicing through flesh. He laughed derisively as a grunt of pain escaped from Fearghal. He sprang up, his shield edge catching Fearghal beneath his chin snapping his head backwards again.

The opposing sides watched the duel closely. Torches were brought to the fighting circle, their flickering red, yellow and orange flames adding to the atmosphere. The difference in the two sides was palpable. While Conall's men cheered loudly, shouted advice for Fearghal and heaped curses and profanities on Odhrán, Odhrán's men were subdued. Most realized that if their commander won, it would be a short-lived victory and they would be quickly overwhelmed and likely slaughtered by an angry mob of warriors and peasants. The more observant noted the villagers replenishing quivers of arrows and Conall's archers moving into positions with a clear sight of their targets. The remaining cavalry were retrieving their mounts. There was to be no escape for Odhrán's men.

Cursing himself for being fooled so easily, Fearghal shook his head and stepped backwards to regain his footing. He felt the sticky blood on his thighs and winced in pain as he moved. His opponent off-balance, Odhrán pushed forward. The taut muscles of his arm powered his sword thrusts and slashes, keeping Fearghal on the defensive, however, while Odhrán was a proficient swordsman, he was also overconfident and arrogant in his abilities. With a shout of victory, he slashed viciously downwards, carving a deep gash in Fearghal's leather shoulder pad. His exultation was short-lived and he cursed as he heard the blade strike iron scales underneath the leather.

In that moment, as Odhrán's sword slewed off Fearghal's shoulder, his shield dropped leaving his neck and chest exposed. Fearghal struck upwards with the head of the axe, catching Odhrán under the chin. Odhrán staggered backwards in surprise, spitting blood onto the dirt, yet quickly moved his shield back into place as it was pounded over and over by axe and shield. Each blow bit deeper into the shield carving shards of wood from it. Forced backwards and sideways, Odhrán grunted under the force of the raven-emblazoned shield's iron boss as it alternated with slashing axe strokes. He desperately hit out at the moving figure of Fearghal, but realized, too late, that he had been maneuvered from his advantage on the high ground and was now fighting uphill.

Slashing at Fearghal's calves and shins, Odhrán hoped to maim his challenger and regain the advantage. His opponent continued his relentless assault, axe and shield moving as one – attacking and defending. Fearghal's persistence was rewarded when he heard a sharp crack as Odhrán's shield split in two. Cursing, Odhrán tossed the shattered shield aside and reached for the dagger in his belt. Another time, Fearghal would have allowed his adversary to arm himself, but not the bastard responsible for Aengus' death. As Odhrán's left hand snatched at the dagger in his belt, the blade of Fearghal's axe chopped downwards, neatly removing his hand at the wrist.

Odhrán screamed. In desperation, he swung the bloody stump at Fearghal, futilely hoping the sticky crimson torrent would blind him, but Fearghal slammed his shield hard against Odhrán's useless arm causing him to shriek in anguish. He smashed the butt-end of the axe on Odhrán's forehead. Stunned, the warrior fell to his knees and croaked a plea for mercy as Fearghal stood over him. There was none. The axe swung one final time and Odhrán's head spun to the side, as his body fell forward.

The dual over, Fearghal placed his foot Odhrán's corpse and turned to face Odhrán's men, "Cowards," he shouted, "you have no honor, but I will not waste my sword on you. Go back to Emain Macha. Tell Macha Mong Ruad that Fearghal Ruad will be calling on her."

CHAPTER 24

AUTUMN 411 B.C.

It had been a quarter cycle of the moon since the battle at Portach an Choirr. Offerings had been made to the goddess and the men were rested. Those needing healing were attended to; the dead were honored and their families assured that they would not be neglected or forgotten. Encouraged by Conall to be open with their opinions, the Chomhairle discussed, at length, how they should proceed. The few that were still uncomfortable with this shared approach were respectfully chided.

Cúscraid listened to the discussion, then spoke up, "We should remain here for the winter and make the journey north in the spring. The island is large enough for the army and our people. We have wood from the road to build a solid defense perimeter."

Nikandros licked the fat that had dripped down his hand from the hunk of meat he had just carved, and said. "You would build us the finest of defenses, Cúscraid, but Ailill and Medb would not be pleased. They would be even unhappier when we started raiding their lands for food and cattle. We've almost two thousand men to feed; the same again counting our followers – and, of course, there's Íar's horses."

Nervously, Deaglán, the newest member of the council, cleared his throat. "Our reception at the Dyke may not be terribly friendly. Odhrán's men will almost certainly have found their way back before us - and bringing his head with them! That's not going to encourage

Macha Mong Ruad to welcome us with open arms."

At the mention of Macha's name, a snarl came from a morose Fearghal, "Who cares what that bitseach thinks? Her time on this earth will not be long."

Íar refilled his horn and drank deeply sighing at his friend, "Do we need to cross the Dyke? From what I hear, it's not a solid, continuous wall, but stops at mountains and rivers. Why don't we just choose a mountain path or follow a river into the North?"

Recognizing the need to reach a speedy decision, Conall said, "We can't remain here. Ailill and Medb would soon set aside their personal quarrel and we'd be faced not with five or ten thousand warriors, but thirty thousand – or more. The coming winter will not protect us from attack, but will make the bogland easier to cross. As Nikandros pointed out, we have many mouths to feed. We still hear rumors of battles to the east. We have little choice, but to move north." Conall paused briefly and then continued, "Besides all that, we're not at full strength. Many of the men are still recovering from injuries. Sickness is spreading throughout the camp; the healers are just able to keep ahead of that. I have no doubt the men will fight if needed, but our losses could be great. We have no forges to repair or replace weapons."

Glancing at Fearghal, he said, "As I see it, we have no choice, but to cross into the land of the Ulaid, hopefully with as little trouble as possible. Macha is not to be trusted, but she is threatened by Dithorba and word will have spread among her own supporters that Fearghal Ruad has returned. The queen cannot be sure how many of her followers may be more loyal to Fearghal and might switch sides. She is bound to know that provoking a fight would only weaken her. While Macha may not make it easy for us, she cannot openly confront us for fear of dividing her own support."

Taking the grunted acknowledgement from Fearghal as agreement, Conall declared, "We'll rest up here for another seven sunrises and then move north. Based on what Cúscraid, Fearghal and Deaglán have told me, the ground will be easier to travel on and will be hardening with the winter frosts. Once across the Dyke, we travel north-east along a wide valley between two mountain ranges.

Our aim is to pass Macha's fort keeping as much distance between her and us as possible. We'll then travel along the west shores of the waters of Uiscí na Fathach until we reach the gleannta of the north-east. Once there, we'll find a secure valley to wait out the winter, re-equip and train our newest recruits."

There was a general rumble of agreement and relief that the direction had been set. Looking at the northern members of the Chomhairle, Íar asked, "Does anyone know how to ride a horse in that land? I've lost a lot of men. Can we convince some more to join us?"

Deaglán laughed, "I think you'll be pleasantly surprised Íar."

"I have a suggestion to add to your numbers." Íar eyed Conall suspiciously. "I think the archers should join your cavalry. They'd be more useful if they were mobile although they may have a challenge controlling their mount while using the bow."

Although he saw the sense of the proposal, Íar groaned, "That's just great, now I have to deal with women in my cavalry - including my sister.

Can we not have something just for men?"

Macha Mong Ruad's face was trippin' her. Cimbáeth and Macha's commander, Cearbhall, both observed this, but chose to ignore it. It was Cimbáeth's opinion that Macha had gambled and lost. They all had underestimated the young ruiri and his battle commanders. The question was how the queen would react to it.

"My scouts tell me that Conall Mac Gabhann and Fearghal Ruad's forces are approaching Gleann na Muice Duibhe," she said, breaking the silence.

Cimbáeth nodded, "My latest information is that a force of some two thousand men, cavalry and chariots, accompanied by their followers is a day's march from the Dyke."

"Two thousand men! What fool sent Fearghal Ruad's old comrades to Portach an Choirr?" A withering glance in his direction showed Cearbhall who the queen blamed, "and under the command of that arse-hole Odhrán Mac Seáin? He should thank the goddess that Fearghal took his head. Now, Dithorba, his sons and supporters openly laugh and point to what they see as my incompetence. I've even heard rumors that some of my own nobles are considering changing allegiance." She considered for a moment, "Can we stop them at the Dyke?"

"You might be able to stop them at the Dyke, but whether that would be wise is another question. Fearghal still has a lot of powerful friends, like the ó Neills and the Ruads. They are not at all happy at how young Deaglán was treated or how Aengus died. They would quite likely throw their weight behind Fearghal if it came to a straight fight, and they of course would influence and put pressure on many of the lesser nobles. Your only advantage, at this time, is that the ó Neills and Ruads loathe Dithorba and his sons more than they dislike you."

Pausing before he delivered his final opinion, Cimbáeth looked Macha in the eye, "Fight Fearghal now and you may as well kiss the throne of Ériu goodbye."

The bluntness of Cimbáeth's words stunned Macha and her head snapped back in anger. "The throne is mine by right," she screamed. While Cearbhall blanched, Cimbáeth remained calm.

Looking pointedly at Macha, Cimbáeth continued, "You should pray to the goddess that Conall Mac Gabhann can influence Fearghal to exercise restraint. Fearghal holds you fully responsible for Aengus' death. However, given time to think, I doubt that even Fearghal would contest your right to be Ard-Righan. Your best ally could be the young ruiri. My informants tell me that Conall's intention is to avoid a confrontation and that he only seeks a path to the gleannta to find a winter refuge for his people."

Cimbáeth waited to let his words sink in and then said, "I am also advised that Conall seeks a Roman named Cassius Fabius Scaeva, who was responsible for his family's murder. As it happens, this is the same person who has been advising and encouraging Dithorba to contest your claim. It strikes me that perhaps we can use Conall to remove the thorn in your side."

Macha thought for a moment then spoke, "Send a courier to meet Conall Mac Gabhann at the Dyke. Let him deliver a message that Macha Mong Ruad regrets the misunderstanding at Portach an Choirr. Say that Odhrán Mac Seáin was acting on his own behalf and did not follow his queen's orders. Extend our thanks for his execution and advise Conall that he and his people are welcome and that he should make his way to the gleannta west of Ráth na Lairig Éadain. Tell him that we also look forward to meeting him, his queen, their daughters and Chomhairle as guests at Emain Macha."

With an eyebrow raised, Cimbáeth said, "West of Ráth na Lairig Éadain? Doesn't Dithorba consider that part of his territory?"

Macha laughed, "It will be an interesting winter."

The winter winds were beginning to make their presence felt, although, on the whole, the past days had been very pleasant. The rain had gone and apart from a few light showers, blue skies speckled with feathery white clouds and the warmth of the sun's rays combined to raise the spirits of the men and their followers. Conall smiled contentedly as he rode Toirneach with Mórrígan cantering alongside. The laughter of Danu and Brighid sitting on their ponies, led by Íar and Nikandros, delighted him.

Intent on making up for lost time, Brion and Áine often disappeared along the forest trails. Both blushed at the good-humored shouts from the men at their disheveled appearance when they rejoined the main group. Conall was glad to see that Fearghal's spirits had risen, due largely to Mongfhionn's presence and attention.

As they approached the Dyke, Conall stopped to admire the earthworks. Even at a distance, the Dyke looked an impressive and formidable barrier. He called Cúscraid and Deaglán forward and passed orders back that the Northern members of the army should come to the front. It was his hope that the guards on the Dyke would be more favorable to their fellow countrymen.

From the Dyke's watchtowers, Cróeb Ruad warriors watched the army approach. The Ulaid glanced nervously at each other, for they had rarely seen an army march in such defined order and with a confidence that could only have come from battles. They quickly sent for the Captain of the Guard.

Behind Conall, Brion, with Áine at his side, led the chariots. In memory of Aengus, each carried a black standard, alongside their raven banners, waving and snapping in the wind. Íar and Nikandros, on their great warhorses, led the cavalry on the flanks. In the center, marched the newest recruits. Determined not to be shown-up by their comrades, they marched resolutely in ranks. To their right and left marched the red and black shields of Conall's men and within their ranks, the archers. Behind the army there was a train of wagons with the tradesmen and camp followers walking alongside.

The captain of the guard was a tall wiry man whose short, grey, rust-speckled hair, belied his age. A longsword hung in a well-worn leather sheath on his back. Eoghan ó Liath commanded the battlements of Gleann na Muice Duibhe, not because of his well-deserved reputation as a swordsman, but because he was known to have a cool head in extreme circumstances. He looked with admiration on the army drawing near, but he knew he had problems.

The Dyke had never been breached and was built to be defended by a few elite warriors until the main Ulaid army could be mobilized. The forces before him were not huge by any means and certainly far less than could be mustered from the Ulaid. However, from the few faces that he immediately recognized, he knew that this was no ordinary cobbling together of warbands. By Eoghan's estimate, his men were outnumbered by at least twenty-to-one. Adding to his frustration was that, so far, his messengers had returned with no indication that help was to be expected or on its way.

A hundred paces from the Dyke, the army halted and Conall cantered forward. Removing his helmet, he shook his head, raking long fingers through his long dark hair. He took his time and appeared at ease. Absently, he mused that, despite Mórrígan's preference for his hair to be longer, he needed a haircut. It seemed to him that his helmet was getting quite restrictive. When he had finished, the others followed his lead and removed their helmets or hoods. As Fearghal removed his, a loud belly laugh echoed from the Dyke, "So, not only can the bastard ride, but now he has a fancy helmet."

Fearghal grinned and shielding his eyes from the early morning sun, shouted, "I see you still haven't been able to grow a decent head of hair or beard, you old arse-hole." A ripple of laugher flowed through the men on both sides of the Dyke as they felt the tension subside.

Conall nodded to Deaglán who took several paces forward, "Captain of the Guard, I am Deaglán ó Neill and I request passage through the Dyke for myself and my friends."

"You must be very popular, Deaglán ó Neill. You've got a lot of friends." Eoghan's rejoinder belied his thoughts – none particularly good. "I have no orders to allow anyone passage through the Dyke and you must know that I cannot ignore my orders, for you or anyone."

At this, Conall urged his great black horse forward, "I am Conall Mac Gabhann, and I am responsible for all before you. My people and men are tired and need rest. We bring no trouble and only wish to find a safe haven for the winter. Many of my men are Ulaid, many you possibly know. We would appreciate your understanding and an invitation to enter."

Not wanting to provoke a fight that would most likely result in the senseless death of many men, Eoghan called out, "I appreciate your position, but my hands are tied. Until I receive orders, I can't open the gate to anyone. Perhaps, I could meet with you and we can discuss the matter?"

As Conall started to reply, another horse cantered forward. A grey-cloaked person dismounted and strode forward until she was within ten paces of the solid, oak gates. Slamming her staff into the solid, frost covered ground, the voice of Mongfhionn rang out along the Dyke, "Who among the Ulaid denies passage to the Sidhe? Do you, Eoghan ó Liath? Must I shatter these oak gates you guard so steadfastly?"

Eoghan rolled his eyes. His morning had just gone from bad to worse. He was not at all happy with the position he found himself in and wondered which goddess he had pissed off. The forces that faced his small band of men were formidable and now a Sidhe was calling him by name. He cleared his throat, "My lady, you know my name, and so you must also know my reputation and that I speak the truth. Even for the Sidhe, I cannot open the gates to the land of the Ulaid. I have my duty."

"Duty I understand. Foolishness I don't." Both sides watched anxiously as the oak staff was raised and the grey cloak fell from Mongfhionn's shoulders. Drawing strength from the earth, the statuesque Sidhe stood in a radiant white dress that took on the red and golden colors of the early morning sun. Then a deep, melodic peel of laughter filled the air, "It would appear, Eoghan ó Liath, that you have earned the goddess' favor. Look to the messenger riding from the north. We will wait on your decision."

In a flowing movement, Mongfhionn gathered her cloak, swung up onto her horse and trotted back to Conall. As she passed Conall, she said, "Let's rest for a bit."

Mid-morning, the gates swung open and Eoghan walked towards Conall's group, who stood by their horses. He rubbed scarred hands through his short brush of hair as he came closer. "Well it seems I won't be worrying about how I would have prevented you coming through the gate. I have a message from Macha Mong Ruad bidding you welcome. She suggests that you and your people travel a few days more until you reach the gleannta."

Glancing at Fearghal, Eoghan continued, "I didn't know about Aengus. I'm sorry."

Fearghal grunted, "What else did she say?" Eoghan recounted the full message.

"The lying, scheming witch. Of course Odhrán was following her orders. That eejit wouldn't do anything unless he had his orders. And as for where she's suggesting we stay, she knows fine well west of Ráth na Lairig Éadain is Dithorba's territory." Fearghal stomped back and forward as he tried to control his anger.

Seeing his friend's pain, Conall drew him aside and spoke calmly, "Our people are tired. We don't have a lot of options if we want to be prepared for the winter storms. I'm accepting her offer. We can consider other plans when we are settled."

Returning to where Eoghan waited, Conall said, "Please send our thanks to the queen along with this gift." As arranged, Cathán walked forward with a beautiful, pale cream horse. On the horse were two chests of gold. "I'm sure, like all rulers, some additional treasure will not go amiss." Surprised, Eoghan took charge of the horse.

As they followed Eoghan through the gateway, he turned to Conall, "This may or may not be of use to you, but where you're heading, there is a deserted village well placed between the valleys, forests and mountains. There's no shortage of water from the local springs and waterfalls. It has natural defenses from wolves, bears - and other animals that might call – if you know what I mean."

"May I ask why the village is deserted?"

Clearing his throat, Eoghan said in an embarrassed whisper, "Sickness. A plague decimated the village – men, women and children. It was a thriving place by all accounts and the trading center for the area - until the sickness came." Seeing the look of concern on everyone's face, Eoghan hurriedly continued, "But that was many winters ago, I'm sure the sickness is long gone. You'll be able to tell, if there are rabbits still about! People don't go near the place, because they say the spirits of the dead still live there. Myself, I think some shepherds were frightened by the howling winds in the valleys." Thinking that possibly he had said a little too much, Eoghan finished, "I'm sure you're not afraid of a few ghosts, and besides, you have the Sidhe with you. She'll keep the spirits friendly!"

There was a moment of stunned silence, and then Conall roared with laughter, "So this is a Northern welcome, lodgings in a plague village that's in the territory of the queen's enemy." Conall slapped Eoghan on the back, propelling him forward, "Well, point us in the right direction and we'll be on our way."

"I'll do better than that. I'll have one of the men guide you - just in case the other northerners with you get lost." Before he left them, Eoghan called Fearghal aside, "I meant what I said about Aengus. I liked the lad. He was a good warrior and if it comes to trouble, there's a lot more like me who might prefer to be on your side."

Fearghal looked Eoghan steady in the eye and said, "Thanks, but it's Conall who's in command and decides where and when we fight."

"Well, you know where I stand. By the way, here's one more piece of information from Macha's messenger. Seemed a bit strange to me, but you'll probably know what it means. He said, 'the Roman, Cassius Fabius Scaeva, is an advisor to Dithorba and is at Ráth na Lairig Éadain'."

Fearghal's hand shot out to grab Eoghan's shoulder. The northerner winced as Fearghal's strong fingers bit deeply into his flesh. "Repeat that," he snarled, "and be sure you're speaking right." Startled and uneasy at the venom in Fearghal's voice, Eoghan repeated the words of the courier.

"Shite, the bastard is still in Ériu." Fearghal's heart sped up as he pondered how to break this news to Conall. The days since the battle at An Portach an Choirr had allowed Conall to get some rest and relaxation with his daughters and his queen. And while Fearghal was pained over the death of Aengus, he found solace in the laughter and smiles on Conall's face. Now that would change.

Soon the battle horns were sounded and orders relayed along the rows of men. Horsemen and chariots charged through the gateway to scout ahead of the main army, while the remainder tightened up their ranks and doubled their pace. Each man's face was a reflection of their leader, who now sat, a forbidding figure, on his warhorse. As Fearghal took up the reins of his own mount, Eoghan stopped him, "What's the meaning of all this? What do I not know?"

"You couldn't have known, old friend, but the queen certainly did. Cassius Fabius Scaeva was responsible for the murder of Conall's family and the slaughter of many families of others who are here. The waters in the gleannta will run red and Conall will tear Ráth na Lairig Éadain down stone by stone to avenge his mother, father and sisters."

"The Hag preserve us, Fearghal. Another blood feud is not what we need. I wish I had never told you."

"Too late Eoghan, Macha has played us all like pieces on a fidchell board."

Cassius Fabius Scaeva was agitated. The view of the valleys and gleannta from Ráth na Lairig Éadain were breathtaking in their beauty, yet today it did nothing for Cassius. He looked, and was, a very troubled man. "Bastard!" he exclaimed, his voice filled with venom and bitterness.

Earlier, that day, Cassius had considered his position as being fairly comfortable. While not close to the luxury and lifestyle of Rome, he had come to think of his current residence as having significant benefits and many opportunities for him to acquire wealth and power.

He had ingratiated himself with Dithorba, who he thought quite dull and not of great intellect. As for Dithorba's sons, he was not sure that between them they had any more intelligence than the Barbary ape that Macha Mong Ruad was rumored to have as a pet. This, however, was a perfect scenario for his machinations and his lust for power and treasure. It was he who, over many months, had assured Dithorba of the injustice of Macha assuming the throne of Ériu. And it was he who had aided Dithorba in drawing like-minded nobles to his cause. That was until the messenger arrived. The throne had been within his grasp, but now his plottings were trickling away between his long, bony fingers, like grains of sand.

His nemesis, Conall Mac Gabhann, had appeared and by all accounts was planning on setting up camp within a short ride of Ráth na Lairig Éadain. Even now, Cassius' ill-concealed contempt for the residents of Ériu, who he still considered barbarians of low intelligence, ranking well below the citizenry of Rome, would not allow him to concede that Conall had outplayed him. With ill grace, Cassius granted that the boy had had some luck with his skirmishes and it would now appear that he had a small army of outlaws and deserters.

Cassius took with a large grain of salt, the rumors that Conall had held off the might of the Connachta. Likely this was just another tall tale sung by drunken poets. The upstart would surely present no challenge to the armies of Dithorba and his nobles, which, in turn, meant no threat to him. But what of Macha Mong Ruad? The queen had proven to be almost as devious as he, though, until now, he had outmaneuvered her. She had the army to match Dithorba and now she had a pawn to manipulate.

Though reprehensible, Cassius was innately clever and as sly as a fox. But now, pride blinded him. Had he given Conall even the smallest amount of credit then he would not have underestimated him.

"Bastard! Bitch!" he swore, startling the guards as he pushed past them and made for the Great Hall.

CHAPTER 25

WINTER 411 B.C.

It seemed to Conall, as he gazed over the green pastures, rolling hills, tall mountains and tumbling waterfalls, that this was a rich and fertile land. If only the biting cold would subside, it would be a very pleasant place to live.

The small crofts, settlements and forts they passed regarded them with a mixture of suspicion, curiosity and amusement. Their guide told them that a hard march would have got them to their destination in three or four sunrises, but with all the wagons and non-military folk it would be double that. Conall did not mind the slow pace. It gave him time to think, and the freshness of the land made everyone's humor much better. The odd flake of early snow, however, was a reminder that he needed to get his people prepared for a northern winter.

The entrance to Ghlean Athain was a narrow gorge opening out into a rugged valley of bogland, forests and waterfalls. There were moors to the north and mountains on the east and west. Groves of oak, birch and sycamore were scattered across the land. Red and purple juices from the berries they picked stained teeth and dribbled down the chins of the children who ran alongside the army. In the autumn sun, the land glowed rust and orange from the hedgerow bushes, heathers and mosses.

Soon they reached Sráidbhaile de Bhiotáille. Its grey stone dwellings and walls looked particularly drab and forlorn against the riot of autumnal colors in the valley. Thatched roofs had decayed, leaving large holes; stones from the dwellings and the enclosing walls had fallen in places, leaving gaps that encouraged a variety of animals to claim the site. As they drew closer, a flock of ravens rose into the sky, their cries welcoming them to their new home. Scores of rabbits disappeared into burrows, possibly in anticipation of being the evening meal. Several sheep bleated and scampered away to join others on the hillsides. And the evening chorus of birdsongs recommenced as if now aware that once again they had an audience.

"Well it seems we've been welcomed by the village guardians." Mongfhionn laughed and guided her horse towards a gap, what remained of the ruined entrance to the settlement. "Hold everyone back. I'll check the village out for anything troublesome." Conall nodded and ran his hand along Toirneach's velvet neck. He watched as the grey cloak of the Sidhe disappeared, perfectly camouflaged against the greyness of the buildings.

Mongfhionn reappeared a short time later, "We should be safe. The spirits of the dead have long since departed. The buildings are suffering from the weather and years of neglect, but are basically strong."

Heaving a sigh of relief, Conall turned to his commanders, "Cúscraid you're in charge of our defenses. Rest the men this evening. Tomorrow we need to establish a sound perimeter and make a start on quarters for the army. Our people can stay in the village. I'll speak with Seanán and the elders later to inform them what I expect." Looking to Íar and Nikandros, he said, "Set up pickets to give us warning of visitors and tomorrow scout out the land to the west and east. Let the hounds loose this evening. They should dissuade any animals – two or four-legged - from giving us much trouble."

Looking at Mórrígan and Áine, Conall said, "Please organize the people to get fires going and dig new fire pits. We'll need a hot meal before sleep takes us and the fires will take the chill out of the night air." Both nodded in agreement and then Conall turned to Mongfhionn, "There are still many who have injuries. Perhaps, you could find Fionnbharr and make sure the injured are cared for."

"As for you two," Fearghal and Brion hung back, having no

desire to be assigned mundane chores, "you're getting off light. We're going for a brisk walk around our new demesne before it gets dark." With wide grins, Fearghal and Brion gathered up their shields and weapons and followed Conall.

For a full cycle of the moon, Ghlean Athain's hills echoed to the sounds of trees being felled, the hammering of oak posts into the already hard ground and the grunts of men hauling rocks to rebuild the village walls. The forge in the village had been relit. Scattered pieces of ore told them a source of iron was close by and a long unused bog iron "mine" was soon re-discovered. Copper and other iron mines were found later in the hills. The constant striking of metal on metal, as tools and weapons were shaped, added to the orchestra of sounds.

The few flakes of snow soon became flurries dancing and swirling over frosted ground, then the flurries gave way to sporadic storms. Conall studied the village from his vantage point on the fort's new walkway.

The village wall had been rebuilt as a double row of stones and stood the height of a man. Sturdy oak gates guarded its two entrances. The village itself had been quite large, so there was space for the additional roundhouses, erected to cope with the large number of camp followers. Beyond the village, pens were staked out and built for the horses and other livestock. A few enterprising young villagers had gathered up a good-sized flock of sheep; Conall knew their meat and skins would be highly sought after in mid-winter.

Conall was especially proud of the army's camp and marveled at how in so short a time, under Cúscraid's direction, his men had constructed a formidable fort. The square perimeter walkway felt solid and reassuring under his boots as he walked, accompanied by his brace of wolfhounds. A double wall of oak stakes rose up from the earth, almost twice the height of a man, and a deep ditch had been dug around the camp and filled with blackthorn bushes and short, sharpened stakes. Within the stockade, quarters and eating halls had been constructed from a mix of rocks, wood and turf. The buildings were basic, but strong, dry and well able to resist the fury of the northern winter.

Already a blue-grey pall could be seen hanging over the camp from the many wood and peat fires and the smell of roasted meat from the cooking pits filled the still air. Some of the northern men had managed to arrange a supply of beer for the camp. They also had discovered a local brew made from winter parsnips or wild sea beet. A rough drink, it made cheeks glow red and burned both mouth and throat as it flowed to the stomach. Conall wryly observed that the custom of many of the men to take a female companion to keep them warm during the winter was now well-established. He sighed at the thought of the swollen bellies and additional mouths to feed that summer and fall would bring.

"We're being watched." The voice broke Conall's train of thought and he turned to face Cúscraid who had accompanied him on his inspection.

"Where?"

"The mountainside to the east… and the high ground south of the village."

Conall laughed, "I feel like a piece of cheese between two slabs of bread with Dithorba to the east and Macha in the south. Do northerners fight during the winter or do they rest and sleep like sensible people?"

Cúscraid exhaled, his breath forming a mist in the chilled evening air, "If we waited for good weather, we'd never get the chance to fight! My guess is that an attack is more likely from the east, from Ráth na Lairig Éadain. Macha will enjoy a peaceful winter at Emain Macha knowing that we lie between her and Dithorba."

Conall sighed, "Post extra guards and ask Íar to organize mounted patrols and to vary their paths so we don't become predictable. You and he should also include the archers in your guard and patrol schedules."

The mountain range of Taobh Builleach stood on the east side of the valley. On its slopes Cassius Fabius Scaeva's horse, which was far superior to the flea-bitten, bag of bones he had during his stay with Eochaidh Ruad, pawed at the frost covered ground. The light had almost faded, but Cassius was confident the horse knew its path back to Ráth na Lairig Éadain - even in the darkness. Besides, it was not the first time that Cassius had ridden within sight of his enemy's camp.

His mood was not improved by his assessment of the progress the bastard, Conall Mac Gabhann, had made in less than five summers. Even with his innate disdain for barbarians, he was forced to admit that Conall had gathered a formidable force. By Cassius' reckoning, there were about two thousand warriors. Although he found it difficult to believe the tales that were brought from the Connachta, Cassius had to concede that Conall's fortifications had been constructed with amazing efficiency and speed. Indeed, almost as well as a Roman army unit.

At first he thought the position of the encampment showed Conall's lack of experience. Were it his decision he would have placed it in one of the many narrow gorges. However, his latest assessment was that its location was deceptive. There was a wide and long stretch of open and relatively flat land in front of the encampment. Its long sightlines made it a perfect killing ground and the land was ideal for the cavalry and chariots. His mind now made up, Cassius returned to Ráth na Lairig Éadain. He needed to gauge the threat from Conall, but to accomplish this he needed to convince Dithorba to risk enough of his men to make it a reasonable test.

"Watch it, arsehole. It's bad enough being on guard duty and freezing my balls off without some eejit dumping snow on me." The sharp northern tongue startled Conall for a moment and then he laughed out loud.

"I'm sorry, it will not happen again."

The equally astonished warrior now recognizing his king stammered out an apology before making a sharp about-turn and moving quickly in the direction of the lookout tower.

"I see you retain the ability to strike fear into your men." Mongfhionn grinned as she mocked Conall, and then turned to Fearghal, "Move you big lug. This wind is biting and you can at least make yourself useful as a windbreak."

Looking to make sure no one was beneath him this time, Conall stamped his boots on the walkway. Even with the additional sheep lining, the cold gnawed at his toes. Mórrígan stood at his side, trying unsuccessfully to make herself so small that the wind and snow would ignore her. Conall pulled her closer wrapping his skins and furs around them both. He looked across the valley, but if he gazed too long at the monotonous whiteness of the landscape, his eyes became blurred and tired.

"Will it ever stop snowing?" Fearghal asked, watching as his breath formed ice crystals. The hairs in his nose frequently froze, making him sneeze incessantly.

"You're asking me? You come from here!"

First the rains had come, cold wet rods that forced everyone to take shelter. Then the rain had turned to sleet – a combination of bone chilling rain, snow and ice. It soaked into clothes and shoes making life a misery. Good humored tussles became bad-tempered brawls over who had the best seats around the fires and fire pits. Fionnbharr and his team of healers had been kept busy tending streaming noses, fevers and sprains as well as broken bones from the unlucky who had slipped in the muddy ice. Later they attended to the purple-black, blood-filled blisters on the faces, hands and feet of those who ignored the numbing wind and cold.

The snow had fallen for almost the full cycle of the moon and if the dark grey skies were anything to judge by, there was a lot more to come. The days became shorter and shorter. In many respects this was a blessing as it meant most just slept and ate. If they were feeling energetic, the residents might take a short walk to squat or piss, although going by the rising pungency in the buildings, Conall had a good hunch that this was becoming less frequent. He made a mental note to have the ceannairí céad remind their men he did not want to be facing an epidemic of loose bowels come the spring. Only the blacksmiths continued to labor, but then, they had the forges to keep them warm.

The laughter of children playing in the snow pleased Conall. The village dwellings had all but disappeared under the deep drifts. The perimeter wall had created a vessel that the snow gladly filled and now only the thatched roofs were visible. Around the army camp, great banks of snow piled up, reaching almost half-way up the stockade. Inside, more drifts rested against exposed walls.

To the south, the valley was impassable. To the north, east and west there lay a deep white blanket. Íar's patrols continued to make their daily forays, but the horses were finding it increasingly difficult to tramp through the drifts. Conall mused, to no one in particular, "Well at least we've an excuse to avoid the feast at Emain Macha. We just wouldn't make it in this storm."

In an attempt to initiate dialogue, Macha and Cimbáeth had invited or commanded, Conall, the Chomhairle and his daughters to Emain Macha as guests at the festival of Imbolg. In any circumstance it would have been impossible to refuse without giving offense. The snow and storms had provided him with the excuse he needed.

As Imbolg approached, Conall was saddened by the inevitable losses from the winter. The sickly, old and very young who had succumbed to the embrace of a silent, but remorseless enemy were buried or burned. The cries of mourning families were heard for many days and nights, before the life of the departed was finally celebrated. As he listened to his status reports, Conall felt slightly guilty that his family had survived, so far, without disease or death.

Among the living, there were always the foolish who neglected to keep warm or covered in layers of skins. Their reward was blackened appendages - toes, fingers, ears and noses, which wept with foul smelling lesions. For the unlucky, it meant the loss of an arm or leg. For the lucky it meant the loss of a few toes or fingers – or death. One unfortunate soul upon waking after a drinking binge found his balls black and threw himself off the guard tower, cracking open his skull on a massive boulder. He was doubly unfortunate as his friends had only painted his balls black as joke.

The winter still had several cycles of the moon before it would relinquish its throne to spring, but the weather in Ghlean Athain calmed sufficiently to make it possible to clear the snow from the inside of the village and fort. Now the air filled with curses as men were hauled from their winter cocoons and forced to train for battle. The unceasing work of the blacksmiths had created a stock of iron ready to be finished into swords, javelins, arrows, helmets and shields. In the village and the fort, life once more was one of repair and preparation.

Dithorba reluctantly agreed with Cassius' argument that they needed to assess the strength of Conall's forces. However, he was not overly happy sending men to attack the fort and settlement. Supremely confident in the strength of Ráth na Lairig Éadain, Dithorba viewed Conall as an irritant. Like many others, the young warrior would die on the cliffs of Lairig Éadain were he foolish enough to attack. He well outnumbered Conall and knew that he could call on many nobles to provide men. Thus, sending his men to attack Conall seemed a waste of effort.

However, Cassius was both persistent and persuasive. In his sly way, he suggested that this would be a good way to get rid of some malcontents and test the loyalty of Dithorba's supporters. Therefore, as winter drew to a close and before the spring rains softened the land, Dithorba dispatched a force of a thousand men to test Conall's defenses.

The gods have a sense of humor. At around the same time Dithorba's men were preparing to march, Cimbáeth arrived at Sráidbhaile de Bhiotáille in his adopted role as Macha Mong Ruad's ambassador. Ostensibly there to deliver an invitation to a feast at Emain Macha, in reality, his goal was to assess Conall's army. However, with a guard of just twenty men, Cimbáeth, unlike Dithorba, had no intention of attacking Conall or indeed anyone else. That said, in the beginning, the level of coolness between Fearghal and Cimbáeth threatened on occasions to bloom into a rage as Fearghal held Cimbáeth partially responsible for Aengus' death.

Mongfhionn had asked – nay insisted - that they accompany

her to the grave of Oisín, Ériu's legendary warrior poet. Few of the party believed Oisín ever existed or was buried on the hilltop overlooking the valley and Taobh Builleach, but they were happy to accept Mongfhionn's word that it was a holy site. The group was small, and included Tadhg ó Cuileannáin, the poet, who had begged to be taken along. They cantered through the gateway and travelled north-west along the valley, hooves crunching along as they broke through the icy crust that had formed on the snow.

The grave site was not much more than some scattered rocks and a cairn said to mark Oisín's resting place. Close by, a small spring gurgled out from the earth and splashed its way down the hillside until its waters finally froze. This was somewhat odd given the cold and inclement conditions. The wind swirled around the hilltop carrying Mongfhionn's incantations into the skies. After she had finished, the group dropped the usual sacrifices of gold into the spring.

It was a pleasant morning, until Nikandros nudged Conall. "Visitors," he said, pointing across the valley.

Conall scratched his ragged beard and ran fingers through long winter hair, "I make it about a thousand men."

Fearghal nodded, "Not enough to make a good battle, but adequate to test our strength. They're obviously disposable. Do we defend the fort or fight them in the open?"

"In the open; it will give us a chance to see how well our new recruits fight in the wall." Conall turned to Íar, "Give the signal; alert Brion and Cúscraid." Íar grinned broadly and sharp blasts of his hunting horn sounded across the valley. Conall then turned to Mórrígan, "Have your archers ready. This will be a good time to see how they fight on horseback."

Mórrígan smiled broadly too, her lips and cheeks flushed red with the winter breezes, "Oh, I think Áine has them well trained."

Cimbáeth who had accompanied them, chortled, "You didn't have to arrange all this entertainment for me."

With a knowing smile, Conall turned to Cimbáeth, "It would seem that you'll get an even better opportunity to appraise my forces. After all, that's really why you're here - isn't it?"

"Of course. My visit appears to have been quite well-timed. My only dilemma is where would be the best vantage point? Here on the mountain-side or on the stockade?"

It was mid-morning by the time they returned to the camp. Dithorba's men were expected to be with them around mid-day. As he rode through the gateway, Brion and Cúscraid were readying the men. They held them as long as possible in the shelter of the fort before giving the command to march to the open land. Brion, Deaglán and Cúscraid looked to the ceannaire céad, each responsible for a hundred men, and shouted, "Stop at five hundred paces from the stockade." Winter boots crunched through the spring snow as they made their way forward.

Having decided to watch from his vantage point at Oisín's grave, Cimbáeth started a small fire to keep his hands and feet warm while he waited. The breeze had died down and curls of grey and white smoke rose to join the clouds. Mongfhionn also remained behind and Cimbáeth wondered if this was because Conall did not trust him. He watched the Sidhe as she stood cloaked in grey, holding her oak staff. Her gaze was fixed upon the men below like a hawk watching its prey. Cold or warm, he sensed she had an aura that made the weather irrelevant. As if sensing his thoughts, she turned and smiled briefly before returning to her watch. Cimbáeth shivered, but not from the cold.

Turning his eyes to the snow-covered valley floor, Cimbáeth watched Dithorba's men emerge from the dense wildwood that swaddled Taobh Builleach. They were arranged in warbands, each with around fifty men. Apart from a few of their leaders, they were mostly on foot. Even at this distance, it was plain to see there was little unity among the fighters; each band jostled, kicked and gouged their way to prime positions. Most wore thick skins, furs and woolen pants in earthy colors of greens, browns, oranges and reds. Along with their axes, spears and swords many carried small round shields. "Drunken fools," Cimbáeth snorted, though he noted several mounted men remained on the open hillside; among them one with a purple cloak worn over his furs.

The contrast with Conall's men was stark. At five hundred

paces from the fort, they halted and formed three ranks, each with two hundred and fifty men. Conall had decided to add a third row to his wall. The rear row rammed three javelins into the ground and then, as the front rows, stood an arms distance from the next man. Red shields, emblazoned with a black raven, rested on the ground, contrasting sharply against the harsh whiteness of the snow. Behind them, ten charioteers controlled their teams of horses, whose steamy breath rose into the air as they snorted and butted each other. After a long winter, the horses were as eager as their drivers to stretch their legs.

Further behind, wolfhounds howled and strained on their leashes. On the left, a troop of horsemen, led by Íar, galloped for the hillside and the cover of the trees. Cimbáeth was intrigued when another group of riders took up a position to the right of the formation. He could just make out the burnished armor and high red plumes of the Spartan's helmet. Mórrígan rode alongside him, wearing her own distinctive, raven-crested helmet.

Finally, Conall and Fearghal, accompanied by a pair of wolfhounds each, cantered to the front of the men. "So they chose to fight with their men," Cimbáeth thought, "commendable and brave, but dangerous." As the distance between the two forces shrank, Cimbáeth looked across to the encampment. The stockade was now lined with the remaining warriors, standing alert, and as many from the village who could squeeze onto the parapet. Soon, the rumble of many bodhráns sounded across the valley. A flock of black ravens rose from the forest and circled, anticipating the feast that was to come.

"Home advantage, Conall Mac Gabhann," he chuckled, and rose to watch the battle.

Conall and Fearghal dismounted and handed their reins to Beacán and Cathal. Conall breathed in, sucking cold air deep into his lungs. He stretched to loosen up muscles that had seen little activity during the winter and was keenly aware of the weight of his chainmail. He turned to the warriors, "No heroics. No risks. If any eejit breaks the shield wall before I give the order, his ceannaire céad will have the pleasure of teaching him a lesson. Are we clear?" The men laughed and roared their acknowledgement. Fearghal and he took their places in the wall and waited.

Cassius Fabius Scaeva shifted uneasily in his saddle. It was the first time he had seen Conall since the attack on the blacksmith's settlement, almost five years past. He watched Dithorba's men gather pace as they were cajoled, cursed and slapped with the flat sides of axes and swords. The beer and other stronger drinks coursing through veins made faces deeply flushed and as they screamed their way across the snow-covered ground, made the fools think of themselves as heroic warriors. Cassius' concern was the manner of Conall's men. As the mob of Dithorba's men bore down on them, the men stood resolutely, almost arrogantly, in their ranks.

At two hundred paces, a flight of arrows arced across the sky. Before they had seen its impact, the archers had kicked their horses forward and were galloping to follow a path parallel to the horde. More arrows were released as the archers passed Dithorba's men. The edges of the formation thinned and became ragged as men fell bleeding onto the snow. The archers wheeled left around the rear of the attackers, letting loose more iron-tipped missiles. Screaming warriors cursed and pushed those in front to move faster, to escape an arrow in the back.

Cassius had expected the archers to continue their circuit and flay the other flank, but was surprised as they went in the opposite direction. He watched, perturbed, as they peeled away and rode east, away from the battle. His mind was not quite as agile as usual in the penetrating cold, and he pulled his furs and cloak tightly around him. His equally cold and restless mount snorted and pawed at the ground, steam rising from its nostrils. Still puzzled, Cassius scanned the other side of the valley and dimly saw a grey-cloaked figure raise a staff. Absorbed in the sight, it was almost too late when he looked back at the riders. In a voice filled with panic, he shouted to his guard, "The bastards are riding for us. Back to Ráth na Lairig Éadain and don't forget you're paid well to protect me." The small group wheeled around and galloped along the forest pathways that crisscrossed Taobh Builleach.

Cimbáeth chuckled, "So you weren't just keeping an eye on me."

Mongfhionn smiled, "A wise king would be advised to watch and learn." Then she turned back towards the camp.

At twenty paces, the rear rank of the wall released a volley of javelins. Totally unexpected, this stunned Dithorba's warriors turning battle-cries into screams of pain. As they stumbled over the dead and injured, the attackers were struck by a second and third volley of iron. The warriors at the front fell by the score, their crimson blood blotting the formerly pristine snow. Facing them, the shields closed rank and waited. The front row held their javelins at waist height, the second at shoulder height and the rear rank pushed their shields hard against the backs of the second row ensuring the wall would stand firm. Pushed by those at the rear who wanted to avoid being brought down by arrows, Dithorba's men trampled over or kicked aside the bodies of their comrades and threw themselves at Conall's men.

The noise of axes, spears and swords banging against shields echoed across the valley. They were answered with ripped flesh as javelins were thrust through skins and furs. The wall stood implacable, a monstrous beast with hundreds of iron teeth, snapping and biting all who ventured close enough. Realization of the hopelessness of their efforts permeated the sprawl of attackers until it reach a tipping point and then the men turned and fled.

Conall shouted, "Now," dropped his shield and sprang forward as he reached over his shoulders to pull his twin axes from their scabbards. His first downward stroke cleaved a long gouge down the back of a retreating warrior.

The ceannairí céad barked to their men, "You know the orders. No survivors," and led them into the bloodbath.

On the hillside, Íar gave his command, "No one escapes," and led his men down the slope to cut off any hope of retreat. As the shield wall dissolved, Brion split his chariots into two groups and swung them left and right to corral the attackers. Long chariot wheel knives sliced the flesh and snapped the bones of anyone foolish enough to come close.

It was a short, brutal and efficient slaughter. The foolhardiness brought on by alcohol had encouraged their assault, but dulled their minds. Thus, the sharp blade that split their skull, opened up their bellies or took their heads from their shoulders may have been rendered less painful by blissful senselessness. No one survived. The piteous pleadings from the wounded were answered with a swift blade.

Quiet settled as Conall removed his helmet and shook his hair loose. He wiped at the sweat on his forehead, but only succeeded in replacing sweat with blood. Seeing Deaglán close by, he called out, "Take Torcán and organize what needs to be done. Strip the bodies of anything that is of value; remove their heads and stake them out north and south of the village and camp. Then burn the bodies. They were foolish men used by a foolish leader."

On the hilltop, Mongfhionn swung long legs over her horse and grinned ghoulishly at Cimbáeth, "Conall will likely have all of Dithorba's men beheaded before I get back. I must ride quickly if I am to have any for a sacrifice." She shook her head, "Such a waste," slapped the reins against her horse's flanks and took off down the slopes.

"I too, hope they are all dead, my lady." Cimbáeth sighed as she rode away. As the ravens gathered overhead, Cimbáeth shook his head. The message he was to give Macha Mong Ruad was all too clear. No mercy and no quarter to those Conall considered his enemy.

Cassius suspected, even without witnessing the outcome with his own eyes, that none of the thousand would be having a meal tonight – at least not in this world. He lost three men from his guard to arrows in the back, but was confident that he had eluded his pursuers. That confidence arose from a deep suspicion that he had been allowed to escape. So he returned to Dithorba with no intelligence worth telling and with no warriors.

Nikandros thoughts were troubled as he led the archers back to the camp. One of Dithorba's men had been badly wounded and tumbled from his mount. Expecting nothing less than a blade as his fate, the warrior had slumped down with his back to an old oak tree, and awaited his executioner.

It was his misfortune that Mórrígan approached, blade in hand. She roughly grabbed his hair and pulled his head back exposing his neck. The man gave no fight, resigned to his fate, but fate was not kind. Instead of a swift cut across his throat, which would have ended his life quickly – if not painlessly. Mórrígan's knife slid slowly, almost sensuously, across her sacrifice's throat opening a deep, wide gash to the bone. His final screams were trapped in the froth of blood that at first bubbled and then spurted from the cut. As blood splashed onto her face and flowed over her hands, the sigils, formerly merely paint, now seemed to rise up from beneath the skin to glow under the shadow of the forest.

The Spartan was glad the others had ridden on and only he had witnessed the twisted smile on Mórrígan's face.

CHAPTER 26

"I'm not going. Unless it's to rip the conniving, treacherous bitseach's heart out," Fearghal shouted, roared and stomped across the dirt floor. Conall's deep sigh reflected the mood of the other members of the Chomhairle felt as they sat around the wooden table in the eating hall. They sympathized, yet were exasperated with their friend.

The cause of Fearghal's current angst was Cimbáeth. Before departing, he had issued an invitation to Emain Macha to celebrate the festival of Bealtaine. He also made it clear that this was less of an invitation than a command from Macha. His counsel was that it would be politic for them to swallow – or at least give the appearance of swallowing - whatever animosity they felt for the queen.

Tired, Conall looked at Fearghal, "We're going. You're going. Accept it. You've told me often enough that I need to be more diplomatic. Well, it's diplomacy now. We'll consider revenge later."

Fearghal scowled at Conall and the rest of his friends, but they sensed his acquiescence before he grabbed Mongfhionn's hand and pulled her towards the exit. She winced in pain; as Fearghal's calloused hand dwarfed her own, in size and strength, but smiled lasciviously, "I will be so bruised tomorrow!"

At the advent of summer, the Chomhairle journeyed south

towards Emain Macha, accompanied by Conall's caomhnóirí. Fearghal and Conall's hounds circled the group, enjoying their freedom while keeping a watch for game or threats. Conall's daughters rode their ponies alongside, laughing and enjoying being the center of attention. The recent birth of Áine and Brion's son had stolen some of their thunder, but they did not seem to mind.

As usual, Cúscraid remained behind to command the defenses of the camp and village. This time he had offered very little resistance or protest and was not at all displeased at missing the festivities.

Bealtaine signaled a time of purification and transition as well as heralding in the new growing season with hopes for a bountiful harvest. It was also a time when spirits from Tír inna n-Óc were reputed to be close at hand. Given that the invitation included Mongfhionn, this did appear to be an attempt to placate the Sidhe. Macha may have thought a feast that honored Mongfhionn, albeit indirectly, would make her more amenable to her ambitions. She greatly misunderstood and underestimated the Sidhe.

The earthworks of Emain Macha lay on rolling grassland. From a distance its appearance resembled a great breast swathed in green velvet, but there its beauty ended. The stench of rotting meat, vegetables and shite dumped into the perimeter ditch assaulted the visitors' nostrils as they entered the gateway. After the clean air of winter and spring in Ghlean Athain, the smell made the party grimace.

The compound was about five hundred paces in diameter. Inside a great stockade, the scene was of ongoing construction, with mud, rocks, stacks of wood and huge piles of dirt, scattered throughout. It was dominated by a massive hall at its center with smaller buildings in various stages of construction placed off to the side. All entrances faced east. The Great Hall served as the residence of Macha and the headquarters of the Cróeb Ruad. As part of the Bealtaine celebrations, a huge bonfire was being erected in front of the hall.

As they made their way to the hall, Fearghal remarked snarkily, "Typical of Macha. The place is going to be more like a summer residence than a fort."

As they approached the Great Hall, a steward descended the

wide wooden steps. Observing the leading group of riders as they removed their quite ornate helmets he surmised that these were the chieftains. The young man at their center had a growing number of scars on the exposed areas of his face, arms and legs and a determined look in his steel-blue eyes. The men and women with him, although somewhat strange to the eye, projected an air of confidence, both in their leader and themselves.

"Welcome to Emain Macha. I am Cian Craobhach, steward to Macha Mong Ruad and Cimbáeth. Should you need anything during your stay with us please come and see me. We have accommodations for you in the Great Hall. Your men can set up camp just beyond the gates." With a sweep of his hand to illustrate his point, he continued, "As you can plainly see there's hardly room to swing a cat inside with all the work going on."

Cian stroked his ginger beard, amply dusted with silver to match his years. "I see you like horses. Personally I don't know much about them, but I can admire yours. As yet, there are no stables within the compound. So, if your men can look after them at their camp that would be best. I'll make sure that whatever feed they require is delivered daily."

Íar nodded to the man, "Not a problem. The weather is turning towards summer so the horses will be happy to be outside. We can erect a corral."

Then Conall said, "Thanks you for your hospitality. I have one small favor to ask. My friend Brion's son is newly born and is quite content to suck at his mother's tit. Sad to say, the same cannot be said of my own. As you will likely discover, my daughters can be a bit of a handful." This brought screams of protest from Danu and Brighid, a glowering look from Mórrígan and raised eyebrows from the others. Ignoring the protests and looks, Conall continued, "To make all of our lives more bearable, I'd like to have ten of my men remain within the stockade – to watch over my girls."

Cian's hazel eyes twinkled. He knew fine well that the duties of the guard was not to watch over two girls – whether they were overactive or not. Seeing no reason to refuse and cause insult to Macha and Cimbáeth's guests, he spoke warmly, "I have no issues with your request. Everyone should be safe in Emain Macha – children and adults." Stepping towards Conall, Cian extended a hand.

Conall smiled, dismounted and taking Cian's hand said, "Looks like we'll all get on well." With this signal, the remaining riders dismounted.

"Deaglán ó Neill, are you just going to stand there and not greet your uncle?" Cian laughed as a deeply embarrassed young man came forward to be grasped firmly by the shoulders. "Your parents and many of the ó Neills will be here for the feast. You wouldn't want me to be telling them how you mistreated me."

The feast was a raucous celebration. The smell of spit-roasted meat, peat fires and beer pervaded the feasting hall. Blue and grey smoke stung and left eyes streaming and rimmed red. The crackle and hiss of great splats of grease falling onto glowing embers mixed with the sounds of good natured banter, singing and story-telling as well the music of many harps and bodhráns. All things considered, the craic was good and the normally staid Ulaid certainly proved that they could match anyone in celebrating.

There was a great cheer as Fearghal entered the hall accompanied by Mongfhionn. A somewhat lesser, but nonetheless loud, bout of shouting erupted as Deaglán appeared. The hush as the dark-skinned Nikandros sauntered in was followed by the usual shouts about his sense of dress. On seeing Conall enter with Mórrígan and their daughters, Cian quickly traversed the hall, and bowed deliberately to Conall signaling to all that this was the group's leader.

"I'll take you to your tables. I've placed you with the ó Neills, the Craobhachs and the Ruads. They're a disreputable bunch of cattle thieves, but they're good company – safe company." Looking at Íar, Cian remarked, "There's usually an ongoing wrestling match in the center circle. Perhaps you might want to consider taking part. No great prizes apart from pride. Although some say there's quite a bit of wagering that takes place."

Íar laughed, "Fill my horn up with beer a few times and I'll show you Northerners how to wrestle."

As the eating and drinking gathered momentum, the results of over-indulgence contributed a definite odor to the atmosphere. Arriving late, as befitted their status, the doors swung open and horns heralded the entrance of Macha with Cimbáeth at her side. The pair proceeded slowly towards the high table, stopping occasionally to have a word or share a drink with a favored noble. As they stopped before Conall's entourage, Macha paused, looked at Fearghal and then Mongfhionn. Fleetingly, her face betrayed her jealousy, anger and frustration, before she regained her composure.

"It is good to see you again, Fearghal Ruad," she said, and then to the Sidhe, "of course, I am delighted to see the lady Mongfhionn. It's a pity my father was not here to greet you. You and he had so much in common."

Mongfhionn looked her in the eyes, "It's Bealtaine, Macha. Your father may yet join us from Mag Mell." She smiled, "As always, I'm sure he would have wise words of counsel for you."

Affronted, Macha fought to control the anger revealed by her flashing emerald eyes. She looked at Conall, "It is not fitting that you should sit at this table while the other high-born nobles and kings sit at mine. Bring your queen and daughters and sit with us."

It was on the tip of his tongue to refuse at the perceived insult to his friends, but he saw the pleading looks in Cimbáeth and Cian's eyes and heard a gleeful Fearghal's aside, "Diplomacy, Conall."

Conall's rose from his seat and exclaimed, "Come, Mórrígan. It would appear that kings and queens are not allowed to have fun with their friends." The roar that greeted him brought a scowl to Macha's face as she turned around and stomped off to take her place at the high table.

The evening's feasting proceeded without incident. All were treated to a cheerful and drunken Íar tossing many Ulaid warriors out of the wrestling circle, as if they were featherweights. He and his friends had accumulated a considerable mound of gold and silver by the end of the night.

The Bealtaine celebrations carried on through three sunsets and were halted only by the limits to overindulgence for all. Conall's band was grateful that they had brought Fionnbharr. His herbal remedies soothed stomachs stretched from the constant bingeing, as well as the inevitable cramps from retching and throwing up. By the end of the feast, Emain Macha resembled – and smelt like, a cesspit. Eventually, sore heads and parched throats improved and the party received a visit from a still pale Cian.

"The queen has requested your presence to discuss some pressing matters before you return to Ghlean Athain," Cian said to Conall. "She would prefer that you come alone."

Conall nodded, "I will be pleased to speak with the queen, but not alone." He thought for a moment, "I will be accompanied by my Queen, Fearghal, Nikandros, and the lady Mongfhionn."

Smiling, Cian turned to exit, "A strong team, my lord. The balance of fear, intimidation, unspoken secrets and beauty will make the conversation highly entertaining!"

As they entered Macha's quarters, it took Conall's eyes a few moments to adjust from the brightness of the mid-day sun to the gloomy room. Nikandros was later to comment that the utilitarian nature of the room contrasted with Queen Medb's accommodations. Macha sat at the head of a thick oak table, to her right stood Cimbáeth and to her left, Cian. A pace behind, stood a tall, older warrior, introduced as Cearbhall Ó Domhnaill, the commander of Macha's armies, although he was plainly subject to Cimbáeth's commands. At the entrance, there stood two hard-faced Cróeb Ruad guards. To Fearghal's amusement, the ape he had gifted Macha in his youth chittered in its cage in a far corner of the room.

As Macha spoke, her face betrayed none of the signs of anger or jealousy at the presence of Mongfhionn. Instead, the countenance and demeanor of the Ard-Righan in-waiting was smiling, welcoming and to the uninformed - sincere. "First, my deepest regrets for the death of Aengus. No matter what you may have heard, I had nothing to do with his untimely death. Odhrán Mac Seáin went beyond his orders. My suspicion is that he was also taking instructions from Dithorba."

Conall admired the neat way that Macha had presented a plausible, if totally false, explanation for Aengus' death while introducing the real issue to be discussed – Dithorba.

Fearghal locked eyes with Macha until she glanced away. "Aengus will be avenged. Odhrán Mac Seáin is dead by my hand. Death will be the reward for whoever issued his orders. Now let's get down to what you really want to speak about, Macha." It was possibly the most measured response that Fearghal had given in his lifetime. He continued, "Your throne is not secure. There has never been an Ard-Righan and there was no provision for this in the agreement settled upon by the kings of the Ulaid - your father included. What's your proposal?"

Macha's lips grew thinner, their blood-red color deepening as sharp teeth bit into them. She was accustomed to using her nimble mind and luscious curves to get her own way, preferring to enthrall and entrap. Fearghal's full frontal assault left her at a disadvantage. She was not comfortable and looked to Cimbáeth.

"Dithorba and his sons are a threat to the throne. As you well know, Fearghal, that family hasn't a brain between them. They have always relied on muscle to enforce agreements and generally this has worked in their favor – until now. They are not used to dealing with events that complicate simple contracts, such as the birth of Macha to Aedh Ruad. In the scheme of things, they would probably have sulked at Ráth na Lairig Éadain for a few years and raided Macha's cattle until the next royal cycle came around."

Cimbáeth waited to gauge the temper of his audience before continuing, "That was until Cassius Fabius Scaeva sought refuge with them and sowed discontentment among weak minds. He saw an opportunity for mischief and profit, and took it. Now, enough nobles and ruiri have pledged allegiance to Dithorba to make civil war a real possibility. That cannot be allowed to happen. It will weaken the Ulaid leaving us open to attack from the Connachta or even the Laighi who it would appear are having challenges and might seek new land to settle. The throne of Ériu must not be allowed to pass from the Ulaid."

Finally, Cimbáeth added as he looked at Conall, "You have no loyalty to the North, but as fate would have it, we have a common enemy in the Roman."

Conall rubbed his chin, "It is well-known that we seek Cassius, but we could just as easily settle our quarrel with an assassin's arrow or blade. What's your proposal? Why should we become involved in your fight with Dithorba? Our debt to the Ulaid was paid when we destroyed Ailill's roadway"

"Your fight is with Dithorba as much as it was with Eochaidh Ruad and Medb. They sheltered your parents' killer as does Dithorba. From what I've learned about you, I very much doubt that an arrow or blade in the back would satisfy your quest for vengeance. Besides, you need to know who gave the orders to Cassius Fabius Scaeva."

At the mere mention of his parents, Conall's eyes grew steel-grey and his body tensed. The warriors in the room sensed the change and their hands moved to their swords. Macha's eyes widened as she took in a scene that could quite swiftly descend to bloodshed and with no guarantee of who would survive.

"You seek the Roman," she interjected, hoping to lower the tension. "I do not wish Dithorba dead, but rather to be chastened. We have common ground. You have an army and a growing population for which to care. In return for your help, Ghlean Athain will be gifted to you as well as Dithorba's lands, including Ráth na Lairig Éadain."

"You have no need of my army. Your own vastly outnumbers mine. Take Ráth na Lairig Éadain yourself. Then you'll be beholden to no one."

Cimbáeth interjected, "On open ground, our men are the best of the Ulaid or any other army. Frankly, we would take heavy losses if we assaulted Ráth na Lairig Éadain. Your recent experience and style of fighting stands a much better chance of success. We seek to use the best tool for the job. Bluntly, that's you and your men."

"And what will you be doing while we are solving your problems?" Fearghal growled.

Macha cleared her throat, "Our forces cannot be seen to start the battle. There are still groups of nobles that, while they give allegiance to me outwardly, also have some sympathy for Dithorba. Our men will keep their distance until the assault is under way. Then they will reinforce you. Dithorba must be taken alive. The

Roman is yours to do with as you see fit."

"And we all know how good your promise of support is."

Conall rested his hand on his battle commander and friend's arm, then said, "There is no trust here, but it is true we do have a common quest. My army will attack Ráth na Lairig Éadain midsummer. My men will not have orders to take any prisoners, save the Roman. If you want Dithorba and his sons alive then make sure your men fight alongside us."

Conall rose abruptly and bowed, "My thanks for your hospitality. We'll take our leave."

Macha's façade finally cracked. Spluttering with anger that anyone should speak to her in this dismissive manner – and in her own fort, she erupted at Cimbáeth, "Why should we allow this upstart to dictate terms to us? We could hold his striapach and daughters hostage. Then he and his men will do what we want."

Cimbáeth shook his head in disbelief, "We were so close."

Then, to everyone's amazement, Nikandros stood up and roared with laughter. He took a pouch from his belt and placed it on Fearghal's now open palm, "My share of the winnings from the betting on Íar. That was our wager."

He looked at Cian, "I'm sorry if what follows causes you trouble. You're a good man, but perhaps you should consider a change of employer to ensure your continued health." Then to everyone in the room he said, "Let us go outside and bid our farewells in the sunshine."

Totally bemused, Macha and Cimbáeth followed the Spartan as he made his way outside. They were greeted by a loud cheer from Conall's caomhnóirí as they sighted their commander. Facing the gates of Emain Macha, and a growing band of Ulaid warriors, the men had lined up, in full battle formation, ten paces from the entrance to the Great Hall. A wave from Mórrígan was instantly greeted by cheers from her archers positioned on the stockade, each with bow drawn and an arrow nocked.

"Shite!" exploded Cimbáeth, although his tone was one of admiration at having been outfoxed, "How?"

Laughing, Conall slapped Cimbáeth on the back and replied, "Not everyone was as drunk as you at Bealtaine! If you look beyond the gates, you will see my horsemen. They followed a day behind us and rested in the woods. They had ample time to replace those who were originally camped beyond Emain Macha. While everyone was celebrating, it was simple to have my caomhnóirí come inside and wait."

Then, offering Macha a severe look, Conall said, "I do not take it kindly when my queen and my daughters are threatened. Sadly, I thought you might be tempted to do something imprudent and so my daughters were taken from Emain Macha a few nights ago. If you look beyond the gates, you can wave to them."

Turning to Cimbáeth, Conall took his hand, "You I trust. This queen I don't. I take it there will be no issues with us leaving? I know your strength and my men have fought against such odds before – and prevailed. You will always be welcome at our camp in Ghlean Athain."

"You play a good game of fidchell, Conall Mac Gabhann. Have a safe journey to the ghlean. We'll meet mid-summer." Cimbáeth sighed and turned to follow Macha who had already stormed back into the Great Hall.

CHAPTER 27

MID-SUMMER 410 B.C.

The quintet of Conall, Cúscraid, Nikandros, Íar and Fearghal looked across the lush valley to Ráth na Lairig Éadain. Dense forests bordered fields filled with grazing cattle and sheep. It was not the first time the group had made the trip.

"Someone picked a great location to build a fort," Cúscraid did not bother hiding his admiration. Rising like a giant, erect nipple from the ample curves of the valley, Lairig Éadain towered above all. On its lower slopes, goats and sheep scampered along narrow trails. To the east, the land swept down a plain to the coast. To the west, the peak overlooked two gleannta. Dithorba's fort sat atop the mountain, defended by closely spaced ramparts and wide ditches. The only path and entrance to the fort faced the coast.

Conall dismounted, plucked a blade of grass and absent-mindedly started to chew.

"Some sheep probably pissed on that," Fearghal chuckled.

Deep in thought, Conall smiled absently then said, "You're the master of defenses, Cúscraid. How do we open this one up?"

Rubbing at his latest, and somewhat discouraging, attempt at a beard, Cúscraid shook his head, "Beats me. We could certainly hide our army in the thick forests that border the bottom slopes, but that doesn't get us inside. Maybe we should just walk up to the gate and ask them to let us in!" He sighed in acknowledgment of the daunting task ahead.

"Look at it, Conall. The sides of that last stretch of black rock are practically vertical, although the rains and ice have had taken their toll on the rock face going by the fissures we can see. Could a force of men, in full armor and weapons, scale the mountain and then assault the ramparts?"

"My horsemen will be no use unless we can breach the outer gate." Íar stated the obvious, then added, "but, once inside, my men and horses could do a lot of damage; the plateau the fort stands on is massive"

"Not a cloud in sight. It's been that way for almost a full cycle of the moon." Conall looked to the clear blue summer sky as he spoke.

"What are you talking about?" Fearghal looked at Conall quizzically.

"Remember the first time we rode here? It was a dark, rainy day and the top of Lairig Éadain was shrouded in clouds. If you didn't already know there was a fort on the mountain top you'd never have guessed it." His eyes twinkling, Conall said, "Mount up. It's time to talk to Mongfhionn about her weather divining skills!"

Cimbáeth arrived mid-summer with about two thousand men. He was met by Conall and Fearghal, the latter grumbling good naturedly, "Hope you brought your own food. We're not going to feed you. And you can keep your hands off our beer – and our women, too."

Conall scolded his commander lightheartedly and shook Cimbáeth's hand, "I must admit I'm surprised to see you. We didn't exactly leave in Macha's good graces, but we're grateful for the additional help."

"Well, I wouldn't expect an invitation to celebrate Samhain! However, I am to inform you that the queen's forces will join us before the battle starts."

Conall snorted, "They may join us, but will they fight with or against us?" Both Fearghal and Conall noted Cimbáeth's uneasiness at the question. Before they could explore this further, Conall had enjoined the tall figure of Cian Craobhach who was attempting to unobtrusively pass the trio, "Cian, perhaps you would take charge of organizing space for the king and seeing his men are settled on good ground in the valley?" Cian nodded nervously and scurried off to bury himself in work.

"I thought that Cian might be here," said Cimbáeth. "Stealing Macha's steward does not exactly help mend fences!"

Conall ignored the dig. "I think we did him a good turn. The man excels at organization and we're getting too big for Cúscraid to see and do everything. Turns out Cian wasn't exactly truthful about his knowledge of horses. The Craobhachs and Íar apparently have a lot in common." At the sound of approaching horse's hoofs, Conall turned and saw Toirneach being led by Beacán; Cathal brought mounts for Fearghal and Cimbáeth, "I hope you can ride."

As they cantered along the valley, Cimbáeth's keen eyes observed groups of men scrambling up the steep sides of Taobh Builleach. It appeared that in addition to armor, shields and weapons, they also carried large irregularly-shaped packs on their backs. He looked inquiringly at Conall.

"Rocks. Each man has the weight of himself in rocks to carry up the hillside as well as his armor and weapons. They've been practicing for a full cycle of the moon now. Nikandros is a hard taskmaster."

A horn blasted the air, diverting Cimbáeth's attention to the other side of the valley where the huge figure of Íar cursed, cajoled and praised his horsemen as they drilled their horses up and down the hillside. "He also has the men ride their horses through the deeper parts of the river that runs along the valley." Cimbáeth nodded, knowing what he was being shown - discipline and strength.

Later, they sat around one of the cooking pits. Cimbáeth sliced and stabbed a piece of roast pork with his blade. As he bit into the slightly charred, crisp layer of skin, fat streamed down his beard to join the other food and drink stains on his tunic. "Well, are you going to tell me the plan? Do we have a plan? Or are we all going to run like raving eejits up Lairig Éadain and hope that the defenders laugh themselves to death?"

Conall's eyes glittered reflecting the flames from the open fire. "I have a plan. I'm just waiting for Mongfhionn to tell me when. Until then, we practice." Across from him, Mongfhionn smiled enigmatically at an exasperated Cimbáeth.

Cassius paced up and down the Great Hall in Ráth na Lairig Éadain. "You're wearing a rut in the dirt." Dithorba looked up from his throne, annoyed. He had not forgiven Cassius the loss of a thousand men and it chilled him to the bone at how ruthless Conall Mac Gabhann had shown himself to be. Not a single man had returned.

"Mac Gabhann is planning something," Cassius scowled unguardedly at the interruption of his thoughts. "The few spies that have managed to survive the arrows from his archers tell me of strange exercises. And now, Cimbáeth has arrived with over two thousand men – most likely Cróeb Ruad."

Dithorba waved his hand to stop Cassius, "Now, you're beginning to exhaust my patience, Roman. Were it not for your weasel words, my sons and I would have accepted, albeit with bad grace, Macha Mong Ruad as Ard-Righan and raided her lands quite profitably for the next seven years. Now I have lost a thousand men and you tell me a growing army is camped in Ghlean Athain. It is fortunate for you that Ráth na Lairig Éadain is unassailable. We can wait until they get bored, go away or fight among themselves."

"We have just three thousand men in the fort. They have almost five thousand – and that doesn't include Macha's main armies."

The Roman was really getting up Dithorba's arse. Irritated at Cassius' lack of confidence in the location and ramparts of Ráth na Lairig Éadain, Dithorba spoke from between clenched teeth, "It has been many generations since the fortifications at Ráth na Lairig Éadain were breached. Even then it was a plague from the Hag that killed the defenders. Now take yourself off before I let you test how steep and high the sides of Lairig Éadain are - with your own body."

"Of course, my lord. Forgive my questions. I do not doubt the strength of the defenses. It is my way of ensuring the king is well protected." Cassius smiled as he spoke, bowed and exited the room.

In his mind, he was unsettled. Logically, Dithorba was right. The fort was as impregnable as any he had seen. However, logic never seemed to matter to Conall Mac Gabhann and the witches that accompanied him. Intuition and a knack for self-preservation told Cassius that it was time for him to make plans for flight.

Conall stepped outside their shelter and looked back at the naked beauty of Mórrígan, her face framed by a sea of red hair, her milk-pale skin contrasting against the straw and rushes on which she lay. She murmured as she drifted towards waking. He wondered if he was fooling himself or if it was wishful thinking that it seemed her belly was rounder, her breasts fuller and her nipples darker these past few weeks.

He stretched and scratched his balls, as he breathed in the morning air mixed with the scents of the fort – some fresh, some ripe and cloying. It was a few moments before he sensed the dampness and saw mist forming on the slopes of the mountains guarding Ghlean Athain. He smiled and called to Íar, who as usual was making sure his horse was brushed, fed and watered. "How're your lungs this morning?"

Íar looked up with a huge grin, "Never better."

The sound of Íar's hunting horn blasted out across the valley. At first, men grumbled and cursed as they rolled off their skins, straw and women. Then, at the realization of the signal's meaning, they sprang into action. Armor was inspected one final time, shields were examined for cracks, and swords and axes were taken to the whetstones for one final sharpening. More than a few were heard to say, "Thank the Hag. No more humping bloody stones up a mountain!"

Cimbáeth had chosen to camp with his men, but now he tramped with his captains across the fields to the fort. He soon caught sight of Conall.

"Now do we find out what the plan is?" he called out. Not wishing for his men to be outshone by Conall's, Cimbáeth had instituted a similar training regime. Although they had not the same time to practice as Conall's men, he was happy that they would more than play their part.

Conall chuckled, "Not just yet, Cimbáeth, but soon. Let's move. I want to be at the top of Taobh Builleach by this afternoon, and the low slopes of Lairig Éadain by tomorrow morning. Can your men keep up?"

After consulting with his captains, Cimbáeth laughed and offered a wager, "A bag of gold says my men will beat you to the crest of Taobh Builleach." Then as an afterthought he added, "But that doesn't include horses!"

Fearghal snorted, "We'll take that wager, but you'd better get going. Conall's caomhnóirí have already left!"

"Cheating bastards!" Cimbáeth barked instructions to his commanders who in turn tore back to their men, shouting orders. Soon both groups streamed from their camps and jogged towards Taobh Builleach.

Before mounting Toirneach, Conall called Mórrígan, Íar and Nikandros, "Get to the top of Taobh Builleach as fast as you can. Make sure there are no eyes to give our position away. Kill anyone you see. I don't care who they are. We can apologize later if we made a mistake." They nodded and ran for their mounts.

Conall turned to Cian, "We can't take wagons with us to haul replacement weapons, shields and arrows. So I'm relying on you to make sure the pack animals keep pace with us."

Cian feigned shock, "I wasn't aware of this!" Then smiled, "don't worry, my men and horses will be alongside you."

Mid-day, under a silver-gray sky and drizzling rain, they reached the bottom slopes of Taobh Builleach. After a brief rest, the armies turned east and scrambled up the rock-strewn hillside towards the crest. Curses filled the air as men slipped on damp grasses and mosses or plunged knee deep into a patch of bog. Mid-way up the slopes, they disappeared into the dense forest that wrapped itself around the mountain. Progress was slower, but drier, under the summer canopy of branches and leaves.

They broke from the forest late in the afternoon and gazed on the rocky summit of Taobh Builleach, shrouded in cloud. Light rain washed sweat from flushed faces and men leaned on their shields to catch their breath. At the sound of horse's hoofs on the rocky ground, Conall wheeled around.

"The mountain is clear as far as we can tell. No real problems. We scared off a couple of young boys herding sheep and goats. Put the fear of the Hag into them and they ran screaming off in the opposite direction to Dithorba's fort." Íar paused to look at craggy mountain top, "Still some ways to go."

Brion came puffing and breathless to Conall's side, bent over double and gasping for breath as he spoke, "Everyone's through the forest. No major injuries apart from a few twisted ankles which the healers are taking care of."

Fearghal chortled at Brion's distress, "Riding a chariot has made you soft."

Scowling, Brion retorted, "I hope you fall into a bog - a deep one!"

As they surveyed the summit, Cimbáeth strode up and joined the group, "Guess we won the wager. Pay up."

"In yer dreams," Fearghal laughed, "Conall's guard was here long before anyone."

"They don't count. They had a head start!" Conall was happy at the camaraderie, but frowned at how quickly this might change. "Get the men moving again. We have daylight left and need to be over the summit and down the slope before dark. Let's go."

With a collective groan, the two armies gathered themselves up and headed for the crest of Taobh Builleach. The mountain was the highest in the gleannta, and the panorama that met them as they rounded the summit was awe-inspiring. To the east was the broad floor of Gleann Baile Éamonn. The gleann stretched as far as the eye could see. Cattle and sheep roamed fields separated by dry stone walls. Many farms lay in ruins and it seemed that nature was slowly repossessing the land as the people moved or were culled by sickness, weather and war. Before them, the dark teat of Lairig Éadain erupted from the valley, pushing upwards to be suckled by the clouds.

The armies set up camp on the bottom slopes of Taobh

Builleach. No fires were lit and the men huddled in small groups just inside the tree line or against the stone walls. It was the end of summer and the nights had a chill that was made more uncomfortable by the persistent drizzle.

Finally, Conall called the Chomhairle, Cimbáeth, and his captains to explain his plan. "We waited until this time because I needed the weather to break. Mongfhionn thinks that the weather will get increasingly worse overnight. I hope she is right." Mongfhionn acknowledged Conall with a nod of her head.

"Tomorrow, we will assault and take Ráth na Lairig Éadain. I'm hoping our plan will take them by surprise and with a bit of luck we should have few casualties. At sunrise, I'll lead my caomhnóirí plus four hundred around the north-western side of the mountain. Once past the lower inclines of Lairig Éadain, we'll scale the black rockface that erupts from the high slopes and upon which the fort is built."

Cimbáeth's reaction was a sharp intake of breath, "It can't be done, Conall. Once you get past the slopes, that rock is a straight climb upwards for at least the height of ten good sized trees. Even if you make it to the top, you'll be wasted and in no condition to fight."

Conall addressed Cimbáeth, his jaw firmly set, "Everyone keeps telling me what can't be done. Tomorrow, my men and I will climb the cliffs and we will scale the stockade. Mórrígan's archers will accompany us and cover us as we go over the ramparts. Nikandros, Deaglán and Brion will also be with us. As you said, Dithorba's main defense is not the stockade, but a series of ramparts, earthworks and ditches that cross the middle of the plateau. Behind that is where he has his main buildings. Once over the outer stockade, we will fight our way to the ramparts and open the gateway."

Fearghal snorted as he looked at Brion, "Well there's one person who'll never make it!"

Brion scowled again, "Arsehole!"

"So what's our role in this besides watching you kill yourselves, collecting what's left of your bodies at the bottom of the rock face and giving you a decent burial?"

Conall slapped Cimbáeth on the back, "Why, you're the distraction!

The clouds should keep us well hidden from Dithorba's men until it is too late. Your job is to attack the gate on the south-east like a bunch of eejits, making as much noise as you can. Try not to get too many killed. The path to the outer gate is too steep and narrow to allow for battering rams, so you'll have to use axes. My men, led by Fearghal and Cúscraid, will provide as much cover as possible with their shields. Once you have opened the gateway, Íar's horsemen will charge inside. By that time I should have reached the main defenses and taken the gateway." Conall paused and then smiled at Cimbáeth, "Of course, if my men fail to open the inner gate, then it will fall to you to take it!"

"Wonderful, so we assault the gate after fully alerting Dithorba's men. Great plan, Conall. I'll see you in Mag Mell!"

The cloaked figure slipped and scrambled down the south-eastern pathway from Ráth na Lairig Éadain. He was heading towards the small cluster of buildings that lay at the mouth of an inlet. It was here that traders, fishermen and smugglers tied up their mix of vessels to offload cargo.

Cassius was not escaping. Rather he was ensuring his options and that the gold he had generously given for services had been well spent. He had been keeping track of the few Phoenician and Greek traders who made infrequent journeys to these isles. By his reckoning, the next galley was expected soon. If all else failed, he meant to be on it.

He made his way to the home of his agent. It was in darkness, but the smell of the peat fire told him the building was occupied. He ducked under the lintel and stepped inside. As his eyes adjusted to the gloom, he became aware of several figures standing in the cramped roundhouse. On instinct his hand slid inside his cloak to feel the comfort of his blade. Cassius' instincts were true, but not quick enough.

A hard fist drove into his belly knocking the wind from him. It was followed by a punch to his chin that snapped his head backwards. His knees buckled and as he fell to the floor, his last memory before unconsciousness was of a wet, mud-caked boot as it kicked him in the face.

There was little wind, so the rain fell straight down in rods as they set out for the western slopes of Lairig Éadain. Dark clouds had settled on the mountain top, blocking the fort from sight and, by the same token, blocking the view of the valley to those inside. As they divided to undertake their respective missions, Conall reminded Íar to ensure his men kept a good watch for any sentries Dithorba may have posted.

Now, Conall breathed against the black rock face. Its rough surface felt cold and wet against his cheek. He was thankful that the rockface was not as smooth as it had appeared from a distance. Most of it rose up in tall columns, but was well weathered, providing good foot and handholds. He glanced to Mórrígan on his right and shook his head. Her ever present guardian, Urard, stood resolutely beside his mistress. Conall tried in vain to persuade the giant that the climb would be too much for him. As was becoming his custom, Urard had simply ignored his king.

Slipping a dagger from his belt, Conall clamped it between his teeth and then stretched an arm upwards to begin his climb. It was a signal for the first men to start their own long, arduous climb. The rest followed in groups of fifty keeping a man's height between each row. Mid-way up the cliff face, Conall's row disappeared from view into the shrouding mist. Muffled grunts and curses were interspersed with strained breathing; each foot or hand-hold gained upwards paid for by muscles that burned and ached. The soft clinking of blades on rock as men tried to carve better grips was often followed by mutters of, "Bastard" or "Arsehole" by those below, as various sizes of rocks, dirt and bird-shite rattled down on them.

Conall grunted as his grip slipped, losing him more skin from exposed knuckles, knees and elbows. He swore at Mórrígan who, apparently more agile, was now almost a full body length ahead of him. Poor Urard struggled, but through sheer stubbornness drove higher with his huge muscled legs. The bellyaching became increasingly louder as they edged closer to the summit of Lairig Éadain and Conall prayed that there were few guards on the west side of the fort. Otherwise, the long and torturous ascent could become a short and painful descent.

Exhorting his screaming muscles to one more heaving effort, Conall finally rolled over the lip of the mountain-top. He looked up to find Mórrígan crouched in front of him, her bow held ready. "Old man," she mouthed. Conall rolled to the wooden rampart and rested against it as he fought to bring his breathing under control. There was no ditch on the outside of the stockade and only a few short paces from the wooden barrier to the cliff edge.

Looking around, Conall hoped that the edge of the cliff was solid or his men would be in trouble. Their luck held almost to the end when one man chose a loose rock for his next grip. His nearest friends reached out, only to claw empty air as he eluded their grasp. Mud and slime worked against them and the warrior slid down the rock face. His body bumped and banged against unforgiving black rock, splashing it red as his head split. Finally, the spinning body struck another warrior as it fell; the two men ended up a mass of broken bones at the bottom of Lairig Éadain.

"Shite. Not a good way to go," murmured Deaglán. Conall nodded grimly, aware and proud that neither of the men had shouted or screamed as they fell. They had died as warriors.

Fearghal, Cimbáeth and Cúscraid viewed the crooked path that meandered its way to the summit and the outer gate of Ráth na Lairig Éadain. It was not much more than a widened goat trail, rutted from the wheels of supply wagons and worn by the tramping of men over many generations. In the stretches with soil and moss, the path was about ten warriors across, but in the rockier terrain, the distance was barely the width of a wagon. A narrow ramp had been hewn from the rocks for the last few paces and widened into a small, flat area in front of the outer gate. It would be difficult to get more than fifteen or twenty warriors into the space.

"The main defenses are about two hundred paces back from the boundary rampart and that's where Dithorba has most of his men. The outer gateway serves as a distraction to give him time to get organized. Quite simple and so far it's been a very effective strategy,"

Cimbáeth informed them.

"Well, it also helps that his fort is on top of a bloody mountain with only one path to the front door!" Fearghal grunted. "So the plan is that I send in several of our men with shields high and javelins in hand. A few volleys of javelins should dissuade the defenders from being too eager to defend the gateway. Especially if it's true that they know the main defense is behind them. You can send a group of your huge brutes with axes to break down the gate."

"Don't forget about the part where we all have to be shouting and screaming like mad eejits," Cimbáeth reminded him. "This had better work or the seanachaí will be entertaining folk with tales of our foolhardiness for a long time."

Cimbáeth walked back to his captains to have them select men for the attack on the gate. Out of earshot, he also told them to let their men hang back so that Conall's men did the larger part of the work – and took the most casualties.

As Cimbáeth walked away, Íar strode past him to stand alongside Fearghal and Cúscraid, "My outriders have come back," he spoke quietly, but urgently. "To the south, there's a force of about twenty thousand Ulaid moving up the coast. They're led by Macha and should be here in one or two sunrises." Fearghal started to speak, but Íar held up his hand, "There's more - news from our village. A company of Macha's men raided the village. They killed about two hundred."

"Shite!" A great cry exploded from Fearghal making Cimbáeth and his captains turn around with a look of concern. "We should've killed Macha when we had the opportunity. Nobody listens to me!"

"Quiet, Fearghal. I don't know how much Cimbáeth is aware of Macha's maneuverings. The deaths of our people, while grave, are not our most pressing concern."

Fearghal gritted his teeth, "Out with it Íar. What are you holding back?"

"They have Conall's daughters. That was the purpose of the raid. The villagers who died tried to stop Macha's raiders."

"Bastards! May the Hag take their souls! Conall will be furious, but we can't tell him until we secure the fort. Agreed?" Íar and Cúscraid concurred. A sudden dread grabbed Fearghal's heart, "Where's Mongfhionn? She loves the girls as if they were her own. I fear Conall's reaction, but Mongfhionn will take revenge to unimaginable heights."

"Mongfhionn was at Oisín's grave. It was her wailing across the valley that stopped the slaughter at the village. As soon as they heard the Sidhe, Macha's men grabbed the girls and fled. I suspect she's on her way here now."

"Bollocks! What a mess. Right, we make sure when we take this fort that our men are the ones behind those main defenses. Íar, when the outer gate falls, drive your riders through. I doubt there'll be much resistance so save your javelins for the main entrance. If all goes according to plan, it should be in Conall's hands. If not, then we'll have to take it. We must make sure our men are through before we 'accidently' close it on Cimbáeth. Cúscraid, you'll take command of the inner defenses while Íar and I talk to Conall. Once we're behind the ramparts then it won't matter how many warriors Macha has brought. They'll never get past us."

Cúscraid nodded, "Dithorba had better have plenty of food and water. Once we take this fort, there's only two ways out; we sit back, defend and hope they all get bored and go home or we come out fighting!"

Dithorba shared his mid-day meal with his sons – Baeth, Bedach, Bras, Uallach and Borbcas. They cursed the weather but, supremely arrogant and confident about the fortress' defenses, were unconcerned.

The fort was by no means an elaborate construction, with more time having been spent on the defensive ramparts and ditches than on shelter for the fort's residents. The area back from the ramparts was dominated by the Great Hall, which also doubled as the king and his family's quarters. The zone surrounding the hall and against the stockade was populated with many simple buildings of various sizes and construction. Most, like the hall, used a combination of the black rock of the mountain and native hardwoods. Immediately behind the stockade was a large area of open ground. Here, there was little depth to the dirt with most of the rock having been scraped clean by constant wear from boots and bróga.

Borbcas pointed out there was only one way in and it was too narrow for an army. Dithorba agreed, but grumbled that on most days his view of three gleannta was unrivalled by any other in Ériu. Now he could hardly see ten paces in front of him. He was also disturbed by the disappearance of Cassius. The Roman had not been seen since the previous night.

The ripping of sheep flesh sloshed down with beer and mixed with their mutual grumblings was brought to an abrupt halt by the clamor at the outer gate. "If it's an attack, the bastards are making enough noise to wake the dead," shouted Dithorba's eldest son as they grabbed their shields and weapons and ran to join their men on the defenses. Orders were barked to the ceannairí na céad, who in turn kicked, shoved and swore at their men to take their places on the ramparts.

Fearghal was correct in his assessment that the outer gate was no more than a delaying tactic. Protected by Fearghal's men's shields, Cimbáeth's brutes made short work of the gate with their great battle-axes. On horseback, Íar's riders were almost at the same height as the rampart and javelins found targets with ease. Following a quick volley of javelins, resistance on the stockade crumbled quickly.

With the gate in pieces, the remaining horsemen galloped up the narrow pathway knocking aside anyone unfortunate enough to get in their way. The slashing blades of axes and swords made short work of the few hapless defenders caught as they scrambled for the main defenses. Íar's horsemen were soon followed by a string of pack horses guided by Cian and his men. The rest of Fearghal's band scrambled up the narrow pathway, rushed through the gateway and poured towards the main defenses.

Torcán's hundred were the last of Conall's warriors, but Fearghal had given him different orders. He was to be the plug in the narrow pathway. So instead of charging forward, his men fell over themselves blocking each other. Even the odd fight broke out as one warrior tripped over another. Their pace was agonizingly slow and was directly proportional to the look of annoyance on Cimbáeth's face. Even though Cimbáeth was happy to see Conall's men face the defenses of Ráth na Lairig Éadain, he was certainly not amused at such a blatantly obvious delaying tactic. He began to worry.

The din of the attackers combined with the shouting of commands and tramp of boots on the wooden ramparts veiled the sound of grappling hooks embedding themselves in the wooden stockade. Mórrígan's archers were the first over and swiftly silenced the few guards. Then they fanned out. Using the cover of the buildings they quickly commanded the high ground.

Conall grunted in pain when he scrambled over the fence and instantly discovered that there was no perimeter walkway to break his fall. Shortly after there was a raft of swearing as men found that they too had to drop from the height of the stockade onto the hard rock surface of the fort. Once over the rampart, they gained the open ground behind the main defenses, and divided into two groups.

One was led by Nikandros and Deaglán. Deaglán was the only one who actually could identify Dithorba or his son's, so their task was to find and secure them. Despite what he had told Macha, Conall had no intention of killing a potential bargaining piece such as Dithorba – or his sons. Meanwhile, Conall and Brion formed their men into two rows led by Conall's caomhnóirí and advanced towards the gateway. Those archers not on high ground walked in a crouch behind them picking targets as they came into range.

On the outside of the ramparts, Fearghal and Cúscraid's men stood in two rows and waited – one row facing forward, the other facing behind. Íar's horsemen trotted along the edge of the ditch throwing volley after volley of javelins at the defenders. On the rampart Borbcas ducked and dodged the iron-tipped missiles. One had already split his first shield. He shouted to his younger brother, "Why is the main force not attacking? They can't have an endless supply of spears to throw. Something's wrong."

His answer came not from Bedach, but from the cries of his men who suddenly sprouted arrows in their backs. In horror, Borbcas turned to see the solid ranks of red and black shields stride rapidly across the largely open and undefended ground towards the gateway. They stopped at twenty paces of the gate and both rows launched their javelins; at the same time the archers used up the remaining arrows in their quivers.

Facing forward, the defenders were taken by surprise. For over a hundred paces on each side of the gateway the picture was one of carnage. Blood stained the wooden ramparts, dripping onto the black ground below. Bedach fell, clutching at arrows in his shoulder and chest; Borbcas took a javelin in the thigh which almost pinned him to the wooden rampart. His last sight, before losing consciousness, was of a tall, dark warrior with a red-plumed helmet and glittering bronze armor scything through his father's guard.

Dithorba's guard of five hundred encircled him and his remaining sons, but was steadily forced back to the perimeter wall. The king cursed himself for his pride and complacency in believing Ráth na Lairig Éadain was impregnable. Looking to the gateway, he watched two sons fall and saw the rampart was lost. He was aware that in the time it would take for his men to descend the ramparts to support him, they would be likely face a force that would well outnumber them.

The two hundred that faced his guard were not attacking with normal Ulaid battle tactics, but slowly and determinedly slashed, stabbed, hacked and bludgeoned their way through. The body count of dead and injured rose rapidly before him. Dithorba knew he was beaten with nowhere to run. To fight on might possibly forestall the outcome, but he was defeated and well aware of that fact. He had a fleeting thought that the roasted meat he and his sons had been eating was probably still warm. Ráth na Lairig Éadain had fallen in a brief moment.

Forcing his way to the front of his men, Dithorba spotted the bright red head of hair of Deaglán ó Neill and shouted, "Enough ó Neill, you have won the day. There is no sense to this slaughter. I will not throw the lives of my men and my sons away for the sake of foolish pride. I will surrender if you will stop this butchery."

Nikandros overheard Dithorba and shouted to Deaglán, "Agreed. I'll inform Conall and have him cease the attack." Looking to Dithorba, Nikandros took off his helmet, letting his long, black, plaited hair fall loose, "You're a wise king. I truly hope you survive."

As Dithorba had surmised, the main gateway fell swiftly. Soon the yard was filled with the besiegers, easily distinguished by their armor and shields. He was impressed by the northerner, Cúscraid, who had immediately taken command of the defenses and was marshaling his forces with uncommon and urgent swiftness. Dithorba suspected that while the day was over for him and his men, it would not be for the new masters of Ráth na Lairig Éadain. He was surprised to see the great gates slammed shut as a group of men led by a young warrior with a scar on his forehead dashed through it.

His musings were interrupted as he spied a warrior with an elaborate helmet stride towards him. The warrior removed the helmet, letting his dark, damp hair fall loose. Most noticeable were the steel-grey eyes that now focused on him.

The warrior bowed, "I am Conall Mac Gabhann. These are my men. Where's the Roman?"

Dithorba blinked, not believing what he had heard, "The goddess preserve me. You mean that this slaughter is all about the Roman?"

"Among other things. Where is he?"

Dithorba took a long deep breath knowing his answer was not going to please the young king, "I don't know. We last saw him a few nights ago." Conall's body twitched slightly and Dithorba added. "If he was here, I'd gladly hand the weasel over. Why do you seek him?"

An angry Conall spat on the ground, "He was responsible for the slaughter of my family and the community where we lived. I have trailed him and fought battles from the southernmost tip of Ériu to here and still he eludes me." He turned away tugging his hair in frustration, then turned back, "I have an agreement with Macha Mong Ruad. We will hand you, and your sons, over to her as soon as can be arranged. I keep my word, so I have no choice in this."

Dithorba nodded, "It is good to have honor. Do what seems

right to you."

As he was speaking with Dithorba, Conall became aware of an agitated conversation between Fearghal, Nikandros, Íar, Brion and Mórrígan. Soon the air was rent by a heartbreaking scream. Conall watched as Mórrígan fell to the ground, beating dirt and stone with her bare hands until they were bloody. He ran across, and dropped to his knee to hold her, "The goddess preserve us Mórrígan, what news can bring this much grief?"

Fearghal put his hand on his friend and king's shoulder and said simply, "Macha has Brighid and Danu."

A great howl of "No!" joined the cries of Mórrígan as Conall's legs buckled and he slumped to the ground. Moments later, he slowly rose, holding Mórrígan, "We will turn this land into a place of blood to get them back."

Conall turned to Dithorba, his face like granite and his eyes piercing, "Provided you give no trouble, you and your sons will be well-treated. Our healers will look after the injured. We need space, so your dead will be found at the bottom of Lairig Éadain. It seems I have no time to give them a better farewell. Make no mistake, cross me and I will execute everyone in this fort. That is my promise." Dithorba nodded and wondered what had caused the young king's demeanor to change so swiftly.

In an ominous tone Conall said to Fearghal, "Let's talk to Cimbáeth."

Cimbáeth at first was angry, then frustrated and now was disturbed. As he and his men stood before the gates and ramparts of Ráth na Lairig Éadain, they heard the wailing of Mórrígan and a great howl of rage from Conall. It was disconcerting to watch the ramparts quickly fill with the red and black shields of Conall's men as they stood side-by-side, erect and watchful; their javelin tips visible over the wooden stakes. Bow staffs soon appeared at intervals along the stockade.

"In the name of the goddess, what is going on? I thought we were on the same side." Cimbáeth's second-in-command was about to speak when the gates of the fort swung open.

Flanked by Fearghal, Nikandros, Íar and Brion, Conall strode through the gateway. From their bearing and the fact that all had helmets firmly strapped on and weapons drawn, Cimbáeth knew this was unlikely to be a pleasant conversation. The only one missing was Mórrígan and as he scanned the ramparts, he soon found her pale face and red hair in the gate's guard post. She had nocked an arrow to the bowstring in readiness; its target was obvious.

He turned to his captains, "You four with me, the rest have the men step back well out of the range of those javelins." With a deep breath, he walked forward to meet Conall.

"Would you like to inform me as to what's going on?" Cimbáeth called out as they got closer.

"Why don't you tell us, Cimbáeth?" Conall replied barely controlling his rage.

"Shite! Let's stop dancing," Fearghal placed his hand on Conall's shoulder, "I'll explain."

To Cimbáeth he said, "I thought better of you. Macha is on her way with twenty thousand warriors."

"Well, we all knew she was going to turn up and most likely after the battle. What's the problem?"

"The problem is that she made a diversion to our village, killed over two hundred of our people and took Conall's daughters."

Much as Conall wanted revenge, the stricken looks on Cimbáeth and his captains' faces told him the blame could not be laid on their shoulders. After a brief moment of anger at Macha, Cimbáeth's thoughts were that his men were about to suffer for an act of which they were innocent. And, in truth, he could not blame the angry father before him.

"You didn't know. Did you?" Conall broke the strained silence.

At that moment, the ranks of Cimbáeth's forces shuffled aside as a grey-cloaked figure on a black horse forced its way through to the front. The Sidhe dismounted and flicked her hood back off her head. "No, he didn't know. But he should have. He has been blind to the flaws in Macha Mong Ruad for a long time."

Cimbáeth shook his head and looked Conall in the eye, "I have no stomach for a fight with people I consider friends, but I wouldn't blame you for taking your revenge on us. We will fight if that is your will."

Angry and frustrated, Conall exhaled, turned and walked back to the gates.

Mongfhionn said curtly, "Gather up your men and leave this mountain or it will be your men's blood that stains this black rock." Then she followed Conall to the fort. With great sadness, Cimbáeth bowed and, accompanied by his captains, walked back to his men.

"It's as well Macha's paying us for this one. We'd not make much by selling such a scrawny specimen. The cinn péinteáilte like to get a good days work from their slaves, and are not known for being kind if they are disappointed."

Cassius threw up again, the sour smell of puke filling his nose. The cramps in his belly added to the pain of being punched and kicked to make him more miserable. Bound hand and foot, he sat in the bow of the oversized curach as it bounced up and down with each wave. The spray soaked him and his distress was deepened by the water and piss that he sat in. He no longer complained or asked questions; already he was sure that several ribs had been broken in response to earlier demands for information. So now he listened.

The last piece of conversation had provided the most information since his capture. There had been no interrogation, no questions from his captors and no explanations offered. Only the clink of gold told him that he had been passed on to his current keepers. He smiled grimly. So it was Macha who had been behind his kidnapping and sale to the slavers. Ruefully, he pondered that once more he had underestimated the native cunning of the barbarians. His Roman upbringing obstinately refused to accept that the barbarians could be as clever as - or even cleverer than he. Just animal cunning, he comforted himself.

He shivered, but not because of the cold sea breezes and incessant rain, but in contemplation of his destination. The cinn péinteáilte or painted ones were people of legend and whispered tales. Contacts made with this strange and fierce people had not been encouraging, to say the least. And now without his gold to bargain with, Cassius Fabius Scaeva was reduced to surviving on his wits. Given his recent experiences, this did not fill him with confidence.

CHAPTER 28

SUMMER 410 B.C.

The driving rain and clouds had ceased during the night. In better circumstances Conall would have admired the panoramic views from Ráth na Lairig Éadain. But the sourness in his belly and heaviness in his heart with worry for his daughters blighted his perspective. A sound to his left alerted him to the presence of Dithorba. "While I remain in Ériu Macha will never be Ard-Righan. And I doubt her nobles and allies will be happy over the current set of circumstances. Trade me for your daughters."

Conall laughed hollowly, "It does not sit right with me handing you over to that treacherous woman."

"Do you have a choice? Make a king's decision. As for my sons and I, we will not be harmed or killed, for that is our Law. Most likely I will be exiled to the lands of the Connachta or the Laighi. My sons will survive, though not as princes."

Macha arrived at mid-day and quickly discovered that her numbers meant little. Her battle commander, Cearbhall Ó Domhnaill, reported that no more than a few thousand men at a time could face the fort. To a man, her advisors asserted that the fort was impregnable. This did not satisfy Macha, who retorted that quite obviously the fort was not unassailable since Conall Mac Gabhann now occupied it! She also thought she had fidchell pieces in Conall's daughters to play. Supremely arrogant, she led her men towards the ramparts.

At a hundred paces from the defenses they halted. Macha, together with Cearbhall, rode out ahead of her men. Cearbhall shook his head in dismay at the daunting defenses. His men would have to bridge wide ditches before they got to the ramparts. There was little question that the solid row of warriors lining the stockade would make that task difficult. Macha merely shrugged. After all, she had twenty thousand men. She could afford to lose a few thousand and still win. However, an icicle of doubt touched her spine, the longer she surveyed the fortifications. She shivered even though the day was sunny and warm; goose bumps suddenly appeared on her arms.

The die was cast when she called out imperiously, "Conall Mac Gabhann. Hand over Dithorba, his sons and this fort to Macha Mong Ruad, Ard-Righan of Ériu."

What Macha had not expected, in response to her demands, were the loud roars of laughter, followed by taunts and shouts of defiance from the defenders. Her face blushed as red as her hair as she listened to the invective and defiance flowing from the fort. She waited, hot, fuming and unnerved at her reception and was about to call out once more when the gates opened. Out cantered Conall on Toirneach. Beside him rode Mórrígan, Fearghal, Nikandros, Íar, Deaglán and Brion, their helmets glinting in the sunshine. Behind them marched Conall's caomhnóirí – a solid wall of ravens on a field of red.

Blinded by hubris, Macha was convinced that Conall would bow to the inevitable and cede to her demands. What she had not anticipated was Conall riding to within a few paces of her, leaning over his great warhorse's black shoulders and the harshness of his tone as he pronounced, "You are not Ard-Righan until I give you Dithorba. Challenge me and perhaps you never will be.

Now, hand over my daughters and those that murdered my people so that I can administer justice."

Nearly incoherent with rage, Macha turned to Cearbhall, "No one can be allowed to defy the Ard-Righan. Attack the fort now." Reluctantly, Cearbhall shouted commands to his captains and Macha's men began to move forward. Conall shook his head in disbelief, turned and galloped back through the fort's gates followed by the others.

Macha's warriors quickly passed her, shouting and screaming curses and encouragement, as they charged towards the defensive ditches and ramparts. The ditches while not filled with stakes or other traps were wide and deep. Cúscraid, watchful on the ramparts, waited until the first rows of men had jumped down into the ditch and then gave the order for javelins.

From the ramparts, a thousand javelins arced through the air. Macha watched in stunned silence as her men were slaughtered without having made contact with the defenders. The cries and moaning of men writhing in agony from the iron spikes that had punched into and ripped open their bodies rose along the ramparts. For many, the yawning ditch became a blood-soaked grave.

There was a marked change in the next cohort of men that paced toward the ramparts. They were slower, more measured and looked for gaps or some protection. But Dithorba had built the defenses of Ráth na Lairig Éadain well and there were few places that a man, let alone an army, could shelter. The next unit met the same fate as their comrades as another volley of javelins was launched from the ramparts.

Behind the stockade Conall shook his head in disgust, "What a waste." As he gazed out over the slaughter, he saw that Macha's force had been well thinned out. It also appeared that further reinforcements were reluctant to take their place. He called down to Íar and Nikandros, "Take your horsemen and chase the rest from the mountain top. Maybe we can stop the slaughter – at least for a short while. I'll send some men on foot to follow just in case they show any resistance."

The thunder of hooves from two hundred horsemen galloping towards her settled the day for Macha. Furious and railing at Cearbhall and his captains' incompetence, she retreated to her camp in the valley below. Her mood was not helped by a constant thudding of bodies, as Conall had the injured and dead cleared from the mountain top – mainly by tossing them over the side.

She had clearly underestimated Conall and had not listened to

Cimbáeth's warnings that Conall would be a ruthless and implacable enemy. Her men, used to dash and slash close combat fighting had little reply to the hail of missiles that were rained down on them before they had even a chance to close with their enemy.

While sorely tempted to cut the throats of her two young prisoners, Macha retained enough sense to know that now, more than ever, she needed to use them to force Conall to his knees. Besides, she doubted that many of her nobles and allies would remain with her if she offended their sense of honor by killing the two girls. Above all things, Macha wanted to be Ard-Righan.

It was another somber night in Ráth na Lairig Éadain as Conall and the Chomhairle discussed tactics. A distraught Mórrígan swung between floods of tears and vowing bloody vengeance on Macha. In the end, she was convinced to take one of Fionnbharr's herbal potions and spent the rest of the night in fitful sleep. The meeting itself was interrupted at times by delegations from his men who were at pains to ensure that Conall knew that they would fight to the Other-world and back to rescue his daughters.

More surprisingly, several representatives from Dithorba's men also approached Conall seeking permission to fight with them. The kidnapping of Conall's daughters had offended many. With a view to the future, many of Dithorba's men knew that their lives would be at risk if Macha was named Ard-Righan. Conall drew Dithorba aside and told him about the discussions only to find that the king had already given his blessing to the men.

The morning sunrise flooded the skyline with red. Not the best omen in the world as such a dawn was usually the harbinger of a stormy day. Beacán ó Cathasaigh, now Conall's personal attendant, came to Conall with a message that Macha was on the move again and her men were making their way up the mountain pathway.

Conall rubbed his head and pulled at his hair in frustration, "Has the woman no sense?" He pulled on his mail and grabbing his helmet made his way to the ramparts.

Fearghal met him, "I suppose you heard. She's back."

"Maybe we can intimidate her or dissuade her men from a fight. Line the volunteers from Dithorba along the ramparts. Then march our men out to the just beyond the ditch and form the wall. Two rows of a thousand men and each with three javelins. Have Íar's horsemen form up on the right flank. As for the archers," he looked questioningly at Mórrígan, "have they been told their role?"

Mórrígan nodded, "I trust them. Áine is on the ramparts with the best."

"Good, I want the Chomhairle mounted and in front of the men. Now let's move."

Macha was accompanied by a group of nobles who, as yet, had not permitted their men to join the battle. They had been shocked to find that Cimbáeth had downright refused to take any further part and had marched his men back to his own fort. As they passed through the outer stockade and onto the ground in front of the fort the nobles gasped. Before them were a thousand red shields locked together and a thousand ravens that seemed to stare at them. On the ramparts, banners had been unfurled and flapped in the breeze; the steady rhythm of bodhráns filled the air.

The wall before them bristled with javelins; the front row holding them at waist and the rear at shoulder height. Behind them on the ramparts were more men shoulder to shoulder. Some of the nobles muttered, "Dithorba's men have joined him." To the right, a cohort of mounted warriors awaited; javelins in hand, ready to pounce on fleeing warriors. In front, the leaders looked confident mounted on their warhorses, the plumes on their helmets flickering in the wind.

An elderly noble spoke up, "Negotiate Macha. If you want the crown of Ériu, negotiate. This is a fight you can never hope to win. This king will give no ground and show no mercy. Return the hostages."

Macha spat, "Never," and ordered her men forward.

The noble sighed and together with the others retired to watch the tragedy unfold. At a hundred paces out, Conall and Chomhairle cantered forward.

"There is no sense to this. Hand over my daughters and the killers of my people, then we can negotiate a resolution to this situation."

White with anger and believing that her men would certainly run at the first sign of weakness, Macha made her fatal miscalculation, "Bring the brats forward." The warriors parted to allow two screaming and kicking girls, each held between two men to be brought to the front. They halted on either side of Macha. "Conall Mac Gabhann, for your crimes against the Ard-Righan, your daughters' lives are forfeit. Cut their throats."

A loud screech of, "No!" split the air making the men holding the girls pause briefly. There was also heard, in that moment, the thudding of iron striking flesh over and over. Macha watched in stunned horror as the four guards sprouted hundreds of black arrows from their heads, throats, arms and chests. In their death spasms, their hands opened, releasing their holds on Danu and Brighid.

Conall bellowed, "Run!" and his daughters dashed for the shield wall that had marched forward to meet and enclose them. As the girls got further away, more arrows, were sent into the men until their blood spattered over Macha and gushed into the dark earth.

The horrific cry had come from Mongfhionn, who now led her horse forward, her face terrible to look upon, "You fool. Did you think you could threaten the children of a Sidhe without consequence? Hear me, for this is the judgment of my sisters and me." The Sidhe pointed her oak staff at Macha.

"You shall reign as Ard-Righan for seven years and no more.
The blade with which you would have taken the lives of these innocents shall be the same blade that will end your own.
As you have tried to take the lives of these children you will bear no children. Your line will die with you because of your shame. From this day until your death, your belly will swell, but nothing living will come forth.
As for Cimbáeth, he chose his queen poorly. His fate will be death by pestilence."

As she sent forth her geis, the skies became darker not with clouds, but with an immeasurable flock of ravens. "Now, leave this field or the ravens will feast on your bodies this day."

The blood drained from Macha's face and she felt rivers of

sweat soaking her garments. Short of breath, her head became light and soon, unable to hold herself in the saddle, she began to fall. Her commanders quickly caught her and carried her from the field. As they did, their men drifted away, their heads bowed and eyes fearful of the Sidhe and the ravens watching from the skies.

EPILOGUE

Once he was sure that Macha would not try something stupid again, Conall had divided the army. One half, under Deaglán and Cúscraid, were located at Sráidbhaile de Bhiotáille to protect the community. The remainder, along with those of Dithorba's men who had chosen to swear allegiance to him, stayed at Ráth na Lairig Éadain. About five hundred men, with Dithorba's blessing, had changed allegiance. The rest of his men slipped away into the gleannta. Dithorba's sons recovered from their wounds, but were not looking forward to being left in the hands of Macha Mong Ruad. The king himself remained stoic about his fate.

It had been many cycles of the moon since Conall had come to an agreement with a very subdued Macha and Cimbáeth. The queen, for now she had been crowned Ard-Righan, had seen her hopes of any final leverage dissipate when Conall mentioned that he knew the whereabouts of the Roman. Apparently, Conall's gold was just as effective in loosening the tongues of the slavers as Macha's was in having them transport Cassius across the sea.

The agreement, about which Macha complained bitterly, but in the end got her what she needed – an assurance that Conall Mac Gabhann would leave Ériu, was simple. She would arrange for enough vessels to carry Conall, his army and people across the narrow sea to the land of the cinn péinteáilte. In return she would get Dithorba and his sons, and a third of all the wealth that Dithorba had accumulated. While she had the crown of Ériu, Macha did not have peace of mind. The dark shadows around her eyes and frequent nightmares were a testament to the constant wrestling with the geis she had been given.

Now, Conall sat at the edge of the cliff-top looking to the coast. The mast tops of the Phoenician and Greek galleys rocked back and forward in the gentle swell of the sea. The feasts of Samhain, Imbolg and Bealtaine had passed and the summer was being ushered in. The northern winter had been harsh and as usual the elderly, the very young and the sickly had been harvested.

A gentle nudge between his shoulder blades broke Conall's thoughts and he turned round to see Toirneach pawing at the ground. "Have they sent you to find me?" The great black horse nodded his head vigorously. Conall laughed, "Fine, let's go down and join the others. I hope you like travelling on a boat!"

The End

NOTES

The *geis* is a key device in Ancient Irish mythology and hero tales such as that of Cúchulainn from the Ulster Cycle. It can be either a curse or a gift and is sometimes both. If someone under a geis violates the associated taboo, the infractor will suffer dishonor or even death. On the other hand, the observing of one's geis (or geasa) is believed to bring power. A beneficial geis might involve a prophecy that a person would die in a particular way. The particulars of their death in the vision might be so bizarre that the person could then avoid their fate for many years. Often it is women who place geasa upon men, and in some cases the woman turns out to be some form of deity.

By the later Celtic period, Ireland was ruled by a series of perhaps 100 to 200 kings, each ruling a small kingdom or tuath. Most kingdoms in Ireland had a hilltop fort which was used either as a permanent residence for the king or as a temporary refuge in times of conflict. They were typically built on the top of a hill and surrounded by a stone or wooden wall. Often these sites coincided with previous Bronze Age burial sites and frequently they showed a lack of respect for these previous monuments, sometimes re-using their stones. Unlike the royal sites (Tara, Chrúachain, Dún Ailinne and Emain Macha), which were made from earthen banks, hillforts had very well constructed stone walls made from close-fitting cut stones.

Hillforts were classified according to how many lines of defense/ramparts/ditches they had and whether they were on a promontory — inland or coastal. As far as possible the forts mentioned in the story have a historical basis. Despite their commanding hilltop locations, with the exception of Chrúachain, the royal sites' primary purpose was cultural and ritual.

Ancient Irish kings came in three recognized "grades", depending on how powerful they were. A *rí túaithe* was the ruler of a single kingdom; a *ruiri* or great king was a ruler who had gained the allegiance of, or become overlord of, a number of local kings; and a *rí ruirech* or king of overkings was a king of a province. Ireland had between 4 and 10 provinces at any one time. They were always in a state of flux as individual kings' powers waxed and waned.

The Ard-Righ or High King ruled over all. The traditional list of High Kings of Ireland is a mixture of fact, legend, fiction, and propaganda. Áed Rúad, Díthorba and Cimbáeth had a quite ingenious and successful agreement. They ruled in rotation, seven years at a time and they each ruled for three seven-year stints. Áed drowned at the end of his third rotation, after which Díthorba and Cimbáeth each took their turn.

Macha Mong Ruad demanded to rule in her father's place, but Díthorba and Cimbáeth refused and battle ensured. In some accounts, Díthorba was killed and Macha forced Dithorba's five sons to build her the palace which became Emain Macha. She married Cimbáeth and the pair ruled for seven years. Macha was the only queen in the List of High Kings of Ireland.

Some authors believe that Dithorba was not killed in battle with Macha, but rather was exiled to Connacht. Sadly, that version also ended poorly for Dithorba as he was murdered by his three nephews. As for Macha, she reined for only seven years and was murdered by Rectaidh Righ-Derg who slew her in revenge for her father's killing of his father. Such is the way of Irish kings and queens. Rectaidh himself was slain by Iugani Mór who was the foster son of Macha. Macha never had children of her own. As for Cimbáeth, he was indeed a victim of the plague.

Long before the Romans thought of building a wall to keep out the Picts (the painted ones) and around the same time that the Great Wall of China was built, the people of Ulster (the Ulaid) built the Black Pig's Dyke or Gleann na Muice Duibhe, which is literally the "glen of the black pig". The dyke itself is a series of discontinuous defensive earthworks built along the southern boundary of Ulster. Remnants of the banks and ditches stretch through South County Down, County Armagh, County Monaghan, County Cavan, County Leitrim and South County Donegal.

Excavations reveal that the original construction was of a substantial timber palisade with external ditch. Behind the palisade was a double bank with intervening ditch. The timber structure was radiocarbon dated to 390-370 BC, so the whole of Black Pig's Dyke may date to that period.

However, the tales from old Gaelic folklore that the dyke was the result of a large boar who tore up the Irish country side with its huge tusks or that it was made by a huge worm wriggling across the countryside, are less factual, but perhaps much more interesting.

Corlea lies at the ancient crossing of the River Shannon where it begins to narrow at the northern tip of Lough Ree. About 30 miles northwest is Chrúachain. The Corlea Bog (Portach an Choirr) and the Roadway are near the village of Kenagh, eight miles south of Longford. They lie near the southern extremity of the raised bog zone which covers extensive areas of central Ireland. Raised bogs have an average depth of 25 – 30 feet. They were indeed menacing worlds of reeds and rushes and stagnant pools waiting to engulf weary travelers. Lights from combusting bog-gas were probably the cause and subject of superstitious awe. In the Iron Age, the area around the bog would have been well wooded.

The Corlea Roadway mentioned in the book did exist. I changed the direction of the road somewhat so that it actually pointed in the direction of the Black Pig's Dyke. The real road ran in an NW-SE direction across the bog for around 1.5 miles and terminated at a small island of dry land. The roadway was constructed of birch substructure and oak surface. The road was 10-13 feet wide, which indicates that it was built to allow the passage of chariots. A short stretch near the centre of Corlea bog has been excavated and showed timbers lying loose and in irregular piles. Some of the timbers were burnt, which suggested that the road had been deliberately and systematically dismantled in an attempt made to destroy it.

When I started writing this novel, a good friend, Maxine Lennon, a teller of ancient Irish stories and who lives in Texas, was at pains to stress that such tales are often adult only! They are mostly of sex, violence and drinking! Queen Medb, her "of the friendly thighs" is one of the main and most interesting characters in *The Táin Bó Cuailnge*, an epic poem from the Ulster Cycle.

Strictly speaking, Medb did not make an appearance until about the first century. However, since she was most likely mythical or a demi-goddess, she was also ageless. As a character she was too hard to resist. Her signature trait being that she was an extremely lustful lady who needed satisfying by thirty men a night! Her negotiation skills were also renowned and to close a deal she would often throw in a night or two between her thighs. Her husband, Ailill, was thought to be her grandnephew.

The remains of the Barbary ape mentioned in the story were actually uncovered during excavations at Navan Fort (Emain Macha). The dating of the remains puts the animal around the time of the story and does appear to suggest that Phoenician or Greek traders were not unknown even as far north as mid-Ulster. Pytheas, a Greek sailor and merchant was said to have sailed to the shadowy Northern Sea and the Tin Island, as Great Britain was known due to its tin mines, around 320 BC. Unfortunately, only the title of the record of Pytheas' journeys – On the Ocean – appears to have survived.

The climate in Iron Age Ireland? There was a period of unusually cold climate in the North Atlantic region, lasting from about 900 BC to about 300 BC, with an especially cold wave in 450 BC during the expansion of ancient Greece. Temperature was about 2 degrees lower than normal. The result in Ireland was that some of the bogland began to dry out.

A Spartan colony in the Republic of Rome? According to Dionysius, a group of Lacedaemonians fled Sparta regarding the laws of Lycurgus as too severe. They founded the Spartan colony of Foronia in Italy, near the Pomentine plains, and some from that colony settled among the Sabines. According to the account, the Sabine habits of belligerence (aggressive or warlike behavior) and frugality (prudence in avoiding waste) were thought to have been derived from the Spartans.

Finally, and possibly the most vexing question raised. Did the Romans visit Ireland? Visit, likely yes. Invade, likely no. Have you seen the roads in Ireland? A Roman invasion would at least have provided a better network of highways! The find of a Roman fort at Drumanagh, near Dublin caused and continues to cause much consternation. But the probability is that the "fort" is more likely to have been a trading post. Given that traders often also played the part of spies, it is likely that there was a better awareness of Ireland by Rome than of Rome by Ireland.

SUGGESTED READING

It proved quite a task to discover how the Ancient Irish lived during the period. One reason was that Ireland was relatively cut off from the rest of Europe at that time, so there is not a great record of what was happening. Finding a map of the period is almost impossible. However, I found the books listed below useful:

    Randy Lee Eickhoff, *The Raid: A Dramatic Retelling of Ireland's Epic Tale*, A Forge Book, Published by Tom Doherty Associates

    Geoffrey Keating, *Foras Feasa Ar Eirinn ... The History of Ireland*, TR and Annotated by J. O'Mahony

    Carmel McCaffrey and Leo Eaton, *In Search of Ancient Ireland: The Origins of the Irish from Neolithic Times to the Coming of the English*, Published by Ivan R. Dee

    Damian Noonan, *Castles and Ancient Monuments of Ireland*, The Daily Telegraph, Aurum Press

    Barry Raftery, *Pagan Celtic Ireland: The Enigma of the Irish Iron Age*, Published by Thames and Hudson

THE CHARACTERS

The Original Settlement in 415 BC
Bréanainn Mac Gabhann (killed 415BC, age 35)
Brónach Mac Gabhann (killed 415BC, age 33)
Conall Mac Gabhann (age 18)
Eirnín Mac Gabhann (age 12)
Fearghal ó Maoilriain (age 30)
Brion ó Cathasaigh (age 17)
Mórrígan Ni Cathasaigh (age 15)
Brocc ó Cathasaigh (age 15)
Bricriu ó Cathasaigh (age 12)
Beacán ó Cathasaigh (age 10)
Niall ó Bric (killed in battle, 415BC)
Rónán ó Bric (killed in battle, 415BC)
Cathán ó Bric (age 10)
Labhraidh ó Cuileannáin (age 17)
Fionnbharr ó Cuileannáin (age 16)
Craiftine ó Cuileannáin (age 14)
Tadhg ó Cuileannáin (age 13)
Torcán ó Dubhghaill (age 16)
Siollán ó Dubhghaill (killed in battle, 415BC)
Uallachán ó Dubhghaill (age 14)
Nuadha ó Dubhghaill (age 11)

The Cróeb Ruad Warriors
Eoghan ó Liath (age 45, Commander at the Black Pigs Dyke)
Odhrán Mac Seáin (killed by Fearghal, age 32)
Cúscraid Mac Conchobar (age 27, joined Conall)
Urard (age 29, joined Conall)
Deaglán ó Neill (age 26)
Aengus Ruad (killed in battle, age 25, 411BC)

The Romans
Cassius Fabius Scaeva (age 23)
Marcus Fabius Ambustus (age 50, Pontifex of Rome)
Quintus Fabius Ambustus (age 29)
Numerius Fabius Ambustus (age 21)
Caeso Fabius Ambustus (age 19)
Spurius Sulpicia Longus (sacrificed 412BC, age 40)
Decimus (killed 412BC, age 32)
Publius (killed by Nikandros, 412BC, age 36)
Gaius Aurelius Atella (age 21, Optio promoted to Centurion)

The Sidhe
Mongfhionn (age unknown)
Danu (executed 425BC by Quintus Fabius Ambustus)
Brighid (executed 425BC by Quintus Fabius Ambustus)

The Spartan
Nikandros (age 25, joined Conall)

Carn Tigherna
Eochaidh Ruad (Ruiri, executed by Conall, 412BC, age 40)
Olcán Ó Floinn (killed in battle by Conall, 415BC, age 38)
Faolán Ó Floinn (killed in battle by Conall, 412BC, age 33)
Treasach (killed in battle by Fearghal, 415BC, age 31)
Sleibhin (killed in battle, 412BC, age 23)

Chrúachain
Medb (Queen of the Connachta, age unknown)

Ailill Mac Máta (King of the Connachta, age 25)
Fachtna (killed by Medb, 411BC, age 38)
Cathal (age 40)

Clárach
Aodh Mac Eochaidh Fionn (age 60)

Emain Macha
Macha Mong Ruad (Ard-Righan in-waiting, age 21)
Cimbáeth (Ard-Righ, age 45)
Cian Craobhach (age 50, joined Conall)
Cearbhall Ó Domhnaill (Commander of Macha's forces, age 47)

Settlement at the Bog of Cullen
Seanán (Village elder, age 50)
Onchú Ó an Cháintigh (age 27, joined Conall)

Curraghatoor
Deda Mac Sin (King at Curraghatoor, age 55)
Íar Mac Dedad (age 26, joined Conall)
Áine Nic Dedad (age 17, joined with Brion)

Knockadigeen
Sláine Ulfhada (King at Knockadigeen, killed in battle by invaders, 411BC)
Breácan (killed in battle by invaders, 411BC)

Ráth na Lairig Éadain
Dithorba (King at Ráth na Lairig Éadain, age 55)

ABOUT THE AUTHOR

Born and bred in Belfast, Northern Ireland, David H. Millar is the founder, president, CEO and Keurig operator of a boutique strategy-consulting group and the founder, managing director, and author in residence of a publishing company that promotes Celtic literature and art.

Millar moved to Nova Scotia, Canada, in the 1990s. After ten years shoveling snow, he decided to relocate to warmer climes and settled in Houston, Texas, where he is a member of the board of directors of the Irish Network Houston.

An avid reader, armchair sportsman, and Liverpool Football Club fan, Millar lives with his family and Bailey, a Manx cat of questionable disposition known to his friends as "the small angry one."

Conall's adventures continue in the second book in the series, *Conall II: The Raven's Flight - Eitilt an Fhiaigh Dhuibh.*

CONTACT THE AUTHOR:
www.aweepublishingco.com
Email: davidm@aweepublishingco.com

Twitter: @DavidHMillar

Facebook: https://www.facebook.com
/pages/A-Wee-Publishing-
Company/601748196610367?ref=hl

Blog: http://www.aweepublishingco.com/david-h-millar.html

CPSIA information can be obtained
at www.ICGtesting.com
Printed in the USA
FFHW020844061019
55416550-61163FF